ALL
THE LONELY
PEOPLE

ALL THE LONELY PEOPLE

Collected Stories

BARRY CALLAGHAN

PREFACE BY
MARGARET ATWOOD

EXILE editions

Publishers of Singular
Fiction, Poetry, Nonfiction, Translation, Drama and Graphic Books

Library and Archives Canada Cataloguing in Publication

Callaghan, Barry, 1937-
[Short stories. Selections]
All the lonely people : collected stories / Barry Callaghan ;
preface by Margaret Atwood.

Issued in print and electronic formats.
ISBN 978-1-55096-790-6 (hardcover).--ISBN 978-1-55096-791-3 (EPUB).
--ISBN 978-1-55096-792-0 (Kindle).--ISBN 978-1-55096-793-7 (PDF)

I. Atwood, Margaret, 1939-, writer of preface II. Title.

PS8555.A49A6 2018   C813'.54   C2017-905877-0
                                     C2017-905878-9

Published by Exile Editions Limited – www.ExileEditions.com
144483 Southgate Road 14 – GD, Holstein, Ontario, N0G 2A0
Printed and Bound in Canada by Marquis.

We gratefully acknowledge the Canada Council for the Arts, the Government of Canada,
the Ontario Arts Council, and the Ontario Media Development Corporation
for their support toward our publishing activities.

Canadian sales representation:
The Canadian Manda Group, 664 Annette Street,
Toronto ON M6S 2C8 www.mandagroup.com   416 516 0911

North American and international distribution, and U.S. sales:
Independent Publishers Group, 814 North Franklin Street,
Chicago IL 60610 www.ipgbook.com   toll free: 1 800 888 4741

For Claire, my Crazy Jane,
Who, at 83, left me too soon.

"What can you do
With such a crazy dame?
She knew, she knew."

—HAYDEN CARRUTH

All the Lonely People

FULL DISCLOSURE

Preface by Margaret Atwood

Barry Callaghan has been a friend since the early 1980s when we both lived in Victorian red-brick row houses in downtown Toronto, near the Art Gallery of Toronto on one side and, on the other, a number of Chinese groceries and garment wholesalers and Grossman's Tavern and the recently closed Victory Burlesque. That's a good frame for Barry's work: his interests as a writer have been mostly urban, with one foot in high art and the other in the hustle and fight-for-your-place world on the fringes.

Our cat used to pretend to be a stray in order to mooch food from Barry and his beloved, the painter Claire Wilks. The same cat used to leap from rooftop to rooftop wearing a bonnet and a pinafore. Did he ever appear at the Callaghan/Wilks back door in full dress? If so, that would have been appropriate: Barry Callaghan has never shied away from a touch of the real-life surreal.

Barry and I are of an age – he was born in 1937, I in 1939 – and thus we both remember a time when the sides in street fights among groups of boys in Toronto were more likely to be divided by religion than by any other consideration. Toronto in the Forties and Fifties was a small, provincial, Protestant-dominated, blue-law city – blue laws governed such things as who could be seen drinking what, where, and when. Catholics – especially those of Irish descent – were somewhat of an out-group. In the boy wars, snowballs with rocks in them were hurled, epithets were shouted, fisticuffs exchanged, turfs defended.

Barry was unavoidably a part of that scene. But he also had a well-known writer for a father: Morley Callaghan had seen much of the literary world, such as Paris, and he'd published in places that were not Canada, such as New York. He wasn't above knocking people down, such as Hemingway, in their famous boxing match. Powerful lessons for a growing boy: you could have the Art Gallery on one side of your personality tool kit, and the pugnacious, tinsel-bestrewn scuffle on the other.

Barry came of age with the sense that there was a party going on somewhere – probably among the haute-Wasps – to which his ilk would not be invited. So what? Throw your own party and make it better. In retrospect it seems no accident that the magazine he founded in 1972 was named *Exile*: a space for those excluded from the party. (There wasn't ever that kind of monolithic literary party in Toronto, which has typically specialized in sub-groups; or if there was, I wasn't invited to it either. But that's beside the point.)

Here is a Barry Callaghan moment. When it came time for Morley Callaghan's funeral, Barry tried to talk the officiants into some Dixieland jazz, because Morley had loved that music. They were having none of it. The service proceeded as usual, with speeches and prayers and boy sopranos, but when the coffin was being wheeled down the aisle, up from the choir loft rose a full Dixieland band, which burst into full throttle. That's when the mourners cried.

Morley never would have pulled a caper like that. Barry did.

As a young man, Barry became, first, a reporter – sent forth to see, to report, and – newspapers being what they were – to cover usually the bad news. But then he morphed into a poet and fiction writer – a writer of short stories, for the most part.

Barry Callaghan was never fashionable. He was never merely clever or witty. He was never "post-modern." He was always off to the side somewhere, pursuing an aesthetic of his own that was not that of the prevailing zeitgeist.

How to convey the flavour of his prose?

You might divide prose styles into the Plainsong – such as Hemingway's *In Our Time* – and the Baroque, such as Faulker or Proust or Thomas Wolfe. For Plainsong writers, less is more. For Baroque writers more is more, and the road of excess leads to the palace of wisdom. Callaghan inclines to the Baroque.

He has never been interested in other people's ideas of good taste. A pie in the face for it, and a knuckle sandwich into the bargain! Beige is not his colour. If he were a parade it would be a Mardi Gras parade. If he were a church it would be a Mexican cathedral, and the more candles and paper flowers and gold ornaments, the better. If he were a musical entertainment, it might be *Gypsy* – there's no business like show business, and when in doubt take off your clothes, but not quite all of them. If he were another writer, it might be Dashiell Hammett crossed with a Jacobean playwright. If he were a sideshow attraction… Will it be the Bearded Lady or the Siamese Twins Joined at the Head, or will it be the carnie who lures you with the offer of winning a Kewpie doll, and, when you lose, gives you one anyway?

And what sort of dessert would he be? Not the plain apple. There would be whipped cream in it, and booze. It would be rich.

His characters have emotions, and they have them all over the page. People cry, including men. People are sentimental and sorrowful and enraged and in love and in lust, as people are. People drink. People wallow in misery and bask in pleasure. People fail. People fall apart. Life is not tidy. Approaching a Callaghan story, it does no good to stick a toe in.

Here you are. Plunge in!

I

Everybody wants to laugh,
Nobody wants to cry,
Everybody wants to hear the truth,
But still they want to lie.
Everybody wants to know the reason
Without even asking why.
Everybody wants to go to heaven,
But nobody wants to die.

—ALBERT KING

BECAUSE Y IS
A CROOKED LETTER

...a motiveless malignancy...
—JOHN MILTON, *Paradise Lost*

THERE'S A HOLE IN THE BOTTOM OF THE SEA

It began over a year ago. I was going to drive to the foothill town of Saratoga to stay for two weeks in a rambling, spacious house and try to have lunch every day at a table under the tent at the old gabled racetrack. I had renegotiated the mortgage on the house and bought a new pair of tinted prescription sunglasses so that I could read the racing form in the glaring sun. C. Jane had packed several oblong dark bars of wax and her slender steel tools. She is a sculptor. I am a poet. We went out the back door of our house, through the vine-covered and enclosed cobble-stone courtyard, and decided to move the car forward in the garage, toward the lane. I turned the key and the Audi lurched backward, breaking down the stuccoed wall, dumping concrete blocks and cement into the garden. I looked back through the rear-view mirror into an emptiness, wondering where every-thing had gone, and I heard the whisper of malevolence and affliction on the air. I did not heed it.

The car was fixed. Mechanics said that wires had crossed in the circuitry. We drove to Saratoga where every morning in the

1

lush garden behind the house I wrote these words while sitting
in the shade of a monkey puzzle tree:

pain and pleasure are two bells,
if one sounds the other knells.

The house was a brisk walk from the racetrack where
shortly after noon grooms started saddling the horses under
tall spreading plane trees, and then they led the horses into
the walking ring and people pushed against the white rail
fence around the ring, the air heavy with humidity. Some
horses, dripping wet, looked washed out, with no alertness in
the eyes. It is a sign, but it is hard to know if a horse is sweating because of taut nerves or heat, so I looked for the blind
man.

I stood against the rail along the shoot from the walking
ring, at a crossing where the horses clopped over hard clay. The
blind man came every season on the arm of a moon-faced
friend, and they always held close to the rail as the horses
crossed, the blind man listening to the sound the hooves made.
"Three," he said at last, "the three horse." The horse was dripping wet from the belly but I went to the window and bet on
the blind man. The horse got caught in the gate, reared, and ran
dead last. A warning, I thought, but before the next race the
blind man said sternly to his friend, "I can't close my eyes to
what I see." I moved closer to him. The other horses he heard
during the day ran well. He called four winners and I strolled
home to the big house and C. Jane and I drank a bottle of
Château Margaux, 1983, a very good year. A few more winners
and I might be able to pay for our trip.

That night I dreamed of butterflies swirling out of the sky and clouding the track. "It's all our lost souls," C. Jane said. The days passed. I worked on poems in the morning and forgot the blind man and the butterflies. I wrote about my dead mother, who would sit in candlelight, her sleeves stained by wax, and play the shadows of her hands like charred wings on the wall.

The sun shone but did not glare. I did well at the track and bought a Panama hat.

One morning, the phone rang and it was C. Jane. She had driven through town along the elm-shaded side streets. There had been an accident. When I got to the intersection I found our Audi had been T-boned by an elderly man from California who was driving a Budget rental car. "I was listening to Benny Goodman on the radio," the man said, "*Sing, Sing, Sing.* It still sounds great." He had gone through a red light, slamming the Audi up over a sidewalk and onto a lawn, smashing it into a steel fence. Marina had stepped from the car unscathed but stricken. The car's frame was bent and twisted and it was towed to a scrapyard where it was cannibalized and then reduced to a cube of crushed steel. There was a whisper of malevolence and affliction on the air but I did not heed it and we went back to our home in Toronto where I was cheerfully sardonic about the hole in our garden wall. "There's a hole in the bottom of the sea, too," I said, and laughed and then began to sing, *There's a hole, there's a hole in the bottom of the sea...*

Like My Back Ain't Got No Bone

Our house was in Chinatown, a red-brick row house built about 1880 for Irish immigrants. It had always been open to writers who dropped in on us for a morning coffee, and a little cognac in their coffee; sometimes I made pasta or a tourtière for two or three editors; and since C. Jane was a splendid cook, we had small suppers for poets from abroad and often we held house parties, inviting forty or fifty people. It was a friendly house, the walls hung with paintings, drawings, tapestries – all our travels and some turbulence nicely framed – but one September afternoon the front door opened and a young man with bleached hair spritzed like blond barbed wire walked boldly in, his eyes bleary, and one shirt sleeve torn. He stared sullenly at the walls, spun around, and walked out without a word. C. Jane was upset. She began to shake and I felt a twinge, a warning, but I was too absorbed in getting ready to give readings in Rome, Zagreb, and Beograd, and then I was to go on to Moscow and St. Petersburg before coming home in late November for an exhibition of C. Jane's sculpture. We decided to relax before I went away by celebrating Thanksgiving at the family farm near a town called Conn.

We loaded food hampers onto the back seat of our new Audi parked in the lane (C. Jane's car was in the garage). I looked back through the broken wall, through the jagged hole. There had been no time to cement the blocks back into place. I felt a vulnerability, as if in the midst of my well-being, I'd forgotten to protect myself. Before she died, my mother had warned me, "People who buy on time, die on time, and time's too short." I checked the deadbolts and locks on the house doors. An old, fat Chinese woman waddled along the lane watching me with a stolid impassivity that made me resentful. She was my neighbour but I knew she didn't care what happened to me. As she passed, I felt a sudden dread, a certainty that she belonged there in the lane, between the houses, and I didn't. I remembered that my father, whenever he felt cornered like I suddenly felt cornered in my own mind, used to sing:

> *rock me baby,*
> *rock me baby like my back*
> *ain't got no bone*

> *roll me baby,*
> *roll me baby like you roll*
> *your wagon wheel home*

THE QUEEN FALLS OFF HER MOOSE

Our farmhouse was on a high hill surrounded by birch and poplar and black walnut woods. The back windows of the house looked over a wetland, a long slate-coloured pond full of stumps and fallen trunks lying between gravelly mounds. The trees on the hills were red and ochre. There were geese on the pond. At dusk, we ate supper in the dining room that had old stained-glass church windows set into two of the walls, sitting under a candelabra that burned sixteen candles. "I think there's a song about sixteen candles," C. Jane said. "Or no, maybe it's sixteen tons, about dying miners, or coal, or something like that." For some reason, we talked about violence, whether it was gratuitous, or in the genes, or acquired, and whether there actually was something called malevolence, evil. I read something I'd written that morning to C. Jane: *I love darkness that doesn't disappear as I wake again but leaps a distance, unseen, and then as the sun sets, draws near. I see someone approaching: emerging from the dark, merging into the dark again.* I smoked a pipe and we listened to Messiaen, *Trois Petites Liturgies de la Présence Divine,* and then we went to bed. I lay awake for a long while hearing the night wind in the eaves and a small animal that seemed to be running up and down the east slope of the roof.

In the very early morning, the phone rang. It was a neighbour from the city, a painter who had made his name by painting portraits of the portly Queen wearing epaulettes and seated sidesaddle on a moose. He was a shrewd, measured, ironic man, but he sounded incoherent, as if he were weeping. "Come home," he said. "Come home, something terrible, the house, it's been broken, come home." I phoned our home. A policeman answered. "Yes," he said, "you should come home, and be prepared. There has been a fire. This is bad." For some reason, as we drove through Conn, I started hearing in my mind's ear Lee Wiley singing over and over: *I got it bad and that ain't good, I got it bad…*

A DREAMBOOK FOR OUR TIME

We pulled into the lane behind our house (after two tight-lipped hours on the road). I felt a terrible swelling ache in my throat: there, alone and in pairs and slumped in sadness, were many of our friends. What were our friends doing there? They came closer and then shied away, as animals shy from the dead. The police were surprised. They were expecting C. Jane's red car (it was gone from the garage), and at first they did not know who I was, but then a detective took me aside. "You should get ready before you go in... I don't know if your wife should go in, it's the worst we've ever seen." I looked through the gaping hole in the garage wall. "She's not my wife," I said. "We've lived together for twenty years."

"Do you have any enemies?"

"I don't know."

"It looks like it."

"Why?"

"Because it looks like somebody's tried to hurt you."

"Really."

"We'll have to go around to the front of the house to get in, they never did break the deadbolt on the back door."

"I've got a key," I said.

"Oh right, sure," the detective said and another cop tried to lead C. Jane away, but she broke free. "No one's keeping me out of my own home." In the kitchen, a long black-handled carving knife had been stuck into the wall over the telephone; two fires had been set, one on the floor, the other on the gas stove, and the house had the sour reek of smoke; papers and broken glass and crockery covered the floor tiles; the television set was gone. In the dining room, the armoire doors hung open, armloads of old family crystal and china had been swept out onto the floor...but I saw that a portrait of me, a painting by Kurelek, had not been touched and I said warmly, "They're not after me, otherwise they would have slashed that."

"Don't be so sure," a cop said smugly. "It doesn't look like you."

"The red car's been stolen," another cop said. "It's just been reported in a hit-and-run accident."

We went into the living room with its twelve-foot high ceilings: the black sofa was hacked to pieces; an engraving by my old Paris friend, Bill Hayter, had been hammered off the wall and lay in a scorched heap; a tapestry I'd brought from Cairo, carrying it through the Black September war in 1970 when I was a war correspondent, was slashed open down the centre; the floor was littered with boxes, broken crockery, papers, broken frames, torn cloth, broken records and cassettes, a Chinese vase and ripped books; the lace curtains in the bay window (*Lace curtain Irish*, C. Jane had liked to call us, since she was Lithuanian) had been set afire, charred; and in the vestibule, a turquoise funerary piece that had once been in a pharaoh's tomb, the pharaoh from the time of Moses, lay broken and beside it a Phoenician bronze bull that had been crushed under a heel, or at least there were well-worn black shoes left beside the bull, and I realized my leather cowboy boots were gone.

"The son-of-a-bitch," I said, laughing grimly, "he's not only cut and slashed his way through my house but he's gone off in my goddamn boots and left me his lousy Goodwill shoes."

"This is terrible," C. Jane said. We shied away from the grand piano. A fire had been set under it. I could see the blackened veneer, the warped lid.

"It's worse upstairs," a cop said.

"Well, lead on, Macduff," I said. The cop looked at me quizzically.

The second floor *was* worse; they had torched a vase of antique silk flowers and a Kashmir carpet on the landing; the word processor was stolen (a literary prize I'd never learned to use, didn't want to use, and was secretly glad to see gone); my books were spilled on the floor, yanked out of their shelves (they'd tried to set a fire in the study by using two books: *Child of the Holocaust* by C. Jane's cousin, Jack Kuper, and *A Dreambook for Our Time* by the Warsaw novelist, Tadeusz Konwicki); in the bedroom, they'd thrown a child's pine pioneer chair through one of C. Jane's large brush drawings of tangled lovers; Chinese porcelain figurines that my dead maiden aunts had brought from Shanghai in the late 1920s were smashed; and they had ransacked the bureau drawers for jewellery...all the silver and gold...rings, charms, bracelets...all were gone...all our bindings of love...

The third-floor studio walls were soot-blackened: dozens of C. Jane's frames and drawings smashed; an enormous black and brown oil painting by one of her former lovers, *Homage to John Kennedy on his Death,* slashed; the sofa-bed springs had been pulled apart with a claw-hammer, the sofa pillows burned; plaster casts hacked open or broken; and the floor was slick with a sludge of burned, scorched, and then doused papers...they'd started a fire in an old Quebec armoire...acting like a fire box, it had funnelled flame to the ceiling and had burned through the roof of the house, the heat blowing out the windows...and all my papers, so assiduously kept over the years – letters, manuscripts, transcripts...twenty-five years of intimacies, words chosen with care, exactitude...a wet grimy ash.

"We had the water on her three minutes after the alarm," the fire chief said. He was pleased, full of self-approval. "Thank you," I said. He had a grey bristle moustache. C. Jane asked me if I thought he trimmed it in the morning with little silver scissors. "When we got here the whole house was full of black smoke…luckily the front door was open, luckily a woman across the road saw the smoke coming through the roof…"

"Who would want to hurt you?" the detective, a Sergeant Hamel, asked again.

"I don't know. All I know is the Dom Perignon is gone." C. Jane went downstairs from the studio and then came back. There were tears in her eyes. She does not cry easily. "It's the piano," she said. The piano had been given to her by her laconic father before he died of throat cancer, a cancer he'd contracted during the War when he'd enlisted as a boy, too young, having lied about his age, and he'd been gassed and buried alive for several hours in a rat-infested trench. A rat had gnawed on his left little finger. He'd told her two things: "Always listen to music no matter what, and never tell anyone you're Jewish." He'd given her the piano, a 1912 Mason & Risch, a mahogany grand with a beautiful fiddleback grain and carved legs.

The fire under the piano had burned down into the hardwood floor and then up an antique silk shawl draped from the lid. When the lid was lifted, the piano was a burned-out, warped, gutted box.

"It's gone forever," she said.

"No it's not," I said.

A standing whalebone shaman, a drummer figure who had the four eyes of the mystic, done by Ashevak, the finest of the Inuit carvers until he died in a house fire, was still on the piano but the drum was broken, the beater scorched black.

"Don't you feel violated?" a newswoman friend, who'd come in from the lane, asked. "Don't you feel raped?"

"No," I said.

"You don't?"

"No, and you're a woman, you should know better. This is a house. No one's entered my body, no one has penetrated me. This isn't rape…"

"Yes, but…" She took off her glasses and then put them back on. She was offended, as if I had been difficult when all she had intended was sympathy. But I *was* being difficult, because I believe, especially in times when there are charred shadows on the walls, that exactness is one of the few ways I can make a stand in the ditch against sentimentality, self-pity, falseness.

"But the rage," she said. "Someone attacked your place in a state of rage."

"It looks that way."

"How do you account for such rage?"

"I don't know."

"Any ideas?"

"Motiveless malignancy," I said. Then a cop, who I noticed had cut his neck while shaving, took me by the arm, smiling a tight little angry smile. "We've got one of them," he said.

"You have!"

The cops, while driving down a lane behind the El Mocambo club, had seen a shabbily dressed man sitting huddled in a doorway, and he was clutching two bottles of Dom Perignon. "We knew right away that something was sure wrong," a cop said. They had handcuffed him. Strung out on crack, he said he would show them the house he had broken into that morning, and now he was in the back seat of the cruiser in my lane.

"I don't know whether I want to see him," I said.

"Oh, you can't see him."

"Why not?"

"I don't want an assault-and-battery charge on my hands, too."

But I did not want to beat anyone. I felt only the torpor that comes with keeping an incredulous calm in the face of brutality. Rage, imprecations, threats were beside the point. I had seen in my life what skilled and sanctioned soldiers or thugs could do to a house in Belfast or on the West Bank or in Beirut. I felt curiously thankful that so much in our house had survived. But I knew some people, and particularly some cops, had their own expectations: I quickly learned that I was a suspect…because I was too detached, too self-contained. "He's got to be in on it," a cop, who smelled strongly of Old Spice cologne, told Sergeant Hamel, who said that he had tried to explain: "No, no. He's a writer. That's what writers do. They stand back and look at things."

WHAT OLD PROFESSORS KNOW

The suspect was named Lugosi ("It looks like he's a cousin of Bela Lugosi," another detective insisted), a young man "of no fixed address." Lugosi had fought in the cruiser, kicking out the rear window, punching, biting and spitting. He had fought at the station. He had seemed driven by rage. The officers had had to go to Mount Sinai Hospital for hepatitis shots.

Sergeant Hamel, ingratiating yet reflective – a cop who did not look at you with that wry solicitousness so close to a sneer that is the mark of the cop who knows we all have a criminal secret – opened the trunk of his cruiser. "They set seven fires," he said. "Firebugs. The worst we've seen." He reached into a bag and took out several small bronzes...funeral ornaments for a mummy's breast from a pharaoh's tomb, a Phoenician clown's head...and then an alabaster fertility monkey from a scent dish...all things that I had bought years ago in a desert town outside Cairo from a disgruntled professor of archaeology who had stolen them from his museum.

"These yours?"

"Yes."

"It's terrible, things like this being broken."

"Yes. Lasting this long, suddenly smashed."

"I want you to think about your enemies."

"I'm not sure I have any."

"You've written a lot, some people are pretty crazy."

"I'll think about it."

I did not think about it.

"We've got to go where there's water," I told C. Jane, and we went, and in the morning we woke up in the Hotel Admiral on the waterfront, and as we sat up, with the dawn flaring red across the water, we were suddenly flooded by light. "I had an old philosophy professor," I said, "and he always talked with his eyes closed, but when he forgot where he was going he'd open his eyes and say, 'Well, we'll lick the lips and start afresh.'"

We went back to look at the house. Standing alone in the sooty squalor of the rooms, I knew we had lost things that connected us to the past, but they would be nothing compared to the loss of the future. I wanted to sit at the piano as I had on other dark and sombre days and play in a minor key. I wanted to shuffle on the black notes, singing, *Rock me momma in your big brass bed, rock me momma like my back ain't got no bone...* but it was charred, and then the expert piano restorer, a man named Rob Lowrey, came into the house, shook hands, and then shook his head as he lifted the lid. "Burned to a crisp. It'll cost more to fix it than it's worth, it'll cost $30,000 if we can do anything, and we can't." He hung his head. "The insurance will never pay for it."

"I don't care," I said, "we'll work out something." Lowrey's men carried the piano out of the house. "If we come back," Lowrey said, "it'll be in a year, and if we come back at all, it'll be a miracle."

"You bring the loaves," I said, "and we'll bring the fishes."

EURYDICE DESCENDING

We lived in the hotel for over two months. It was small and elegant, charmingly run by young women, and one wall of our room was glass facing over the water, facing Ward's Island and Hanlan's Point. Every day we came back to the room after sifting through rubble and refuse in the house, and we sat and stared as the sun leaked out of the autumn sky, and then we dressed for supper...it was a determined elegance of spirit, a determined refusal to yield to the lethargy of dismay, regret, self-pity, or blame (all the questions asked by the police or insurance adjusters – even the simple question, Why? – contained a hint of blame, of accusation...and it was even suggested by a friend that we had asked for it: our house had been too open…and another friend wondered whether we wouldn't at last learn that such expansiveness, such openness in a home, was a vanity, and vanity was always punished), but we did not blame ourselves. We ate well at a table beside the wide harbourfront window and watched the island airport lights flicker on the dark water. There was a pianist who played out in the lobby, out of our sight, and it was like listening to the ghost of our piano playing, our piano being rebuilt, and ironically, we knew that before our house could be rebuilt, it had to become the ghost of itself: walls washed down, the quarry-tile floors stripped, the broadloom ripped out, the hardwood floors sanded…as if a deep stain had to be eradicated, as if a cleansing had to be done (and all the while, we went through the dreary listing of each broken or missing thing…each thing the ghost of a moment from the past – like counting razor cuts on the skin that were so fine they could hardly be seen though the wounds were deep to the bone). Papers had been hosed down by the firemen and letters turned to sodden ash in my hands; rolled drawings were scorched funnels that fell apart…leaving only a drawn fingertip, a lip…all stacked in a hundred boxes piled in the basement… two lives, boxed and stacked, and then, a few days later, the police told us that they had arrested a second man, named Costa. In a determined gesture toward normalcy, we bought a new television set and put it in the kitchen, a dead grey eye but a promise of sound…

On a crisp December morning we woke and ate breakfast and watched the long, lean harbour police boat leave on patrol. The harbour was icing over but there were still geese on open patches of the gunmetal grey water. We drove to the house and discovered that the back door was open, the television set was gone, some jewellery trinkets and a fox fur jacket were gone. We had been robbed again (when a house has been hit, a cop on the phone said, the word goes out on the street: thieves know television sets will be replaced, and an empty house is a sitting duck). So we were being watched. We were a word on the street, a whisper of affliction on the air.

A detective came by to dust for fingerprints. He was wearing a narrow-brimmed hat, a brown suit with narrow lapels. He was lean and close-mouthed, gruff and meticulous. "Yes, ma'am," he said. "No." Dust and fingerprints. For a moment, C. Jane said she thought she was losing her mind, except she couldn't stop laughing quietly, and she mumbled to me, "Go ask Jack Webb if he thinks we'll ever catch these guys."

"No," the detective said. "Not likely. You got the first guys but not these guys."

I could see that this affliction was going to go on for a long time. I could hear the blind man talking to the butterflies. Disconsolate, I went back to the hotel, and then down to the shore, to the breakwater in front of the hotel, and I sat watching single-engine planes drop out of the watery grey sky to the island airport. I'd finished a new poem, my dead mother following a dogwood trail:

> until she reached brushes and eelgrass,
> a cover of slate grey water.
> She undressed and slid
> down a stone shelf
> into the shallows,
> dragging shore-slime and fronds,

and splashed cold water over her belly and breasts,
staring at the sky
moth-eaten by light, pale stars.
She eased into the slough.
It had the feel of ointment
as she scissored down
to the braided roots on the bottom,
eyes closed, ears singing,
her drowning voice filling her lungs, swelling,
until the sound became a searing light
behind her eyes
that drove her crashing
into the air,
gulping down the dark
as she crawled ashore.

GUMBY GOES TO HEAVEN

We knew that this tawdry, soft mockery of our life was going to go on for at least a year: certainly, we would outlast it if only because we could still laugh, that raw laughter down the snout, the *Haw* of laughter at laughter itself – but I was now full of a dark rankling alertness to all kinds of signs and signals of affliction: for instance, one day at Dundas and University Streets, I saw through the car window a tall memorial monument to the dead airmen of the War. I was suddenly enraged. I heard myself hissing the name of the very rich man who had paid for the monument. *Hal Jackman*...a local man known for his wealth, his collection of antique lead soldiers, and his sterling political connections, a man who had used his connections to erect a monument to his moneyed influence, and his trite taste. Children had nicknamed it *Gumby Goes to Heaven*, after the cartoon character, Gumby, who had been steamrollered flat by life. In every aesthetic sense, since it was safe, so conventional, so banal, the monument was a sculptural affront to all the men who'd fallen out of the sky on fire, the lost souls it presumed to celebrate. I could rebuild our house, and someday – if Rob Lowrey could work his miracle – I would play the blues on the piano, but I was going to have to confront that self-serving monument for as long as I lived in the city. It was a permanent offence, a tin-soldiering view of life and death.

Luck Bird in a Monkey Puzzle Tree

Before Christmas, on a cold, clear day, we drove to the Old City Hall (a dank labyrinth of pea-green and pallid yellow court-rooms) for the preliminary hearing. We had not thought much about the two men who were doing dead time in the city jail (my own contact on the street, a musician – a black horn player I'd known for years – told me that six men had been in the house, that six men had been in C. Jane's stolen car). We wondered about their faces and pondered the old question: was this a hired hit? And if so, who hated me so much? And if money for the moon plant and crack were the motive for the break-in, was the raging assault on the house a malignancy without malice?

We sat in an overheated room with the fire chief, several detectives and officers, a woman who said she was Lugosi's girlfriend, a Vietnamese bricklayer who had come face-to-face with Costa as he hauled suitcases full of our things out the front door, hauled them out to be fenced and melted down by some scumbag uptown swine who fed off junkie break-and-enter kids...melting down our bindings of love...and the woman who had seen the smoke and turned in the alarm, a stout woman who was the desk clerk at the Waverly Hotel on Spadina Avenue where Lugosi had rented a room, another woman with confetti in her hair who sat beating a tin cup...

As we went up the wide marble stairs to wait outside Courtroom H, a courtroom next to the marriage bureau, I was told several things by several people: that when looking for Costa, two officers had cornered a man in a cappuccino bar on College Street and the man had flattened them both, driving one cop into the street through a plate-glass window...the detectives confessed that they felt very sheepish about this; also, Lugosi had checked into the Waverly Hotel before breaking into the house and he had checked in under my name; the house had been cased by a man, a light-skinned black man, named Bo...and Bo – who was known to the cops – had probably been in the house at least once before it was hit; Bo apparently had his own business cards – "Surveyor and Estimator" – and would work for any "interests" who would hire him; Lugosi had come back into the hotel after leaving the house in the morning, waving a blowtorch, threatening to set fire to the hotel "just like he had torched a house on Sullivan Street;" several men were waiting in a blue car at the hotel and got into C. Jane"s car without Lugosi and drove off; Costa had made several trips to the fence who operated out of a Dunk-A-Donut shop on lower Spadina Avenue during the night using C. Jane's car; Lugosi's old girlfriend, saying he had done her grievous harm, not only wanted to testify to that harm but also said she could explain why he had savaged our house: it was all, she said, because of an incident in August when I was seen taking the ferry to the park on the island in the city harbour, and Lugosi, who worked with a punk rock band, had spoken to me and I had snubbed him: "He said he would get you for that." The only problem was, I hadn't been on the ferry to the island for four years and in August I had been writing poetry and handicapping under a monkey puzzle tree in Saratoga.

As the afternoon passed, as we waited to be called into the courtroom to at last look into the faces of the two men, to say to them and to the court what we had been through, what we had lost inside ourselves, what music and private liturgies had been stilled, we listened dryly to the sullying confidences of the street while very young couples – most of them black and surprisingly alone, without friends or family – strutted by, beaming, untarnished and newly wed. The woman with the confetti in her hair beat on her tin cup. Then, after all the witnesses had been heard in the closed courtroom and the afternoon had waned, we sat alone on the bench, uncalled, in silence: the doors opened and Sergeant Hamel, looking pleased, explained that everything had worked out to his satisfaction. "The two of you are unnecessary. It's being sent to trial." Lugosi was led to the elevator; slender, head bowed, penitential; Costa, less shrewd, smirked with bravado and stared brazenly at C. Jane. The elevator doors closed, and so, with nothing left to do in the shadow light of the Old City Hall corridors, we went Christmas shopping.

"This is all lunatic," I said to C. Jane. "Everybody's doing what they're doing without ever asking why."

"Because Y is a crooked letter," she said.

On Christmas Eve, after we were told that the sanded hardwood floors in the house had been stained, we stood at midnight in the vestibule, pleased with the wet, dark sheen. "It'll go beautifully with the piano," C. Jane said.

On Christmas Day, though there was no furniture in the house, we moved out of the hotel, leaving the waterfront behind. Two old Chinese women stood in the lane watching us unload books and papers and clothes. The women said nothing. One was wearing a T-shirt under her open jacket. There was lettering on the shirt:

IN FREEDOM
LUCK
BIRD

I realized that in our four years of living in Chinatown not one Chinese neighbour had ever spoken to me, not even the people who ran the corner Mom and Pop store, who sold me cream and detergent and paper towels. We had handed dimes and quarters back and forth, but I didn't even know if they could speak English. I was angry at Lugosi and Costa but loathed the political culture that encouraged people like the two old women to close in on themselves in a language from another country. Getting to know such neighbours would be like climbing a monkey puzzle tree.

Separate trials took place in February. The Crown Attorney, a pert young woman, was eager: she had a solid case; break and enter, theft and arson, fingerprints and a witness. She thought she could get a substantial sentence. A plea bargain was struck: Lugosi would not contest his guilt if I would agree to five years. "Yes," I said, "I suppose five years will do." (But what, I wondered to C. Jane, did five years mean? – What did this curious attachment of penitential time to a crime mean?...Not the inflicting of corporal pain, but the religious notion of "serving time" in a monkish cell; and I recalled the idiotic notions of my childhood catechism and the confessional – two years off in the purgatorial fires for...five years off in purgatory for...we were pale souls smiling wanly, innocent but sullied by an eyeless fire-bug desert god who was always itching for a final conflagration.)

We sat in an almost empty courtroom. Two men I'd seen around the Waverly Hotel sat beside me, and a lone woman, and a detective. Lugosi sat in a box, head down. I looked at Lugosi for a while and felt little or nothing: no witnesses were called before Judge David Humphrey. Police photographs of the house were entered as evidence of wilful havoc and the seven fires. At the court's request, I had written a note about what it was like being a victim. It was for the judge to read. Time, I told the judge, was our punishment, too. Guilty of nothing, we were being punished. Time was the real bond between criminals and victims: "Having survived three months' dislocation we realize how disruptive the devastation has been...the endless sorting through drawings, papers – charred, destroyed, these are the tissues of our life, our spirit. We have been robbed of time, it is a robbery that goes on and on…Creative time, insights – those fleeting moments of inspiration – they are gone forever…The dispiriting loss of time – and we cannot help each other – for C. Jane, as an artist, has suffered exactly the same loss as I have. We are doing time, and we get no time off for good behaviour. The terrible irony is that these two men may well do less time than we will. For us, the loss of time spirals…each week implies a month of lost writing, sculpting…every two months a half-year, a half-year two years, a year will become five. Together, we may do more dead time than they will. There is the real crime committed against us…" The judge expressed his stern dismay; C. Jane said nothing; Lugosi said nothing. He was sentenced to five years.

A few weeks later, Costa was tried. His defence was hapless: he said that all the damage had been done by Lugosi after he'd left the house for the last time at nine o'clock in the morning. The fire alarm had been turned in at 9:03. That meant Lugosi had savaged the house and set seven fires on three floors in under three minutes. The judge shook his head, embarrassed by the ineptness of the argument. Costa was a young immigrant, a crack addict, a child of the moon plant, his life ruined, on his way to the brutality of prison. I wanted to say something but had nothing to say. The judge told Costa that he was sentenced to two years in a dark clock, the penitentiary.

BETWEEN THE STRUCK KEY AND THE STRING

"At last," C. Jane said, "I feel safe." She stopped looking for addicts in the windows at night where she'd see only her own reflection. We took no pleasure in the sentencing. It had to be: the arson demanded it; the police – for their own morale – needed it; as victims we were witnesses to it; but we took no pleasure. Vengeance, like jealousy, is a second-rate emotion, which is why I told the Crown Attorney that I had always found the old Jewish tribal stories of bloodletting and sacrifice – "an eye for an eye, tooth for a tooth" – so twisted. "Esther was a murderous lunatic," I said. "Esther who?" the Crown Attorney asked. I was no pacifist, but vengeance gave me no pleasure, no satisfaction. We felt only a hollow in the house, and the need to fill it with laughter, meditation and music. But every morning, all day, there was only repairing, hammering.

Drilling.

Waiting for workmen to show up.

Waiting. Life as repair.

Realizing the repairmen were padding their bills.

"What d'you care, Mac, it's all covered in the insurance." Expediency. Grease for the wheels. Nothing done on time, time meaning nothing, till in the summer we went to Rob Lowrey's to see the piano: it had become, in our imaginations, more than scorched fiddleback veneer and charred legs; after opening the lid on its inner parts, so scarred and warped and twisted by fire and supposedly beyond repair – it had become the embodiment of our own renewal. Mahogany could be turned and trimmed, as we had turned ourselves out for dinner every night at the waterfront hotel, but only we knew the ashes, the soot we could still feel on the covers of books, taste on our breaths. So the piano had to be cleansed and brought back to life. The stillness that lies between the struck key and the string, the stillness that contains the note, had to sound.

Rob Lowrey, who had said in dismay that restoration would require a redeeming miracle, greeted us with a subdued eagerness, a caution that comes from dealing with damage. But he had a solid, rounded playfulness as he moved quickly and soundlessly into the aroma of varnish and glue in his workroom, standing in his white apron, obviously relishing his young workers' bashful way of laying their hands on wood. There were men at several pianos, each striking a note, listening, head half-cocked, then malleting a tuning peg into a pin plank, threading thin wire through the peg...slowly tightening, tuning the treble and then the heavier bass strings...twenty-four tons of tension in those strings, all our anxiety struggling toward the inner harmony that is always the mystery of the piano, the piano in tune with itself.

I stood staring into the hollow guts of our piano as if I were looking back through a jagged hole into the months that had passed, the veneer peeled down to the glue-stained frame and new wood held by vises, the bridges and ribs, the pin planks all laid out...and Lowrey, smiling, said, "September. We've had to send the legs to Cleveland. No one here can carve those old legs..."

"September?"

"Don't worry," he said. "It'll play like a charm."

"I'll have a party, then, open up the house."

"Why not?"

We felt safe: the lane and the garden were floodlit at night, the garage door could be opened only from inside, the garage wall was rebuilt, all the glass doors had jamb-bars, the rooms had been wired to an alarm system of motion detectors, and we were now four: we had got a young, powerful golden retriever, and called him No Name Jive, and we'd got a regal Irish setter, C-Jam Blues. They slept with us and whimpered if they weren't petted but snarled at any sound outside the door and chewed our shoes as we retrieved our losses.

We had been fortunate to have a good man – fair and accomplished – as our insurance adjuster: a man with close-cropped hair and alert eyes, John Morris. His efficient cheerfulness puzzled us: more than for a priest, it seemed to me, disasters came like tumbleweed across Morris's desk...an endless array of mishaps and malevolence that he had to adjust. Perhaps, I said to C. Jane, that is what a priest really is or should be: an adjuster. In his middle years, he had heard every slick story and dealt with every scam, yet, for all his rigour, he had been sympathetic, and the insurance company had accepted all his recommendations. We would never recover all our losses, but the company was going to honour their obligations without argument.

To Erewhon and Back

But as we prepared to drive south again to Saratoga, to renew the ritual of daiquiris in the garden and the saddling of the horses in the walking ring, and the blind man, our insurance company, Trafalgar, announced it would not renew its coverage, shedding us, leaving us completely vulnerable. So be it, I thought. Our agent tried to make arrangements with other companies. To her astonishment, to our rage and sudden fear, no one would insure us. Not Trafalgar, not Wellington, not Guardian, not Laurentian, not any company approached. At the same time, the mortgage company wrote asking for confirmation of fire insurance, a condition of the mortgage. Without insurance the mortgage would be called. Never mind the blind man. We would be broken by debt, driven out of the house. "Because," I was told, "you're a controversial writer, even I remember what you said about the settlements on the West Bank, the bigots in Belfast." This was worse than any street thuggery. Even our insurance adjuster, unbelieving, tried to get us insurance with his contacts: the answer was No. There was nothing to be done. Though I had paid house insurance into the industry for twenty-five years, as soon as I was hit – as soon as what I was insured against happened – those companies all closed down on me. Insurance men weren't low-life junkies, strung out and hooked on crack; no, I raged at C. Jane, they were the blue suits, the actuaries money-crunching the odds on death, shrewd men who were kissing cousins to the California auto insurer for Budget Rent-a-Car – who still, a year after the Audi had been compacted to the sound of *Sing, Sing, Sing*, owed us $1,200, and still they refused to pay, stalling and stalling until time, the statute of limitations, the clock would run out. These men were bigger sharks than any dipso break-and-enter kid: these were men who had earned their pinstripes, men who intended to leave us twisting in the wind, defenceless. I knew where I was. I was in the land of Erewhon, Samuel Butler's Erewhon (Nowhere misspelled backwards), where "ill-luck of any kind, or even ill-treatment at the hands of others, is considered an offence against society, inasmuch as it makes people uncomfortable to hear of it. Loss of fortune, therefore…is punished hardly less severely than physical delinquency." We had committed an offence by becoming victims. The insurers were going to punish us in ways harsher than any druggies had ever dreamed of…the motives behind their institutional malignancy were clear. "The insurance companies are protecting themselves," a broker with pale, almost colourless eyes said with disarming openness. "If you weren't who you are, there'd be no problem."

"If I wasn't who I am," I said to C. Jane as we drove past the monument to all the dead airmen, "I'd blow the bastards up."

Then our adjuster found us a sensible, elderly, experienced woman in the insurance business – who reminded me of the way good bank managers used to be: she did not have an MBA from a business college and she was unafraid of her own judgment – and the problem was solved.

"What's required is a blind eye," she said.

"Of course I understand…I'm a nobody," I said, and we both laughed.

She wrote on the form: "No known notoriety." I let out a raw laugh, a loud *Haw*, down the snout.

"How come you don't think like these other gonzos around here?" I asked.

"Actually," she said, "I was not born around here. I was born outside Munich, on the edge of Dachau, but that's another story." The woman winked. "They make very good porcelain in Dachau, you know."

The house was insured by Chubb.

BEYOND FIELDS OF ASPHODEL

On a September Saturday afternoon, two men levered the legless and lidless body of our piano onto a sling and lowered it out of a truck onto a trolley and rolled the trolley into the house. They malleted the pins that hold the legs and set the piano in the bay window, all the light catching the grain, so that Rob Lowrey could tune the strings, and then in the early evening, Doug Richardson, a friend for more than thirty years, came in. I had known him back in the days when I'd hung out with a woman called EveLynne in a black dance hall close to Augusta Avenue, the Porter's Hall, run by a gap-toothed man called Kennie Holdup, and Doug had played his horn there, and now he played flute, too, and he had a pianist with him, Connie Maynard. "You get to christen the keys," I said, as Connie sat down and worked through several chord progressions, and then stood up, beaming: "Very nice. Beautiful sound. Quiet touch."

"Quiet, I like quiet," Doug, who had an impish wit, said. "I hate noise, noisy cars most of all. Expensive cars are noisy. Who'd want a Ferrari? How could you ever hold up a bank in a Ferrari?"

The house was beginning to fill with friends carrying flowers and wine, crowding into conversation in all the rooms, friends who were writers and newshounds and gamblers, editors and the two carpenters who had meticulously trimmed the house, professors and maître d's and film producers, and after C. Jane said, "This'll be strange, being hosts at our own resurrection," I drifted happily from room to room pouring wine, all the slashes on the walls healed, while hearing – I was sure – each note unlocked from the stillness between struck key and string. I introduced Sergeant Hamel to the crowd. He bowed in a courtly way from the waist. Doug, mischievous as ever, stopped honking on his sax and spread-eagled himself beside the door. "All niggers up against the wall," he cried. Everyone laughed and the laughter was an acknowledgment that there is a little larceny in all of us, and in the cops, too. I had given Sergeant Hamel my new book of poems and he said he wanted to hear something said aloud because he didn't know how to read poetry. "It's not like reading a report," he said. With Doug and Connie on the piano backing me up, I chanted in the voice of Sesephus the Crack King, a whacked-out hustler:

> *Get down, get down,*
> *you got to get down*
> *on your hands and knees*
> *and keep your ear close to the ground.*
> *There are druggies*
> *who honey-dip around parking lots*
> *playing the clown*
> *instead of the clarinet, looking for*
> *peddlers of high renown*
> *as in H,*
> *or dealers doing sap of the moon plant,*
> *crack and smack. I used to dial a vial*
> *myself,*
> *a little digital digitalis,*
> *the speed I dropped*
> *absorbing the absence*
> *in the air*
> *with a light so rare*
> *it baked the shadow of despair*
> *on a wall that wasn't there.*
> *God almighty, it was a time*
> *in fields of asphodel...*

In the early morning hours, after our friends had sung a last song around the piano and had gone home and C. Jane had gone to bed and the dogs were asleep, I stood on the upstairs back porch staring down into the darkness of the lane, the dark split by a shaft of light from the new high-beam lamp on the garage. The two thieves had come up on to the porch out of that darkness to break and enter into our lives, but as I stood there staring at the light I remembered my childhood and how at night when the light from a kitchen door fell across an alley-way, I'd crouch on one side of it – as if I were a mysterious traveller – and then I'd leap through the light and go on my way unseen, unscathed. The year had been like that light; we had leapt through it and with our secret selves intact we were now travelling on.

II

What he has now to say is a long
wonder the world can bear & be.
Once in a sycamore I was glad
all at the top, and I sang.
Hard on the land wears the strong sea
and empty grows every bed.
—JOHN BERRYMAN, *The Dream Songs*

THE BLACK QUEEN

Hughes and McCrae were fastidious men who took pride in their old colonial house, the clean simple lines and stucco walls and the painted pale-blue picket fence. They were surrounded by houses converted into small warehouses, trucking yards where houses had been torn down, and along the street a school filled with foreign children, but they didn't mind. It gave them an embattled sense of holding on to something important, a tattered remnant of good taste in an area of waste overrun by rootless olive-skinned children.

McCrae wore his hair a little too long now that he was going grey, and while Hughes, with his clipped moustache, seemed to be a serious man intent only on his work, which was costume design, McCrae sported Cuban heels, and lacquered his nails. When they'd met ten years ago Hughes had said, "You keep walking around like that and you'll need somebody to keep you from getting poked in the eye." McCrae did all the cooking and drove the car.

But they were not getting along these days. Hughes blamed his bursitis, but they were both silently unsettled by how old they had suddenly become, how loose in the thighs, and their feet, when they were showering in the morning, seemed bonier, the toes longer, the nails yellow and hard. What they wanted was tenderness, to be able to yield almost tearfully, full of a pity for themselves that would not be belittled or laughed at, and when they stood alone in their separate bedrooms they wanted that tenderness from each other. But when they were having their bedtime tea in the kitchen, as they had done for years, using lovely green and white Limoges cups, if one touched the other's hand then suddenly they both withdrew into an unspoken, smiling aloofness, as if some line of privacy had been crossed. Neither could bear their thinning wrists and the little pouches of darkening flesh under the chin. They spoke of being with younger people and even joked slyly about bringing a young man home, but that seemed such a betrayal of everything they had believed had set them apart from others, everything they believed had kept them together, that they sulked and nettled away at each other, and though nothing had apparently changed in their lives, they were always on edge, Hughes more than McCrae.

One of their pleasures was collecting stamps, rare and mint-perfect, centred, balanced perforations, and no creases or smudges on the gum. Their collection, carefully mounted in a large leather-bound blue book with little plastic windows for each year per page, was worth several thousand dollars. They had passed many pleasant evenings together on the Directoire settee arranging the old ochre- and carmine-coloured stamps. They agreed there was something almost sensual about holding a perfectly preserved piece of the past, unsullied, as if everything didn't have to change, didn't have to end up swamped by decline and decay. They disapproved of the new stamps and dismissed them as crude and wouldn't have them in their book. The pages for the recent years remained empty and they liked that; the emptiness was their statement about themselves and their values, and Hughes, holding a stamp up into the light between his tweezers, would say, "None of that rough trade for us."

One afternoon they went down to the philatelic shops around Adelaide and Richmond Streets and saw a stamp they had been after for a long time, a large and elegant black stamp of Queen Victoria in her widow's weeds. It was rare and expensive, a dead-letter stamp from the turn of the century. They stood side by side over the glass counter-case, admiring it, their hands spread on the glass, but when McCrae, the overhead fluorescent light catching his lacquered nails, said, "Well, I certainly would like that little black sweetheart," the owner, who had sold stamps to them for several years, looked up and smirked, and Hughes suddenly snorted, "You old queen. I mean, why don't you just quit wearing those goddamn Cuban heels, eh? I mean, why not?" He walked out leaving McCrae embarrassed and hurt, and when the owner said, "So what was wrong?" McCrae cried, "Screw you," and strutted out.

Through the rest of the week they were deferential around the house, offering each other every consideration, trying to avoid any squabble before Mother's Day at the end of the week when they were going to hold their annual supper for friends, three other male couples. Over the years it had been an elegant, slightly mocking evening that often ended bittersweetly and left them feeling close, comforting each other.

McCrae worked all Sunday afternoon in the kitchen, and through the window he could see the crabapple tree in bloom and he thought how in previous years he would have begun planning to put down some jelly in the old pressed glass jars they kept in the cellar, but instead, head down, he went on stuffing and tying the pork loin roast. Then in the early evening he heard Hughes at the door, and there was laughter from the front room and someone cried out, "What do you do with an elephant who has three balls on him?... You don't know, silly? Well, you walk him and pitch to the giraffe," and there were howls of laughter and the clinking of glasses. It had been the same every year, eight men sitting down to a fine supper with expensive wines, the table set with their best silver under the antique carved wooden candelabra.

Having prepared all the raw vegetables, the cauliflower and carrots, the avocados and miniature corns-on-the-cob, and placed porcelain bowls of homemade dip in the centre of a pewter tray, McCrae stared at his reflection for a moment in the window over the kitchen sink and then he took a plastic slipcase out of the knives-and-forks drawer. The case contained the dead-letter stamp. He licked it all over and pasted it on his forehead and then slipped on the jacket of his charcoal-brown crushed velvet suit, took hold of the tray, and stepped out into the front room.

The other men, sitting in a circle around the coffee table, looked up and one of them giggled. Hughes cried, "Oh, my God." McCrae, as if nothing were the matter, said, "My dears, time for the crudités." He was in his silk stocking feet, and as he passed the tray around he winked at Hughes who sat staring at the black queen.

WITHOUT SHAME

Only one thing is more tragic than suffering,
and that is the life of a happy man.

—ALBERT CAMUS

Alice Kopff and her brother, Lyle, owned a bakery shop. He was
thirty-six, she was thirty-three. He baked the breads. She was the
pastry chef, a pale, plain woman who was so constantly bright-eyed
and ebullient that Lyle said, "Sometimes I think you must be one
of those happiness flashers for Jesus."

"Not likely," she laughed.

"But even after the funeral…"

Two years earlier, their mother and father, who had opened the
Kopff & Kopff Bakery Shoppe after coming to Toronto from
Dresden, had died of smoke inhalation. A fire that had broken out
behind the ovens had crawled quickly across the floor, trapping
them in the kitchen. They had suffered severe burns to the face.
Their coffins had been closed. During the funeral mass, Lyle, arms
folded, holding on to himself, had said, "It is incredible to me that
our mother and father who, as youngsters, survived the wartime
firestorming of Dresden, who had then made of their life…not fire
but bread…should here, among us, nonetheless die of fire…"

Alice, veiled and dressed in black, had wept in her pew as if she
were inconsolable, yet after the service, standing out in the sunlight
on the church porch, she had lifted her veil and looked delighted

as she took hold of every hand extended to her. Lyle thought she had lost her mind.

The eager young parish priest, Father Dowd, was disarmed by what he thought was her avoidance of the vanities of grief and whispered to her, "I'm glad that you..."

"Yes," she'd called out, "a gladness..."

That night, over a supper of cold meats, Lyle had asked, "What came over you?"

"Nothing."

"What do you mean, nothing?"

"Nothing. Nothing's nothing."

"No, it's not."

"Yes, it is, plain and simple."

"I just wondered," he had said mournfully, "how, with both Mother and Father fresh in the ground, you could be so happy?"

Crossing her knife and fork on her plate, she said:

> *As I was going out one day*
> *My head fell off and rolled away.*
> *When I saw that it was gone*
> *I picked it up and put it on.*

Then Alice got pregnant. No one knew who the father was. She would give no name. Lyle was furious. "The shame." He pounded the granite countertop beside the cash register with his fist: "This is a complete betrayal of everything Mother and Father stood for."

"Maybe."

"Maybe what?"

"Maybe not."

"Maybe yes. And who'll look after the child?"

"There'll be no problem," she said.

She bought an old black wicker pram at a thrift store. She wheeled it, full of freshly cut flowers, up and down the street, to and from the shop.

"I think I'll call the child Happy," she said. "If it's a girl, she can be a dancer, and if it's a boy, he can play second base for the Yankees – Happy Kopff at second base."

"Happy's not a name," Lyle said.

"You could try being happy yourself," she said.

"I am happy. Who says I'm not? However, I'm no fool."

"Meaning I am," she said.

She folded her hands across her stomach, and then with a pouting, playful little smile, she said again, "There'll be no problem."

"Of course there's a problem."

"No, there's not."

"It's awful, it really is, you're without shame."

When she told Father Dowd that she was pregnant, but there was no problem, he said, "No, no, there is certainly a problem, a problem that requires at least some regret, some weeping."

"You mean confession?"

"At least."

She said she would not go to confession, for she didn't like confession, but promised Father Dowd that she would say an Act of Contrition alone in her room. "I'll put penance to bed with me," she said, smiling. And for four days she went without lunch and for four days she did not put flowers in the pram, and, when she said hello to neighbours passing in the street or to customers in the shop, she did so with a contrite pout. But then one morning she appeared at the shop with a little red tear painted under each of her eyes, like a doll's tears, and she stood in the shop kitchen delighted to be laughing again, through her painted tears, tears that by the end of the day, because of the intense heat from the ovens, had run in streaks down her cheeks.

"You look goddamn insane," Lyle said.

She shrugged and said, "Don't be silly, I'm happy as a lark," and she turned on the radio to listen to the baseball game while she worked. On the way home she bought two large bouquets of flowers for the black wicker pram. She did not, however, wheel it up and down the street. "That'll come soon enough," she said.

When she was taken to hospital and went into labour, she was three weeks early. It was a breech birth, the boy child coming out feet first, dead.

She overheard Father Dowd say to Lyle, "The child's soul has gone to limbo."

At the undertaker's, she told the priest, "He's right here in my heart. My heart's alive in him."

One week after the burial, she came into the bakery in the morning, her long hair tied in a single thick braid. She was wearing a smock that was baby blue. She said she was going to come to work wearing her baby-blue smock every day, like she was going to wear her tears. She laughed a shy little laugh. Lyle said sternly, "Why not wear normal white? Wipe the slate clean."

By closing hour at the end of that week, when the kitchen and counter staff were convinced she was going to be as easygoing and cheerful as ever, as Lyle stood with his arms buried up to his elbows in a vat of flour, they circled around her and rapped their pastry brushes, spoons, and even a rolling pin on the granite counter and gave her a clap of hands.

She was so moved by the applause that she untied her braid, letting her hair hang loose. Then, once she was at home, she wheeled the pram out to the centre of the front lawn and filled it with potting earth. The next day she bought and planted an ornamental dwarf pine – "a pine that will grow green all year" – and she surrounded the fingerling branches of the pine with red and white impatiens.

"The colours of the resurrection," Father Dowd said, trying to cheer Lyle up.

"The pram's morbid," Lyle said.

"A touch, it is that, perhaps," the young priest said.

"Morbid," he told Alice.

"Not at all," Alice said. "Everything can be made to be happy," and then she broke into a grin, with her hands on her hips, as if she were challenging him.

He said nothing. But he told Father Dowd, "I think she's maybe hysterical."

Father Dowd said, "I don't know. Perhaps something quite profound is at work in her, not just the acceptance of God's will, but out of the darkness, out of the sin and death that was the birth, has come the renewal of a joy that is inherent in death. It is the mystery of the Cross, is it not?"

That weekend, on the feast of Corpus Christi, Alice baked a five-layer chocolate-mocha cake for the priests at the parish church of the Blessed Sacrament. She carried the cake in a white cardboard box to the parish house. Father Dowd, standing in slippers at the door, said he would offer a prayer of thanksgiving for her at Mass.

"For my child, too," she said.

"Of course, and if there's any need, any emergency, call me."

"Life is an emergency," she said, eyes bright.

A few weeks later, she had the shop delivery man carry five cakes to the Knights of Columbus church basement Friday night supper. After some confusion, the Knight Exemplar, realizing the cakes were a gift from Kopff & Kopff, doffed his plumed hat and happily ordered that the cakes be carried to the kitchen for cutting.

"Isn't Alice Kopff a Christian to contend with?" the Knight Exemplar said to his fellow Knights, as coffee and her cakes were served.

"Isn't Kopff a German-Jewish name, the two F's?" one of the Knights asked.

"As far as I know she's completely Catholic."

"Not that it matters."

As the Knights seated in the round, ten to each table, discovered coins in their cake and cleared icing away from their prizes, the Knight Exemplar, moved, said, "I have always liked to think that we men, as Knights in the army of our Lord, have not lost a sense of where we come from, that God's dirt is under our nails. But suddenly I realize what it is that some of us have lost, and that is – the delight at finding a penny in our cakes, the delight that a child knows in discovering there are grace moments in life…"

"Alice is a wonder," Father Dowd said, and after Sunday Mass, as Lyle waited for her in the emptied church, he thanked her from the altar for what he called her "generosity, her infectious irrepressible lightness of spirit," smiling down at her as she, seated alone in the pew that had become her usual place at Mass, smiled up at him.

"I think I might go to confession," she said.

Over lunch, Lyle said, "That priest, Father Dowd, he's got some kind of thing about you."

On some nights, particularly weekend nights after they had worked hard all day in the heat of the kitchen, Lyle heard, after supper, what he thought were moans from her bedroom, and he was sure that she was talking to herself. He couldn't tell by her tone, as he stood at the bottom of the stairs, whether she was angry or not – or perhaps she was praying – but he gave no thought to going silently up the stairs to listen: that would have been an invasive intimacy, and he shied away from any intimacies if he could (there had been women in his life but he'd liked best those who had expected the least from him). He stayed at the bottom of the stairs. Her moans sounded almost sexual, or like she was in pain, yet there was certainly no one with her in her room (he'd spent several hours, off and on, wondering where, in what room, she had bedded down with an unknown man, and when – and for how long? When had she been out of his sight, and could it have possibly been in her own room – under his eye, so to speak – without him seeing? The possibility filled him with panic; could he, in his own house, have had no idea of what was going on?). Rattled, he didn't know what to think, especially in the morning when she appeared for her toast and coffee looking well-slept, refreshed, with no clouding of sleeplessness or pain in her eyes.

"I must remember to water the flowers in the pram," she said. "My little dwarf pine."

"It looks ridiculous. It's not a pot."

"Then what is it?"

"It's not a flowerbed."

"It's a deathbed," she said firmly.

They divided the morning newspaper. He took the editorial section, she the sports pages.

"The Leafs lost," she said.

"Oh yeah."

"In sudden death," she said.

He put his page down. "We've never talked very much, have we?"

"You mean talking talk, or real talk? We've always talked talk, if we had to."

"Real talk," he said.

"Well, I wouldn't know what to say."

"No."

"Or why."

"No."

"Mother and Dad never seemed to need to talk very much."

"Yes. I always thought that that's what was so sane about them," he said. "I mean, they seemed, I don't know..."

"Together."

"I suppose it's because of them I've always known it was okay to have nothing to say."

"We're kind of accomplices," she said.

"You mean the shop?"

"No. In solitude. We are accomplices in solitude."

He looked into her eyes, at her painted tears, and said, "You know," laughing, an unguarded laugh that she had almost never heard from him, "sometimes I think you are right out of your mind."

She laughed, too, her sprightly laugh, and said, as if she needed to somehow reassure him, "If I'm out of my mind, it's all right with me."

><><

On Sundays, after the taking of Communion, when the congregants turned to each other in their pews to shake hands, to embrace, she didn't notice – as she eagerly clasped hand after hand – that some parishioners, confronted by her relentless goodwill, shied away from her.

Father Dowd noticed, and he wondered – the next time she came to confession, and she was now coming once a week though she had little or nothing to confess – if he shouldn't try to speak to her about how dangerous candour is, how it does not bring out the best in most people but makes them feel inadequate, and he thought he should suggest that she be less effusive, less delighted by her own enthusiasms.

After Mass, however, out on the porch steps, when she took Father Dowd in a two-handed clasp, exuding all her open generosity of spirit, her seemingly guileless goodwill, he couldn't resist: he held her with two hands himself.

"More and more there is a gladness in my heart," she said as she backed down the stairs, calling out, "and don't forget to pray for my son. He's not in limbo. I don't believe in limbo."

One of the other priests, Father McClure, after lunch, as if he were having an idle thought between pitches as they watched a baseball game on television, said, "You know, Father Dowd, I'm not sure we should encourage that woman, all that ridiculous gushing good feeling... And those painted tears. Please..."

Father Dowd didn't answer. Someone hit a home run for the Blue Jays and Father McClure stood up, clapping, enthusiastic.

><~><

For the annual Field Day held in the gym at the parish school, Alice sent, by the Kopff & Kopff delivery van, eight large icing-lathered cakes to the grade school homerooms – each of the cakes seeded with nickels, dimes, quarters, and one silver dollar. Lyle, as he banged his fists together in exasperation, told her, "This is not good. Not for you. Not for me. The expense, the expense to us out of pocket, and all the hours you take to make those cakes…"

Seated at her work table, she was building a tall cone of chocolate profiteroles, each pastry ball filled with cream – "wiring" the balls together with spun caramel. "For a person like me, who is a pastry chef," she said, looking up at Lyle through filaments of caramel, gold in the light, "making a cake is as easy as falling down. Besides, I'm sure you've noticed that our business has probably tripled… The wives of the Knights of Columbus have done us no harm…"

"For Christ's sake, they call you the Cake Lady."

"That's better than calling me a whore, which some did."

"And you think gladness of heart is a defence…?"

"I don't think like you do, not at all. I don't need to defend myself. I'm guilty of nothing."

He sighed, opened the ovens, and went back to ladling mounds of dough into the fire, singing over and over a gay little ditty that was trapped in his mind: *I got plenty of nothing and nothing's got plenty for me…*

He tried to find in his head another song to sing.

He couldn't.

None of this is fair, he thought, unsure of what was unfair as he stood among pleased customers who were lined up in front of the pastry showcases.

"Dessert is such a pleasure," he said to a woman, startling her as she waited by the cash register. "Isn't it?"

"Yes. Yes, it is," she said defensively.

"Have a chocolate mousse tart," he blurted out, "on the house."

"Why, thank you, thank you. What an unexpected surprise."

"Yes," he said and gave her a big smile, pleased with himself.

Several teachers at the parish school, however, were not pleased with Alice's cakes. They had not anticipated that several students, with more cake than they could eat, would start cake fights in the halls, lobbing gobs of icing against the walls, smearing cream across the chalkboards, fighting over the prize monies. And one irate mother complained that bigger boys had bullied all the quarters and silver dollars out of other children and had offered the money to her daughter if they could touch her bare breasts and she had let them touch her. She had come home sick from too much cake and icing, her jeans' pockets heavy with coins and her training bra lost behind the playground chain-link fencing.

No one told Alice about these children.

Many parents did not want her told. They said it was terrible, given her generosity, that she – who had asked for nothing in return – should be blamed for the evil inclinations of some unruly children. "It is unbelievable that a guileless spirit should be told to stop," one parent said at a meeting in the principal's office, "and told to stop with all the meanness we can muster."

Lyle got up from the living-room sofa. He heard her moaning, a deep pulsing moan that he could not ignore. He stood at the bottom of the stairs, listening. He felt a chill come over him, something deep, a ground chill. He had cocked a cold eye on her that morning and he had been astonished to see how frail she was, her skin translucent, almost a glazed tint of blue beneath the skin. He realized that she had been eating less and less, looking more and more pleased the less she ate.

He undid the laces of his shoes and in his stocking feet went stealthily up the stairs to her bedroom door that was ajar. She was sitting naked in shadow light in a rocking chair. He could see that she was cradling a bundle of white in her arms, but he couldn't tell if the bundle was blankets or whether the blankets contained a doll, and for a shuddering moment he thought, *What if it's the child?* knowing, since he had seen the boy in its tiny coffin, that it was not the child. She moaned again but she had, at the same time, such a contented look on her face, a look of such stillness and calm that he felt confused and ashamed for having, like a sneak in his own house, looked on her in her nakedness.

My God, he thought, hurrying downstairs, *I've seen her like she's never seen herself.*

That week, a parent who was a lawyer announced to Father Dowd and the school principal, and then to the press, that his daughter – "a young girl having every expectation of becoming a successful teenage model" – had broken a front tooth on a penny in the Field Day cakes. At a small press conference on the school steps, he announced that he was suing the school and Alice Kopff for twenty-five thousand dollars. "I intended to be a model," the chubby girl whined, showing a gap in her mouth to a photographer from the *Sun*.

Confronted at the shop by two newsmen who had been sent by their papers to speak to her, Alice said simply, "I have done what I've done in memory of my own dead child."

"Is that why the painted tears?" a reporter asked, snickering. "And what was the child's name?"

"His name is a secret."

"And the father?"

"He's a secret, too. He doesn't matter. That we do good is what matters. That we do good. Any priest will tell you that."

"What about the lawyer, the twenty-five thousand?"

"I don't know about any of that."

The following day in the parish house, Father McClure slammed the *Sun* down on a table in front of Father Dowd.

"Do good," he cried, "do good! Any priest will *not* tell you that..."

He was red in the face.

"Relax. Watch the baseball game."

"Baseball... Do you realize what's going on, Father Dowd? There's upheaval in the classrooms, lawsuits, we're giving scandal to the church in the press, and we're here, you and me, yelling at each other..."

"I don't know," Father Dowd said. "She only wishes well, she only wants people to be happy."

"Happy!" Father McClure said, almost sneering. "The message of the Cross is not happiness. Jesus did not die happy."

It was the week of First Communion for the first-grade students at the parish school. Alice worked late Thursday and Friday, working by herself at the big stainless steel oven. The heat in the kitchen was intense. *We could use more air,* she thought. There would be almost three hundred parents and children at the Communion reception after Sunday Mass. Alice, going about her work, felt feverish and she knew that her face must be flushed because Lyle, before leaving the shop for home, had taken a long look at her – as if he thought he should caution her – but she had put her finger to her lips.

Then she had blown him a kiss and he had blushed.

On Sunday morning before the eleven o'clock Mass, the Kopff & Kopff van arrived at the side door to the reception hall. The delivery man carried in flat box after flat box stamped COMMUNION CUPCAKES: five hundred little cakes in round fluted paper cups. She enclosed a handwritten note to Father Dowd, explaining that these cakes were not only an original recipe, but just before the mould trays had gone into the oven she had taken a wafer of white chocolate and pressed it in under the cap of each cake so that when the cakes were baked the wafers would melt, would transform completely and become the cake, white and unseen, while still being chocolate, which, as best as she could understand, was what happened at Communion.

She wished him every happiness in Jesus.

The Communion cupcakes were a huge success, not just with the children but with the parents, too.

Father McClure was apoplectic.

"This is outrageous. This diminution, this belittlement of the Blessed Sacrament… She has to stop. An end must be made of it."

Father Dowd reluctantly agreed and telephoned the Kopff house.

Lyle said that she had had a coffee with him, watered the flowers in the pram, and then had gone to the shop, saying that she wanted to sit alone on that Sunday afternoon in the empty kitchen.

"She looked very happy, almost blissful," he told Father Dowd, who hurried to the shop and, finding the front door open, went in, hesitated, and then stepped around the cash register and counter into the kitchen.

"Welcome to the inner sanctum," she said.

She was sitting in front of the big oven.

"I have been so happy all morning," she said. "I'm so happy I could die. I could die and be happy with my little boy."

He hesitated, afraid that any admonition or any cautioning word, would seem petty to her. He wanted to say something serious, but only as a warning of what to expect from Father McClure and others like him.

"Have a cupcake," she said.

"Not just now."

"Well, some white chocolate then," and she handed him a tray of white chocolate wafers. "I'd be very hurt if you didn't have one," she said.

He took a wafer, bit into it, and swallowed.

She closed her eyes. He licked a leftover sweetness from his lips.

"I call to mind," he said, almost in a whisper, "two lines of poetry I like very much…"

"Yes… I like poetry, too," she said, smiling, eyes still closed.

"So do I," he said.

Then he said softly,

A perfect paralyzing bliss
Contented as despair.

Folding her hands, she said, "I don't know what that means."

"Well, perhaps neither do I. It's hard to know the meaning of what we say or do."

"All I know is that everything means more than we think it does," she said.

"I suppose," he said. "I suppose that's true. Though my friend, Father McClure, likes to say that all of this means less than meets the eye."

"I spy with my little eye," she said, opening one eye and giggling.

"Yes," he said.

"That's what I've always liked about you," she said.

"What?"

"There are people who say yes and people who say no. You nearly always say yes. Mind you, I said yes once and look where it got me."

"Where's that?"

"Pregnant." She laughed, taking a wafer of white chocolate herself. "And ever since, I've learned to live with death being alive in me."

He lowered his eyes for a moment. Then, he almost whispered when he said, "About the Communion cupcakes…"

"The idea was so simple," she said.

"Yes, I guess it was."

"I guess so."

"Well…" and resenting Father McClure, his sneering tone, he stood up, saying, "I must go…tickets for the baseball game, a 1:30 start. A kind parishioner gave me tickets for the Blue Jays game…"

"That," she said, standing up to shake his hand, "was my dream, you know."

"What?"

"That my boy would play second base for the Yankees. Happy Kopff at second base…"

He felt not only a sorrow for her but something harder, the loss of something he'd never had a chance to have.

He stepped out of the shop into the relief of afternoon sunlight.

>≕⚊≕<

Father McClure heard the nearby sirens in the parish house. He put his stole around his neck, ready for the worst, and hurried after the fire trucks.

Father Dowd, at the baseball game, was unhappy: the score was 3-2 for the Yankees.

Father McClure gave the Last Rites to dead Alice in the back of an ambulance. Father Dowd came home, pleased because the Blue Jays had beaten the Yankees in extra innings, 4-3.

>≕⚊≕<

"Our estimate," the Fire Chief said to the press, "is that somewhere between 1:30 and 2:00, a fairly rare but known form of spontaneous combustion occurred. The technical name is pyrolysis, the transformation of a compound in dried-out old wood that is caused by heat. It seems the old wood over the big oven just burst into flames. You might recall the same thing happened in Perl's Kosher Deli on Bathurst Street last year. She didn't have a chance, the whole place turned incendiary, it went up in flames in no time flat."

The funeral Mass at Blessed Sacrament was said by Father Mc-Clure. It was so crowded, with children especially, that latecomers had to stand on the church steps. In the pulpit, Father Dowd spoke of Alice's unblemished goodwill and how the goodness of spirit can be infectious just as her mysterious generosity of spirit – born out of great loss but unsoured by loss – had been infectious in the community. Many in the pews wept as he lamented her passing: "She was so much on the side of life."

Standing by the black limousine that was about to carry her coffin to the burial yard, Lyle thanked Father Dowd and said, "You know, what's a mystery to me is that my family has been in one firestorm after another. First in Dresden, then my mother and father dying by fire, and now this. Alice up in flames."

"Well, no, I hadn't thought of that," Father Dowd said. "There seems to be so much I haven't thought about her. I have the feeling I may have let her down."

"Maybe."

Lyle wryly laughed so loudly that Father Dowd looked at him with concern.

"Maybe," he said, "it'll be me in the fire next time."

That evening, Lyle transplanted the impatiens and the dwarf pine out of the black wicker pram to the lawn, kneading the earth around the root. Then he emptied out all of the potting earth and put the pram at the curb for the garbage pick-up in the morning.

He remained inside the house for a week. One night he thought he heard her moaning in her room and he went to stand at the bottom of the stairs, even though he knew that she was not there. A second time, he blew her a kiss. "I owed you one," he whispered. He saw no one for the week, not until the estate lawyer knocked on the door.

Over coffee and afternoon bitters, the lawyer explained that Alice's will, though very simple, was complicated.

She had willed all her goods and possessions – a substantial account at the bank, her half-interest in Kopff & Kopff Bakery Shoppe, all her recipes, and her half-interest in the family house – to her dead child, Happy Kopff.

"Happy…"

"Don't worry," the lawyer said, "it's complicated, but we'll unravel whatever she's done."

PIANO PLAY

Al Rosenzweig was called Piano by his friends. He agreed to meet with me to eat a smoked meat sandwich at Switzer's Deli. Piano was a big man who appeared affable because he was slow-moving and because of his ample pink cheeks and jowls. I knew he was a killer. The police knew he was a killer. They couldn't prove it but they said they knew that after the Magaddino family from Buffalo had tried to kill Maxie Baker outside the Town Tavern so that the mob could take over the gambling that was controlled in Toronto by the Jews, Al had driven to Niagara Falls and it was believed that he had strangled two of Magaddino's men with piano wire. But he was not known as Piano because of the wire. It was because he played the piano at a Bathurst Street high-rise social club for survivors of Shoah every Thursday night, where he liked to sing Irving Berlin and Cole Porter songs: *Let's do it / Let's fall in love…*

As I arrived at the table Piano was singing to himself. He looked up and said, "Take a pew with a Jew."

We ate our smoked meat sandwiches, and then I said to him, "Piano, I know business is business but we both know Solly Climans for a long time. He's a good guy."

"So he's a good guy. I even knew his father, Fat. I booked his father's bets, too. But he owes money, too much money."

"I'm worried about him."

"Why worry? If he pays, he's good."

"He's beyond scared, Piano. He says he's gonna commit suicide."

"He ain't gonna commit suicide."

"I believe him."

"You believe him?"

"Yeah, I believe him."

"Jews don't kill themselves."

"Believe me, he's gonna kill himself."

Piano wiped his lips with his napkin.

Drumming his fingers on the table, he began to hum *Birds do it, bees do it,* and then he said, reaching out to touch my hand, "Jews don't kill themselves. They sometimes kill each other but, believe you me, they don't kill themselves."

He shrugged, as if I should have known we were helpless before a truth, a truth that allowed him his amiable consideration for me.

"Do yourself a favour," he said, "try a little dessert, a cheesecake. It'll look good on you."

OUR THIRTEENTH SUMMER

I was a child during the war and we lived on the upper floor of a duplex in what was then called a railroad apartment, which was a living room at the front end and a sunroom at the back end and a long hall with rooms running off the hall in between. The apartment below was the same.

"The same," my father said, "but not exactly the same."

A chemist and his family lived there. He was an expert in explosives, working with the war department. He was not old but his hair was white. He told my mother that he was working on "a bomb so big that when it hits, when it blows, the war will end up on Mars."

He was called George Reed. He was a chain-smoker and his teeth were yellow and irregular. He had a port wine stain on the back of his left hand. He often kept his left hand in his suit coat pocket. He didn't talk much. He seemed to be shy and reticent but I always felt that he disapproved of me, disapproved of all of us, but he didn't want to be forced to say so, and so he hid how he felt behind his shyness. Sometimes his left hand fluttered in his pocket, and sometimes he couldn't stop it fluttering, not once it got going. "It's like he's got a trapped bird in there," my mother said.

As for his wife, I heard my mother tell my father once that "she looks like someone who's been swept over by sadness and has gone strange."

She was from Vienna. That's what she had told my mother and father. I didn't know where Vienna was. "That's where it all began," my father told me. "Hitler's town, except she's Jewish." She was short and had thick black hair. When she talked she got excited. She leaned down and breathed into my face, she peered into my eyes, like she was looking for something that was way beyond me, beyond my mother and father, like she didn't know what she was looking for and yet she was sure it was out there, whatever it was, long gone and lost. And one day she breathed in my face and said, "I'm not Jewish," and her son, Bobbie, told me the same thing. "My father's English and nobody's Jewish." Bobbie and I played to-gether on the front lawn. He had his father's wine stain on his neck, just below his left ear. We played war games with toy soldiers and tin tanks in the rockery. There were no flowers in the rockery, only mud and stones because the landlord refused to spend money on flowers. He said money was too scarce because of the war. But Bobbie and I didn't want any flowers. We wanted the mud and the stones. We could spend a whole afternoon shifting our soldiers from ledge to ledge, country to country. We took turns being the enemy. Whenever he had to be the Germans, even though they always lost, he would say, "Don't tell my mother, don't let my grandfather hear us."

Every day at ten-thirty in the morning and at four in the after-noon his grandfather came out of their sunroom, which was below my bedroom. Bobbie said he slept there and studied his books there with the shades down and then he would come out and take one of his walks, shuffling in his slippers from our house to the end of the street and back. He never spoke to Bobbie. He never spoke to me. He was dressed all in black, in a black suit. He had a long pale face and a long blade nose. He sometimes wore a black broad-brimmed hat and sometimes a shiny black skullcap, and he had long curls of hair that hung down beside his ears. He didn't wear shoes, he wore his black leather slippers.

"If he isn't Jewish, I don't know who is," my mother said.

"We're not Jewish," Bobbie told me.

"Sure you are, you gotta be," I said.

He punched me as hard as he could in the chest. When I got my breath, when I wiped away the tears that had come to my eyes from the punch, I told Bobbie to put up his dukes. My father had taught me how to box. He had bought me boxing gloves, and kneeling down in front of me he had sparred with me, teaching me how to jab and hook, and how to block punches and take a punch. He'd hit me really hard two or three times. "That's so he'll understand that getting hit never hurts as much as he thinks it's going to hurt," he told my mother. "Once you know that, then you won't worry about getting hurt and you can learn how to hit and hit real good."

Bobbie put up his fists. I flicked a left jab in his face. He didn't know what I was doing. He didn't look scared. He looked bewildered, helpless, as he tried to duck his head. I hit him with a left hook. His nose began to bleed. He tasted his blood, he looked astonished, and then when he saw blood all over his shirt, he was terrified. "My mother will kill me." He began to bawl, but he was afraid to run into the house. His mother came running out. Her black hair was loose and long and flying all about her head. She screamed and pulled Bobbie behind her, to protect him, but I didn't want to hit him again. I felt sorry. I wished he hadn't hit me and I hadn't hit him.

"Why?" she screamed.

"Because he said I was Jewish," Bobbie said.

"Because he's Jewish? He's not Jewish," and she swung and hit me in the head, knocking me down. She hauled Bobbie into the house. I looked up from where I was, lying flat on my back, and the old grandfather, who was wearing his skullcap, was standing by their open front window, staring at me, twisting one of his long curls in his fingers.

Later, when I told my father what had happened he said to my mother, "I know they're terrified. I know they're from Vienna, but that's not the point." And he went downstairs and stood very close to Mr. Reed and said through his teeth, "If either one of you ever hits my boy again, I don't care how big your bomb is, I'll knock your block off."

><del>~~</del><

There was a Jewish family up the street, just north of us. Mrs. Asch was plump, almost fat. She wasn't too fat because she didn't waddle, but she had a huge bosom and she would hold my head to her chest. Mr. Asch worked with furriers. He was, my father said, "a cutter." It sounded dangerous, like he should be a character on *Inner Sanctum Mystery* radio. But he didn't look dangerous. He was small, had pasty-coloured skin, a round closely cropped head, and always wore his skullcap, even under his hat. He came home every evening at six-thirty, sat down looking sullen, ate cold chicken that was shiny and pimpled in its boiled white skin, and drank Coca-Cola. We never drank Coca-Cola in our house. "Rotgut," my mother called it, so I drank Hires Root Beer, telling my friend, my pal, Nathan Asch, that it was a kind of real beer. He didn't believe me but sometimes we put aspirins in it to give it a boost and he drank it with me, usually saying,

"This is living," and we got a headache that we called a hangover.

Nathan, who was plump like his mother, had one leg shorter than the other. He wore an oxblood boot with a double-thick sole and heel. He couldn't run very fast and he could hardly skate at all, and so, because I wanted to be a baseball pitcher, he was my catcher. His sister, Ruth, who was a lot older and very pretty and worked in a fur salon modelling coats, had bought him a big round catcher's glove. It was the best glove anybody on the street had and Nathan knew it. He was proud to be a catcher and I was proud that he was my catcher because he was good at blocking any curve balls I threw into the dirt.

On the weekends when Bobbie Reed's mother and grandfather walked up the street together to the grocery store on Dupont Street, they would pass the Asch house, and most of the time in the summer the Asches would be sitting out on the front porch listening to Mel Allen broadcast the Yankee games on WBEN Buffalo, or Ruth would have her portable record player set up by the porch stairs, playing Frankie Laine singing:

> I must go where the wild goose goes,
> wild goose, brother goose, which is best,
> a wandering fool or a heart at rest...

and the old man dressed in black would sometimes get a hitch in his step and hesitate and glance up the walk to the porch. He always wore some kind of white tasselled cloth under his suit coat that looked like a piece of torn sail. If Mr. Asch was sitting on the porch, he'd glower at the old man and if Mrs. Reed looked at him, then Nathan's father would get up, still small no matter how tall he tried to stand, and he'd push his chin out and down and spit. This seemed awful to me, particularly because Mr. Asch was no good at spitting and whatever he hocked out of his mouth it always went splat and sat there on his own porch stairs. I didn't understand why he was so angry and why he was spitting at a woman and I didn't understand spitting on your own stairs. I didn't understand any of this at all. The second time it happened, I asked Nathan and he said, "It's because Bobbie and the whole bunch of them tell everybody they're not Jewish. My father hates them for that."

"I never heard the old man say he wasn't Jewish," I said.

"He don't say nothing," and Nathan shouted, "You don't say nothing," hoping the old man would hear him. "You might as well be from Mars."

I watched Mrs. Reed thrust out her chin and quicken her stride as the old man unbuttoned and then buttoned his suit coat, shuffling away from us. He looked bonier and sharper in the shoulder blades than I'd thought he was, but then, I'd always thought of him as slumped through the shoulders and he wasn't slumped. His shoulders were very straight, though he did push his feet along the sidewalk like he was tired when he walked.

"Just look at him like he's not there," my mother said. "That's best."

"But he is there," I said.

"So you say," she said and laughed.

About two months after Nathan shouted at the old man it was time for Nathan's birthday. August was always a big month for the kids on the street. August was the last month of the summer holidays. Nathan's birthday was at the beginning of the month and Bobbie's birthday was at the end, and all of us were always invited to wear paper hats and blow whistles, bob for apples, eat cake and play hide-and-seek down the alleys between the houses after dark, before we went to bed. I didn't like my birthday because it was in February and it was too cold to play outside. But this year Nathan's party was different. It was smaller. There were kids there that I didn't know and the kids I knew and expected to see weren't there. Nathan told me that this wasn't going to be his real birthday party. His real birthday party was going to be his *bar mitzvah* because he was turning thirteen and he was going to be a man. After we ate the cake and his mother's cookies, when I said goodbye to him at the door and he thanked me for my gift – a Yankee baseball cap my father had brought from New York – he said, "I can't see you so much anymore."

"What?"

"My father says I can't see you so much, not now that I'm a man."

"Why?"

"'Cause you're a *goi*."

"What's that?"

"One of the *goyim*. You eat unclean food so you got unclean hearts."

When I came home early, surprising my mother, she was standing alone out on the sidewalk under a street lamp that had just come on. I was crying quietly, not quite sure why because I had done nothing wrong, or maybe it was because Mrs. Asch was never going to hold my head against her big bosom again. The Reed front windows were open and there was loud music coming from the windows as I told my mother what had happened with Nathan and she folded me into her arms and said, "There, there. There's nothing you can do with some people." She sounded very sad but

I could tell she was also very angry. As we walked up to our door into the duplex I could hear the music and see the Reeds spinning and twirling, Mrs. Reed with her head thrown back, laughing, and I asked my mother, "What's that they're doing?"

"Waltzing," she said. "That's the way they dance in Vienna, they waltz."

"Like that?"

"It can be very graceful," she said.

〜〜〜

At the end of August, Bobbie turned thirteen, too. I was playing more and more by myself. Once or twice I lay on my bedroom floor with my ear to the floor to see if I could hear Bobbie in the old man's bedroom below me but I never did hear him. Sometimes I heard the old man complaining and singing a kind of moan and once, as he was going out walking, he paused beside the rockery and looked down at me as I lined up two Lancasters at the bottom of the stones. I looked up and he looked down. "Bombers," I said. Another time I had my baseball and my glove beside me and I asked, "Hey, you wanta play catch?" He looked startled and then he laughed. Not a loud laugh, but quiet, like a chuckle. "You speak English?" I asked. He took two steps away and then stopped, turned around, and said in a voice that seemed to be as much heavy breathing as it was a voice, "Of course," and then he kept on walking without looking back.

I asked Bobbie if he was going to have a *bar mitzvah,* too. He sneered at me and said, "Of course not. What d'you think I am?" Then I realized that every night, just before supper, Bobbie and his father were putting on boxing gloves in their living room and Mr.

Reed, who probably didn't know anything about boxing, was trying to teach Bobbie how to box. One late afternoon as I stood out on the lawn watching their heads and shoulders duck and weave, I realized that the old man was standing near me and he was watching, too.

"Hi," I said.

He just looked at me, a strange look, like for a minute he thought I was someone else that he was surprised to see, but he didn't say anything. He sighed and went into the house.

Two days before his birthday, Bobbie's mother stopped my mother and me. Usually they said something nice to each other without meaning it, but this time his mother didn't bother. She said, "From now on, nobody calls Bobbie Bobbie anymore. His name is Robin. A man's name. Robin Reed." Bobbie looked kind of mopey, so I said, "Well, Robin, I don't hardly see you anymore, not even on the weekend."

"I go with my father on Saturdays now."

"Where?"

"To his lab. He takes me to his lab."

"What for?"

"To teach me chemistry, to teach me what he does."

"Terrific," I said. "He makes bombs."

"He doesn't let me make bombs," he said. "Not yet."

On the afternoon of his birthday, I was all alone. My father was away again and my mother was out shopping. Mr. Reed came home early, his head down, his left hand in his suit coat pocket, fluttering. I thought he was home to get ready for the party, but not long after, Robin came out onto the front lawn wearing boxing gloves and carrying another pair for me. I thought it was really strange, the gloves were the exact same colour as the wine stain on his neck. He said his father had told him that he had to box me before there could be any party. "He says I'm turning thirteen, you know."

For the first time in my life I just suddenly felt all tired, like my whole body was tired. And sad. I tried to laugh while the two of us stood there with great big gloves hanging off the ends of our arms, but I felt so sad I was almost sick. Though I could tell right away, as soon as Robin put up his gloves, that he was still the same old Bobbie, that he didn't know how to box at all, I only remembered the last time I'd hit him, the blood, and how sorry I felt. I was half leaning toward him while I was thinking about that when he swung a wild looping left that caught me behind the ear and knocked me down. I wasn't hurt, and he didn't know that I knew he couldn't hurt me no matter how hard he hit me because my father had taught me how to take a really hard punch and not to be afraid. So I got up and pawed the air around Robin, trying not to let him hit me, not really punching him because I felt too tired even if I had wanted to punch him. He cuffed me a couple of times, but he didn't know how to punch off the weight of his back leg, so I staggered a little. I saw that Mr. Reed was standing in their front window, his hands flat on the glass, a great big glad smile on his face, but the old grandfather had come out onto the cement stoop beside the rockery. He had on his broad-brimmed black hat and he stood with his arms folded across his chest, the torn sail hanging out from under his arms. He was silent and intent. I let Robin take a bang at my body. I was glad my father wasn't home. He'd have been ashamed and angry and I would have had to fight, had to really beat up Robin or Bobbie or whoever he was. Instead, I wanted to cry. Not because I was hurt. I just wanted it all to be over so that I could cry and so I sat down on the lawn and stayed there because no one I loved could see me, no one I loved was there to make me do anything I didn't want to do. Robin, totally astonished, turned and ran into the house, ran into his father's arms.

I got up and went down the lawn to the sidewalk, sat on the curb and slowly undid the laces to the boxing gloves with my teeth and pulled the gloves off. I wasn't really sniffling. The Reeds were crazy if they thought I was going to get up and go to Robin's birthday party, but I didn't know why they were actually crazy. Then I heard shuffling leather slippers behind me. I thought he'd gone into the house, too, to be with them, but he was standing close behind me, and when I turned and looked up I was almost angry at him but he was smiling, looking down from under the wide brim of his hat and shaking his head with a kind of bent sorrowful smile.

"It's not so easy to hurt you," he said.

"Nope."

"You would make a good Jew."

"How would you know?" I said, real sharp, "You're not Jewish."

"No, that's right," he said, smiling a little more, and then he leaned down and whispered, "I'm the man from Mars."

T-BONE AND ELISE

He heard her coming up the back-porch stairs out of the rain, and then her laughter as she stepped in her open-toed spectator heels along the dimly lit hall of the small house he rented not far from the lakefront rail lines. Holding her coat close, she came into the kitchen, heavy-breasted, a sauntering woman who had gone out for a few minutes to enjoy the freshness of the early morning rain.

"It's more like a mist now but it's still coming down," Elise said.

"Who was you laughing with out there?" T-bone asked.

"Myself," she said. "Me and Philomena. We had a good laugh."

Her camel-hair coat fell open.

She had got out of bed naked, put on her coat, and gone out onto the porch, carrying Philomena, the rabbit puppet, under her arm. T-bone was seated at the kitchen table. He was in his shorts, wearing a Blue Jays T-shirt and a nylon stocking cap on his head, trying to keep the previous night's *conk* in his hair.

"I know it's none of my business an' I only know you since last night," she said, "but I don't like you doing what you're doing to your head like that."

"I do what a black man got to do, girl. I gotta keep my wig-hat on."

She opened a bottle of Jack Daniel's that was on the table and poured herself two fingers of drink, neat.

"You go to kick-starting on the bottle like that," he said, "and you gonna end up with a lifetime home in the ground."

"I bet you're no slouch with the demon yourself," she said.

He had a clouded whiteness in his left eye but with his good eye he fixed a stern look on her. She sat in silence with the rabbit, Philomena, and she let him stare at her until he broke the stillness by saying, "Yes, you is okay," pouring himself a drink. "I'm gonna fry us up some T-bones. A T-bone and onions beats all for breakfast."

"You some kinda dude in the morning," Philomena said. She was sitting up straight on Elise's fist.

"I be the morning man," T-bone said, leaning up close to the rabbit, "an' you is *one* smart-mouth mothafucka."

"I come from a whole family of motherfuckers," the rabbit said. "Elise, here, she got the gift of tongues, man. She got hat boxes full of the likes of me."

They had met at two in the morning on the outskirts of town. At that hour, after playing a gig, T-bone often went for a drive alone in his van, "to slow down the bloods and come to some easement of mind." He'd stopped to fill up at the AC-DC Gas Bar and Groceteria, where the fourteen trucking lanes of the 401 cross with the overnight commuter highway, 427. He was standing at pump Number Nine of the eleven cement Self-Serve islands, each island a pond of halogen light in the dark, and he was staring at island eight where a woman – as she pumped gas into her red Passat – wore on her left hand, hanging head-first down, a puppet glove, a floppy-eared rabbit. He saw the rabbit's upside-down mouth flap and heard a voice by his right shoulder ask, "What's happening, man?" He called across the cement island, "Be cool," and when the woman, still holding the gas nozzle to her tank, turned to look at him, he said, "You one of them ventriloquists, like on TV?"

"Maybe."

"You wanta do some personal damage?"

He racked his nozzle.

"He's one of them nighttime crazies," the rabbit called out.

"Not me," T-bone said, coming across the island. "Ain't nothing crazy 'bout me."

"I foresaw you, I foresaw who you were, coming on at me like you just done," she said.

"You saw me?"

"Right. Ain't nothing secret about your style."

"What's my name then?"

"T-bone, T-bone Duflet," she said triumphantly.

"How'd you know that?"

"Check out your wheels, man."

He turned to face *T-bone Duflet & His Blues Band* in gold-on-black letters on the side of his van.

"There I be," he said, laughing. "Goddamn, there I be, big as lightning."

❦

He shifted his black iron-ware pan on the gas burner fire as he fell to telling her about his home farm and his father and how he loved his father and how he had watched his father die slowly, the dying being so slow it was like studying rain. "There be all kind of rains," he said. "Rain in your heart, and there's rain that comes out of the woods in sheets and in the springtime they look like ghosts, long tall ghosts, and that's what white people was like, too," he said,

73

"ghosts," and he winked at her, "long and tall." He started telling her about his Uncle Lazarus. "I was a Lazarus by name, too, until people took to calling me T-bone at the piano. But meanwhile," he said, "my uncle was a man who had himself an alligator mouth and because of his mouth he'd got his own self in trouble with a good-looking, fine as wine white woman. A lot like you she was," he said, "except way back then the sheriff, he lit out after Lazarus, his dogs whooping. When they finally did corner old Lazarus's humming-bird ass, the sheriff he hollers, 'You're a dead man, Lazarus,' and Lazarus come up into the open from between two trees and calls, 'I been betwixt and between before.' The sheriff shoots him but he comes back one more once from between two other trees like he's never been shot. 'You're a dead man, Lazarus,' and the sheriff shoots him again but Lazarus with a moaning cry keeps coming up while they say he's running farther away, coming back, and run-ning away in the rain till they never did find him or find his ghost." Pleased with his own storytelling, pleased with a look of curiosity close to dazzlement that he saw in her eyes, T-bone said, "Lazarus, he keeps coming up every springtime, he be one of those long tall moaning ghosts of rain," and then he whispered song words to her,

...consumption killing me by degrees
I can study rain

In the low lamplight of his bedroom they had undressed, unhur-ried, at three in the morning. The bed had newel posts. She had looked around for a place to rest Philomena, and then had sat the puppet straight up, alert, like a sleeve over one of the posts. In that shadow light on the bed she had lain back and drawn her knees to her shoulders, trying to take him deeper, and he had cried, "You mine, baby, you is all mine," but she had thought, the pain of his deepness giving her pleasure, *No, this is mine*, and she had rolled him over, surprising him with her unexpected strength. Sitting on top of him she said, "Mine, mine all the time," arching in release, falling forward over him, kissing his neck, saying, "Turn up the light, baby, I wanta see you. I've never been in bed with a black man before."

"You is here with a lady killer," he said, laughing.

"Don't you worry yourself," he heard Philomena say from down off the post. "She's so quick you won't know she was here til she's gone."

As he reached for the light, she eased off his body, sliding down between his feet, to sit beside Philomena.

"Here I am down at the deep end," she said, surprised to see that half the width of the wall beside the bed was a mirror.

In a fuller light, with his eyes accustomed to the light, he said, "Mercy! Jesus, Lord," leaning forward to look at her more closely.

Below the glitter of a single rhinestone set in her navel, he saw that she had shaved all her body hair, she was bald at the cunt except for a razor-thin line of black hair. "It's called the California cut," she said.

He drew his finger along the line of hair. "Ain't life a bitch," and he rolled her over onto her stomach, buckled her knees, and hoisted her hips and entered her, saying, "Gonna get me some more trim," not with the lunge of the earlier hour, but slowly, and then he heard from behind her shoulder, the rabbit, "You sure she wants to do this this way?"

"Lord Jesus," he said and collapsed on her back, and she burst out laughing and he laughed, too, saying, "Next time, the rabbit stays in the next room."

She took over and took him into her arms. "Sorry about that. It's just my way of talking. Can't help it, it's me. It's how I do."

With her cheek against his neck as they lay together, she felt a moaning song inside his throat. When she asked what was the matter, he said, "Never you mind, girl, it be raining..." She didn't know what to say, so she said, "Not telling's unfair." He had hauled back out of her arms at being told he was unfair, but he laughed as if by laughing he was putting something protective between them, a protection being necessary because they didn't know each other at all. Then, with a sudden bitterness of tone that took her aback and made her wary, he said, "Ain't nothing more foolish looking than a black man with his head on a white woman's shoulder."

They sat up together on the edge of the bed, facing the mirror, her legs bent open, the rhinestone in her navel a point of light in the mirror.

"I got no axe to grind. I don't need to take nothing from you, T-bone," she said, "'cause I got nothing to give more than what I already gave."

"Fair 'nough. But maybe I oughta check you out with the rabbit!"

Elise laughed and took both of his hands in hers and put them to her lips.

"What you do with these hands of yours, the way you play, is beautiful. Beautiful, man."

"How you know?"

"I've heard you play before. I didn't just say hello out by the pumps for no reason."

"Your rabbit said hello."

"My rabbit does what she's told or she better watch out."

Still facing the mirror, she said, "I hate mirrors. My mother, she used to look in the mirror after she'd had a drink and she'd say like she was real angry that she was looking for the child she'd lost, my twin sister who'd died beside me being stillborn. Sometimes she'd see my sister in the mirror and talk to her all night just like we're talking now, trying to get her to come out from hiding behind the glass. And if my mother was drunk enough she'd call her out by her name, Lisa, and then she'd call her a coward for staying back behind the mirror. She'd put her arms around me and hold me and call on Lisa to quit acting like some kind of ghost, but by then Mother had got so altogether confused in the circles of her own mind she'd hold me and call me Lisa instead of Elise, like she was holding a dead girl who had come back to life in her arms."

"Hey, I wasn't holding no dead girl," T-bone said as he brushed her blond hair away from her eyes and then laid her back on the bed. "No dead girl be rattling on my bones." Taking her in his arms, he entered the cradle of darkness, hearing her say, "Oh Lord."

><del>~~</del>~×

With the morning rain a chill had taken hold in the kitchen.

T-bone turned on the stove's gas burners, put slices of black bread in the toaster and two steaks and onions in the big pan, and got himself warm by wearing his tuxedo suitcoat – the same coat he wore every night while playing at the Black Swan Blues Bar – a coat that was one size too big for him, the sleeves hanging down to his knuckles. He'd worn the old coat for years and he told her he thought it had once belonged to an undertaker because of the broad black silk band sewn around the left sleeve. "Unless maybe it was a suit for a one-armed man and when he died that's how they sewed the sleeve back together."

He did a little shuffle dance of delight at his own wit in front of the stove.

"We're some pair in the morning," she said. "I drink an' now you dancing."

"We's the best, girl. All I wants from life is some whisky, loose shoes and some dancing bootie."

"I got two left feet," she said, laughing. "I caught the heel of my shoe out there on the porch. Thought I snapped it off. They say if you break the heel off your shoe in the morning you're gonna meet the love of your life by night. But I didn't break my heel."

"You breaking my heart anyway, woman."

"Wasn't looking to break nothing last night. I was only looking to gas up and go home."

"Uh-huh."

He shook lemon pepper onto the two T-bones and onions, set them down on a platter between two plates and poured two glasses of bourbon, but instead of sitting down he shied away and started to poke about the kitchen as if he were looking for something that he had forgotten, his shoulders slumped inside his coat.

She let him turn in a circle and turn in a circle again and then she said, "What are you looking for? What you lose?"

"Captain Hook," he said. "I'm looking for somebody I lost when I was a kid. I'm looking for when I believed back then that I was this dangerous mothafucker who had seen Captain Hook on TV on a Saturday morning and I had killed Captain Hook with one blow of my fist to his eye-patch. And when I went looking under his eye-patch I find that this small snake is nesting right there in his eye socket and that snake snatches out, bites me on my cheek and I got me a small scar." T-bone touched his cheek. "Right here that I tell people is a birthmark but I'm telling you that it is the mark of the snake's tongue."

"You expect me to believe that?"

"You believe what you believe, like some days you dream what you gotta dream. You got no choice."

Elise reached out and took hold of him by the sleeve that had the black silk arm band. "The night before yesterday," she said, "I was sound asleep but I dreamed my bed was gone. I was asleep in mid-air, that's what I dreamed."

"What's that supposed to mean?"

"I don't know. You study rain an' I study the way some things sometimes show up wanting to be something else – like a girl sitting on a bench who is trying to be real by thinking she's a violin. I dreamed that once. But I try not to dream."

He hit the table with the heel of the knife, making her flinch and draw back. "Try staying alive."

"What?"

"That's what I deal with. Day by day. All that other shit's too much for me."

"What shit?"

"Shit for brains."

"I think you been drinking too much of that morning whisky."

"Don't whisky me, man."

"I'm just saying."

"So, tell me this. When Philomena is talking," he asked as he cut into his T-bone, "is she talking to you or is that you talking to yourself?"

"Sometimes she talks," she said, "and I don't know what she's saying til she says it. Sometimes I have to whack her on her head."

"Sometimes, sometimes…"

"*Sometimes I'm happy,*" she tried singing, "*sometimes I'm blue…*"

"Yes, you are," Philomena said.

"I think I have to go and get my clothes on."

"Sometimes," T-bone said, "I close my eyes and I see that you and me, we aren't nowhere to be found. Like my daddy say when he want me outa the house, 'Make yourself scarce, boy.' And what I found out in life is that being scarce is being free."

"You playing scarce with me?"

"Girl, you is fine, one fine woman this morning."

"I ain't nobody's woman. Not yours, not my momma's, not nobody's."

"You keep going on like that an' you gonna get rain in your heart."

༺‿༻

Elise had left her skirt, her sweater, her panties on the floor at the base of the mirror. She slid her hand inside her coat and touched her breast, thinking she and T-bone should leave off all the talk and get together again in bed, but she was afraid that if she went to the bedroom she would find Lisa and her mother sitting in the mirror waiting for her, so she knew there was going to be no more tussling in his bed. She wanted to get dressed, fast. She felt she was getting a chill.

"My time ain't most people's time," T-bone said. "The night-time be the right time for me. The rest of the time is day, and they's different people that live in a different city in the day time. Some peoples feel 'fraid at night, Sweet Jesus," he said, clapping his hands, staring at her out of his clouded eye as she sat with the rabbit puppet in her lap. "Even so…"

"Even so what?"

"Like I just said, I woke up thinking about my daddy."

"You think your daddy would like me?"

"The deal is, can you remember my daddy?"

"How could I?"

"'Course you can't, that's the point. The whole of his life was the nighttime. My ghosts don't talk to your ghosts. You got daytime ghosts."

"I got Philomena," she said.

He began to laugh, and laugh loudly, so loud he could hardly talk for laughing. She started to laugh, too. She had no idea what he was laughing at but she laughed along with him.

"Maybe we should go back to bed so I can T-bone you one more once."

"No time," the rabbit said, rising up from her lap.

"Shut your mouth," she said, rising up, too, and she smacked Philomena on the head. Philomena fell forward, whining, saying to Elise, "It's morning, you got to go. You got a performance this afternoon."

"A performance?" T-bone asked.

"Yes," Elise said. "I do kids shows. Birthdays in the garden, that kind of stuff. Love it. The kids love it. They talk to Quack Quack the Duck and Mister Magoo…whatever glove I've got on my fist, whatever face. It's hilarious. Those kids want to know some mean things about life…what's going on…"

"An' you tell them…"

"I explain the whole world, man. Or at least, Quack Quack the Duck does… It's easy."

"All that politics and shit?"

"They don't think life's shit, they think it's funny, in a serious kind of way, the way kids are."

"And Philomena listens…"

"Philomena never just listens – she sits behind me and smiles."

He reached across the table to Elise and took her hand, lifting it to his lips. "Serious is as serious does, girl. What I do is sing the song." And he tasted the soft flesh between her fingers, tonguing the little web of flesh, holding her eye with his, and then he said, almost growling at her, "You don't know…you can't know nothing about me, nothing about what I be doing when I play, when I sing the song, 'cause when I sing about all the ghosts I got in me… I am one fucking Lazarus…"

He picked up his knife and fork to finish eating his steak. She had not touched hers. She had a feeling that came at her from out of nowhere, a feeling that she could taste death in the onions, on her lips. She took a lipstick from her pocket and while T-bone cut up his meat she half-turned away from him and reddened her mouth. She took a deep breath and licked her lips. She liked the taste of lip gloss, and also the taste of damp from the garden. She said she was going to get herself dressed and go out and take a little air again on the porch, with Philomena. "Looks like there's a break in the rain."

She had intended to saunter out of the kitchen but instead hurried to the bedroom, and with her back to the mirror she got dressed quickly. Philomena, lying on the bed, said, "He's singing that fucking consumption song again…"

She put on her coat in the kitchen, hugging it close around her hips. She picked up the puppet and her car keys.

"That's a good-looking T-bone you leaving there," he said.

Elise said that maybe she would come back another night but not to eat. He gave her a humming laugh of approval. "Yes, yes," he said. She started down the dark hallway, Philomena hanging head-down as she went. "So long, big guy," Philomena said. "It was real."

T-bone, who was working hard with his knife around the bone of his steak, listening to the *click click* of her high heels, called out, "Don't forget. Sweet meat's closest to the bone," and he wagged his knife at the door to the hallway that she'd left open. "I got to get me a light in that hall, man." He took a sip of whisky, picked up the bone and chewed on it, sucking the bone clean.

"An' I don't need no loose shoes."

He was in his bare feet.

INTRUSIONS

1

Dusk, and once again Mildred Downs, dressed in a black blouse and a long black skirt, sat in a rocking chair on the front verandah of her stone house. She clutched a blanket around her shoulders and settled her Siamese cat in her lap. The dark green blinds in the windows of the big house were drawn. When she wanted to close herself off completely from the street, she unrolled a canvas awning down to the old wisteria that grew along the verandah railing, clusters of pale mauve flowers hanging from the vines.

Her husband had drowned in the spring in Lake Scugog, and since then she had taken to sipping sherry in the afternoon and green chartreuse at night. Sometimes on hot nights she put a cube of ice in the chartreuse. She slept fitfully at night, afraid that if she fell soundly asleep she might forget to wake up. She believed that several light sleeps during the day were good for her. She liked to sit as still as she could in the rocking chair, holding the cat in her lap. "I can keep my body so breathless," she whispered to the cat, "that I don't even hear the beating of my own heart." When she slept, she moaned and rocked in the chair.

As soon as she fell asleep, the cat leapt to the floor, went down the flagstone stairs and crossed the lawn and climbed into the tall sugar maple tree. Her son, Henry, was standing in the shadow of the awning. He was lean and angular and in his early thirties and he had his mother's pale, almost colourless blue eyes. He didn't like the cat. "Let it fend for itself," he told her when she woke up and wondered where the cat was. "It kills birds." As he said this, she touched the hollow of her cheek and sighed. "There are hard truths," she said. "Hard truths you've never had to deal with, thank your lucky stars." He stepped back into the shadow of the lowered awning, tying the cord into little loops. He offered to make tea. "No," she said, "I'll have a glass of sherry. There's a time for everything."

"So there is, Mother. So there is. Go back to sleep."

When she woke, the sun had gone down. Though it was a moonless night, the sky was blue. She heard the shrill cries of children chasing each other in the dark at the back of the house. *They sound like seagulls,* she thought. She was angry. She had heard seagulls crying when they'd brought her husband's body ashore, broken by rocks in the cold lake. Bloated lamprey eels were fastened to his legs and stomach. "This is unfair, this is unfair," she had cried over and over, beating her fists on the sand. "Goddamn unfair." She had boarded up the windows of their summer cottage, nailed the doors shut, then suddenly, with an air of vengeful disdain, she had sold it at a loss. "Let some other fool get the blood sucked out of him."

The screeching children were at the side of the house, hooting and crying. Mildred picked up a small mallet. There was an oak end table by the verandah railing and, on the table, a brass bell from the bridge of a small yacht. Henry had bought the bell years ago in a pawnshop and had given it to his father as a birthday present. His father, who had been a ham radio operator and built small-scale model schooners as a hobby, had laughed and said, "Whenever there's trouble, bang the bell. Lord knows, no one will come, but bang the bell anyway."

Mildred banged the bell. She listened to the echo clang down the lane. Then there was silence. Her heart was pounding. "You stupid children," she called out, "get away from here. You're a menace. I won't have it." She held her breath, listening. When she was certain the children had crept back through the trees, she went into the house and called upstairs to Henry, opened the liquor cabinet that was inlaid with copper and tortoiseshell, and poured two glasses of sherry. She always had Hunter's sherry before supper.

Henry stood in the centre of the living room, facing the drawn blinds in the bay windows. He had long arms and large hands and a loping stride that made him seem boyish. Mildred adjusted the hour hand in the brass *boulle* clock on the marble mantelpiece and then lit a match. "It's bad luck," he said, "to chase young children away. They'll come back to haunt you." She lit the six candles of a candelabra that was standing on a side table. Like his mother, he had high cheekbones and hollows in his cheeks and something mournful in the way he stood with his head cocked to one side. "I've come home for good," he said. "I'm home to stay for good."

"Have another sherry," she said. "And whose good do you have in mind?"

"I need a whisky," he told her. "I need something strong."

"Well, water it down," she said. "Your face flushes all red when you drink whisky. Your father couldn't drink either, he was always flush-faced."

Since her husband's death she had held off loneliness and the panic of loneliness with a stern composure, a composure that gave her a severe but attractive dignity. Some mornings when she woke and lay in bed with her eyes closed, she was sensually aware of her own stillness, her repose, and in repose, she thought she could actually feel the comforting weight of silence, a weight like the spent body of her husband after he'd made love to her. That was when she had felt closest to him, when he'd lain exhausted and thankful on her body. She regretted that she had not learned this composure earlier because her husband, Tom, so bluff and good-natured and full of yearning and rash bursts of generosity, had always embarrassed her, suddenly giving her gifts and wanting to know her thoughts. "If I talk to the whole world on my radio at night, why can't I talk to you?" he'd said, sitting beside her on the bed. "So tell me what you're thinking." This had left her feeling sheepish and guilty. Twisting the silk straps to her nightdress, she hadn't known what to say, what he wanted to hear. "I love you," she'd said at last, but he'd said, "No, no, not that. What are you really thinking?" She had hugged the pillow and said, "Nothing," and he had yelled, "Don't lie to me. Not in our own bed." Now, she wished that instead of telling him the truth and weeping, she had been able to confront him with the stern composure she'd shown on the day that they had buried him. Even the winds had been still on that day on the high cemetery hill, so that the sun had felt closer and stronger and, shielding her eyes with her hand through the prayers, she had felt suddenly in touch with her own strength. The very earnest priest had said, trying to console her, "Well, he's in the embrace of God." She had startled him, saying, "He wanted to know me and I don't think he ever did, because he didn't know he knew all there was to know, and that's a fact."

"A fact?" he said.

"That's right. And facts hurt."

She turned away from Henry and put her glass of sherry on the side table and laid her hand on a small hunched dark bronze figure standing to the side of the candelabra. "Your father was a generous man," she said. "I remember when we were in Paris and we went into a gallery somewhere around rue du Bac and I had always loved Rodin, and there it was, this very maquette of the big Balzac statue that's up by La Coupole, and so he bought it for me. Oh, that was years ago when no one wanted Rodin and you could get him for a song. He was a very kind and generous man."

"La Coupole?"

"Really, Henry. You shouldn't be coming home, you should be going away, out into the world, out of yourself."

"My father didn't know any more about La Coupole than I do."

"That's no tone to take toward your father."

"He didn't give a damn about Paris. He wanted to go to Vladivostok."

"Where?"

"Vladivostok. With Nikolai."

"Oh, that dreary little man. He had one of those dreadful flat faces. Thank God he disappeared. I still wish I could find out what he stole."

"He didn't steal anything. He just took off. And that's what Dad wanted to do, too, though I guess he did it the only way he knew how."

"Oh," she said and clapped a hand over her eyes. He let her stand there like that, her long bony fingers covering her eyes, and then he said softly, "You're peeking, that's not fair," and he laughed, saying, "I miss old Nikolai." He had been the gardener around the house and summer cottage, a hunched old handyman who'd been in the Czar's navy as a boy in Vladivostok, and then he had worked for years in mining camps inside the Arctic Circle. At the cottage he'd crouched on his haunches at the end of the dock and told Henry about men who had got lost in the deep Arctic nights of deep snows, and then when they were found in the spring they were only skeletons hanging by their snowshoes, the shoe-webbing tangled in the top branches of the trees after the snows had melted. He'd seen a government handbill that had said: COME TO SASKATCHEWAN and because he didn't know where Saskatchewan was, he'd gone, working on a feed-and-fertilizer tanker out of the Black Sea. But he'd never gotten to the prairies. He'd said, "Even men who have two good legs dream they are crip-ples," and he'd laughed and tousled Henry's hair, and Tom had said, "What a terrible hard life you've had, Nikolai."

"Hard, okay," Nikolai said. "But no terrible."

"No?"

"No. You'll see. In one hundred years it could be very beauti-ful, this life."

Then, Nikolai was gone. There was no word, no note, only a pair of canvas work gloves tacked to the garden shed door. For weeks Tom was strangely unsettled. "I think somehow he was my legs," he told Henry. He talked for hours in the night to towns all over the world on his ham radio, suddenly angry and berating people he didn't know, people he had never talked to before. Then he wandered into the spare room that his wife had covered from floor to ceiling and wall-to-wall with mirrors, a black steel ballet barre bolted to the wall – and when he'd walked into the room and found her limbering up wearing black leo-tards, seeing that her image disappeared down reflected tunnels of cold light, he'd said, "Jesus, it's like being swallowed up inside a Fun House."

"This is my room," she'd said. "I expect to be left alone." He had gone out onto the verandah and given the bell one good clang and had never spoken of Nikolai again.

"He had a flat face," Mildred said. "You cannot trust people with flat faces. Your father had a good nose, what they called an aquiline nose, and a good firm jaw."

"And he had a good life," Henry said softly.

"Yes," she said, ignoring the wryness in his tone, "but you're too morbid about him. It's morbid the way you ring that bell in the morning and sit scrunched up in his chair in his study with the door closed, suffocating with those model boats. I never understood the hours he gave to those boats."

"He sailed the seas in the palm of his hand, Mother."

"It was the oddest thing," she said. "I saw him staring so hard one day at a boat in his hand and he suddenly crushed it, and then smiled at me as if he'd made a mistake, some kind of big mistake that had nothing to do with the boat, like when we were children and did something wrong and we wanted it to be right, but you knew it never could be right."

"He had his own reasons. I never understood why he was so generous."

"It seemed perfectly straightforward to me," she said.

"Maybe it was a kind of despair," he said. "Maybe he gave things away so he could be sure that there was at least a little generosity somewhere in the world. That's when I felt close to him."

"It's not how I knew him."

"No?"

"He was never desperate with me."

The cat leapt into her lap. "It's strange, Henry, that you should feel so close to him and not to me because I was the one who always made sure you were sent away to the best boarding schools. Let me tell you, your father's generosity was just his way of hiding away from all of us. He hid who he was, and he turned whatever he gave us into a kind of blackmail. We were always in his debt. Sometimes, when I couldn't stand it anymore, I mean his silence, and I was just about to scream at him, he'd suddenly give me something so beautiful I wouldn't know what to say. So I wouldn't say anything, and he'd get really mad at me. And sour and sullen. All those gifts of his became like little deaths, hoarded little deaths. And, certainly something died in me when he died but now I don't owe him anything. And," she said, reaching out to Henry, "you come home from one of the finest teaching positions in the country, with no woman and no ambition. It's preposterous. Your father became a rich man by making men believe they owed him something, and now you come home as if you owe no one anything, not even an explanation. It's unfair."

"Of course, it's unfair," he said.

"What do you mean, of course? You had everything, everything I could give, and now that you're home you insist on sleeping in the attic room, as if somehow you're in the wrong house, trying to hurt me."

"Why would I want to hurt you, Mother?"

"I just feel it," she said with a little coquettish whine. She lifted the cat out of her lap and pulled a quilted comforter around her legs. A window was open and there was the tang of early snow in the air. "I don't know," she said. "I honestly don't know why you'd want to hurt your mother."

"Well, if you don't know," he said, touching her shoulder and then her cheek, "who does?"

He poured himself another whisky.

"You know what Nikolai used to tell me?" he said. "It was some kind of old proverb... *If you meet a Bulgarian, beat him. He will know the reason why.*" He laughed so hard he got a stitch in his side and had to hold his breath until he could straighten up. He stood in front of her, stirring the ice cubes in his glass with his finger.

"What a terrible habit, Henry," she said with a little curl of disdain in her lip. "Where in the world did you pick that up?"

"Out in the wide, wide world," he said. "At school. You pick up all kinds of bad habits from children. They attach themselves to you, they cling to you." He tugged the cord to one of the green blinds in the front bay window and it clattered up into a tight roll, but there was no sudden burst of light. It was the dead of night outside. "Don't you think," he said, "that this is all a little too deliberate, I mean keeping the blinds down all the time?"

"This is the room where I sat after he died."

"In the living room," he said and laughed quietly.

"I swear I don't know what's going on in your mind. I don't know why you say the things you do or what you think about anything."

"I may not know either," he said.

"Well, it's not necessary to mock me," she said, brushing a wisp of hair away from her face. "It's not necessary to come home and mock whatever contentment and control I've been able to find."

"Are you content, Mother?"

"At least I know how to show some composure. Now take your finger out of your drink."

"You love to talk to me like I'm a child," he said, watching the cat lick its forepaws.

"Well, you are my child."

"I am indeed," he said.

"Well, don't forget it," she said.

"I won't. I can't."

She sipped her glass of sherry and settled into a heavy wingback chair, her eyes closed. With her head to the side, she was soon asleep. He began to hum, a dirging sound, and then to sing quietly, staring down at his mother:

> *My eyes are dim,*
> *I cannot see,*
> *I have not brought my specs*
> *With me,*
> *But there are rats, rats,*
> *Big as alley cats,*
> *At the door, at the door…*

2

He stood in front of the large bathroom mirror, drawing silver-handled brushes that his father had given him through his hair, and then buffed his nails and went downstairs to the dining room where his mother, with a silk shawl around her shoulders, sat at the long oak table. She'd recently taken to ordering in meals from a local French restaurant, Le Paradis, who'd delivered soup and duck confit to the back door by bicycle courier. He was late, having changed his shirt and trousers after playing games with children in among the trees behind the house. She was reading a slender book and seemed in a state of such repose that he hesitated on the last stair, unsure if he should enter the room and disturb her silence. She looked surprisingly frail and shrunken, as if she had never been young, and as he rubbed his big hands together he found it hard to believe that he'd ever come out of her womb, come out from between those thin thighs, but then she stirred and snapped her book shut. He strode to the table, saying with loud heartiness, "And what are you reading tonight, Mother?"

She closed her eyes, straightening her shoulders, and then smiled warmly, looking up as if she were pleasantly startled and had just seen him for the first time in a long while. "About Saint Teresa," she said.

"I didn't know you went in for the lives of saints."

"I don't," she said, lifting the lid of the silver soup tureen, preparing to serve him. "I found it among your father's books."

"Really," he said. "I didn't know he went in for saints either."

"He certainly did," and she smiled coyly.

"I don't know, I get my saints confused, but wasn't Teresa the little girl who slept with her mouth open until one day a bee flew into her mouth? It buzzed around but it didn't sting her?"

"I really wouldn't know."

"And Christ is the bee with His blessed little stinger."

"He is?"

"Sure, but He's come and gone. The rest of us got stung."

She handed him his bowl of soup, a steaming fish soup, and for a moment he lost his breath because he thought he saw an eye floating in the broth, but it was only a bubble that suddenly broke, and with relief he said, "Well, what does little Miss Teresa have to say?"

"It's quite wonderful," she said, ladling soup into her own bowl. "She says that if God hadn't created heaven for Himself, He would have created it for her."

"There's a ripe little bitch."

"Oh, I don't know."

"You think that's wonderful?"

"I find it amusing."

"Sounds like she's having a wet dream," he said and spread his napkin over his knees.

"Really. You can be so crude," she said and scowled.

"All right, a dry dream," he said.

They ate in silence, their knives and forks clicking on the bone china, the cat scratching and mewing by the back screen door. He wondered if the cat had brought a dead bird to the doormat again. As his mother cut her meat into tiny pieces, he suddenly felt queasy and had the uneasy sense that he was on the verge of swirling into deep sleep, slipping down into an inner twirling cocoon, the walls of this cocoon just beyond his touch. Afraid that he was going to pass out, he almost reached out to hold on to his mother, but then the spell passed and she crossed her knife and fork on her plate and said, as if there'd been no silence between them, "I think we should take coffee in the other room. And the chartreuse." There was a slice of veal on his plate, untouched, but he got up and followed her.

They sat in maroon leather easy chairs in the living room, with a silver coffee pot and a silver plate of little meringue biscuits on the pedestal table between them. "You still haven't told me," she said, "why you've come home, why you've quit teaching."

"Home is where the heart is."

"Don't be facetious."

"You want me to tell you the truth, now that we're done with supper?" he asked.

She dabbed the corner of her mouth with the napkin. "I'm not sure," she said.

"Let's just say that when you love children too much you make childish mistakes."

"Do you?"

"Yes, you do," he said. "That's what love is, a mistake. All the best things we do are mistakes."

"I did my best with you," she said.

"That was probably a mistake, so who could blame you?"

"I honestly don't know what you're talking about, except I know your father would not agree with you," she said.

"Oh yes, he would," he said, getting up and coming around behind her chair so that he could lean over her, into the lamplight. "Yes, he would. He did all the right things all his life and he knew every one of them was completely wrong. He should have been a man of the sea, a real captain, instead of frittering his life away with all those hours of dreaming, making his model boats, his little toys." And then he whispered in her ear, "That's where his heart was, with his toys."

"Oh," she said. "Your father was not a childish man. And he certainly loathed people who made mistakes." She straightened her collar. "Imagine, thinking you could know what was in your father's heart better than I could, the woman who listened to his heart in his bed. I can still sometimes hear the pounding of Tom's heart."

"Ah, yes, the bed," he said. "It all begins in the bed."

"What does that mean?"

"Nothing," he said and he took a cigarette from a black lacquered box. He lit it from the candle on the mantelpiece, blowing a smoke ring. He watched it dissipate. Then he blew another ring.

"You can't say something like that and then just say 'Nothing.'"

"What's there to say?" he asked. "That I used to lie there on my bed when I was a boy, pretending to be asleep, watching you watch me?"

"What do you mean, watch you?"

"Just that. You stared and stared, with some stern little hairball of a thought inside your skull. How could I know what was eating at you?"

"I loved you very much," she said.

"Of course, you did. You were my mother. It's just that I hadn't seen that look of yours for a long time."

"What look? When?"

"When the headmaster at the school agreed that I should quit teaching boys, he stared at me a long time and all I kept thinking was, where have I seen that look before?"

"What look?"

"Your look," he said. "Distaste."

She sat with her eyes closed. He stood blowing smoke rings in the silence, and then, after a long time she said softly, "Put on some music, Henry. A little Schubert, perhaps. Schubert is so simple, so intimate, so much the way the heart is." She set her cup and saucer aside. "We'll have to get to know each other again, Henry. Do you still have trouble sleeping? I used to listen to you when you came back as a boy from boarding school. It was frightening, listening to a grown young man cry out in his sleep."

"Sure, it's frightening," he said. "Sometimes I used to walk through the student dormitory at the school," and he drew away from her, a pained look in his eyes, "early in the morning, before dawn, listening to the smaller boys cry in the night, but it wasn't so much crying. More like a whimper. It's terrible to think that a child, free in his dreams, ends up whimpering."

"And what do you think's wrong with them?" she asked.

"They know they have two legs but they think they're crippled."

They sat listening to Schubert.

"I think," he said at last, "I'll take a bath."

In a little while, she snuffed the candles and went upstairs, pausing at the top of the stairs. She heard a voice and slowly went down to the end of the hall and stood by the bathroom door, listening to a low intoning that soothed and enticed her, so that without thinking and full of curiosity, she quietly opened the door to the large tiled room, the window filled with hanging potted plants, and saw Henry in the big old claw-foot tub, reading aloud:

> Hear the tolling
> of the bells, iron bells!
> What a world of solemn thought
> their monody compels.
> In the silence of the night,
> how we shiver with affright...
> at the bells bells bells...

"How beautiful," she said, "how very beautiful." Then she saw that Henry was surrounded by his father's model boats, all of them afloat. He rose out of the water, glaring, and the book slipped from his hands and sank. Water streamed from his naked body, swamping the boats, and she was astonished at how much black hair there was all over his body, wondering as she backed out if he could really be her child with all that hair, murmuring, "His boats, his silly little boats."

Henry screamed, "How dare you, how dare you!" as she backed down the hall to her bedroom.

3

Through the following week, she slept late in the morning and began to take a sip of sherry before coming downstairs. She wore the same black blouse for three days. He wasn't sure if she was washing in the morning. Then she appeared for lunch wearing a black lace mantilla around her head. She ate very little, only green salads and bowls of steamed rice with honey, and she insisted on carrying the cat in her arms from room to room, though the cat mewed and sometimes struggled to get away. Henry watched her, head cocked to the side, with an almost languid aloof sadness, as if he were bored, and he played with a little silver pocketknife while he sat silently across from her in the late afternoon on the verandah. There was menace in the way he toyed with the tiny knife. It looked like he was trying to frighten her, but he was only keeping his nails clean, the cuticles cut back. He didn't want to frighten her at all. He only wanted to watch her, in silence. He wanted her to feel his presence. The weight of it. The bulk of it. "I am a bit of a bastard," he said to her quietly one day, but she said nothing. The cat started to spit. She let the cat go.

Then, one afternoon she kicked her comforter away from around her legs and suddenly pulled the cords to all the blinds in the living room, flooding the room with light. "You're just like your father," she said. "You think I owe you an apology. You want me to feel as if I'm in your debt, but I'm not in your debt. I am your mother."

"Whatever you say," he said and opened the door to the verandah. The late-blooming asters were fading. He sat outside, and she came out, too. They sat side by side for a while, bundled against the chill of a sudden east wind, saying nothing, until at dusk, because it was so cold, they went in and she poured a glass of chartreuse and a glass of whisky. "Cheers." In the bleak light from the bay windows, he saw that a large painting on the east wall was hanging crooked and when he straightened it there was a clean slash of white left on the wall. "We can't have that," he said. "It looks like a scar." He moved the frame so that it was crooked again and the scar was hidden. The painting was of barley fields and a setting sun that was bathing a white stone cottage in a sepia light.

"That's my painting. I love it," she said with sudden eagerness.

"It was hanging crooked," he said, tapping the ornate frame with his forefinger. "It's only the same old stone cottage it's always been."

"Only a stone cottage to you," she said.

"That old butcher general, Kitchener, he used to say the heart of the empire was the stone cottage."

"The empire, my foot. What the devil do we know about empires?"

"We know," he said, "that they fall down," and suddenly he sang out:

> *London Bridge*
> *Is falling down,*
> *Falling down,*
> *My fair lady-o.*

"There are times," she said, "when you sound like a lunatic."

"It's my childhood," he said. "A childhood song. Anyway, that's what's lovely about anyone's childhood. It was always a little on the lunatic side."

"You think so?" she said coldly.

"Sure. As soon as you grow up, everything turns into a lie, a good sensible lie, so everybody can get along. There are even crippled men who will tell you they've got two good legs," and he laughed.

"You are a lunatic," she said.

"Too long in the noonday sun," he said.

"There was one summer month," she said, "before I got married, that I rented a stone cottage. Alone. I was very happy there alone. That's the truth and it's still true, even if you think everything's a lie," and she closed her eyes, saying, "You are much crueller than your father."

The cat was curled in her lap, staring at Henry, purring. "Tomorrow's my birthday," he said, but she did not answer and he realized that, with her empty glass in her hand, she was sound asleep. He took the glass out of her hand. "You should pay more attention, Mother," he said sourly. "You never paid attention." The cat leaped away as he stood up. He wanted to hurt the cat, beat it with a stick, break its back. He didn't know why he hated the cat because he didn't really care about the birds that it killed. He cared about the mess of bone and feathers on the mat. He felt so enraged that he suddenly wanted to cry, to beat his fists on the table, overwhelmed by sorrow, by a terrible sense of being cheated. "I don't care, I don't care, I don't care." He felt ice cold. He saw himself hanging by snowshoes tangled in tree branches, upside down, gleaming in the spring sun, a skeleton. He began to sing:

There are rats, rats,
Big as alley cats,
At the door, at the door...

Early the next evening, with his loping boyish stride, he hurried up the front walk carrying a cardboard box. His face was ruddy from the wind. He'd been away all afternoon. "Hello, Mother," he called, but as he got to the top step she said, "Hush, hush, only badly bred children yell like that." He gave her a dry laugh and went into the house. She could hear the faint crying out of children in the trees back behind the house. She suddenly wanted to cut down all the trees, so the children would have to go away forever. They would have no place to hide. No place to seek.

In about half an hour, Henry came out onto the verandah. Her head had fallen forward and she was dozing with a smile on her face. He banged the ship's bell, two good clangs that re-sounded down the lane, and she bolted up, dazed, crying, "Tom, Tom." She sounded so vulnerable, so afraid, that he suddenly felt reluctant and full of remorse though he'd done nothing to her, nothing except wake her up, but then she wheeled on him with disdain. "You're not Tom. You're not my Tom." He said, "No, no," and laughed and took her arm. "I'm glad you stopped wearing that damned mantilla," he said and led her into the house and down the dark hall, past the cabinet of rare porcelain that Tom had bought for her.

"Henry, I think your life has been too easy," she said, "so easy that you've turned into someone quite hard." They went into the dining room. She had regained her composure as she sat down at the head of the table, facing the French doors to the garden. "No, not hard, Mother," he said. "Hard's the wrong word. I've just learned to love kids the way my father loved his toys." The chandelier lights were on. He'd lit the sideboard candles and set the long table, covering it with a lace cloth and laying out silver and

Crown Royal china. She was too startled by the light and the table to say anything. She sat with her mouth open, gaping at an enormous birthday cake. "Close your mouth, Mother," he said. "Or you'll get stung." On top of the cake, she saw a ship made of marzipan, surrounded by little candles. "I knew you wouldn't want to forget, Mother," he cried. "You wouldn't forget my birthday," and then she heard shuffling and muffled giggling outside, and someone clanged the bell out on the porch as the French doors were thrown open and a huddle of small boys, all wearing coloured paper hats and blowing their new plastic police whistles, broke into the room, crying, "Happy birthday, Henry, happy birthday…"

They sped around the table, squealing and banging into one another, terrifying the cat, picking up forks and plates and waving them in the air. They also had wooden whistles with rolls of paper attached to the ends, and when they blew, the paper unfurled into long coloured stingers and they spun around her, bees stinging one another with glee. *Buzz… Buzz…* Henry, beaming at his mother, drove the silver cake knife into the heart of the icing, crying, "How do you like my little darlings, Mother?" She clasped her hands to her throat, unmoving, stricken by a pain, a closure on her lungs that she had not known since childbirth, a pain that burned through the arteries in her neck so that she felt her collarbone was cracking, and she tried to choke the pain off with her hands as the boys piled cake on their plates and let forkfuls of icing slide onto the carpet, hooting and hurdling over one another, clutching at her legs, fat little boys fastening on to her ankles until she closed her eyes and cried, "It's unfair, it's unfair."

Seeing her stricken, Henry pried her hands from her throat. Two of the boys let go of her legs and backed away. She began to pound the table, pounding with her eyes closed, her face ashen, whispering, "It's unfair, it's unfair." All the boys were backing away, not just from her but as if they were suddenly uncertain of Henry, even afraid of him. He was enraged by the wariness in their eyes and yelled at them, telling them to go away. As they trailed out of the room, he pulled his chair in front of hers and sat down. Their knees touched. He looked at her thin legs, shaken by how thin she actually was, and how big he was. "How in the world did I get born?" he asked, and reached to the cake, flicked a fingerful of icing into his mouth, and said, "Look, Mother…"

She stared at him, her mouth open, her pale eyes unblinking, and he put a finger full of icing in her mouth.

"Look," he said, as she licked his finger, "in a hundred years life could be very beautiful."

BETWEEN TRAINS

It was a small train station. I sat in the stifling stillness of the waiting room, staring at junk food vending machines until the storyteller came in and sat down and offered me a drink from his silver flask. "Bourbon," he said, "Knob Creek," sitting back in his chair, waiting for me to say something about whatever it was I had on my mind about stories, because that's what he had agreed to come down from his house in the hills to talk about after I had called him up, telling him, "I'm between trains."

I didn't say anything, I watched the old man's eyes, and I guess it looked like I was wondering whether I could trust him, but it wasn't that – I was wondering if he trusted me on first meeting, so I said, to relieve him of any idea that he was going to end up under obligation to me, "I've got no story to tell you or for you to look at to read. I was just hoping to hear something from you."

He leaned forward, smiling in a confiding kind of way, and said, "You just sit still, because I always thought the best storytelling, in case you were going to ask, is still as still water."

I looked him in the eye, pondering, and wondering if I should get myself a soda from one of the vending machines, but instead I said, "I don't know any stories like that," and I reached for his whisky flask.

"Trust me," he said as I took a swallow of whisky.

A moment or two passed, and then, as if he had been testing the silence, and he had decided that it had become our silence, he said, "This is a story I'm going to tell you that's about a real death, and how anything that's really real in the past – like a death – keeps coming at you out of the future, and this story happened at the racetrack where there was this young trainer who was wanting to ingratiate himself with an old trainer, and the young fellow said – because he knew that there'd been a death in the family – 'I hear your brother died,' and the old trainer says, 'Yes, that's right.' The young trainer asks him, 'And how long has he been dead?' So the old trainer says, close up to his ear, 'If he'd lived till Saturday he'd be dead a year.'"

He looked me in the eye and I looked him in his eye.

"Is that a story?" I asked.

"Sure, it is."

"If that's a story then I really am between trains."

"We're all between trains," the old man said, "but if that won't do, then I'll tell you what another writer once told me in Paris when I was about your age. He told me how he was talking to a small group of schoolgirls and he told those girls that any good story, when you get right down to it, is all about brevity, religion, mystery, sex, aristocracy, and plain language. And so, sure enough, one of those girls wrote him a story for when they met the next day, and the story she wrote went, 'My God,' said the Duchess, 'I'm pregnant. I wonder who did it?'"

He held up his hands as if he were under arrest. This stopped me from either laughing or complaining. He closed his eyes and sat back in his station house chair. I took another drink of whisky. The storyteller and I sat as still as still waters could be.

DREAMBOOK FOR A SNIPER

I was his priest.

That's what he said, standing in front of my church, St. Peter's Church: "You are *my* priest."

I was not sure by the sound and feel of him that he had ever prayed. He certainly was not seeking forgiveness.

The chill composure in his pale hooded eyes was not the look of a man wanting absolution. Yet he insisted he needed a priest.

"A walk might do us good," I said.

"Stretch the mind," he said.

We went for a stroll along Bloor Street, a clutter of shops on both sides of the street.

When he saw himself in a storefront window, he said, "I have eyes like ghosts."

He had large bony hands, he cracked his knuckles as we walked, and he wore a black leather finger-glove on his index finger.

"What's that?" I asked.

"A glove."

"I can see that. What's it for?"

"To keep the finger warm. Safe. My trigger finger."

He touched the glove to his nose.

He had a crooked nose.

Women, he said, liked his nose. "Lonely women, the kind of women who like to look after things they think are broken," but soon it was clear, when I asked about who his friends were, that there were no women in his life.

Sitting in the Whistling Oyster café, he sang to me:

momma cooked a chicken
she thought he was a duck
she set him on the table
with his legs cocked up

He wore, even while eating in the café, a black borsalino hat.

"A sensible man wears a hat in this country," he said, "and here you are, hatless?"

"Yes."

"That's strange for a priest. They always wear hats in the movies."

"They're old B-movies."

"My father died under his hat, hit by a car. His hat rode on his coffin to the grave. I, too, am to be found under my hat."

✖

As a soldier, he'd worn the blue helmet of the Princess Pats in Bosnia, and in the Medack Pocket on the Croatian border. He'd come home as a hardened master sergeant who appeared to be modest as a hangman might be modest. After a thirteen-month tour of duty, he had decided to set up his own eponymously named, one-man company – Earlie Fires, Animal & Pest Control – telling me in his unhurried drawl, "I keep down the vermin."

He also told me, as if he wanted me to understand that he had moments of dark uncertainty, that he sometimes woke in the morning in his bedroom, naked, in a cold sweat, staring at a porcelain cat's face on the wall, the face a clock.

He said the cat had "an evil smile" and a pendulum tail. He could hear the wag of the cat's tail: *te-duh te-duh te-duh*... "You know, like the beating of my heart."

I told him he didn't have an evil smile so his heart could not beat like that.

"Believe me, nothing's what you think it is. My heart beats like that."

It was the way he talked that caught my ear, the way he closely articulated each word, with not a slur, not a mumble, and the way he sounded – the tone, a kind of sandpaper dryness. I kept telling myself, *That's the sound of dried blood*, though I wouldn't exactly know what that means, but it's what I kept telling myself, *dried blood* being sandpapered.

>———◦

We sat on the back porch of his house of an early summer evening.

Shad flies clotted the window screens. Hundreds of little silver shrouds. He pointed to two old elms towering over the porch, boastful, like they might be old relatives: "They survived the blight, the Dutch elm disease."

Crows were nested in the high branches, he said, and rats at the roots. He took me by the elbow, about to give me a warning. "Rats don't just run in the slums and on the waterfront but in the fine parts of town, too, fat rats because of good people doing good works," and he chuckled, tweaking my arm, the fatness of the rats a joke on me, on God in His good works, and especially on "people of civic goodwill composting garbage heaps in their backyards.

Compost, it's fast food, takeout," he laughed. "The heaps are honey pots. Adam rat and his Eve in the Park." There was no compost heap in his yard. But several neighbours had theirs, he said. One was an old man who had apparently survived the death camps. And the heaps had their rats. To get rid of the rats under his elm trees, Earlie had baited the nest holes with *THRAX* and then he'd waited, cradling his shotgun. As the rats came up for air in twos and threes, he'd sat in a canvas summer deck chair – and he showed me the deck chair that was still out on the lawn – BLAM…by five in the afternoon…BLAM…sixteen rats were dead, the bright red casings of fine-bird shotgun shells scattered in the grass amid their bodies.

"I raked up the dead rats, raked them into their own heap, drenching them with gas, and lit them on fire."

He had fed and stoked a slow-burning fire for more than an hour.

His next-door neighbour, and I've seen him since, is a dour old man who had been propping up the white heads of peonies in his back garden, and Earlie said, "He's an old man who has lived alone beside me for years in his squat little house. He's always out there, puttering around, looking bent and half-bewildered, a mumbler. On that afternoon he had been standing with the wind blowing smoke from my fire across our fence into his garden, into his face, and he stood there, the wind thick with the rancid sweet smell of burning flesh, with ash, until he began turning in circles, beating his breast and pulling his hair, stricken-looking, and he started in on this nasal chant: *Yiskaddal veyiskaddash…* And I'm screaming at him, because I can see he's caught up in some kind of chant for the dead, 'You crazy old man, you're crazy. Can't you tell the differ-ence?'"

The next day as we sat in the Whistling Oyster he said his right eye, what he called his crosshair's eye, hurt. It hurt so much that he put his hand over the eye to hold it in darkness. He wanted me to know he worried about his eyes. "I trust my eyes," he said. "For me, seeing *is* believing. Whatever it is. It *is*. Real, more than real, if it is in my mind's eye. I *am* the sniper."

"You're a sniper?"

"So they say."

"You picked off men?"

He drew little moon circles on his paper napkin,

humming to himself, *momma cooked a chicken...*

When I said I didn't understand what he meant by momma cooked a chicken with his legs cocked up, he shrugged, not looking up, and replied, "How come she thought he was a duck?" as he drew the + of the crosshairs of his telescopic sight into each circle. Then he told me it was more important for me to know that sometimes, when the pain in his eyes was too much, he played the flute. Then, with a kind of staccato intensity, he told me how he'd come to learn about harmonious musical intervals, how they could be expressed by what he called perfect numerical ratios. And how all phenomena, he said, tapping the table with his leather trigger finger, like I should know that his leather finger was his lethal finger, all the things around us follow the patterns of number, showing me what he meant by drawing it on a napkin, showing me that the sphere, the circle, was of course perfect, but no circle was more completely human (he smiled a wry, surprisingly satisfied smile) than a circle with a crosshair in it. But most beautiful of all – and he took off his hat – was a tetraktys of crosshairs (which I had never heard of),

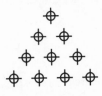

an image, he said, of eternal harmony. And, just as I decided for sure that he hadn't called on me to own up to some terrible crime, but, astonishingly enough, he was outlining for me his idea of what perfection was, he said, "Look, you're a priest, you understand these kind of things," and though I told him right away that nothing is more overrated than the understanding of priests, he carried on breaking it all down for me, telling me how the monad (primordial unity), the dyad (the energy of opposites), the triad (introducing potential), and 4 – the four seasons, the four essential musical intervals – all completed a progression: 1+2+3+4=10, what he called the tetraktys. It was, he said with a big wide sweep of his arms, the actual numerical model for the kosmos, "the whole damned kosmos" and then he wagged his leather trigger finger at me again. He was now having a very good time with himself, let alone me. It was also, he said, the symbol of the human psyche, "that enraging, frightening, exhilarating space where men have gone in head-first to create some kind of harmony out of the most horrific pain, like the craftsmen for the coliseum in Rome. Did I know about them? Artisans, artists who sculpted brass cows big enough to hold a man in their bellies, giving the cows a hinged lid that they opened. And then the man, tied in a fetal position, they put him in the belly, the lid was closed, and a fire was built below the brass cow's belly, a fire so they could slowly roast the man inside alive. But what's fascinating," he said, holding me by the wrist, "is that the craftsmen had shaped the mouths of the cows into six small flutes, so that the roaring screams of the dozens of roasting men in the stadium were turned into harmonious song – bursts of light-hearted flute music, pure notes from pure pain, harmonies that filled the air until there was a last drawn-out dying note, a long B-flat."

As I put his napkin of crosshaired circles in my pocket I thought, *What in the world is going on? Where does this man want me to go with him in his mind, and why?*

Then he said: "Ten is the tetraktys. Ten is complete fruition. And the question is – can ten killings be a fruition?"

〜〜〜

We were walking along Bloor Street, a crowded downtown shopping street that was all in sunlight, the men wearing linen jackets, seersucker and white suits, and the women summer floral dresses. I had decided in the morning to not wear my Roman collar. He had said immediately as we'd met: "You're not wearing your dog collar."

I said, "No. No because as far as I can figure out you're not wanting me to hear your confession."

"Confession," he snorted, "of course not. The yellow dog's got nothing to confess. I'm a virtuous man."

The yellow dog was new to me but I let it pass as we crossed an intersection against the stoplight. He said he'd been having a hard time with the light, with his eyes, "a lot of pain, ordinary little things, light bulbs going on and off, light stinging off the chrome hubcaps of parked cars. The same kind of sting of light my father showed me one afternoon when I was a child, showing me how to burn ants alive, burn them with a magnifying glass, frying them like he did one by one until he got bored and poked the nozzle of a can of 2-in-1 lighter fluid into their nest hole, pumping the fluid down, and then he lit it with his Zippo lighter and kept injecting fuel into the fire·hole. The mound burning to black sand, burning the bodies to black nubbles." Then he took me completely by surprise, plunking his borsalino on my head as if we had become secret sharers of his head and all that was in it – "and so you keep this under your hat, now," he said, with mischief in his tone and a menace I'd not yet seen in his eye. "You keep it strictly between us. That's how my father kept me company in the hills, hills that were called the Medak Pocket, when I was crawling in the tunnels – the wormholes – tracking the scent of human fear. I'd always gone into the tunnels calmly, my lieutenant saying, '*Sometimes I think someone freeze-dried your nerves,*' going deeper, trying to 'hear' the terror of the killer hiding in there. And I'd always pick a time when I knew I was close to the man, a time to laugh, to snicker, so that the man would know a devil was coming after him, and some started screaming before I ever got to them, boys gone half-mad, and, it was a long time before my own fears at last took me tight by the throat, when I was suddenly dead sure that I was being buried alive. It just heaped up like someone shovelling dirt in my brain that I was being betrayed, maybe by my lieutenant, maybe by some hill country militia thug who was waiting for me to come up out of my hole, waiting for me with his 2-in-1 flame-thrower to burn me alive, to sting me, so that now when I wake up I sometimes wake up with my body sopping wet..." and he reached across and snatched his borsalino from me and jammed it on his head – "and I stand in the corner of my bedroom, naked, wearing only my hat, freezing in a night sweat although it's already noon and I'm trying to calm myself, calm down because I've been awake all night, not falling asleep until dawn, the Glock under my pillow, death close to my ear. It's like having crabs on my bones. A clutch. Not panic. A desolation. Something nameless. I empty my mind into a stillness. It's a stillness where singing helps. I found that out while I was crouching down in the stench of a sewage ditch stacked with naked bodies, *Oh death, please sting me, and take me out of my misery,* listening to myself – listening since I can't seem to shut myself down, singing and mumbling in my mind, a running, loping, barking dog. That's my mind, running low to the ground, nosing under a log, a gangly yellow dog between the bushes, sniffing at the legs of a little girl who's got freckles and her mother, two refugees straggling along the edge of the road, looking at me, looking at my blue helmet that looks to them like a piece of the blue sky had fallen down between them as they carried on trying to find some small flat stones. Wanting the stones to throw at birds, to kill the birds for food. All the fields scorched to stubble, and the trees blackened, the branches settled by small white butterflies, clustered. Shanks of blackened rope. Skull bones tied into the branches of the trees, a bit of blue sky in the bones. Butterflies in the skulls. Each a stillness. Like an empty thought. So empty I needed a priest, I needed a sane priest," and he eased up very close to me, almost cheek by my cheek, whispering, "Make no mistake. In the Pocket we weren't peace keeping, we were fighting. For our lives. The whole place was overrun by crazy true believers, priests and mullahs and tribal wackos. Children flensed to the bone by flame-throwers. *Pray for us.* Buckets of men's testicles marinated in kerosene – set up as fire pots at night, as landing lights for airplanes. *Pray for us.* Water poured from a tin cup, a final blessing over a bald but heavily bearded old priest propped up on the steps of a monastery. *Pray for us.* His severed hands, severed feet, crossed in his lap. *Pray for us.*

"And all the time I was trying, I was trying as hard as I could to step into the skins of those farmers, to get into the skins of those shopkeepers, those tribal priests, trying to step into their shoes like you're trying to step into mine. That's what I hoped then and I hope now. Trying to make what I'm saying fit. Into something. Any kind of shoe. Anything other than the ineffectual moral arrogance of trying to keep, by the barrel of an empty gun, another man's peace! Which is exactly how I dropped into the line of sight of this warlord who was in charge of the local airstrip. I was out on the tarmac, and there he was, a completely drunk fool crying *fuck fuck fuck fuck fuck* while I stared at his shoulder insignia. Serbs? *Who were they?* Drunk on malignancy. One saying over and over, 'Flowers, flowers thanks to God, are in bloom, no clouds.' Saying that they thought they were going to have to shoot me, a Blue Beret, me with no permission papers where there were no permission papers for anything, so they said they were going to have to shoot me or else someone would shoot them. It was necessary since what was necessary is necessary and what is not necessary is not and the crazy warlord nodded. And there I was, pointing at my blue helmet, and I kept pointing until I worried they might think I was telling them to shoot me in my head. The drunk militia captain, whose fly was open, told me, 'Mister, please, your helmet, you take it off, yes!' I took it off. 'Put on helmet.' I put it on. Without waiting for his orders, making mock, I took it off, I put it on. 'You go play your game,' the furious captain said, 'and you wake up dead.' Leaving me with nothing to do but to shrug and say, 'Your fly is open.'

"The captain cracked me across the shoulder with the butt of his AK-47. My blue helmet fell into the mud. 'Now helmet is off. You are lucky. You know why? Why is a very big question,' the captain said. 'Is most important question, Why? Why? Why? Why?' he screamed.

"Then, he smiled. 'Fuck.' He took hold of my hand, the pupil of his eye black to the core, and I looked into that blackness. The cold in his hand a biting cold. A cold that was not the hand of death. It was the cold hand of evil. (I look at myself every morning in the mirror, my priest, waiting to see if my eyes have gone black.) That was the sign of evil, the blackness of the eyes, that cold hand.

"The captain, he saw an old man sitting by the side of the tarmac, sitting there braiding flower stems into a bouquet. He went over and shot the old man. Dead. 'Jesus Christ,' I yelled, 'why did you do that? Why?' He said, 'Exactly. Why? Now you are a philosopher.' Waving his arm, 'You go. Pass freely.' Before I could go he laughed, holding up a weighted sack. 'Here is freedom,' saying he had in the sack the severed head of another warlord. 'No trouble,' he said to the sack. 'You too are free.'

"He bowed to me. Courteous. A fellow soldier. 'Fuck,' I said, banging my helmet on the tarmac like I was crazy. 'What a fucking thing to do!' He screamed, 'Fuck you to fucking hell. You do not want to be on bad side with me.' Saluting. He gave me the V for victory sign, telling me, 'Come into my hills, I will kill you too.' I didn't know what to do. You're a priest, what can you do? Pray? Good works? There was nothing I could do. Not then, and not later at a crossroads when I saw that the head of the other warlord had been taken out of the sack and mounted on a pike, eyes closed, the mouth open and stuffed with oxlips and violets.

"A mouthful of flowers at a crossroads. A shrine to all those numbed men out there with their need, their inexplicable crazed need for utter cruelty, trying to keep a peace where there was no peace, no battle lines, only skirmishes, fire-fights, hordes of refugees and camps, and militias made up of stupid ordinary men who were not just killing each other but decapitating, raping, and dismembering. Killing off the boys, the babies, trying to kill the future, gang-fucking the women and girls to contaminate the bloodlines, to infect the heart, to sow hatred.

"And nobody wanted our Blue Berets, not even the local priest who, totally stripped down, bald-ass naked, bicycled across the air-port tarmac to his gutted church, crossing the air to ward off out-siders, to keep us away as he passed the airport's tiny lounge where an officer who had flown in from Brussels stood and spoke to us, to his Blue Berets: '...very well, they choose to suspend the accepted rules for conducting civilized warfare. Well, if two play at the game – and that is what they are doing – then those two sides are in violation...we abide by rules...'

"'Does that mean we are civilized, sir?'

"'That means we are to enforce the peace by engaging in no retaliatory aggressive action, not against either side, we are to stand between...'

"'Between is where, sir?'

"'Where it has to be.'

"'Could that be anywhere, sir?'

"'Anywhere is where it is.'

"'Yes, sir.'"

He invited me more and more into his house, his family home, where I realized he talked about all houses the same way. Houses were alive.

"There is life, teeming life," he said, "moving in the cellars. Vermin in the walls, from the dust mites we can never see in our beds to the raccoons playing hide-and-seek under the roof."

He had a large bookshelf full of books on woodworms, rodents, centipedes, squirrels, ants, cockroaches, and especially termites. And it was the termites who seemed to fascinate him the most, largely because of the way they built huge insulated housing hives. It was like, he said, they had their own military point men. They'd send out blind feeders – their own Blue Berets, he called them – who set up forward positions, stone-cold blind but still able to somehow survey the hills.

And then there were the infiltrating carpenter ants, sawing into support beams and the floor scantling, tunnelling and leaving only tiny mounds of superfine sawdust in the corners of a house. Apparently he had had his own infestation in his own house – ants nesting in the wood framing above the basement concrete blocks.

He had sprayed all six of his rooms and the basement with a chemical called antheletymene, and then he sat down, watching and waiting for them to come out of the walls. He told me that the stillness in which he sat was like his stillness as a sniper: as he'd waited for men to come into his x line of sight, but the antheletymene had turned out to be so strong, so toxic, that his nerves had turned to neon lighting in his brain. He could feel his heart ricochet in his rib cage. He must have been taking the chemical in through his pores as if he were an ant himself, and it had brought him to his knees, listening to snakes whistling.

Not long after he told me about the ants, he went on the porch into the house to get a glass of water, and then I heard him yelling. I found him in front of a floor-length mirror in the hall, berating himself in the mirror. "But I wasn't yelling at myself," he told me later. "I was yelling at a man who was yelling at me, a killer, and, because I wanted nothing to do with him I took off my hat, and then put it on, trying to get my hat off and on before he could get his hat off and on, but he spread his fingers against his side of the glass, like he wanted our fingertips to meet, and they almost did, but I pulled back because he had widened his eyes into the kind of eyes that I've seen before – the eyes of a man who has seen oxlips and knows they're a sign of spring in the mouth of a dead man. And I'd no sooner yelled at him, 'You don't scare me,' than you came along, asking me, 'Can I help?' – 'Help? What d'you mean *help*?'"

><~~><

Earlie gave me a drawing, a drawing he says of the man he saw in the mirror. The man has the nighttime stars of Van Gogh in his eyes, stars crisped to black. I feel the insurgent embrace of suffering in his face. It bleeds to the edges, or perhaps I am wrong. Perhaps it is terror.

><~~><

What he said, so matter of fact it was kind of frightening, was that listening to snakes whistling was just like being back in the Medak Pocket, like he was tracking the palpable scent of human fear, of panic, "following my nose, nosing around outside of a small field hospital that the UN had set up close to a gutted farmhouse and an abandoned orphanage.

"A half-track had ground razor wire down into the mud, but after the rains, the wire had risen up. I saw a sliced-off toe, like a white bud about to flower in the mud."

Apparently he'd kept the toe bone as a souvenir. To remember how they grew things there.

"And how they have butchered their own lives, and I can see it all but I can't see the answer to the question, the *Why?* Which is why I want you to imagine the dead carts I've seen upended in the mud. I want you to step into my shoes, see that there was still a dead body in one of the carts, the long handles sticking straight up in the air like prongs to a tuning fork (I thought it'd be perfect to find Beethoven between the prongs, brooding on the B-flat harmonies of Moscow on fire), the *clack clack clack* of .50 calibre machine-gun fire up in the hills, *clack clack,* it was like the tapping of a blind man's cane in my brain, the red tracers streaking into the trees clumped behind the orphanage, the walls that had been buckled in by mortars, the fruit trees between the orphanage and the open graves in full bud – white and lemon-yellow – the same white and lemon-yellow as the gay spring scarf I saw on a nurse after I walked through a skeletal-standing doorframe of a house whose front wall had been blown away, a television still on in the back room, blaring so loud I'd slid along with my back to a wall to see who was watching the TV and what I saw was CNN, this reporter with his wacko angular Australian twang, his tone of pained urgency as he told me that mass graves and a concentration camp had been found outside a village just ten minutes away, and I thought, Yes, because I'd been at that concentration camp ten days earlier just ten minutes away from where I was now in a back kitchen where a nurse, a Red Cross band on her head and a white and lemon-yellow scarf around her shoulders, a woman who looked to be in her late thirties, was lying on her back on the floor with her legs spread and angled in the air, angled like you could hang your washing on her ankles, and between her legs there was a naked boy – a stripling boy of ten or twelve with thin wrists and narrow buttocks – a boy, perhaps from the orphanage – and standing there against the kitchen wall, cradling my rifle across my chest – I couldn't believe how glistening white her thighs were – and the boy's body, too – their embrace a stillness in my mind's eye, and I thought – I should report to CNN, I have found a still-ness, a toe that is in bud and a stillness – until she turned her head and, looking sluttishly pleased, she winked at me, as if she was sure I would understand why she was there having a beautiful boy-child fuck her, probably for the first time in his life, down there in the tile and plaster rubble, down there in the reek of cordite.

"I went back out into the yard – I wasn't sure whether I was pissed off or aroused – a yard that was attached to the field hospi-tal that was flying our blue flag, to eight cots in the hospital, three corpses on the cots, and one squat, heavy-shouldered, iron-haired nurse. Sheets caked with blood covered the sick and injured, not the dead. The corpses were naked (nothing, it seems to me, so con-veys the lousy vulnerability and dead-eyed futility of struggling to live as a limp penis lying along the thigh of a dead naked man). Without thinking, I laid my hand on the shoulder of a corpse whose face was yellowish green, his left eye closed below a wound in his forehead, his right eye open, staring straight up. I shut my left eye and stared down, sniper to sniper, I thought, as the nurse, who had liverish bags under her eyes, said, 'You want to do something good?'

"'Sure,' I said, 'I'm a good man.'

"'You find the one with the hammer, you kill him.'

"'Like a good man should,' I said.

"She turned to a man lying on a cot. His wound over his collarbone was running pus. She applied a poultice that smelled of sulphur. It looked like a goat's or sheep's liver.

"'Jesus Christ, what's that?' I asked her.

"'Is poultice,' the nurse said. 'Do your own business.'

"'I'm going,' I said, 'to check out the orphanage.'

"'The hammer. Not forget. Do something good.'

"So, my priest, like I set out to find you in your church, I set out to look for the hammer in the orphanage to do something good out there among the fruit trees, some burned to a bone crisp, others loaded with white and lemon-yellow buds and I thought – though I didn't smoke – I had this crazy thought that in a movie about my life this would be the time, the place, to stop and smoke a cigarette. And then, in the movie this would be the moment, with me standing there relaxed and guileless, I'd get shot by an unseen marksman, shot as I took my first deep satisfying drag, and in my memory's eye that shot taught me to always keep an unseen marksman in my mind's eye, sniper to sniper.

"In the orphanage, in the dining hall, under the wall icons of two saints with fire-eyes inlaid in silver – on the other side of several rows of polished oak dining-hall tables – I found a dead woman lying on the bloodstained linoleum floor, a young naked woman, spread-eagled. Nailed alive to the linoleum, naked and nailed down, at her hands and feet, with long roofer's nails – nailed and raped.

"Until she was dead.

"Her bones were still in her skin…but not because she hadn't tried to rise up out of her skin's skin…her back was still arched up off the floor, surging in a last attempt to get loose of the nails…her mouth wide open, her perfect white teeth, eyes bulged out of their sockets. An empty Champagne bottle by her foot, the room stifling. Shit and rotting flesh. Flies. No white butterflies. Wobbling fluorescent green flies. Hundreds of them. I wanted to get my own bones out of my own body, sickened, in a fury at the futility of young bodies piling up till the trenches overflowed. The rats feeding. Then a pause in the clock happened. It always happens. A little cuckoo bird sings… Time. Peace. Except, there's always a rat in the clock. There is always a rat in the clock behind the bird – behind the door – (the bird thinks he has found his escape hatch, so dumb in his memory that he springs out and thinks this every hour on the hour) – and the bird sits out there and he sings, but always the spring goes CLICK and the pause is done even before the mustard gas and the smoke and ash from the furnaces settle and the bird gets snatched back into the clock and the door slams shut, CLACK – and it is Hello Pol Pot, *Pray for us*; Hello Churchill, the Crisper of Dresden, *Pray for us*; Hello Stalin, *Pray for us*; Hello Pinochet, *Pray for us*; Hello Mao, *Pray for us*; Hello Hitler, *Pray for us*; Hello to all the Doctor Kissingers and Strangeloves. And then, sometimes – except for the moving hands on the clock – there is that pause, that calm. There is a lull in which, as soldiers, as Blue Berets, as peacekeepers, we sit tall in our tanks at a crossroad, models of rectitude, but soon the rats begin to feed, rape, behead. They are the generals, the police, the bishops, the mullahs, the rebbes, the tribal militias... And so, what was I to do? What good was to be done for my iron-haired nurse? What was required? What is required as the door slams shut, CLACK, and it all begins again, the eruptions begin again, the buboes, as the unbelievable becomes all too believable, when a woman disembowels a man and tries to stuff his live baby son into his stomach. I was outraged, I, who can sit in utter stillness for three or four hours – letting all the anxiety drain out of me, absolutely relaxed, not limp – relaxed into focus, complete focus, coiled for action in my mind's eye, trusting my eyes since *seeing* is believing, coiled yet at ease, as if I felt the moment before and the moment after happen at the same time – a moment so satisfying – and so prolonged in its tension within that stillness, in the ⊕, the × of the crosshairs, that once or twice I almost did not pull the trigger, wanting to hold on to the feeling, but as I told you, my priest, O my priest, the decision I made – not just to disobey my orders but to kill certain men, and one woman – was taken in all intellectual awareness, a decision to act, and by completing the act, completing its virtue, my own act of what I might call virtuous violence."

"Ah yes," I said to him. "Aquinas, a matter of intellectual virtue independent of morality."

"Perfect," he said. "I was not wrong to have sought you out. You get the point exactly, intellectual virtue independent of morality. Which is why I have let you look into my eyes. I've let you see my ghosts, feeling no rectitude, as I rehearse in my mind how I hunted down, on separate occasions, split off from my squad, those I intended to kill. So let us make no mistake, my priest, I knew exactly what I was doing... *I have not only seen evil but more important, I understand that I have seen evil.* I have seen it in an offering of oxlips in a dead mouth at an empty crossroad. It's not the thought that counts, it's acting on the thought. I tracked nine men and a woman who had become monsters of evil. Monsters. Not machine-gun jockeys. But monsters who believed they were safe, safe to go back up into their hills, confident that those of us who were there to keep a peace would not only never kill them but would protect them from each other. But not me. I drew each one of them into my crosshairs, into the magnifying circle of my telescopic sight. I was their intimate, up close, as God is with us, up close, as God is our intimate from a great distance. Patient. Absolutely patient. Setting up the perfect shot from a distance, so that no one would know where the shot had come from, I shot them dead in their shoes. I eradicated evil.

✦ – the hammer, seated on a kitchen chair, bearded, lifted his hand. Perfect. He'd been to the market. He held a slice of bread warm from his wife's oven, then slumped over his kitchen table, bleeding from the mouth into a soup bowl

✦ ✦ – the airport warlord, sitting cross-legged on the stone step to his village well, petting a dog, his string bag full of tomatoes, and then his body jerks back, the dog licks blood from his blown-open throat

✦ ✦ ✦ – a man, an ex-doctor, who was known as the Stitcher because he stitched up the mouths of people he was going to kill, once sewing a live mouse into the mouth of an old woman, driving her insane

✦ ✦ ✦ ✦ – a professor, smiling, pleased with himself, offering a book to his wife as I'd seen him offer the hand he'd severed from a six-year-old girl to a guard dog on a chain

✦ ✦ ✦ ✦ ✦ – the woman who disembowelled a father so that she could then try to bury alive his baby son inside his stomach, the father, of course, left still alive for this ·

✧✧✧✧✧✧ – a tinsmith at his worktable wearing a leather apron, making a breadbox, who had used his soldering irons to burn out the eyes of a mullah, shot from behind, blowing out forehead, bone, and eyes

✧✧✧✧✧✧✧ – the man who'd sowed a playing field outside the front door of a kindergarten with land mines and then had hurried all the children out to die as they tried to run and dance through the mines, shot clean through the heart as he sat at home with his own children

✧✧✧✧✧✧✧✧ – a woodsman who was a militia gunner who cleaved a woman's skull from crown to chin with a power saw, gutting it and then placing her hands, severed at the wrist, in the skull, shot between the eyes as he took outdoor Communion

✧✧✧✧✧✧✧✧✧ – the gas station attendant who, as a captain, drowned men by forcing a nozzle into their throats and then firing them up as human bombs (my only near-miss), his jaw blown away

✧✧✧✧✧✧✧✧✧✧ – and finally, the commandant who drowned a prisoner every day in the camp cesspool, shot as he bathed in a mountain pool, shot in the shoulders so that he could not swim to stop himself from slowly sinking

"Ten times, my priest. I killed, my priest, ten people.

"And my killing them was an act as impersonal as a hangman is probably impersonal, unlike the killing of someone like my mother or father – or you – would be personal, but then. of course, I can't kill my mother. I never knew my mother. And I can't kill my father because he is already dead. He died just before I went into the army, though he still moves around in the house. I know him by his step. I hear the creaking of the floors, his step slow and hesitant, his presence like an incursion, a shadow moving in and then moving out of me along with my other ghosts. I've decided that refugees are just more living ghosts, like those ten ghosts, who inhabit me the way vermin inhabit a house. They leave behind a superfine trail of sorrow, a sorrow that heaps up and sits heavy on my mind, especially in the morning when I find myself not refreshed by sleep but overcome at the beginning of the day by an unfathomable ache, by what I believe is not despair, something beyond *Why?*"

"What is that?" I asked.

"It is a sense of desolation."

"It is a state. It is virtue in desolation."

"Consider that, my priest. Could you live there in that state as I do? Could you live there alone?"

"No, I could not," I said. "I'm a priest."

⚞⚟

Again, we were on the back porch. Earlie was wearing his black hat and he had bought me a borsalino as a gift, so there we were, two men sitting side by side on a back porch, sitting under two old elm trees wearing our hats. And he was playing his flute. A simple melody, a pure pleasure to hear, a song he'd heard in the hills outside Daruvar.

I asked him if I could give him a gift, if I could make a blessing, a sign of the cross over him?

He said, "No, not over me. If you want to bless the garden, be my guest."

I did.

Then, putting down the flute and after a silence, he said, "My father told me that memories are a ladder and if you walk back and forth under a bad memory you get bad luck. Some men, he said, live under a ladder all their lives. I killed those ten people, I make no bones about it. I am not sorry. I live under the ladder of their deaths. I regret nothing.

"Every day I draw a deep breath, take off my hat, and look into it.

"My beautiful borsalino hat.

"I bring the hat up to my face.

"Eyes open, I cover my face with darkness.

"I smell my smell.

"'Yes, that's me,' I say, as I say to you now.

"Then I go to the kitchen,

> momma cooked a chicken
> he thought he was a duck
> set him on the table
> with his legs cocked up

"And I eat ice from the refrigerator.

"Ice is good for the soul, it brings down the swelling."

DÉJÀ VU

I wonder what I'll do now that I have seen the room where I was born in several black-and-white B-movies where there is a hotel room in the east end of town by the railroad station and there is a single iron cot against the wall, and on the floor, an old leather suitcase made up into my child's bed, and outside, a hotel sign that flashes on and off, which, after my mother, a brunette with high cheekbones has gone downstairs to the bar, turns out later in the movie to be the Hotel Rex. The bartender, a retired light heavyweight boxer with a moon face and a bent nose, has always favoured my mother for her beautiful skin. She smiles at him. "Peaches and cream," she says, touching his hand, and then touching her cheek, "Peaches and cream. That's how life should be." She smokes a Camel, tapping her ash into a heavy glass ashtray, and she blows a smoke ring and turns on her barstool, crossing her legs, and says, looking me dead in the eye, "Don't you worry, boy, when the world ends, the world's gonna end on B-flat."

CROW JANE'S BLUES

Crow Jane, who was a singer in the local after-hours clubs, was walking down Spadina Avenue, her hands in her pockets. There were chrome studs on the lapels and cuffs of her jean jacket. It was nearly midnight but there were five bandy-legged boys playing stickball on the sidewalk in front of the Silver Dollar Show Bar and across the street, in the doorway beside the Crescent Lunch, some immigrant women, probably cleaning-women, were huddled around a homeland newspaper. Their warm laughter touched the loneliness that Crow Jane had felt all week, a loneliness that left her with a listless sense of loss, but she wasn't sure about loss of what, and that was why she was out walking around her old haunts, looking into the show bars from the old days, threading her way through the late-night street hustlers who were standing half out in the street between the parked cars, and for a moment she felt good, seeing herself years ago the way she used to slow-walk down the street knowing where everything was – the upstairs bootlegger who kept the beautiful Chinese twin-sister hookers who put on a show every midnight, and over on Augusta Street, behind the fruit stalls, there was heavy-jowled Lambchops, the Polish-Jewish giant who hired himself out as muscle to the after-hours clubs. But then, watching a tall white girl in front of a hat shop, the way she primped her hair with pleasure as she caught her reflection in the glass, Crow Jane hunched up and put her head down, suddenly disconsolate. When she looked up, the girl was gone.

An empty bus pulled away from the curb and she turned and wandered back up the street, into the Silver Dollar Show Bar where a lithe black girl wearing a silver sequin halter dress was on the stand. Crow Jane sat in a darkened corner drawing circles on the tabletop in the dampness from ice-cold beer bottles, and as she sat listening, the revolving coloured lights made the singer look like several women at once, all of them afloat in a wash of light, and Crow Jane thought, *She's light, lighter than me, and I bet some slicker salesman gave her momma an old black and white TV to see those black breasts and this here's the daughter of that old black and white TV,* singing with her head back, eyes shut, opening memories up inside Crow Jane, the night long ago when she wore a dust-rose shirt and had gone up the two flights of stairs on College Street to the small dance hall where two big old women wearing sweatbands and bloated by bad food took tickets at the door. She'd danced with a narrow-hipped, long-legged white girl called EveLynn, and in the lingering light the white girl had said after they'd gone home and Crow Jane had sung for her in a moaning whisper just like this girl singing here in the Show Bar, *And yes, she'd said, in the lingering light is where I do like to touch, touch you, ten years ago almost, lying back on the white sheets of the big cannon-ball bed, her nipples small, the pinky-brown of white women, and yours are plum-coloured, she'd said, lying in that bed every night, with her legs spread like a wishbone and, Baby, I said, I got sweetening', I mean in my time I've sung the song, I been lying up with the shades down just holding on to holding on, but you come high-heel sneaking in your sling-backs into my life and now I got high on sunshine,* and the singer on the stand was isolated in a small spotlight, just her face, a black face on a white moon suspended for a moment in the noisy room, *But sunshine don't get it all the time 'cause a long time* ago it was that I was with you, my little sweetenings, an' we got to always come home to the cabbage, which is why I always to this day every night sing the song how you were my love who brought me the cherry that had no stone, 'cause stones and cabbage is how I most remember my old beat-up hand-me-down days, when I be a little girl pedalling my fool self on my tricycle along the long hallway, dead end, man, I learned early to make the tight turn when you come to the end, so I see this girl so sharp up there in her spotlight of silver sequins looks like me in all the places I already been and turned back from, 'cause you see even my mind got hallways, I mean sometimes I lean back singing a song or lying up with another woman, all the good womens in this world, or poppin' pills, and them pills look like lemon-yellow bowling balls rolling down inside my head, an' sometimes when I get scared, when some sucker comes at me leering with the big hard-on in his eyes, I just sit there talking baby talk we used to talk, me an' EveLynn looking at each other side by side, studying on each other, real close, that blond hair of yours on my shoulder an' ever since then I got all the cabbages and none of the kings, an' I been down along the long hallway, pedalling on my tricycle with the bell on the handlebar that don't work, just goes fhzz fhzz like my daddy's old Ronson lighter that got no flint, railroad halls we called 'em, but nobody knows that no more 'cause nobody rides them trains, which is why I like the mouth harp sound, harmonica you called it, white words for black birds, lonesome trains and pain, that was my daddy since back then the onliest work a black man bagged was Pullman porter which my daddy was for a while till insomnia set him down, the clickity-clack inside his head he said, an' I mean he had the light on the whole time, he put pennies on his eyes when he went to sleep an' said I ain't dead, the light jess don't go out, and Crow Jane, listening to the voice on the stand in the small room of the Show Bar, was reminded so much of herself that she decided she wanted to talk to the younger singer, thinking she'd buy the girl a drink, hold her hand a little like she was holding hands with herself, and scribbled a note inviting her to the table. Crow Jane gave it to the waiter. The singer read the note and with a shrug flicked it back behind the piano, *and that too is cabbage, boiled cabbage heads, the state of shredded stink, which is bigger than big, all the cabbage-stinking long halls of the world with a Raggedy-Ann kid on a tricycle going* fhzz fhzz *at the dead-end dirty window that don't look out on nothing but back alleys, mean mealy living, man, like daddy drinking whisky, which kept his eyeballs on all the time, bulbed outta his headbone before he died, looking on the lookout for what never was, only him always sitting on an afternoon with his hair conked to get it straight, looking at me he'd say, Sweet Thing, when you're black stay back an' if you're brown stick aroun' but if you're white you're right, all that sour self-laughter of his, an' sometimes when I was with that white girl, I think he did tell it true 'cause I loved her an' black weren't beautiful then, baby, nigger heaven was nowhere, there was just my old daddy sitting on his rusty dusty listening to the "Salt Pork Blues" on the old 78s, his hair straight with lye under the stocking cap and even then, me only being a little girl on the downside of ten, I saw that a grown man sitting with a woman's ugly rolled stocking like a circle of surgical tube on his head was weird, trying to dude himself into the land of seersucker soul, arctic power, whitener was what he was up to an' drove himself stone blind on booze an' left me, little girl sucking wind the day he died, gone down like the light comes up, always the lights come up, ole young girl up there singing so pretty, I got a baby way 'cross town who's good to me,* and then she stepped down, taking the hand of a lean black man wearing a knitted wool cap, strutting a silver-handled cane and a T-shirt that said SPADE POWER. Crow Jane liked that. *I can dig it, I can dig it,* and she laughed, wishing that she knew them but it was closing time and people rose and straggled out and Crow Jane suddenly had the feeling that all her past was emptying out of her head, leaving her alone at her table in the corner, staring at the rough ceiling painted black, the water pipes and heating ducts all exposed in the light, *And that one time, I don't know why me, but they put my picture in the paper, big, full-face, singing at a festival over on the island, an' I felt good an' I said, Daddy, you may be dead and down but there I be, I is, big as lightning on the page for all to see who I am 'cause I am, Crow Jane has sung the song, the* fhzz, fhzz *is finished an' I took that clipping from the paper, an' I said to myself, EveLynn, wherever you are hiding in this here old city with your kids or whatever, I'm looking you in the eyeball, big, and I am the queen of darktown and I may not be having a ball but I'm still strutting, an' I wanted it bigger, so I scissored out that head of myself and took it down to one of them blow-up-yourself picture places an' I say, man, I want this big for framing, hang myself over my head in my bed, two feet by three I said an' he shrugs, and when I come back there I am, mounted on cardboard, an' I can't find myself for the looking, my whole face just gone to great big grey and dark dots an' I say, where'd I go, man, I don't see myself at all, an' he says that's what happens when you blow yourself up outta some newspaper, you disappear into dots, 'cause if you look close that's all you was in the first place,* and so the only thing to do was go home, still wanting to take the singer's hand and hold it to her cheek, sweat and perfume on the woman's neck, and to look into the other woman's eyes, but when Crow Jane went by, walking slowly, it was like the singer looked right through her, leaving Crow Jane suddenly alone in the doorway, facing the darkness of the street in the cool early morning air. She walked up Spadina. A big milk transport truck rumbled by. She went past a closed restaurant in which a fat-bellied man was all alone swabbing the floors, wearing a stringy undershirt and torn pants, and he waved a grubby hand and when she shrugged with disdain he mouthed a curse at her through the glass. Fog had come in off the lake and she could hear her own footsteps in the empty street.

ALL THE LONELY PEOPLE

1

They met at an Inuit sculpture gallery. She started talking to him as if they were casual old friends. Her name was Helen. As they walked around a whalebone bird with two heads, he said, "Don't you see? They were after the spirit already there inside the bone. What emerges is in the bones." When they went for coffee she sat very straight in her chair and several times she opened her pocket mirror and looked at herself, touching her lipstick with her little finger, as if she were never sure of herself. But after their first week together, meeting in the late afternoons at his small bookshop and walking in the speckled light of the heavily treed parks close by her big old family home, she suddenly disappeared without warning, phoning first from Boston and then from Palm Springs, where she had old school friends. "Don't worry about me, Gene," she said. "Now that my parents are dead, the one thing I know how to do is look after myself." She had been married to a scholar, a specialist in Anglo-Saxon riddles. "And he said I made him feel like he'd done something wrong. He was quite unfair, saying that. We just didn't agree anymore."

One afternoon, on her return, she came and sat in Gene's long narrow bookshop, staring at the walls lined with books, some of them old and rare and locked behind glass doors. "It's a little like a tunnel in here," she said, smiling, but she didn't ask to see anything and didn't open a book. Later, while they were in the upstairs sitting room of her house listening to Ravel, she said, "Does it bother you that we haven't made love?"

"No," he said, taking her hand.

"I think we should make love. I've chilled some white wine."

Her large bedroom at the back of the house was filled with light. There was a polar-bear skin on the floor and panel mirrors on the wall beside the brass bed. "Do the mirrors embarrass you?" she asked.

"Why should they?" he said shyly.

Later, when they were resting in bed, she said, "You know, my husband made up a riddle about me."

"What was it?" Gene asked.

"I don't know. It was in Anglo-Saxon. No one knows Anglo-Saxon. Anyway, was I good?"

"Yes," he said.

She had been silent while they made love, watching herself in the mirror.

"What else could you say?" She closed her eyes, touching the inside of her thighs.

"I could say no."

"No, you couldn't," she said, pulling the sheet up to her breasts, which were smaller than he had imagined. "What do you think about women's lib?"

"I don't think about it at all."

"I think it's awful. What was quiet desperation is now noisy desperation. By the way, could I have a photograph of you, a nice one?"

"Sure," he said, pleased.

"Did you look?" she said, sipping her wine.

"Once."

"I love to look. Sometimes I feel I'm watching someone who's not me with her legs up in the air."

She smoothed her hair away from her face.

"What did you see?" she said.

"I don't know."

"Come on. Don't be shy."

"You've got just that little bit of blond hair between your legs, like no hair at all."

"No, I mean in the mirror."

"I was surprised at how big I looked, when I was going into you."

The following week, Helen said she didn't want to make love. "I could tell you I have the curse," she said, "but the truth is I want us to know each other better before we make love again." She led him through the house, opening up small formal sitting rooms, the breakfast room and the library, and china cabinets filled with figurines and albums that had pages of photographs of her father. "I don't use most of the rooms but I like to keep them like they look as if they're lived in." She had become a collector of things and one night she got undressed slowly at the bottom of the stairs so he could watch her walk up the stairs wearing black lace underwear and a black garter belt. She said she'd bought them at an auction in Palm Springs because they had belonged to the famous preacher Aimee Semple McPherson. Then, in the bedroom, she made love to him, telling him to stand with his back to the mirrors. He felt a warm unsettling surge, as if he could throttle her as he stood with his hands on her shoulders. He wanted to see her face but could only see the flood of her auburn hair and the small of her back and buttocks.

They lay in bed listening to music and she said, "Did your father ever tell you anything? I mean, we all remember something our fathers told us after they're dead."

"Sure."

"What?"

"Get a good lawyer."

"Why in the world would he say that?" she said, laughing.

"He was an honest man who liked life."

"So?"

"So, he was foolish about himself but not about other men."

"Anything else?"

"Anything else what?"

"Did he tell you anything else?"

"Always keep a clear head."

"What did that mean?"

"He was a salesman and he always warned me to watch out for fast talkers. 'Keep a clear head and don't get fooled,' he used to say."

"That was all?"

"Just about."

"What else?"

"You won't like it."

"Maybe I will, maybe I won't. What else?"

"When I was about sixteen he told me that it was just as easy to fall in love with a rich girl as a poor girl."

"Oh, I don't mind that," she said.

"No?"

"I like being rich and I don't mind being loved. What a shrewd man your father must have been."

"He should've been a preacher."

"You mean he was religious?"

"No, not at all. He was just good at preaching a good game. Some guy fast-talked him for all his money with a scheme about a machine called Super Scoop that would give you scoops of ice cream like you were getting Cokes at a Coke machine."

"No kidding," and she buried her head in the pillow, laughing.

"Sure. Super Scoops. He didn't want me to believe anybody because he believed everybody. He believed in everything."

"My father," she said, "only believed in himself."

"What was his problem?"

"Since when was believing in yourself a problem?"

"You just said it like he didn't believe in anybody else."

"I don't know who else he believed in. God and distilled water."

"What?"

"Distilled water. He went all over the world and wherever there was bad sewage he got big business selling distilled water. Then it all got so big and so successful there was nothing to do but retire."

She sat up, a silk bedshirt falling away from her shoulders. She cradled Gene's head, caressing his throat. "Father became a gardener, planting in the yard, and even buying a small lot of vacant land close by so he could build a rock garden. But after that Portuguese boy was drowned downtown in a sink – remember how it was such a big story in all the papers? – killed by that lunk-head who had sexually assaulted the boy, my father then discovered the death penalty. He was determined to bring it back, and he came alive like he'd never been before."

She got out of bed, gathering her underwear, and said, "He became such a big public speaker. It was his whole concern and he sat for hours reading, rolling a ball-bearing between his fingers." She had a dresser drawer packed with his collection and she spread old yellowing photographs, engravings, and accounts of condemned men on the bedsheet before him. "They're up in the attic, too," she said. "Boxes and boxes, and rare old books. Maybe you'd like to see them, but it's so hot and narrow up there, you'll get a cramp in your back."

She sat quietly for a moment, touching her thigh, and then she crossed her legs and stroked her instep. "Bad arches. I've always had bad arches. He used to say, 'You should wear support shoes.' It got so he watched everything like a kind of cop in the months before he died. He accepted all invitations to speak about death and the penalty and sometimes even paid his own expenses."

There was a jar of very expensive cream on the night table. She was sitting on the end of the bed, hunched over, and he took the cream and began to rub it into her back, kneading the muscles that were surprisingly hard, even knotted. For a moment her whole body seemed to relax, and she let out a deep sigh, not so much of relief but aloneness, and, lifting her long hair, he kissed the nape of her neck. She shivered and became rigid again. "It gave my father pleasure," she said. "That's exactly the way he put it. It gave him pleasure arriving in an unknown town, having his hand pressed by eager men and women, the hushed attention when he spoke about the way we could kill a man, and then there was the applause and appreciation from the local police. He kept all the photographs from those trips, there in the album I showed you, cut into ovals like rows of eggs, smiling in all of them, serene. 'Not the look of a condemned man,' he told me the week before he just dropped dead in the street."

Gene was sitting cross-legged and holding her from behind. "You know what's weird around here?" he said. "The place is full of vases. Vases everywhere and there's never any flowers."

"My mother told me never to sleep in a room with flowers. They steal the air."

"So why not when you're awake?"

"Stealing's stealing, day or night."

"You know what else I couldn't figure, looking at all those albums?" he said.

"No."

"There're no pictures of your mother. There's only that photograph hanging in the sewing room."

The sepia portrait had been trimmed into a triangle and framed in rococo gilt. Between the frame and the wall there were old palm fronds curling over the face of a woman with high cheekbones and wide eyes and a shining forehead.

"Mother wasn't a Catholic," she said, "but she always went to Mass every year on Palm Sunday. She never said why but she always laughed quietly when she went out the door and said every donkey has its day."

2

As they walked late one night from her home, Helen asked, "Were you born anywhere near here?"

"Sure. And I still live in the same house."

"You're kidding. Nobody I know but me lives where they were born."

"You want to see where I live?"

They went south along shaded streets, the houses dark and the windows long and lean. Bicycles were chained to verandah railings. A police car passed by and came around the block again, slowing down. "The trouble with the police is they think everyone is a criminal," she said. "They're corrupted like that. Imagine having to live with a man looking for the criminal in you." She suddenly called out caustically to the cop, "Anything I can do to help you, officer?"

"That was wonderful," Gene said as the police car moved away.

"It was not. We should be left alone. We should all be left alone and not bothered."

"I meant you were wonderful."

She took his arm. They had to step off the sidewalk twice to avoid lawn sprinklers left on all night. "It's against the law, you know," she said. "Leaving that water on. But there are laws that just don't apply to some people and nobody knows it better than that cop. Nobody's more class-conscious than cops. Ever notice that?"

They crossed an old footbridge over a ravine. "No," he said, "but this is it."

"What is? The ravine?"

"No. The street along the other side. I grew up by the ravine. It runs right through the centre of the city."

She stood looking along the deep length of ravine darkness. "It's like a scar," she said.

"It's a secret place."

"I love secret places. I love it when people take me to their secret places."

There was a heavy, chilling mist and the few bridge lamps were dull and shimmering. He held her close. "This was a lousy little two-storey town when I grew up down here," he said. "Everything was two storeys, tiny ambitions." They heard foghorns down at the lake. She brushed her lips lightly against his hand. "But then I found out there were people down there in the ravine and some were on the run, fugitives from their families or from the law, and winos. You could find a drunk on the side of the hill any morning and these drifters fascinated me, living under the old iron bridge in their own little cardboard and plywood shelters. Even in the winter they were there, and it's like they were angels loose in the ravine, living under a big iron rainbow. I've always wondered what it must be like living under any kind of rainbow."

The front lights were on in his house and they went inside. "It's still a fine sturdy place," he said, showing her the sitting room. "Of course, the rooms are narrow in these old homes. I just seem to live a narrow life," he said, laughing.

"Do you always leave the lights on?"

"Yeah."

"All night?"

"Yeah. My father used to do it."

"Why?"

"'Leave a light on for your mother,' he used to say."

"Where was your mother?"

"She left him a note one night and took off."

"Just like that?"

"Yeah. She told him life was like a hat shop. So he said leave a light on in the shop, maybe she'll miss her old hat."

They were sitting at the back of the house in a glass-enclosed room crowded with plants, vines, and creepers, and the room was lit by a ribbon of neon light around the window ledge.

"It's strange in here," she said.

"I find it settles me down," he said. There was a little white wicker chair in the corner and she sat in it, surrounded by leaves and ferns. He sat on the edge of an old leather easy chair.

"You sit in here watching the plants?" she asked.

"They probably watch me."

"You know, sometimes I feel my father's watching me."

"Out in the bushes."

"What bushes?"

"It's just a family joke."

"So tell me."

"Well, it's not really a joke. I mean, my father and I once, when I was a boy, got lost up north in the bush country and we sat up all night in the dark listening to the goddamndest noises that put the fear of hell in us. From then on that's where he said the dead hang out – in bush country, or in the bush leagues."

"What in the world are the bush leagues?"

She was sitting curled up in the dark corner, arms around her knees, feeling a damp weight on her thighs. The closeness in the air frightened her. She wanted to be comforted.

"The bush leagues," he said, settling back into his easy chair. "That's baseball. When you're not good enough for the big leagues you play in the bush leagues."

"Did you play in the bush leagues?"

"No, but my father was a sandlot third base coach, the local leagues. He was wonderful, the way he got so dressed up. His team had these kind of cobalt-blue uniforms with yellow stripes down the legs and WORLD MEDIA BROKERS in yellow letters on the back, and he used to scream at the umpires."

"He sounds like a man my father would've hated."

"I don't know. Maybe. It was all wonderful play-acting for him. Sometimes he got all confused on the field." He closed his eyes and she felt as if she were slowly easing away from him into the dark earth smell of leaves and ferns. "You see, he'd wave his arms around like a windmill, waving a runner home. And when the runner got called out by a country mile so everybody saw he'd made a mistake, he'd scream, kick the dirt, and finally the umpire would pump his fist, yelling, *You're outa here, you're outa the game.* He'd laugh, patting his hands together like a pleased boy. That was the beautiful thing, see? To him it was all a game, it had nothing to do with life. That's what he used to say: 'Life's real, kid, and playing baseball is playing for time. You get thrown outta life and what you are is dead.'"

"And your mother never came home?" she asked, her voice almost a hush.

"Nope. That was real. About a year after he died I got a telegram saying she was dead, too."

"But you still keep the lights on."

"Well, you can't turn your back on the dead," he said, laughing again. "They may be out there lost in the bushes."

He stretched his legs. They sat in silence for a long time. Then she said, "I think I feel ashamed."

"Ashamed of what?" he said, reaching out to her shadow in the corner, but she was farther away than he thought.

"Nothing. I just feel this need."

He rested his elbows on his knees, his hands hanging together, staring at her shadow in the shadows. There were always raccoons outside in the alley at night. He could hear them, up from the ravine, rummaging for food.

She said fiercely, "I want to make love."

"What?"

"I need to make love."

She stood up and stepped out of her skirt and panties, and still wearing knee-high black boots, stockings, and a garter belt, she lay down on the floor, her head in the shadows, knees up and spread.

"Here?" he asked.

"Here," she said, "and hurry."

He was in his stocking feet. He couldn't grip the tiled floor. Her head was by the chair and she was holding on to the wicker legs. "It'd be better with you on your hands and knees," he said. She got up and crouched over so that he held her shoulders, half squatted over her haunches, and he made love to her until she shuddered in small spasms and let out a keening wail. When she sank down he lay on her, filled with the perfume in her hair. She said, "You didn't come, did you?" and he said, "No." She sighed and said, "That was unfair, making me cry out like that."

3

The next day, she went to Palm Springs. She sent a single rose with a note to the bookstore. He sat alone in his house at night, waiting for the phone to ring. He knew she would be all right. He just wanted the phone to ring, but she didn't call. There was a lot of rain, and dampness seeped into his bones. It was hard to sleep. Two weeks passed. Then she called late one night and said she was home and that she had been drinking. "No, it's not because of the rain," she said. "I don't care about the rain. For tonight I care to be alone." A week later, at about two in the morning, she called and said, "If you come over, I'll take you to one of my secret places."

The streets were empty as they walked. "It's funny," she said. "The whole time I've been away I was thinking about my mother. I should've known her but I didn't know her."

"Me either."

"But yours ran away. Mine stayed put and never seemed to be anywhere. We used to sit in her bedroom and hardly talk. She always wore nylons with seams and she'd run her hands along the seams, over and over, trying to get them straight. But they were always wobbly. She began going to bed early, you know, eleven, ten, then right after supper, closing the day down earlier and earlier until she never got out of bed. Father took her her meals, more courtly the more he was out of her life. She seemed content, except she always said: 'Watch out, watch out.'"

"For what?"

"I don't know. She was so firm about it, indifferent to everything else except watching out. Nothing ever happened to her and nothing's happened to me, or maybe it has. But my always watching for something big to come along, well, somehow everything has seemed so small."

She drew close to him in the night air. After a while they went to an all-night restaurant. "This is it," she said. There were booths at the back and a horseshoe counter with full-length mirrors alongside the take-out stall. They sat at the counter in swivel chairs.

"You know," she said, "I came in one night and there was an old man in a homburg hat sitting here." They ordered the Golden Crispy Waffles from the big glossy menu. "I mean, he had a cribbage board and cards and we played for an hour, and the next night he was back but I didn't want to play again. I could see he was counting on it, but he'd forgotten to wear his hat. He was bald and I distrust men with shiny heads."

A boyish broad-shouldered cop had walked along the mirrored wall to the take-out stall. He asked for a double-double coffee. "There's a sweet tooth," she said. "A sweet-tooth cop."

A man who had a lopsided gait had come in behind the cop. He hurried to an empty chair and pocketed the dollar bill that had been left behind as a tip. Then he sat down and the waitress bawled at him, "Hey, I hustle too hard for my tips. I hustle and I don't care if you're a retard or not."

"How do you like that?" Gene asked her.

"Like what?"

"A little case of theft."

"They'll work it out," she said. "Leave them alone and they'll work it out."

The man sat staring into an empty coffee cup. There was a lipstick mark on the rim of the cup and he touched it. Then he picked up a crust of cold toast and ate it. "I don't care," the waitress said, walking over to the cop, who came back, lumbering slowly, looking a little flushed. The waitress said, "It's my tip." The cop sat down, speaking quietly to the man, saying, "It's her tip, you see. It's hers. You can understand that. You have to give it back." The man shook his head stubbornly and drew little empty egg shapes on the countertop. The cop moved the knife and fork away.

"That's really strange," Helen said. "That's what my father used to do at every meal."

"What?"

"We had to take the knives off the table until after he said grace."

"Where the hell did he get that idea?"

"I don't know. But it sure gave a funny feel to eating when we picked up our knives."

"Come on," the cop said, "be a good guy. You've got to give it back." The man fumbled and took the dollar from his shirt pocket. He gave it to the cop who handed it to the waitress who came over to Helen and said, "I'm sorry, but it's mine, see, because I gotta hustle."

The cop stood up and said quietly, "Come along now. It's probably best if you go home." He caught sight of himself in the mirror and flushed, as if embarrassed at how big he looked, and then he frowned and said, touching the man on the shoulder, "Come on now. It's all for the best." The cop held the door open for him.

The waitress said, "I don't trust cops."

"I don't trust cops either," Helen said.

"But the cop," Gene said, "handled it beautifully."

"I don't like cops," Helen said firmly. "I don't like cops."

"Well, maybe so, but the cop worked it out."

"Don't patronize me."

"We better go," he said.

"Yeah, okay," she said, rolling her napkin into a little ball. She dropped it into her empty coffee cup. He left the waitress a good tip.

"Well," she said at the door, "how do you like our first disagreement?"

"It happens to the best of us," he said.

"And the worst," she said, laughing. "I'll make love to you tonight, okay?"

"We'll see," he said, and put his arms firmly around her shoulders as they hailed a taxi. At home, he started to take off his shirt. "No, no," she said, "I want to be good to you. You can't say no to a girl who wants to be good." He was disappointed. He wanted to soothe her. "You want me up against the wall?" he said, laughing.

"It's nice, isn't it?"

"Yeah, except this time I want to watch."

"Whatever you want," she said and knelt down.

"How come you want to be so good to me?"

"Maybe it's in my nature," she said, smiling, and held him firmly by the thighs.

He could only see her hair over her hunched shoulders and the soles of her shoes, and his own unhappy look in the mirrored light.

Two days later, she called and said she had found a superb pheasant pâté and for him to come over. He decided to bring her a single rose. "Well," she said, taking the long thin box, "where will I put that?" She placed it into the umbrella stand and took him into the library where she showed him the photograph of himself he had given her. It was on a side table, scissored and fitted neatly into an oval upright silver frame. He was smiling in the photograph and looked very handsome.

"Don't you think it's a beautiful frame?" she said. "I got it last time in Palm Springs." She cut two little pieces of pâté and put them on delicate china plates. She was wearing a black dress buttoned to the throat, with puffed sleeves, and a handkerchief at her wrist, under the sleeve.

"Don't you like the frame?"

"Yes, of course. It's very fine. Not the look of a condemned man, either," he said, smiling. She gave him his plate of pâté, paused, and went over to a carved oak cabinet.

"I think we should have a little something from my father's stock, Denis-Mounié. My father told me it's the cognac of the diplomatic corps."

"To your heath," he said. "We've never toasted you, and today you look very beautiful."

"Do you know," she said, "with all the things we talk about, we've never talked about politics? Everybody talks about politics."

"That's right," he said. "And it's only fair."

"What is?" she asked gaily.

"That we should talk about politics."

They discussed the news in the papers, whether the mayor now looked better after a small operation to correct an overbite and whether there should be a citizens' police review board, and then they walked to the vestibule. The rose was in its box, upright in the umbrella stand. She stood beside him at the open door, holding his hand. He kissed her lightly on the cheek. "Leave a little light in the window," he said. She laughed and they said goodbye.

He saw her again a month later out at the airport when he was coming in from a New York book fair. He would have called out to her but she was moving too quickly, and with all her composure, to catch a plane. It was the last time he saw her. But he had occasion to drive by her house one night. The house was in darkness. In spite of himself he stopped, waiting to see a light come on. Over the months, he often went out of his way to pass the big house, and one night the lawn sprinkler was on, but the house remained dark.

DOG DAYS OF LOVE

Father Vernon Wilson was an old priest who led a quiet life. He said Mass every morning at the side altar of his church, read a short detective novel, had a light lunch, and went out walking with his dog. He was retired but he always made a few house calls to talk to friends who weren't bothered by the dog, and though he had a special devotion to the Blessed Virgin and the Holy Shroud of Turin, he didn't talk much about faith.

He was still spry for a man in his early eighties. He gladly let the dog, a three-year-old golden retriever, set a leisurely pace on a loosely held leash, sniffing at curbs and shrub roots and fence posts. He'd had the dog for a year, a local veterinarian having come around to the parish house of an afternoon to leave the dog as a gift, telling the housekeeper, "I've always wanted to give Father Wilson a little dog. I always felt so at ease with myself and the world whenever I'd gone to him to confession."

In all his years as a parish priest, Father Wilson had never imagined that he might want a dog, and he certainly did not know if he could, in accordance with diocesan rules, keep a dog in the parish home. The new young pastor, Father Kukic, had at first said, No, no, he wasn't sure that it was a good idea at all, even if it was possible, but then the diocesan doctor had come by to give the priests their autumn flu shots and to check their blood pressure, and he had said, "No, no, it's a wonderful idea. I urge you, Father Kukic, if it's not usually done, to do it. It's a proven fact, older people who have the constant company of a dog live longer, maybe five years longer, maybe because all a dog asks is that you let him love you, and we all want Father Wilson to live longer, don't we."

"I'm sure we do," Father Wilson said.

"Well," Father Kukic said, trying to be amiably amusing, "there could be two sides to that argument."

"Father Kukic," the old priest said, feigning surprise, "I've never known you to see two sides to an argument." He clapped the young priest on the shoulder. "Good for you, good for you."

"I'm sure, too, that the dog will be good for you," Father Kukic said.

"I'm sure he will," Father Wilson said, but he was not sure of the situation at all. On their first night walk together he kept the dog on a short leash, calling him simply, "You, dog…"

Then, after ten or eleven days, Father Wilson not only let the dog sleep on the floor at the end of the bed in his room, but sometimes up on the end of his bed, and then one morning he announced over breakfast that he had decided to call the dog, Anselm. "After the great old saint," he told Father Kukic, "Saint Anselm, who said the flesh is a dung hill, and this dog, I can tell you, has yet to meet doggy dung on a lawn he doesn't like."

"Oh, really now," Father Kukic said, and before he could add anything more, the old priest said, "But then, look at it this way. It's all a matter of perspective. Most people get Saint Anselm all wrong. He was like the great hermit saints who went out into the desert. They renounced everything that gave off the smell of punishment and revenge, and so they renounced the flesh, but only so they could insist on the primacy of love over everything else in their spiritual lives…over knowledge, solitude, over prayer…love, in which all authoritarian brutality and condescension is absent, love, in which nothing is to be hidden in the flesh…"

Father Kukic sat staring at him, breathing through his open mouth.

"You should be keeping up on your spiritual reading, Father. That's Thomas Merton I was giving you there. You should try him."

"Wasn't he something of a mystic?"

"My goodness," the old priest said, "I think Anselm and I should go for a walk, get our morning feet on the ground."

They walked together every morning just before lunch, sometimes in the afternoon if it wasn't too hot or too cold, and always at night, just before CNN at ten. "If you're going to be in touch, if you're going to keep up with your parishioners," he told Father Kukic, "you've got to know what the trash talk is, too."

When he visited homes in the parish, leaving the dog leashed on a porch or sitting in a vestibule, he talked candidly about anything and everything, pleasing the parishioners, but more and more as he and Anselm walked together, and particularly when they stopped to rest for a moment in front of a building like the Robarts Research Library, he leaned down and patted Anselm's neck and said quietly to him, "Good dog. Now you look at that. There's real brutalism for you. That's the bunker mentality of a bully." He scowled at the massive slab-grey concrete windowless wall, the cramped doorway under a huge periscope projection of concrete into the sky. "This is the triumph of the architecture of condescension," he said, pleased that he'd found so apt a phrase for his thought, and amused and touched, too, by how Anselm, looking up at him, listened attentively, and how the dog, at the moment he had finished his thought, came up off his haunches and broke into a cantering walk, striding, the old priest thought, like a small blond horse.

"Beautiful," he said, "beautiful."

Parishioners and shopkeepers soon took for granted seeing them together.

The only times that Anselm was not with him, the only time he left the dog alone in his bedroom, was when he said Mass at the side altar early in the morning or when he went to visit a parishioner sick at home.

Once, while he was away on a sick call, Anselm had chewed the instep of a shoe he had left under the bed, and a week later he had swallowed a single black sock.

That had caused an awkward moment, because the dog had not been able to entirely pass the sock and Father Wilson had had to stand out on the parish-house lawn behind a tree and slowly drag the slime and shit-laden sock out of the dog.

"Anselm, my Anselm," he had said, "you sure are a creature of the flesh."

But it was while he was at prayer that he felt the closest to Anselm.

It was while he knelt at prayer before going to bed, kneeling under the length of linen cloth that hung on the wall, a replica of the Holy Shroud of Turin, that Anselm had sat down beside him and had nestled his body in under his elbow so that the old priest had embraced Anselm with his right arm as he had said the Apostles' Creed, feeling deeply, through the image of the dead face on the Shroud, the Presence of the Living Christ in his life. And now, every night, they knelt and sat together for ten minutes, after which Father Wilson would cross himself, get into bed, and Anselm would leap up onto the bed and curl at his feet so that as he went to sleep, the old priest was comforted not just by the heat and weight of the animal in his bed but by the sound of his breathing.

His devotion to the Shroud, however, had not been a comfort to his young pastor, Father Kukic, who had snorted dismissively, saying that when a seminarian in Paris he had travelled through the countryside one summer, and as a believer, about to be ordained, he had been embarrassed to come upon a church near Poitiers that had claimed to house "one of the two known heads of John the Baptist," and another that had said they possessed "a vial of the unsoured milk of the Virgin."

"The unsoured milk...I like that," the old priest had said, laughing.

"Well, I don't, and no one else does either," Father Kukic said. "It's embarrassing."

"Only a little."

"And as for your cloth, no one had ever heard of your Shroud 'til somewhere back in the 1500s."

"Not mine, Father. Our Lord's."

"Oh please."

"The thing is this, Father, there are certain facts..." and Father Wilson had patiently tried to describe the two images on the Shroud – the front and back of a man's wounded body and his bearded face, his staring eyes and skeletal crossed hands. And how all this, after experts had completed a microscopic examination of the linen, had revealed no paint or pigment that anyone knew of, nor did the image relate to any known style...and furthermore, "Somehow, the Shroud is a kind of photographic negative which becomes positive when reversed by a camera – the body of a man somehow embedded in the linen as only a camera can see him – a way of observing what no one could have known how to possibly paint."

"These all may be facts, Father, but they prove nothing."

"Exactly, my dear Father. But you see, I prefer facts that add up to a mystery that is true rather than facts that add up to an explanation that is true."

"Like what?"

"Like the Virgin Birth."

"Nonsense. That's a matter of faith."

"No, it's a matter of temperament, Father."

They never spoke of the Shroud again.

There were nights through the winter when the old priest, before going to sleep, felt, as he told Anselm, "nicely confused." Kneeling under the Shroud, knowing how dark and freezing cold it was outside and staring up into the hollowed dead yet terrorized eyes of the Christ, he felt only warmth and unconditional love from the dog under his arm, and after saying his prayers he took to nestling his face into Anselm's neck fur, laughing quietly and boyishly, as he hadn't heard himself laugh in years, before falling into a very sound sleep.

At the first smell of spring, he opened his bedroom window and aired out his dresser drawers and his closet, breathing in deeply, and pleased to be alive. He gave Anselm's head a brisk rubbing and then, having borrowed the housekeeper's feather duster, he took down the linen Shroud that had been brought to him as a gift by a friend all the way from Turin, dusted it off at the window, and then laid it out for airing over the sill as his mother had done years ago with the family bedsheets.

In the early afternoon, leaving Anselm asleep, he went out alone to visit an elderly couple whose age and infirmness over the long winter had made them cranky and curt and finally cruel to each other, though they still loved each other very much. He hoped that they would let him, as an old friend, go around their flat and open their windows, too, and bring the feel of the promise of spring air into their lives again.

When he returned to the parish house, he was exuberant, enormously pleased with himself, because his visit had ended with the elderly couple embracing him, saying, "We're just two old codgers waiting to die," laughing happily.

Opening the door to his room, he let out a roar of disbelief, "Nooooo, God." Anselm was on his belly on the bed and under him – gathered between his big web-toed paws – was the Shroud. He was thumping his tail as he snuffled and shoved his snout into the torn cloth. The old priest lunged, grabbing for the Shroud, yanking at it, the weight of the startled dog tearing it more, and when he saw, in disbelief, that the face, the Holy face and the Holy eyes of the Presence, were all gone, shredded and swallowed by the dog, he raised his fist – hurt and enraged – and Anselm, seeing that rage and that fist, leaped off the bed, hitting the floor, tail between his legs, skidding into a corner wall, where, cowering and trembling, trying to tuck his head into his shoulder, he looked up, waiting to be beaten.

"Oh my God, oh my God," the old priest moaned, sitting on the edge of the bed, drawing the ruined Shroud across his knees.

He could not believe the look of terror and, at the same time, the look of complete love in the dog's eyes, and for a moment he thought that that must have been the real look in Christ's eyes as He hung on the cross, His terror felt as a man, and His complete unconditional love as God. But before he could wonder if such a thought was blasphemous, he was struck by a fear that, having seen his rage and his fist, Anselm would always be afraid of him, would always cower and tremble at his coming. As a boy, he had seen dogs like that, dogs who had been beaten.

He fell onto his knees beside the dog in the corner where, night after night, he had prayed – saying the Apostles' Creed, affirming his faith – and Anselm had sat there, too, waiting to go onto the bed to sleep. He took Anselm's head in his arms, feeling as he did his trouser leg become warm with an oily wetness – the dog, in the confusion of his fear and relief at being held, having peed. The old priest hugged him closer and laughed. Anselm came out of his cower and stopped trembling. Rocking Anselm in his arms, he was about to tell him he was a good dog and shouldn't worry, that he loved him, but then he thought how ludicrous it would be for a grown man to talk out loud to a dog about something as serious as love, so he just sat in their wetness holding Anselm even tighter so that Anselm would understand and never doubt.

DREI ALTER KOCKERS

(THREE OLD FOGIES)

1

ZOL GOT, HORUKH HU, MIKH
HITN FAR PAYN UN SHMARTSEN

*May God, blessed be He, protect
me from anguish and pain*

• Yiddish prayer, said over the challah every Sabbath •

Herschel Soibel, born in the Jewish quarter of Lublin and brought up on the Street of Furriers, was from a pious family prominent among Hasidim in the trade for fur hats.

At Herschel's *bris*, when the rebbe cut his penis, the women were astounded to hear Herschel let out a deep sigh.

His father rejoiced, saying he had heard in his son's sigh the call of the *tzaddik*, he had heard Ezekiel, the righteous man: "He shall reap the fruit of his own righteousness..."

At the age of three Herschel could read and write, by four he could cross-stitch, and at eight, he sat at a small desk on the weekends where he read the Torah. Using a porcelain inkwell, he wrote up bills of sale for heavily bearded men dressed in long greasy gabardines, men who spat into their palms before clasping hands on the price of a *shtreimel,* a broad-brimmed hat made from the tails of seven sables. Herschel handed any man leaving the shop a card that had printed on one side: *Beware of the Wisdom of Fools...In Our Hearts We Know Our Hats* and printed on the other side: EZEKIEL 18:20.

><del>~<del>×

In 1943, the Soibel family of nine, among the last Jews alive in the Lublin wartime ghetto, were driven out of their apartment by men with riding crops and bayonets and herded through the streets into cattle cars. They were transported to Auschwitz.

><del>~<del>×

Each Soibel packed and carried a small suitcase or a satchel; in Herschel's suitcase, a silver menorah, and in his father's satchel, silver Shabbat candlesticks. Paper money was sewn into the lining of dresses and suitcoats.

"Wherever we're going, we'll negotiate," Herschel's father said. "Among the *goyim* there's always a price."

The train came to a halt in the night, the cattle-car doors were unsealed, and an SS officer strode up the ramp to the doors, crying, "*Aussteigen.*"

Stupefied men, women, youths, and children stumbled down the ramp under floodlamps to be met by two thin SS officers who said, "*Gut gemacht,* here are the men who will help you," pointing to Jews wearing prisoners' stripes. They belonged to a labour crew that was called Kanada by other prisoners in the camp because

Kanada was a dream-country and to work in this crew meant that the men not only got their loaves of bread but fresh kosher sausage – and also they received a daily ration of vodka. From time to time they were allowed an uneasy sleep – five or ten minutes – in the grass on the embankment beside the train tracks.

The Kanada crew had to haul the dead from the cars to trucks. Then they stripped the living and pushed and bullied the infirm who were naked and naked mothers who were delirious, the addled naked and the naked young, and the naked elders into line-ups onto the road that led from the ramp to the crematorium, yelling, "You'll have a shower, you'll see, you'll feel better."

After the arrivals had been cleared away, the crew portioned-off all the bread, the marmalade, the meats, and pickled herring they could empty out of broken-open satchels and suitcases. The few men, women, and youngsters who had been cordoned off to the right of the condemned, those Jews selected to live, were sent to the barbers from Zauna who were waiting to shave their heads. They were deloused and given their stripes. Most of the jewels, rings, bracelets, brooches and gold watches ripped out of the piles of clothing were handed over to officers who filched gold for them-selves and sent the rest to Berlin to be melted down to help pay for the war.

After the clearing of the ramp, several of the Kanada crew stretched out under the shade of old chestnut trees that lined the last run of rail track up to the camp, and one of the well-fed crew asked, with sudden concern, "What'll we do if they suddenly run out of Jews, if the trains stop coming?"

Herschel's family was fed into the ovens in the camp. His mother, father, and four girls on the first night, and over the months, his two brothers were burned in the ovens, too.

One day at dusk, Herschel saw, in the play of falling light, the face of an angel in the smoke rising from the stacks – he was sure it was Ezekiel's angel, the avenger – but then the face turned to ash.

He asked an elder, a gaunt rebbe: "If the angels have gone up in smoke, has not God, too?"

The rebbe, without looking at him, said: "*A mensch tracht, un Got lacht.*"[1]

⋊⋉⋊⋉

In 1945, on a cold winter's morning, as Soviet armoured divisions crossed the Vistula River and advanced into Poland, the prisoners in the camp were rousted out of their lice-ridden bunks in the barracks. They were herded onto backwoods roads to begin a long death march west, into Germany.3

Herschel, losing several toes to frostbite, survived the march.

Outside Bratislava, after the Nazi surrender, he celebrated his *bar mitzvah* birthday in the back of a GI troop truck. The GIs were black. One gave him a bottle of Coca-Cola. A rebbe blessed him and said, "God is good."

Herschel said, "Beware of the wisdom of fools."

"I am not a fool," the rebbe said angrily, "and neither is God."

"And so why," Herschel demanded, "are the Nazis not dead in their iniquity? Why are we, in our righteousness, dead, like my papa, like my mama, dead?"

---

[1] A man makes plans, and God laughs.

In a squalid displaced-persons camp outside Vienna, Herschel told a Red Cross nurse something an old prisoner had told him: "There are three truths: One, you can only trust life itself by believing lies – 'Have a shower, you'll feel better.' And, two, just as profoundly absent as the presence of God is the absence of privacy – 'If you are sleeping six starving men to a bunk, never mind the lice, the leg cramps, the snoring, it is the shit…these men shat all over themselves and each other in the night. And just as they never say God's name, they never speak of this shit.' And finally, shoes. 'A man with no shoes is a man who has no future.'"

Herschel told this to the Red Cross nurse after she had tried to stroke his arm.

"I don't want to be touched," he said. "Nothing frightens me, only human kindness makes me afraid. May *Hashem* forgive me."

He drifted out of the displaced-persons camp and went to Vienna, where he worked for a fence as a runner, carrying gold to be melted down. "Behind everything there is always an oven," Herschel said.

He became a small-time fence himself.

He let it be known: for Herschel, a deal was a deal, a contract a contract. He was unforgiving. He cut the cheek of a young *shvindler* who cheated him.

"You're a hard man," a buyer from Prague told him.

"I'm only fourteen."

"Even so, you're a hard man."

"I wish."

In Toronto, he worked as a masseuse-boy and towel attendant at the Grange public steam baths, and then as an apprentice to Nathan the Fish Monger in the Kensington Jewish market, becoming expert in beheading and deboning huge carp. He stood the fish heads on a rack behind him, the eyes staring, accusing. At seventeen, Herschel, working during the day for Morris Fisch, a furrier on Spadina Avenue, enrolled in night classes at Harbord Collegiate where the other students were nearly all the sons of refugee Ukrainians. For generations, Jews had owned farm lands in the Ukraine and one young man's family had worked on a Jewish farm. He called Herschel a "Kike." Herschel spent two nights in jail and was expelled from the school for chopping off the Ukrainian's little finger with his deboning knife.

"I wanted to put his finger in with the fish heads."

"Such a scandal is what Jews don't need," Morris Fisch said. He was the owner of Cadillac Furs, Tri-bells, a semi-pro basketball team, and a contributor to the mayor's re-election campaign. He threatened, over coffee with the mayor's assistant, that if charges against Kerschel were not dropped, he would publicly name a bunch of local Ukrainians as *Kapos*, black shirts, and war criminals, but he also offered to send Herschel to Israel to work on a kibbutz.

"For you to make *aliyah*," he told Herschel, "to live in the Holy Land, this could be everything."

"It could also be nothing," Herschel told Fisch. "They don't wear hats in Israel. It's too hot. They wear stupid caps. Me, I'm from a family of hatters."

He showed Fisch a *Toronto Star* photograph of a hockey crowd in the lobby of Maple Leaf Gardens and said, "Look, a thousand men all wearing hats, fedoras. For the money you'd waste on me in Israel, make me a loan instead for a shop."

"You're going to sell *shtreimel*?"

"In Lublin, we were pious hatters. Here, I will be a stylish hatter."

"And I," Fisch said, laughing, "am Alice in Wonderland."

Herschel, who had no idea in the world who Alice was, told him what Ezekiel said: "*Ki lo echpotz bemos hamis neum Hashem Adonai vehashivu vichu.*"[1]

Fisch didn't understand Hebrew, so he said, "What's that mean?"

"It means, 'Get a new life.'"

><--><

He changed his name to Harry Sable of Harry Sable Hats and opened a small store on Spadina Avenue. After a photograph of the Tri-bell basketball players wearing pearl-grey fedoras with a black band appeared in the evening newspapers, Morris Fisch and several furriers, sportswriters, hockey players, gonzos, and gangsters became his customers. When, after some three years, the young Catholic bishop – Emmett Carter – who had a reputation for elegance, let it be known in an interview in the *Catholic Register* that he'd bought a black fedora at Harry Sable Hats on Spadina Avenue, parish priests began, of an afternoon, to drop into the shop. Through the years, he sold hats to skaters in the Ice Capades, to Sammy Davis Jr. when he played the Barclay Hotel, to Sammy Luftspring, the boxer who had become a bouncer at the Brown Derby tavern, to Joe Kroll, the Argonaut quarterback, to Maxie

---

[1] For I desire not the death of him that dieth, saith the Lord God, return ye and live.

Baker, the gambler, and to Al Rosenzweig, bookmaker, *a far-brecher*[1] enforcer for loan sharks and the Jewish mob. "I once took a finger myself," Harry told Al. Harry had met Al at the Victory Burlesque Theatre, next door to his hat shop, when both had gone to see the Miss Sepia Top Hat Colored Girls Review "direct from Chicago." Harry had said to Al, "There are two ways you can tell about a man. Look at his woman, look at his hat. The man who's the boss in his bed is to be seen wearing a good hat." He gave a firm tug to the brim of his fedora.

Harry and Al became abiding friends, sometimes sharing a Cuban cigar in a smoking room Harry had outfitted for clients above the shop, or they'd meet at Switzer's across the road from the shop for chicken soup with matzo balls, a smoked meat sandwich, and then a strudel or a cheesecake. They discovered they shared not just an enthusiasm for hand-rolled cigars but for Frank Sinatra and Peggy Lee, especially songs by Irving Berlin. Once a month, telephoning from the upstairs smoking room, they hired expensive call girls and listened to Sinatra and Lee on Harry's collection of $33^1/3$, vinyl long-playing records, and drank schnapps.

Harry's other indulgence, which he did not share with Al, was shoes. "The future is mine," he would say, happily confessing that there was something perverse he didn't want to know about himself – a man missing half his toes due to frostbite who wanted to own hundreds of pairs of shoes. "I don't go nowhere but I look good doing it." He often shopped for shoes with baseball players. "Ball players like hats and they like shoes. On the other hand, jazz musicians, they don't care what's on their feet. It's a thing you can notice."

---

[1] A criminal.

Over the decades, Harry did not move from Spadina Avenue and he did not renovate his shop.

"Who needs to? Me is me. I'm a fixture. My shop is me. I can change where I live but not my shop. People believe they know me, they do know me," and he would point to a sign in Gothic script over the door: *Beware of the Wisdom of Fools… Harry Knows His Hats.*

Surprising himself in his sixties, he married a young Jewish widow he'd met on a gambling junket to Puerto Rico. After two weeks of being married, he'd asked her why she wore false eyelashes even to breakfast and she'd accused him of being barbaric because he refused to stop wearing a hat at breakfast. "That's only for *alter kockers*," she'd yelled. Once a week, of an afternoon, she went to a tanning salon. "All the time, even in December, she was brown as a nut." The marriage lasted six months. "She was too much sunlight," he told Al. "The sunlight got in my eyes. I come from the dark forests. Anyway, sometimes a loss is a gain."

As his later years went by, Harry, though successful and secure, had fewer customers. Not many men wanted to wear hats. Very few men wore fedoras.

"Looking back, it was stylish Mister Jack Kennedy who did it to us," he said to Al, nodding sagely. "Everything was out in the open, bravado, the big bare-headed smile, so what happens? Kennedy, he's wearing no hat, so he gets shot in the head…"

Harry settled into semi-retirement. He took a spacious two-bedroom apartment on north Bathurst Street in a 14-floor concrete slab high-rise (which was really 13, he pointed out to Al, because there was no 13th floor). All the tenants were Jewish: Shoah survivors like himself, ultra-orthodox Hasidim ("hardcore," he called them), disaffected Israelis, and Jews who'd abandoned South Africa. "I'm in Little Tel Aviv," he said, "which may or may not be a blessing. But where else should an *alter kocker* be?"

His only difficulty was in resettling his parrot. The parrot, a big bird of intense red and green feathers and a bold head, whose cage and perch were in the second bedroom, had been a gift – after Harry's marriage had failed – from Humberto Escobar, the Puerto Rican third baseman for the Blue Jays. For five years, Humberto had bought Harry Sable hats for himself and for his brothers and cousins in San Juan. The parrot, called Humbo in honour of the third baseman, had lived with Harry for seven years in his duplex flat in the old Annex area. Harry had come to feel enormous affection for the bird. They would sit in the stillness of an hour – at times watching eye to eye – and in these moments of enigmatic silence Harry had taught Humbo how to say the names of concentration camps, and the numbers of their track lines. The squawking of those names gave Harry the only leave for laughter that he'd ever felt in his life about death. On several afternoons, since teaching Humbo the names, he had tried to explain to Al what it was like to see in his memory's eye a rigid SS officer, immaculate in black, and to hear him squawk *Auschwitz, Auschwitz,* but Al said he didn't need to know any more about the SS than he already knew, and what he knew was from the movies. He, too, thought hearing the parrot was hilarious, and so once a week Harry and Al would go for a walk with Humbo on Harry's shoulder, and sometimes on Al's shoulder, too.

"Humbo's one happy bird," Harry would say.

The parrot, however, did not like the high-rise elevators. He became aggressive and even abusive in the elevators, repeating the names of the camps over and over again,

"Auschwitz, track 29.

"Belsen, track 16.

"Treblinka, track 9.

"Dachau, track 3."

Humbo unnerved and outraged many of Harry's new neighbours.

One day Harry was riding the elevator up with Humbo. A fat man with slack jowls and very dark, almost black, eyes was riding with them. Harry, out of the corner of his eye, thought there was something familiar about the man, and though he couldn't immediately place him, he was sure that they had met. Perhaps it was the hat. He was wearing a Harry Sable.

"Nice hat," Harry said dryly.

"Thanks."

"*Dachau, track 3,*" the bird called.

"Quiet," Harry said.

"*Belsen, track 16.*"

"Someone might wanta kill that bird," the fat man said.

"Do I know you?" Harry asked.

"*Auschwitz, track 29,*" Humbo cried.

2

Jakov Przepiorko, born before the war in Warsaw, was a street orphan. "Born with soot in his hair," a policeman said, "*bist a draykop.*"[1] When asked where he came from, the boy replied, "Out of town." An old rebbe, known not only in the schools but on the street as an expert on Hebrew grammar and as a mathematician,

---

[1] A spiv, a con man.

took him by the arm and asked as they walked toward the cemetery, "Which town?"

"I won't tell you," Jakov said, "so you can't send me back."

"Back?" the old rebbe said, tilting his *shtreimel* forward. "You don't fool me. Your mother was a dirty brothel whore in Krochmalna Square."

"Children have been swapped," Jakov said, "Maybe Abel for Cain. *Es regnet – Gott segnet.*"[1]

The old rebbe, who came from a family of *shtetl* horse traders, got him a job tending the horses of several Jewish droshky drivers. Jakov fed, watered, brushed the manes of the horses, and cleaned the pus, caused by coal smoke from household-stove fires, out of the horses' eyes.

He also had to oil down and keep pliable the drivers' leather whips.

After a month at this work, sleeping on a straw pallet close by the horses so he could steal their body heat, Jakov – following the precise instructions of the rebbe – presented the drivers with a detailed bill. He asked for his money. The drivers rolled the bill up in a ball and refused to pay him.

"Complain what you want. Tell the rebbe, we'll whip the shit out of you."

He backed away from the stalls, the drivers wagging their whip handles at him. He was grinning and they thought he must be weak-minded. But he was grinning because he had, on every day of the month, been stealing money from them, stealing from the iron box they kept hidden behind the heavy harnesses hanging on the wall of the stable. He had stolen two groschen pieces a day.

---

[1] It rains, God blesses.

During the month, using the stolen money, he had also begun to lend money, going into Hasidic *yeshivas*, into the quarter around Krochmalna Street – the street of *gonifs, shvindlers*, and hoodlums – demanding interest of 25 percent, one groschen to four.

At the age of fifteen he was in business, carrying a black book, a ledger, that contained a careful listing of the names of his debtors.

Over glasses of tea he told the rebbe about the droshky drivers and about his black book. The rebbe, drawing his long gabardine around his ankles, said, "Let me tell you about a precious gift we Jews gave to royalty, royalty all over Europe. It's about mathematics, this gift for money you have, since for you, how to add and subtract is something easy. It was not always so easy, not for us, not for the *goyim*. Unbelievable it may be now to our eyes, but a thousand years ago when we and the Christians did such calculations as those you are doing in your book, they were written in Latin and Hebrew. You can imagine maybe how it was to keep ledgers, to keep count, let alone compound interest by Latin numbers. Impossible," and reaching for Jakov's black book he turned to a blank page and wrote:

$$
\begin{array}{r}
XXIV \\
-IX \\
\hline
XV
\end{array}
$$

"Who could conduct business in such clumsiness? Also, it was Christians, not Jews, who were forbidden to travel from place to place. We Jews were free. Free to go one day, free to be expelled the next day. And we took from the Arabs their numerals and added to them our *galgal*, our little *wheel*, the decimal point, that allows us to do columns of figures. We became the accountants, the keepers of compound interest and prosperity. We were hated by the Christian traders but treasured by all the great barons and royalty in their courts. No matter the hatred now, do not forget that your gift for money that makes you money is a blessing unto the Jews, a blessing still." And he laid his hand on the cloth cap covering Jakov's head.

"I, too," Jakov said, "should wear a fur hat, not a *shtreimel*, it doesn't have to be only tails but, for sure, a sable hat."

⤐⤏⤜

Jakov saw:

A Death's Head mounted on a stake at a ghetto gate.

Tanks, flame-throwers, and machine guns.

And behind the gauleiters and the guns, in the city proper, gutted apartment houses like giant ruined and blackened molars.

For five years, Jakov – like most Jews in the Warsaw ghetto – had narrowed his shoulders and narrowed his eyes, constricted in his daily business. But he had done well. "I am no fool," he said. "I know how they dream. They intend to kill us all."

At twenty, he was tall, muscular, and agile – very quick on his feet – and brazen: he was curt, crisp, and a successful con man: "I hold one hand out, my fist is in my pocket."

In 1943, as the uprising in the ghetto against the Nazis collapsed, as tanks blew out whole apartment floors, as soldiers went door to door with flame-throwers, as they gunned down folks on the run, as the Nazis razed the ghetto, making it into a deathscape, Jakov escaped down into the underground, nearly suffocating as he inched forward through the sewage, the stench of slop and shit, at last getting out of the city into the woods. Once he was in the woods, however, entranced by the stillness and distracted by the twittering of birds, he was clubbed unconscious by a partisan who wanted his shoes, a partisan who stripped him naked and tied him up and left him in the grass for the Nazis.

><---><

In Auschwitz, Jakov was ordered to work with the Kanada section crew, the "blue" commandos of Jewish prisoners who were in charge of herding Jews out of the cattle cars. He worked diligently. He was then moved to the "red" section – where he helped to undress Jews who, on final inspection, had been selected to walk naked on "the road to heaven." In his mind's eye, he could not help himself, he calculated the day-to-day number of naked bodies – an arithmetic that enraged him – but then on waking each day, he was relieved to be alive, and with increasing anger he willed himself to work beyond his exhaustion. An SS officer recognized this consuming rage to live in Jakov and promoted him to the *platzjuden*, those who were in charge of a sorting area, a kind of flea market for gabardine coats, violins, artificial legs, corsets, menstrual rags, irons and ironing boards. Shortly after that he was given a stool among the *goldjuden*, prisoners who cleaned and sorted gold teeth that had been pried from the jaws of the dead. Finally, he became one of several *Kapos* working under a Jewish "commandant." Few prisoners were surprised that he was made a *Kapo*. Everyone, Jews and Nazis, felt in him a cold implacable fury, a fury far deeper than anger. And even more unnerving to other prisoners, he seemed to have a faith in that fury – a faith that it was his fury, if only he could keep it constant, that would carry him through from day to day, it was his fury that would keep him alive. When he heard another *Kapo* say,

"We will all die. We are dead men on vacation in a life that has no meaning, no God," Jakov said: "If God created the world and created us in His own image, then this place is either proof that He is a complete failure, or this is His place, too, and there is a way to stay alive here on His terms. I do not intend to die, so I assume God is not dead."

><><

Once a month, between trains, as several of the Kanada crew stretched out on the grass under the chestnut trees and drank watery coffee and vodka, an SS officer, to amuse himself, allowed – under very close guard – two prisoners to play Russian roulette with a Colt .45 the officer had taken from the body of a dead American soldier outside the town of Casino in Italy.

A prisoner who played and came out of the game of roulette alive was given two bottles of vodka on top of his regular ration, and two days off with no work, with nothing to do but drink.

The men who chose to play roulette were usually in a state of exhausted hysteria, feverish in their sleeplessness, or they had become *muslimmen* – men who were apathetic and yearning to die – or they were hopelessly drunk.

Jakov had played the game three times, against three men who had put the muzzle in their mouths. The third game had been played on the evening before the camp had been rousted at dawn by Soviet armoured divisions advancing out of the east. All the prisoners had been forced to begin a march double-file down snowbound back roads into Germany.

Several *Kapos* were strangled in the night by the marchers, but not Jakov, who – remembering how the partisan had snuck up on him in the Warsaw woods – kept an eye peeled, watching every-one.

Between two snowbound villages, Jakov Przepiorko and Herschel Soibel had trudged through the snow side by side. They had hardly looked at each other but Herschel had said, "You're a plump little rat."

Jakov, saying nothing, had fallen back in the line.

>~~~<

In Toronto, Jakov Przepiorko became Jake Piorko. For more than a year, with a fake driver's licence that he'd paid for with a gold tooth, he drove a half-ton delivery truck for Future Chicken, a slaughterhouse on Spadina Avenue. He was the only Jew on the trucks. The other drivers were black. Within weeks, he was run-ning a card game in a locker room behind the Future Chicken killing floor. When one of the drivers said to him, "You ever smell anything like this joint, man?" he only smiled.

He began to lend money at high rates to the drivers who had lost at cards, and then he made a loan to a butcher who worked on the floor. "Don't make me draw blood," Jake said, trying for a small joke as he gave the butcher, whose apron was splattered with blood, the money.

"You want blood I'll show you where the blood is," the butcher said, and he took Jake to the Prince George Hotel, whose owners had connections to Meyer Lansky. In the hotel, a weekly high-stakes poker game was dealt by a man with waxen fingers, Harvey "The Heeb" Laxor, who, seeing Jake's camp numbers on his arm, said, "No explanation necessary," and introduced him to Maxie Baker. "Mr. Piorko," The Heeb said, "meet a gambler."

"We Jews," Maxie Baker said, "we bookies, we run all the heavy games in town. We cover the horses, the whole kit-and-kaboodle from which we intend to keep out the Magaddino connection. You'll find out who they are. The *lokshen*[1] Mafia we don't have nothing to do with since a Jew always looks out for a Jew."

"As it should be," Jake said.

"And so, that's what's with me, I'm telling you, and so what's with you? You're from the camps."

"You were there?"

"It's a fact."

"Facts count."

><—><

Jake never spoke again about Auschwitz. With help from Maxie, he set himself up as a businessman whose business happened to be loan sharking. In time, except when he had to go down lanes or into backrooms because his clients looked dishevelled and disreputable, he conducted his business from comfortable booths in three fashionable downtown restaurant watering holes – the Silver Rail, the Savarin, and Bigliardi's. Uptown, he had lobster once a week in the House of Chan, and then he went over his black ledgers with meticulous care, bringing all interest on debts to the decimal point, licking the tip of his 4H pencil, a habit he had picked up from his old rebbe in Warsaw.

For almost a year, he ponied up protection money to cops on the vice squad at 52 Station, paying them off over lunch at Sai Woo on Dundas Street, and because Maxie had shown him a section in

---

[1] Noodle.

the income tax code that referred to "all bribes, under-the-table payoffs, and illicit gambling income" as taxable, he paid his income taxes religiously, every April 30.

"They're no different than us," Maxie said, "it's all business. The government. All they want is the *vigorish*, their percentage of the take." Jake took his percentage and, identifying himself as a professional gambler who accounted meticulously for his expenses – especially his "entertainment" of the police and his forest-green Mercedes – he assumed the air of a grim, well-fed taxpayer who was in the good graces of his government. He allowed himself only a wry smile when he told his bank manager, who wanted to know (because the police would want to know) where all the cash was coming from, "I, too, lend money." The manager had said, "Thank God you're not laundering drug money," but had then apologized because Jake had looked offended. "I got a knack for making bankers feel stupid," he later told a hooker who asked him what he did for a living. "As for living, that's what I do at all cost."

Working out of fine restaurants, taking a compulsive pleasure in eating foods deep-fried or cooked in butter, and having a love of wine and vodka, too, he grew jowly and plump, and then fat, weighing some two hundred and ninety pounds, and he soon became known among gamblers as Fat Jake Piorko.

He gave cash in an envelope to the United Jewish Appeal, as did other mobsters, but he did not go to temple and he never let his photograph be taken, not even when Cy Mann, his clothier on Avenue Road, asked him if he would like a memento snapshot of himself with Bill Cosby, the comedian, another Lou Jacetta customer who flew in regularly from Philadelphia to have Jacetta make him a suit. Jakov said "No" with such a surprising burst of anger that Mann said, "Jesus, you sound like you'd like to hurt me."

"No, no," he said, "sorry, but my hurting days are behind me."
He left the tailoring shop and never went back.

On four occasions, however, he had had to hire Al Rosenzweig
– the Piano man – to hurt four men, to collect bad debts.

"We understand each other," he'd said to Al.

"Yes. Business is business."

"A loss can be a gain," he'd said.

"Give or take a knee," Al had said, smiling.

><><

Over the years, Jake lived alone in several two- and three-bedroom
apartments. In each, Jake had painted all the walls and woodwork
white, and one or two of the rooms had always stood empty, with
no furniture at all. Standing in those stark empty rooms, he always
felt a peace he could find nowhere else.

On two occasions, when a delivery boy and then a hooker had
got into his rooms and seen how he had surrounded himself with
next to nothing, and the hooker had said, "This is no way to live,"
and the boy, "Wow, what a way to live!" he had cancelled his rental
agreement and moved. He didn't ask himself why, he only knew
that he had suddenly been overcome by an anxiety – a question,
What a way to live? – a ringing of numbers over and over in his ear,
a tumbling of numbers – 27,609 – his exact calculation, his camp
calculation of the naked dead he had seen walking "on the road to
heaven." His anxiety only went away when he had closed the door
and secured the deadbolt on a new apartment.

A marriage late in life, a marriage of six weeks when he was
fifty-nine, had failed, a marriage to one of his hookers. She was
twenty-six and he'd been seeing her for two years. To his surprise,

evening after evening, he had found her young plump nakedness strangely moving, a nakedness almost too painful, too pink, too soft, too pliable, and he would stare at her as if she were a discovery, as if, in her youth, something was being reborn in him. When they made love, she made him forget how fat he was. He had given her all the money that she wanted and they had married at City Hall, but six weeks later, astonished at how intimate and easy she was, he had tried to cum in her from behind, and she'd said, "No, no. Not the dirt-track road. That's a private road. That's for my boyfriend." He said, "You mean you're still seeing him?" and when she said "Yes" with a shrug he hadn't tried to hurt her; he had been enraged but also surprised at her guilelessness, and so did not want to hurt her. He had just told her to get out. When asked by the apartment superintendent where his wife had gone, he said, "She was good till she went bad," and he moved to another apartment.

Having gone into semi-retirement, he'd taken an apartment on north Bathurst Street. He'd grown weary, was tired, deeply worn out, not so much in his bones but he felt his tiredness was somehow in his heart. He was eating only one meal a day, and he'd lost weight, some sixty pounds.

One morning, looking in the mirror, he said, in angry distress, "Sixty pounds, that's the weight of a six-year-old boy."

He slammed the mirror, cracking the glass.

><><

Enraged, Harry was weeping, he was almost incoherent as he explained to Al Rosenzweig that someone had broken into his apartment. "Which was easy enough, since, among Jews, I didn't think I'd need a deadbolt lock. But that someone, they took nothing. They wanted nothing but to hurt me. They killed Humbo, they beheaded my parrot. The fuckers, the goddamn fuckers, I can't believe it. The goddamn fucking Nazi shit chopped off his head..."

Al looked around for the body of the bird, or the head. *Does a bird like that bleed?* He didn't see any blood.

"No, no, never mind," Harry said, "I know who did it. Son-of-a-bitch, I knew I recognized him in the elevator. The fat shit, that bag of suet, that *schmuck*, he hated the bird..."

"Who?"

"Upstairs. The fuck, he lives one floor up. He should have been killed years ago, a goddamn *Kapo*. He knew I'd know once I saw him, and he was wearing one of my goddamn hats, can you believe it? He's standing there under one of my hats, and he says to me in the elevator looking me right in the eye, 'Someone should kill that bird,' and he fucking well did...I fucking know in my bones..."

"Maybe you know," Al said, trying to establish a calm, "maybe you don't."

"I know. Believe you me, I know."

"You I believe, but even so, maybe you're wrong. You gotta be careful about who you got in mind."

"Piorko, Jake Piorko. Maybe him you know already. Somehow he's heavy into the rackets."

"Piorko I know."

"What d'you know?"

"I done business with him. He's a shark. All his life he loans money to losers, all kinds of losers..."

"You two've done business?"

"A taste here, a taste there. Nothing big."

"I'll give you big. I'll tell you what I want, not just as a friend, you being my friend, but as a business proposition. Kill the fuck."

"Harry, I'm older, I'm not so strong, cut it out."

"Cut out his fucking heart, I say. This isn't just me Harry talking to you 'cause he killed my bird, beheaded him, *chop chop*, like they did in the camps, this is Herschel. This is Herschel from the old world, before, when you didn't know me and you didn't know what it was like, I wouldn't want you to know, except now, so that you understand, to watch a Jew eat the bread of a Jew, to watch a Jew take the hand of a Jew and lead him to the ovens, he deserves to die."

"He's already gonna die, he's too old to live. He must be ninety-fucking-years old."

"I want *you* to kill him. I want my old pal Piano to wire him."

"No, no, this we don't talk about like pals, you and me. This is business."

"I'm talking business. It's a contract. I'm a businessman, you're a businessman. Ten thousand…"

"Ten thousand what?"

"Ten thousand bucks. To kill him."

"A bird. You want I should kill Fat Jake over a bird? I can take a finger, you want to really hurt him. OK, two fingers, but it offends me, you gotta understand. It cheapens me. This is a bird," and Al stomped his foot. "This is like less than *treyf*,[1] you want me to kill a man for a bird that even someone starving would not eat?"

"Naw, for ten thousand."

---

[1] Unclean. "Every animal that has a split hoof not completely divided or that does not chew the cud is unclean for you; whoever touches the carcass of any of them will be unclean." LEVITICUS 11:26.

"You think maybe because you know I wired a couple of guys that I don't take life seriously? Believe me, I take it serious, life. I'm alive, make no mistake."

"I'm serious. If the bird's not good enough for us to do the deal, so kill him for all the Jews…he was as ruthless as they got. A Jew cruel to Jews, to help the Nazis, he gave death to Jews and what does he do the second time when I meet him in the elevator…"

"You meet him twice…?"

"I saw it in his face, the first time, but I forgot till I remembered the next day who he was, my plump little *Kapo* inside that fat fuck and I tell him, 'I know you.' Then the bird starts screaming, 'Dachau, track 6, Auschwitz, track 29, I know you,' saying, 'I know you' like I just said it to him, and Piorko goes nuts and grabs the bird by the throat, trying to strangle my bird, except I got Piorko by his throat, telling him, 'You fucking *Kapo*, how come you're not dead?' He should be dead."

"Maybe so, but no one did."

"No one did what?"

"Killed him. No one cared enough to kill him and now you do. I got two *alter kockers* trying to strangle each other in the elevator…"

"He was trying to strangle Humbo dead but, instead, he chopped off his head."

"And so now where is the bird?"

"At the vet's."

"They're gonna put back his head, or what?"

"Cremate him. Put him in a jar."

"Cremate?"

"Yeah, for me to keep. An urn. What else have I got to keep? Twenty-five hats? Two hundred shoes? Bullshit. You kill him.

Forget the bird. Like Ezekiel said, 'He that hath spoiled by violence, he that hath given forth upon usury: shall he then live? He shall not live, he shall surely die, his blood be upon him.' I make the price. Ten thousand. Cheap at the cost for all the Jews."

⋙⋘

On the third Thursday evening of every month, if he was free from business obligations, Al Rosenzweig was found playing the piano for an hour at the Bialik North Bathurst Street Social Club for Ladies and Gentlemen. He played at a white baby grand Yamaha piano, gift of the Junior Ladies Auxiliary, in a long, somewhat narrow recreation room on the "penthouse floor" of a Senior Citizen apartment house. The rec room had a small bar and parquet dance floor, several easy chairs, styled in blue or white leather – the colours of Israel – and ten or twelve card tables with four chairs at each table.

Marvin Rosenzweig, Al's father, had retired to this high-rise house but after six months he died of a heart attack. Al had been told "in confidence" by a horse-faced woman wearing a *shatl*, a wig, that his father had "broken his broken-down heart" while "doing sex" with her closest friend, an eighty-year-old widow, "once a slut always a slut" – a story that both astonished and pleased Al. "What a fucking way to go," he'd said. "Exactly," the old woman had replied, slapping her wrist coquettishly.

When asked by the officious manager of the apartments what his father, who had emigrated from Berlin in the 1930's, had done for a living, Al said, "Newspapers. He moved from the *Star* to the *Telegram* to the *Globe*." It was Al's own joke because his father and his mother – who had come together in a marriage arranged by a rebbe in Berlin had, for forty years, sold newspapers from inside a small wooden, forest-green newsstand at the corner of the King and Bay Streets banking district. His father had also scalped theatre tickets, and hockey and baseball tickets. It had been a very lucrative sideline. "He had his window on the world," Al would say, "so he met a lot of interesting people. You know what he said about Fred Astaire? He said Astaire was so good he could give dancing at the end of a rope a good name."

Al amused himself by letting slip what appeared to be little confidences, especially amused if – like the Astaire story – these confidences were not true. He didn't believe inquiring strangers like the apartment manager deserved the truth; he believed men and women did what they had to do and then faced the truth. "It's like we said when we were kids: you show me yours and I'll show you mine. You learn, pecker to pecker, that what you got is what I've got, no matter." When he was asked by the manager how he had learned to play the piano, he said, "I was taught by myself to play by ear, like I play my life. Later, I was taught about music by an Irish choirmaster."

"A Catholic?"

"Yeah."

"And where was this, may I ask?"

"A church at Bloor and Bathurst, St. Peter's, the one on the kitty-corner to Honest Ed's Emporium and Bargain Store."

"Ed Mirvish I know. His wife collects glass eyes. From Catholic I know zilch."

"Don't worry about it."

"What's to worry? I'm too old anyway to worry. Catholics already they gave me grief."

"Me also," Al said, "I got a little grief from them myself."

"And you were born where?"

"Palmerston Avenue."

"Palmerston! So you were born here, so there you are. You play the piano. For me, this is enough."

"I don't carry none of that camp baggage," Al said.

"You're a Jew?"

"I'm a Jew but I'm not Jewish."

"This I don't understand," the manager said.

"Neither do I. That's the point. I just do what I do, I play the piano, Jewish can look after itself."

✖︎✖︎✖︎

The choirmaster at St. Peter's church, Harry O'Grady, had taught Al how to read music and, as a gift, had given him *The Songbook of Negro Spirituals*, which Harry liked to sing, and standing together at the piano, arm in arm, they would shout out,

> *Ezekiel saw a wheel a-rolling*
> *Way in the middle of the Lord*
> *A wheel within a wheel-a-rolling*
> *Way in the middle of the Lord*
> *And the little wheel run by faith*
> *And the big wheel run by the grace of God.*

Al and Harry had met because, as a youngster, Al had played floor hockey in the winter in St. Peter's basement with his friends from the streets around the church. "Nobody plays floor hockey anymore. It was a great church basement game. You had a sawed-off broomstick and this heavy felt disc with a hole in it…and if you lost the game you could beat up the other team with your broom-stick."

Al learned several spirituals from his songbook, but it was play-ing by ear that gave him looseness of spirit, even joy as he trusted his ear, trusted his intuitions – hearing all the melodies, the chords, emerge without calculation as he hit the keys. "It's like walking downtown without knowing where I'm going. If it feels right to turn right I turn right, if it feels right to turn left I turn left. I trust myself. Even when I play only on the black notes it turns out okay."

⤛⤜

Al had dropped out of Harbord Collegiate to drive a truck for Donnie Ryan, an Irish cross-border bootlegger and cigarette smug-gler.

Drinking Bushmill's whisky at the Hibernia Social Club in the Clinton Hotel and learning songs like "Who Put the Overalls in Mrs. Murphy's Chowder" he met a girl, Agnes Egan. She cap-tivated him, telling him that her body was God's sacred vessel and then giving her body to him with no remorse at all, only pleas-ure, saying, "It's a sin between me and God, so I'll look after that." Because he made her pregnant, they married at City Hall and drove to Niagara Falls for their honeymoon – riding under the great falls on the *Maid of the Mist*, holding each other, soak-ing wet, seeing bits and pieces of rainbow light all around them in the mist – and Al decided he probably loved her, saying that he'd never seen such light. She clung to him and said she'd never seen such light either.

"Hail the light," he cried, happy.

"Shush," she said.

When Al returned to work, Donnie the bootlegger took him aside and told him he was fired; first, for fucking a Catholic girl, and then for marrying a Catholic girl.

"Regard me as old-fashioned," the bootlegger said with an amiable wink of menace, "but you can't be nailing Our Lord Jesus Christ to the cross and then be nailing our women, too."

Al, at a loss for words, a loss that made him feel as if the things, the faces around him had gone numb, started to grin, and grinning he knew that he was going to do something, though he didn't know what he intended until he was in the midst of doing it.

Al broke Donnie's nose.

Then he threatened to kill a righteous young rebbe who said God would curse his iniquity, He would punish such a marriage.

Al asked, "What kinda Jewish shit is that?"

The young rebbe said, "Ezekiel 18."

At the birth, Agnes and her boy child died, the child born strangled on his own cord, and Agnes dead from peritonitis.

Al said, "This is bullshit," and went to find the young rebbe and beat him with a sawed-off broomstick, cracking his ribs and collapsing his lung. "You got to believe God is crazy if you believe He strangles a child. You gotta be a lunatic to believe that," he told his father.

"There's a lotta lunatics," his father said.

"Count me out."

"In life, you gotta count for something somewhere," his father said.

"In life," Al said, "if I've got a thing with God, then it's me and God, it's not rules made up by somebody else. I've got what I get, I do what's to be done and I face up to it. That's it. That's all. Period. Punct."

To which his father said: "*Gott bestraft die, die es verdient haben.*"[1]

And his mother said: "*Es gibt niemanden, den Gott nicht bestraf.*"[2]

"I don't believe any of this. I don't believe God punishes anyone."

⤖〜⤔

After Maxie Baker was attacked outside the Town Tavern by Johnnie "Pops" Papilia, who was working for the Magaddino family out of Buffalo, Al's father – who knew Baker because he bought newspapers from Marvin at the kiosk after doing his banking at the Imperial Bank on Temperance Street – introduced Al to Maxie.

Al said he liked Maxie's hat.

"It's a Harry Sable," he said, "one of my only indulgences. A man should wear a good hat."

"I'll get such a hat," Al said.

Maxie took off his hat and looked into it, as if there were something to be learned by looking into his hat. But he put it back on his head and laid his hand on Al's arm. "We'll take a little sun. Here we are, three Jews down among the bankers. I'll tell you something about the rich. The rich are rich because they play poor, they give nothing away. They leave it to the poor to be generous, to give away what they ain't got."

"At big interest, too," Al's father said.

---

1 God punishes those who deserve it.
2 There is no one God doesn't punish.

"The vigorish," Maxie said, "it's the national treasure. You know *The Treasure of the Sierra Madre?*" he asked "I love it. I love Humphrey Bogart when he says, 'Conscience. What a thing. If you believe you've got a conscience it will pester you to death. But if you don't believe you've got one, what can it do to you?'"

"Bogart was a great actor," Al's father said, "great playing tough guys."

"Your father tells me you know how to be tough," Maxie said, putting his hand on Al's shoulder. "You don't brood. Brooding is the killer."

"If you happen to want to be a killer," Al said.

>~~<

"You play a helluva piano," the hunched old man said. "But I need to interrupt." He had laid his hand on Al's shoulder. At first, Al didn't move. Then, as he turned slowly on his stool he could tell the old man was a little drunk. He laughed. But there was also something cruel to the curl of the old man's lip. He looked, to Al, like a man who wanted to hurt someone, and if not someone, then he wanted to hurt himself. Al said, "This is supposed to be a happy time…" but the old man had stepped onto the small dance floor and said to the seniors in the room, "Today is August 2nd, sixty years to the day of the liberation of the camp at which I was an inmate – and several in this room, too – the camp at Treblinka."

He straightened his body, drawing his heels together.

"Every day, ten times a day sometimes," the old man said, "when we were standing at attention on the Roll Call Square, thousands of us sang this song they'd drilled into us, singing till we were perfect, just like they wanted us to be, like a choir," and he began to sing in a droning monotone, in German, which Al understood:

> *This is why we are in Treblinka*
> *Whatever fate may send,*
> *This is why we are in Treblinka*
> *Always ready for the end.*

A man at the back of the room called out, "Nobody needs this, sit down," and a woman yelled, "Shut up, sit down," but the old man kept on singing, unforgiving in his insistence, unforgiving of the other old people in the room, unforgiving of himself and, at the same time, insistent on his own humiliation.

"Stop," a man screeched. "For heaven's sake. You old fool."

> *Work is our existence*
> *We must obey or die.*
> *We do not want to leave...*

Someone threw a cane. The cane clattered against the piano as the old singer slumped into the stooped old man that he had been. Al said *Jesus Christ* to himself as he saw, sitting in an easy chair in the front row, Jake Piorko, looking weary but bemused, his jowls hanging loosely. Al spun on his stool and to break the awkward silence, he played and sang,

> *Embrace me, my sweet embraceable you,*
> *Embrace me, my irreplaceable you,*
> *Don't be a naughty baby,*
> *Come to papa, come to papa, do...*

Al knocked, the door opened, and he stepped into Jake Piorko's apartment. He took off his hat and brushed the nap of the pearl-grey crown with the forearm of his suitcoat. He said, "You need to know who I am."

"What're you talking? You I know. I hired you, for God's sake."

"But even so, you need to know who I am."

Hands on his hips, Jake leaned forward on his toes and looked into Al's eyes. "I know you," he said grimly. "You I seen a hundred times, it's in your eyes. So what's on your mind?"

"A bird. A parrot."

"That fucking bird. You're here because of that big-mouth bird? Dick Tracy would die laughing."

"Maybe you should be a little cautious."

"You're telling me, a ninety-year-old *alter kocker* who has out-lived Hitler and a bunch of other shitheels who'd like my fucking head, that I should be cautious. You gotta be kidding."

"I don't kid."

"This, you'll pardon the expression, is strictly for the birds."

"There's a contract."

"So, you'll break my ninety-year-old arm. This is pathetic. You gonna kill me?"

"It seems."

"Likely story."

"That's what I want to know. What's the story?"

"I got no story. Nobody who comes out of the camps has got a story. We got details. I got seventy years of details. You're talking about I killed the bird. Sure, I killed the bird. This is an insult. You know how many thousands of men I seen killed."

"That's part of it."

"And so?"

"He says you were a *Kapo*."

"Big news. I'm supposed to worry, now, at this age, because back then, up to my nose in watery shit, I didn't swallow? That I'm alive? Fuck. I smell that shit every day of my life. Men. Women. I smell it on you. How do you like that? And he thinks that that bird of his is some kind of joke on somebody. It's no joke. And he thinks I should be sorry, for anything..."

"Even so, we got a situation."

"Me, I'm all tired out. So you got a situation."

"That's right. A contract is a contract. I got to do what's got to be done. Otherwise it's an embarrassment."

"An embarrassment?"

"That's right."

"I can't believe this. I'm losing my mind."

"Maybe so."

"You're fucking *fermisshed*. You want contract, I'll give you contract. All my money, what am I gonna do with it? Whatever he offered, I'll double it up. Turn it around, you want someone to kill, kill him! Put a parrot on his headstone."

Al put on his hat. "I can see I made a mistake," he said.

"The only mistake is if you don't take my price."

"I come to you," Al said, flushing with anger, "with a situation, to see if there could be some way to deal with this situation, and you make me a *shmear*, a cheap bribe that would make me a whore."

Jake sat down, crossed his legs, spread his arms, and looked around the room as if Al were not there, as if their confrontation was only a pause in a long weariness, and he turned back to Al and said, "Take off your hat, you're in my house."

Al was so taken aback by Jake's curtness that he took off his hat. Then he smiled indulgently at his quick compliance, but before he could say anything Jake said, "I tell you the kinda detail you don't know nothing about. People talk about the camps, how all the deaths had no meaning, so God had to be dead, or maybe He never was. I got news for you. I said it then, I say it now. God was there. Auschwitz was as much His place as any other place, maybe more of His face was there than anywhere. I was no *tzaddik*,[1] I refused to quit. I wasn't about to die, not in my own mind. I lived. I played the percentages. I stayed alive. The God of that place was with me, percentages that are a blessing, that's what a rebbe told me."

"Talking to God is crazy," Al said, uncertain of how to respond to the cold fury in Jake's eyes.

"So I tell you what I propose. Just like in the camp. Roulette."

He went to a side-table drawer and took out a gun. "Obviously I never lost…and so the deal is, I'll play and the stakes are this. If I win, I get whatever Harry put up for this job, plus the twenty that I offered you, which you now pay to me, but you don't have to do nothing."

"But if you lose…?"

"I lose what I could've lost seventy years ago." He turned and opened the door to one of the empty rooms in the apartment. "In here," he said. "Here I got everything going for me."

Al, following him and seeing only an entirely empty white room, said, "There's nothing here."

"You sure?"

"Nothing is nothing."

---

[1] Confused.

"Maybe God's here."

"There's no God."

"Say hello to *Hashem*,"[1] Jake said. "We got a deal?"

"I make you the contract."

Jake cracked open the gun, dropped six bullets into the palm of his hand, set one back into a chamber, and gave the cylinder a hard spin.

He put the barrel of the gun in his mouth and stood watching Al watch him. Jake took the barrel out of his mouth and with a contemptuous knowing smile said, "I think you're really gonna let me do it."

Al started to grin. He was playing the situation by ear, feeling sure of himself, that whatever was going to happen, it was going to happen as it should. Jake said, "Goddam, the way you're watching me, you're no different than the fucking SS," and he shoved the barrel in his mouth, pulled the trigger, and blew out the back of his head.

><><

Harry and Al met in Switzer's Delicatessen. Harry was wearing a beautiful broad-brimmed black hat with a grey band, Al a caramel-brown felt fedora.

They ordered their usual chicken soup and matzo balls, smoked meat sandwiches, a side of young dills, and cheesecake.

They said very little as they ate.

They ate, as did several orthodox men in the restaurant, while wearing their hats.

---

1 A Righteous One, who calibrates justice correctly.

After coffee, Harry handed Al an envelope, ten thousand dollars in cash.

"Maybe this is how life ends," Harry said. "Two *alter kockers* sitting together with lots to say about nothing. Mind you, if we were wops we'd have nothing to say about a lot."

Al handed the envelope back to Harry.

"There's no contract. What I did was nothing. It's got to be null. I was there, but I wasn't responsible."

"You sure about this?"

"Sure I'm sure. He loses, I lose, you win. As it should be."

"Except I got no Humbo, Humbo is dead. That fucking *Kapo*, he was no different than a Nazi…"

"He told me I was no different than the SS…"

"Out of his mind. Have a Rémy Martin on me?"

"The drink of princes."

"Believe me, Al, you're a prince."

"Sure," Al said, "but wipe your lip, Harry. You got mustard on your lip. A guy with such a beautiful hat does not look good with mustard on his lip."

THIRD PEW TO THE LEFT

A man of about seventy came into a downtown bar every late afternoon, a small man who wore slacks and a sports shirt in the summer and a cardigan sweater over his shirt in the winter. His hair was white. There was a feeling of wry beneficence in his smile. He seemed to wish people well and to wish himself well. This had something to do with his being an old priest who drank, and sometimes he drank a lot if people at the bar bought him drinks.

The woman who was the bartender always called out cheerfully when he came in, "Hello, Father Joe." He smiled, pleased to be welcomed, but perhaps not wanting everyone to know that he was a priest. He took a chair by a small table in a corner, a table almost no one ever sat at unless the bar was crowded and usually it was crowded late at night, long after he had gone home to St. Basil's, a residence close to the bar and close to the university, a home for young seminarians and old retired priests.

I had gone to the university and had been married in St. Basil's Church so I called out, too, "Hello, Father Joe." He smiled but it was the smile of a man who expected to be left alone. Sitting by myself at the bar I always sent him a drink, a Scotch and soda over ice.

"Cheers," he said quietly.

One day I was feeling so alone at the bar that I couldn't help myself. I went over and sat down beside him. He was surprised, but at ease. "You're a fine-looking amiable old priest," I said. I had been drinking since noon.

"You're a fine-looking ruin of a man yourself," he said.

"Perfidy's upon us," I said.

"Not likely," he said. "Relax."

I did. I told him that I'd been a student. He said that he'd been a teacher. I'd studied languages and literature, I said. He said he'd taught philosophy. I asked him how, after all these years, he liked being a priest. He said he liked it fine. I asked how he liked the new right-wing bishop, Father Ambrozie.

"I dunno," he said.

"The mad Pole's given us a stern Serb," I said.

"Now, now, let's be looking on the bright side. At least you know now exactly where you stand. You can thank the Pope for that."

"Thank you, Pope," I said.

"Have you been drinking?"

"A little," I said.

"I drink a lot," he said. Then he touched my hand. "Don't worry," he said. "It has nothing to do with any spiritual crisis. I don't go in for that class of thing."

"Where you from?" I asked.

"Pittsburgh. Many long years ago, when it was a tough town. My father was a tough man, a steelworker. How about you?"

"Here," I said.

"You're from here?"

"Here."

"I haven't met anybody from here for years," he said.

"Well, you have now," I said.

"Good. It's good to be in touch with roots," he said.

"I'll tell you the truth, Father. As far as I'm concerned, that's a shoe store nobody remembers."

"Well, at least you've got your feet on the ground," he said, trying to stifle a laugh. I wagged my finger at him and he winked at me and I waved at the bartender, telling her to bring us two more drinks.

"I've a weakness for cheap jokes," he said.

"I've a weakness for cheap whisky," I said.

"You might say that makes it even for us," he said. "Myself, I lean to the good whisky, when I can get it."

"Well, they don't serve you slouch whisky in here," I said.

"No, they do not."

We smiled at each other.

"Well, now that we've got that settled," he said, sipping his fresh Scotch and soda, "what's your claim to fame?"

"Coming in third."

"What's that mean?"

"No matter what I've done in my life I've always come in third."

"Yeah, so what are you currently third at?"

"Advertising. Consulting," I said.

"Which is it?"

"Both," I said. "When I'm not consulting I advertise that I do."

"You do?"

"Yes."

"And this is where literature gets you?"

"Like a patient etherized upon a table," I said.

He laughed.

"I used to know some poems by heart," he said.

"What happened?"

"My heart gave out," and he laughed again, saying, "Forgive me, I can't help it."

"Neither can I."

"Do you know what forgiveness is?" he asked.

"No," I said.

"When you know that you have nothing left to lose and you pass it on."

"Boy, I should've studied with you," I said.

"Maybe not," he said.

"Philosophy, right? What'd you teach?"

"For openers, Plato, Aristotle, Thomas Aquinas... It was wonderful, talking about how God's mind worked, and then I used to leap right up to the twentieth century, to our own time, to Maritain..."

"What happened to what's in between?" I asked.

"Nothing," he said.

"Yeah, but where'd it go? Where'd Descartes go?"

"Nowhere. I left him right where he was."

"You can't do that," I said.

"I did," he said.

"Didn't anybody say anything?"

"They did not. Anyway, I used to tell them, 'We all know the trouble with Descartes. He put de cart before de horse!'"

"Oh, God, you didn't!"

"I did," he said. "And why not? It's a corny joke, but it's got me out of some tricky situations. Anyway, when you think about it, this business about 'I think therefore I am' is rather profoundly dumb. After all, God thought and therefore we are and since we are, we think. What else could we do but think – go bowling? And if we think too much we probably end up like your man

Woody Allen, talking ourselves to death. It's what the wise boys call ennui…"

"The wisdom of hell," I said, laughing with him.

"I don't know a lot about hell," he said. "That's why I drink. Any time I get anywhere close to hell I take a drink."

"But you're in here every day," I said.

"Yes," he said.

"Jesus."

"Yes," he said, lifting his glass, "and isn't He a help, a wonderful fellow. Forgave us, and died for our sins."

"You're kidding," I said.

"I don't kid about Jesus," he said.

"I don't mean that, I mean the way you said it."

"How'd I say it?"

"Like He was the guy next door."

"You drink too much," he said.

"Says who?" I said, drawing a circle with my finger in the dampness on the table.

"Never mind, I don't want to ruin our nice talk. I don't want to know why you think you drink."

"No?" I asked, disappointed.

"I might be interested to know why you think you love," he said. "But that would take a couple more drinks and they're not going to give me any more. Orders from on high, eye in the sky."

"You really think I drink too much?" I asked.

"How do I know? I hardly know you."

"Maybe it's true," I said.

"Maybe."

"Maybe a lot of things are true."

"Could be, you never know. Not until you know."

"Not until the fat lady sings," I said.

"The only fat lady I ever knew," he said, "was my mother, and she lived to a ripe old age. Ninety-two. She had a fine philosophical bent."

"I used to like talking philosophy," I said.

He smiled, his mouth taking a little turn, wishing me well.

"You did, did you?" he said.

"Yep," I said.

"If a tree falls in a forest when there's no one there, does the tree make a sound?... That kind of thing?" he said.

"Yeah, that kind of stuff," I said. "And poetry, the half-deserted streets, the muttering retreats of cheap one-nighters in sawdust hotels... Something like that."

"I never went in much for poetry. Limericks were my speed," he said.

"There was a priest who taught me, Dore or Dorey, something like that," and Father Joe nodded as if he knew who I was talking about, "and he had the whole of 'Prufrock' off by heart. He'd stand up in front of us and roar that thing out. I never liked to admit it back then but I envied him. He had this light in his eyes like he was lifted right out of himself. And then he said something I've never forgotten. I mean he said about the end, where you feel like you're a pair of ragged claws scuttling across the ocean floor – and I don't know about you, Father, but that's exactly how I feel when I've drunk too much – he said, 'Hell probably isn't fire or anything like that, it's probably being those claws inside your own head and hearing them...'"

"Don't be so hard on yourself," he said.

"Hard?" I asked.

"Yeah," he said.

"My father always said I was too easy on myself."

"Well, it's a matter of perspective. The truth is tricky."

"Do I dare to eat a peach?" I blurted out.

"There's a time for everything," he said.

"I guess there is."

"Time for me to go," he said, standing up, "I think."

"…am not Hamlet, nor was meant to be," I cried. "Am an attendant player—"

"Thanks for the drinks," he said, straightening his shirt collar.

"Right. Any time," I said.

"And the chat," he said.

"Any time."

I was wounded. I was sure that he had grown tired of me. Then he said gravely, "It's a long time since you've been to confession. I can tell. A long time."

"I suppose it is," I said, startled.

"After a long, long time it's harder," he said, leaning close to me.

"I don't know."

"Listen, the time'll come when you'll want to go to confession…"

"I doubt it," I said.

"Sure. It'll come, but don't worry about it. When the time comes, I'm your man."

"You think so?"

"I know so."

I stared at the circle I'd drawn on the table. "Yeah, well, do you want me to go to confession or do you prefer I tell you the truth?"

"Confession," he said, laughing. "I told you, the truth is tricky."

Over the next three or four months we saw each other almost every day. We got used to knowing that at the end of the afternoon, for about forty-five minutes, we were together in the same room. We said a word or two but we never had a long talk again. I never went to confession. I bought him drinks. He drank them. I consulted. I drank and told myself one or two small truths and turned down a free ticket to see the new Woody Allen film. "It's got to do with Descartes," I told my friends. "He and Woody…put de cart before de horse." Nobody laughed. "Get off the bottle," one of them said.

Then, Father Joe was not there. I asked the bartender if she knew where he was. She said, "Father Joe's been sick. He died. The funeral's tomorrow." I went to the funeral at St. Basil's Church. The bishop, Father Ambrozie, didn't go. I didn't mind. I knew where I stood. Third pew to the left.

THE HARDER THEY COME

Crede Doucet had his mother's very pale blue eyes, but he was long in the jaw, lean and bony, and gaunt. She was plump. His father, Eldon Doucet, a well-known lawyer, who also was long in the jaw and lean said, "How come he never has a good word for me?"

"He envies you," his wife, Madeleine, said, "the way you're so satisfied with your own life."

"A man gets what he deserves," he said, unbuttoning his blue serge vest, as he always did at the end of the afternoon, sitting down in his wingback chair.

"Sometimes, Eldon," she said, "you sound more like a judge than a lawyer."

"Life," he said, running his hand through thinning hair, "is like politics. Once you start explaining, you're finished, and I've been trying to explain myself to that boy for years."

"We don't agree. And he's not a boy. He's twenty-seven."

Because she turned away, Eldon thought he had upset her but she had only turned to admire the sitting room's new pinstripe wallpaper, a paper she had picked out at Ye Olde Shoppe to mark their thirtieth wedding anniversary.

It has a quiet dignity, she thought. And even better, a necessary dignity.

"I never really knew my father either," Eldon said. "He was a man who liked ballroom dancing and ties. That much I knew. He had hundreds of ties. Before he died – perhaps it was some kind of joke – he gave every last one of his ties to a charity drive for the homeless."

She poured him a cup of strong green tea. No milk. No sugar.

He believed green tea was good for his bowels. He worried about his bowels.

He watched for a yellowing under his eyes.

He watched for blood in his stool. Liver spots on his skin. He said he wasn't worried about being dead, it was whether dying would humiliate him, how he was going to die.

"I rather liked my father," she said, holding a well-watered Scotch. As usual, she had been slow-sipping all evening. "He was a nice man, nice to every woman he met except my mother. Then I grew up and got over her disappointment. I discovered I had my own disappointments."

"Growing up isn't enough."

"It helps."

"Crede's a grown man and you still encourage him, still think he's going to be some kind of real singer, keeping all those scrap-book pictures of him. There is no second Tony Bennett. And singing Bennett songs in falsetto is ludicrous."

"He has a wonderful voice," she said. "I love his voice."

"Even I know, only blacks can sing falsetto and get away with it."

She surprised him. She slipped off her shoes and touched his thigh, saying, "I think he'll be mostly like you when we're dead?"

"Maybe. Maybe not. It's all in the family, in the blood," he said. "But calling him Crede, just like my father, was likely a mistake. I didn't know how different he'd be. My father was a hard, practical man. It's like Crede's turned his back on who he is, hanging out at the racetrack. Nobody goes to the track every day, only layabouts."

"And the owners," she said wryly.

"He should own up to how he's wasting his life."

"Maybe so," she said. "Maybe so."

He said nothing.

There were times when saying nothing was best. He worried that he might have sounded petulant.

"You used to sing sometimes yourself," she said.

"Never mind my singing. He has to take hold of himself."

"Anyway, come to bed."

⊱∼⊰

In bed, Eldon was puzzled by the quiet care she took to make love to him, as if she were gently amused, so that he was self-conscious and made no sound, afraid to sigh, watching and waiting as if something quite separate from their lives was going to happen, and he was so upset and softened by her agreeable smile as he drifted off to sleep that he wondered how he might get close to her again... He believed they had been wonderfully close... But the next morning, as she left for her swim at the Rosedale Ladies Club, she said, "Don't you think it's nice the way we can accommodate each other without too much emotion?"

That night he made love to her with a cold fury that frightened him. It was like the fury he felt at times in the courtroom as he closed in on some despicable lying cheat slouched on the stand, a fury that one day had caused him to say out loud, triumphantly, before the bench, "This is how we keep the low-life down," eliciting a reprimand from the judge. He eased off her body in their bed and went to sleep staring straight up at the ceiling, feeling helpless after she said, "That was nice," and kissed him lightly on the cheek. "Sleep tight," she said.

It was a Saturday afternoon. She and Crede were sitting in the garden, under an apple tree. She planted the tree after he'd been born. It was her favourite corner of the garden, protected from the wind by the tree. Eldon stood alone at the back of the garden by the peony beds. He was looking to see if the blooms were heavy with black ants. Black ants brought peonies fully to bloom. Sitting at a wrought-iron table that had a glass top, Madeleine was playing double solitaire.

"When did you start wearing your bathrobe out to the garden?" she asked Crede.

"I dunno."

"Naked underneath!"

"How'd you know?"

"A mother knows when her boy is naked."

"Red eight on the black nine," Crede said.

"I almost never beat this game," she said.

"Why play? Nobody beats double solitaire."

"That's not the point. The point is you keep playing or else you just quit. You wake up in the morning, 'So long, solitaire.' Like someone says *so long* in the night. You wake up and say, 'So long, too...' And no one answers. You're on your own."

"I'm here."

"And your father's here. We're all here."

"King on the ace. Of clubs."

Crede lowered his head and said quietly, "Long live the King." Then he laughed and she shushed him, saying, "We are being quite naughty about the man I love."

"I know, I know."

"The thing is, your father, when he wakes in the morning, he's always afraid that something will have gone missing in the night, afraid everything won't be exactly where he left it. Myself, I'm disappointed that a whole night has gone by and nothing has got lost, that everything's where it was."

"And still is," he laughed as she raised her empty glass and said, "Your father plays life close to the vest. It's his nature."

"Red queen on a black king," he said and reached under the table for the whisky thermos and poured her a drink.

"A well-watered Scotch does one right," she said, as if explaining. "Thank you."

"Think nothing of it."

"In the old days, this," she said, holding the glass high with an air of triumph, "would have been laudanum. All the respectable ladies of the time got blissful indeed on laudanum. Opium got a lady through the day."

"Sometimes I think you're happy being unhappy."

"Who said I'm unhappy? It's just that when I'm cold sober I hear the *tock tock* of the clock. Too loud, too clear. *Tock. Tock. Tock.* Drive you crazy. *Tock. Tock. Tock. Tock. Tock...*"

"Cut it out."

"Why? *Tock. Tock.*"

"It's irritating."

"It's the sound your father's heart makes at night."

"Now, you *are* drunk."

"I am not. Your father listens to his liver and his heart but he keeps his eye on you. He likes to laugh sometimes but he told me he thinks you want to kill him."

"He's who he is and I don't want to kill him. I just don't want to be him. That's all. He thinks he's gone missing in my life if I don't end up like him."

"Maybe in the morning I'll be among the missing persons."

"That sounds goddamn unhappy to me."

"No, no. You've got it all wrong. My idea of hell is being locked up for life in a room with a happy man. A world of sunlight, with no moon. Who could stand it?"

"God?"

"Nonsense. God sneaks around in the dark in secret."

His father, flipping open the gold lid to his pocket watch, called out, "Two o'clock. Watch the heat. The double peony blooms are spectacular, full of ants."

"Oh good," she said and stood up and began to waltz alone on the grass, holding the hem of her dress with one hand, circling Crede, singing, holding her whisky glass with the other,

My heart cries for you,
sighs for you,
Please come back to me...

as she pointed at his father with the glass that still had a swirl of whisky in it. "And don't forget he's a detail man," she said, taking hold of Crede's arm, "and such are the details of my love and disappointment."

She laughed, as if her laughter were an admission that she had found satisfaction in an acceptance of who she had become while her husband, not knowing what she had said, came toward them, handling the weight of his pocket watch. With a look of approval at the laughter, he, too, began to sing:

Who threw the overalls
In Mrs. Murphy's chowder,
Tell us or we'll shout,
Shout all the louder...

⤞⤝

Two weeks later, Madeleine was found in her bathing suit with her neck broken, dead, sprawled on the sky-blue tiles of the Rosedale Ladies Club swimming pool. The caretaker had drained the pool for repairs and had forgotten to lock the door into the room that glared with summer light from the wide glass roof.

"Sometimes," the caretaker said, "even when it's filled with water you feel you're diving into the sky. She mustn't have looked down."

The coroner said, "She took a dive," and ruled Accidental Death.

For two afternoons Crede sat in the garden under the apple tree. He had a feeling that just behind him, if he were to whirl around, he would find an open seam in the air, open to a silent scream he knew was there, a scream he was trying to hear. But he did not hear it. He waited, and torn between fury and lethargy, aching with loss, he sat hunched through two afternoons of drizzle, hollow-eyed, bedraggled, bleak, as close as he had ever come to what he thought was prayer or despair. On the second day his father stood for a while beside him in the light rain, but then said, "For Christ's sake, man," and went back into the house.

On the morning of the funeral, Crede showered, shaved with a straight razor, scrubbed his hands, and trimmed his nails until his forefinger bled. Sitting on the toilet, he licked the blood from his finger. He liked the taste of his blood. He had always licked the blood whenever he'd cut himself as a child. His mother had told him his saliva helped to heal the wound. He liked the idea of healing himself.

At the Requiem Mass in the cathedral he looked flushed, eager and enormously pleased as he tilted his head to look back over the crowded pews. "You look like you're counting the house," his father said sternly, admonishing him, but then added, as if happily content with a public respect being shown to his family, "It's really quite a crowd."

During the Mass, Crede stared straight ahead, moving his lips, but not, his father realized, to the lilt of the prayers. "Are you talking to yourself?" he asked, gripping the pew. Crede smiled and patted his hand. "No, not to myself." Then he startled his father by leaving the pew and getting into the line going up to Communion. His father knew that no one in the family had gone to confession for years, and though he was not ardent in his faith, he nonetheless believed in rituals. After all, he said, the Law was made up of those rituals that had been codified through centuries of inquiry, just as the Church through its Councils and Encyclicals had codified itself, always looking back to and consulting its great Fathers, Aquinas and Augustine, as the Law looked back to and consulted its great Fathers, Gladstone and Holmes.

"You're in a state of sin," Eldon whispered to Crede, who was back beside him in the pew, and then he went rigid with indignation as Crede stepped out and into the aisle again, going back up to the altar, to stand alone on the carpeted stair – something he'd obviously arranged with the Monsignor. But there'd been no consultation with him, no consideration of what he might have wanted; Eldon had been left out and he tasted a sourness come up in his throat. "Goddamn my bowels," he said as Crede concluded the celebration of the Mass by singing in falsetto the *Panis Angelicus*.

> *Panis angelicus*
> *Fit panis hominum;*
> *Dat panis coelicus*
> *Figuris terminum;*
> *O res mirabilis!*
> *Manducat dominum*

Surprisingly moved, he thought to himself, *Got to admit it. In Latin, his falsetto's okay.*

>~~~<

Eight months after his mother's death, stepping out of the steaming shower stall in the morning, shivering with the shock of cold air, Crede put on his heavy white terry cloth robe with a shawl collar and his soft black leather slippers, brushed his closely cropped hair, and then paused at the head of the stairs below the stained-glass window, the strong morning light dappling his skin with rose and emerald petals. He listened to his father shuffling barefooted behind his closed bedroom door, getting on and off the scale that he kept beside his bed.

"First thing in the morning and he's checking the weight of the world," he said to himself, laughing quietly. He yelled out, "I think you're getting slower and slower each morning," as he went down the carpeted stairs to cook breakfast, which he now did every morning, cracking four eggs into a bowl and reaching for any one of the copper pans that hung from the steel hooks over the stove.

They ate across from each other at an old pine table, with a single pink rose between them in a pressed-glass vase that his mother had bought. The breakfast room had a sliding glass door to the garden and the door was full of morning sunshine, the soft light falling on his father's flushed pink face.

"Well," said Crede wryly, "here we go again, alone together."

Eldon looked at his plate. "I must say," he said, touching the yellowing pouches under his eyes, "I am not ready to be alone."

They sat in silence, neither eating.

Then, "You cook a good egg, Crede. Your mother always cooked a good egg."

"You make it sound like she was a good egg."

"She was herself a damn good woman," Eldon said, smoothing rosehip jelly onto his toast. "In her very own sweet way, she could deal with things. She could deal with me and she certainly dealt with you." He bit into the toast and chewed slowly. "I'd call leaving you all her money a damn good nest egg."

"I wonder what bothers you most," Crede said. "Whether it was Mother leaving me the money, or not telling you she was going to give me the money."

"What bothers me," his father said, slipping his knife into the heart of the jelly jar, "is that you not only refuse to work but you don't have to work."

"I sing," he said, lifting the pink rose out of the vase, putting it to his nose, and inhaling deeply with his eyes closed.

"You haven't worked anywhere for over a year. Not even a church hall. Playing the gentleman punter at the track..."

"I sing my heart out every day," Crede said, opening his hand to his father:

> With no star to guide me
> And no one beside me
> I go on my way.
> After the day, the darkness will hide me...

He snapped the long green stem and handed the rose to his father. "Put this in your lapel."

"A rose by any other name," Eldon said softly, with stern control, then, buttoning his vest for the trip downtown to his office, he said: "Don't forget, tomorrow is Wednesday. Wednesday night."

Crede got up, giving his father a wry little smile. "I won't forget. Maybe we should do a joint together before she comes."

Putting the rose in his lapel, Eldon said, "Ridiculous. Who in the world do you think I am? Do you know I spent yesterday afternoon with Senator Mulroney in my office? Life's little fixer. He believes in nothing except his own smoothness, but there he was, courting me. When I looked at myself in the mirror this morning I saw what I believe in."

"And what's that?"

"Me, and I liked what I saw. I see a lot of me in my neighbours but I'm not so sure I see much of you in me."

Eldon had quick darting eyes and a small cleft in his long chin that gave him an air of severity, which he himself saw as dignified and women seemed to find attractive.

He always wore a dark double-breasted suit with a grey silk tie, and carried his gold pocket watch in his vest. He believed the only slight he'd ever suffered, a slight in the sense that someone had actually hurt him and laughed in his face, was the day after Crede had been born, when he'd felt something so close to a seizure of light-headed gaiety, a feeling of affirmation, that – in a moment of spontaneous playfulness – he'd worn a pair of his own father's spats to his law office. His partner had laughed, telling him: "If only you were a nigger you'd look like a pimp."

He'd never forgiven his partner his hoot of loud laughter, and unbuttoning the spats that night he'd decided – thinking what a fine judicious man his father had been – to call his son by the name of Crede – to make sure that what he stood for and what his father had stood for (if nothing else, a stern sense of decorum) would continue. But now they were both dead, his wife and the partner – a pair of spats in the ground, he'd suddenly thought at the requiem Mass, a little afraid of his own levity as he grimly held on to the pew, touched by an unfamiliar sense of pity for all their lives – as if for a moment he believed that their lives were only caprice, a coming and going, a buttoning and unbuttoning. Despite the indignation he'd felt alone in the pew, he had been moved almost to tears by his son's singing at the end of the Mass, admiring his determination, his loyalty to his mother. *Panis angelicus*, he thought. *Bread of the angels.* He wasn't quite sure what it meant. Bread was the body of Christ? Perhaps. And the Blood? He knew all about the blood. He felt pleased with the way he'd reasoned out the moment. He decided to drink a glass of wine.

At six o'clock on that afternoon, Tuesday, Crede – who had been to the racetrack and had come home and showered – stood on the veranda wearing his white terry cloth robe. Through the leaves of the dwarf cherry tree he saw his father step spryly onto the flagstone front walk. Eldon was in a very good mood. After two weeks in court, he had, that afternoon, completed the successful defence of two old friends, two well-known stockbrokers who'd been charged with embezzlement. He'd proved that the investigating detectives had lied, and had lied under oath. His two friends, set free, had been astonished, and together, the three men, arms around one another, had broken into a song they had learned as boys at camp, a Lake Simcoe summer prep school for youngsters whose parents intended them to become barristers, brokers, bankers, and perhaps politicians at a cabinet level.

And now, here he was, feeling almost giddy, at the front door to his fine home, being greeted by his son, who was looking so smilingly fresh and handsome. He even thought that Crede wearing the white bathrobe was amusing. Eldon lifted his right arm and heartily sang out his camp song:

> Oh dear, what can the matter be,
> Three old maids got locked in the lavetry.
> They were there from Monday till Saturday.
> And nobody knew they were there.
> The first one in was Elizabeth Bender.
> She just went in to find a suspender.
> It flew up and hit her feminine gender.
> And nobody knew she was there....

Eldon stopped singing. He shuffled his feet on the flagstone, looking pleased but sheepish. "Oh well," he said, "the word is you're the singer in the family," and he strode up the veranda stairs, past Crede, and went into the house. Crede, taken aback, not knowing what to say, followed but went upstairs to his room where he sat down in a crouch, his robe falling open, legs apart. He saw himself naked in the long mirror on his closet door. He shook his head, as if seeing himself for the first time, startled by how dark his hair was against his pale skin, and how lost in the darkness was his cock. He said quietly, wistfully, "Mother."

><~~><

Within eight months of Crede planting flowers on his mother's grave, within eight months of the silences he and his father had shared, feeling each other's awkwardness, his father said, "Enough is enough," and brought his new lady home for high tea, fixing Crede with a look of stern satisfaction as she'd said, "My name is Grace."

She had thick black hair and a supple shapelessness, and though she was dressed in a tailored dark suit and wore black leather gloves – gloves that were out of fashion but gave her an air of profession-alism – there was a sly impishness in the way she sat on the arm of an easy chair and, while smoking a gold-tipped Nat Sherman cig-arette, said, "I never inhale, I just like the gold tips."

She sat smoothing her dress on her thigh, artfully detached and drawn into herself, aware that in her silence both men were watch-ing her. "You're staring," his father said, and Crede said, "Yes, I sup-pose I am. Sorry."

She rose and offered Crede her gloved hand and then, kissing him lightly on the cheek, said, "There's no need to be sorry. Only men who don't know what they have done should say they're sorry." Her hair caught all the light from the sitting-room bay window. Then she said: "The wallpaper in this room looks just like a bank manager's suit." She smiled, amused by her own audacity, and his father seemed to be amused, too.

"That wallpaper was thirty years in the making," Crede said, "but never mind."

><\~\~><

It was Wednesday evening – his father's time to be alone in the house with Grace. As dusk came on, Crede had taken a glass of white wine with pâté and Cumberland sauce and then he smoked a joint before driving east, past the soybean mills and courier depots, and a spray-painted scrawl on a precast concrete wall: GOD IS DEAD AND HE DOESN'T CARE, out to Ashbridges Bay, to the old gabled racetrack on the lakeshore. He had a reserved chair in one of the clubhouse boxes. He sat with his arms folded as he watched the line of horses and their leads come up out of the dark tunnel from the paddock onto the track.

He loved, in the closing light of dusk and the light from the overhead flood lamps, the sheen of sweat on the chest muscles and forelegs of the horses, and was certain he could tell, as he peered through his big army war-surplus binoculars, whether a horse was ready to run well or whether it was washed out, dripping sweat. He liked to see a prick to the ears of a horse and never bet on fillies.

Sometimes he left his box and went onto the clubhouse floor to feel the mood among the players. Wearing one of his elegantly cut double-breasted Milan linen jackets, he stood listening among men whom he had casually come to nod hello to over recent years, familiar faces with no names. He liked the brief intimacy of their shared intensity that required no names, that required only a willingness to listen and then to play and then forget among fast talkers with their pocket computers who fed each other fractions and formulas, their fingertips smudged with ink from the Racing Form, all locked into their own systems of speed ratings and past performances, as if somehow – in trying to win – there were ways to locate a length lost in a past race that would, if found, correct and ordain the future and save them from disappointment. And he laughed, thinking of the blackness that welled out of these men after each race, after each loss, the acceptance of disappointment, the yearning for pity, and yet there was a resilience, too, and a courage, the resiliency his mother had shown playing double solitaire.

Crede, standing among these men, heard two of them agree that the favourite, the 6 horse, was going to win. He said out loud, "Only dead fish swim with the current," and a wiry little man who was known as Eli the Bat said, "Welcome to the fish market." There was tight-lipped grim laughter. Still, Crede knew that there was something luxurious to be felt in even the smallest win, a glee, and Crede believed he was going to win: *You think you're dead in the water and suddenly you're afloat and it's like a blessing. I can see that. A confirmation of oneself.* He made his bets without hesitation but none of his hunches fell into place. He swallowed hard when he lost the third race by a neck.

All that evening, as the track became an oval of light suspended in a vast darkness, he had to fight off an increasing sadness as, inexplicably, he lost race after race. Yet with each loss he also felt a desperate eagerness, a determination to keep on playing in anticipation of a win until – at a point in the ninth race, he suddenly leapt to his feet, ready to lose, yet throwing his hands into the air as the horses lunged around the turn into the stretch, unable to stop himself from yelling as the horses pounded toward the wire, and then, when the numbers of the first three horses crossed the wire, he could hardly believe what he knew to be true – there were his three numbers, three numbers that he had bet, and as he stood there, alone, flooded with a feeling of affirmation, as if some truth deep within himself had been confirmed, he could see the winning horses set in a stillness apart from the rest of the field as they had crossed the wire. It was as though they had been positioned there at the wire at the beginning of the race, foreordained, as if he had tapped into the order of things, as if life were not just caprice and consternation played close to the vest but life could be a moment of long shots, too.

The payoff for the Triple would be enormous, and he gave a little pump of his fist, but then in sullen wonder he put his fist up to his mouth, muffling his voice as he said, "Shit," suddenly suffering a chill. The Inquiry sign had come on, the thin red neon letters: INQUIRY. His father's favourite word. An inquiry had been called. Under his breath he cursed the stewards and hurried downstairs to the clubhouse floor to stand among other shuffling men who were watching the replay on a television monitor – the horses coming out of the gate from three angles. It was clear to Crede before the decision was announced that his number 4 horse had bumped with the 5, taking the 5 out at the beginning, coming out of the gate and veering into him. It didn't matter that the 4 would have won anyway, or that the 5, at 30 to 1, had no chance – the 4 horse had accidentally interfered. He said aloud to himself, "It doesn't matter," but someone close by snarled, "Goddamn right it matters," because the stewards took the 4 horse down, and though he had won, he had lost. It was disqualified. "Just a minor detail, man," Eli the Bat said bitterly, and Crede suddenly yelled, "I'll fucking detail you, you bastards," surprising the other men who were used to disappointment as he hurried out of the clubhouse filled with outrage, as if, worse than being cheated, he had been taunted and mocked by a promise unkept. "Fucking jockey probably went in the tank." He drove home.

When he came to the house, marching across the lawn and cutting through a flower bed, he tracked wet garden dirt into the front door and along the hall and up the unlit stairs. Filled with a desperate eagerness, a desperate anticipation – just as he had been ready to lose as the winning horses had come to the wire – he stood holding his breath outside his father's closed bedroom door, listening to laughter and little whelps *like goddamn puppy love.* Suddenly the dark stairwell seemed like a vast hole he and his father had lived in and shared and gone up and down in each day, elbows flared to ensure breathing space. As he opened the door and crossed the line of the threshold to the dimly lit bedroom, that forbidden place from his childhood, a place of whisperings and broken breathing, in which the naked woman spun up and around and over his father, her hands held out, he felt a terrible sense of exhaustion and wanted to cry out some word of helpless remorse in his anger so that his father would understand that a cry at least could fill the emptiness that had been between them since childhood, but seeing Grace's breasts and his bewildered father struggling, ungainly and sprawling under her in his marriage bed, Crede yelled, "You horse's ass."

Grace, seeing who it was, sank back against the propped pillows and smiled. "Welcome to the scene of the crime," she said, putting her hand lightly on the old man's shoulder, but Eldon screamed, "What? You sonofabitch." Crede, rocking on the balls of his feet, unsure of what he was going to do, stared at the white hair on his father's chest. *White, for Chrissake, as a lamb, and his skin hanging, his whole life hanging loose off his bones like he had the skin of an old woman.* Crede suddenly wanted to reach out and cradle his father and rock him, as if he were a shrivelled child, but his father, as if slowly recollecting a rage, said, "You sonofabitch, you sonofabitch. You come in on me naked, you dare," and he jack-knifed up off the bed, both fists punching the air. As he fell back onto the sheet, Crede, who'd spun away astonished, said, "Jesus," and when Grace leapt off the bed, landing in a crouch, he laughed, but then they both heard the rattle in the old man's throat and stared at the gaping mouth, the wide eyes, and saw that his father was dying, if not already dead. "I didn't ask for any of this," Crede said, shaken, his eyes filling with tears as he drew the woman to him, holding her hard by the wrists. "I didn't want this."

"No, no, of course not," she said. She drew her hands together so that they seemed to be caught in prayer.

⤖⤙

For the funeral in the cathedral, motorcycle policemen wearing white crash helmets with plastic visors directed traffic, and despite a freak early snowstorm, heavy and wet, an overflow of mourners clustered outside on the steps of the cathedral. The mayor was there and senators and the deputy prime minister. A judge and the city director of roads were among the pallbearers.

Crede walked down the centre aisle beside the burnished oak casket that had been mounted on an aluminum rolling caisson, the casket covered with calla lilies, and then he stepped into the front pew. The choir sang the *Kyrie.* The priest, an aged man with strong cheekbones and alert eyes in pouches of pale flesh, went up into the pulpit and read from a prepared text, praising what he called his father's rare fidelity, that "uncommon bond to the common weal, that duty to oneself – such fidelity being a belief that can become a beatitude," he said, "because this fidelity is a good life so arranged that it melds into all our lives…this fidelity, the virtue of the good soldier, leads us onward as intimates as we embrace each other in the shadow of death."

After the *Miserere,* the priest raised his hand and made a sign of the cross, then motioned to Crede, who stepped alongside the coffin and placed both hands on the dark shining wood and sang, all alone, by special dispensation, because it was not a Catholic hymn:

> *Amazing Grace, how sweet the sound,*
> *That saved a wretch like me;*
> *I once was lost but now am found…*

As Crede walked down the aisle behind the coffin, he nodded with the stern assurance of the deeply aggrieved to men and women he did not know, nodded as if they were old friends, or if not friends, then neighbours. He let people shake his hand and he stood on the curb beside the hearse, stroking his smooth cheek with his long fingers. The wet cold wind carried heavy flakes of snow that melted on his face and bare head, snow that refreshed him. Water trickled out of his hair, down his brow. He thought he caught a glimpse of Grace wearing a veil, making her way toward him between men and women bundled up against the wind and snow, clustered into small groups. *It's just like the track*, he thought, *clustering for comfort,* and several well-dressed women reached out and offered their condolences.

After riding out to the burial yard, past the Chick 'n' Deli and U-Haul and Koko the Muffler King, the several limousines eased to a stop near an open grave. Surprisingly few mourners had actually come out to the grave, among them two women he'd never seen before, both young and quite beautiful, standing apart and apparently a little perplexed by each other's presence. After a shovelful of dirt had been cast into the grave, Senator Mulroney took Crede's hand in his and said, "Your father was a man of means who always meant well."

"Yes, yes, he was well-meant," Crede said, and when Senator Mulroney looked puzzled, he added, "That's what they say about a horse who tried really hard but finished last." He turned away toward Grace, who had stepped out from between two grey turreted tombstones.

"Well, Grace," he said, "how are you?"

"Never mind me," she said. "How are you?"

She held out her gloved hand and he shook it and saw that she was wearing a silver bracelet, inlaid with amethysts, that had belonged to his mother.

"Well, everything went as he would have wanted," he said, "and he'd be relieved."

"Your father would've liked all the arrangements."

"Yes, if he hadn't been a lawyer he'd have been a flower arranger."

"Now, now. I thought you sang beautifully," she said.

"Not sure my father would have approved. To him, I was just doing black face."

"Black face?"

"Never mind, private joke."

He looked down at her little ankle rubbers as she stood in the snow, and he laughed. "You should have boots," he said. "I'm surprised my father didn't buy you some boots," and he took her arm, helping her as they stepped around the small polished marble modern stones that were laid flat in the ground, some lost under the snow. "I think it's terrible," he said, "the way they won't let us put up real tombstones anymore."

"They're so expensive, though," she said, "and such a waste of real money."

"But each tombstone's like a story," he said, "a little story we leave behind about our lives. It's terrible that he's just going to have an ordinary marker – Eldon Doucet – like a little headline in a local news-sheet – like he was nobody."

"He certainly wasn't a nobody," she said as they turned along the lane toward the lead limousine.

"It was awfully good of you to come," he said. She lit a Nat Sherman cigarette.

A gust of wind lifted loose snow over the tombs and a lone skier suddenly appeared gliding between Dutch elm trees, poling over a rise and down around a tall cylindrical black monument.

"Jesus," he said, "a cross-country skier."

"Now, I've seen everything," she said.

The skier, wearing a white suit and goggles, coasted down an incline, swooped around a russet marble slab, and then poled past the small domed crematorium.

"I'll be damned," he said, bewildered by a sudden remorse, bewildered by a recollection of how he had wounded his father, and for a moment he couldn't believe that his father was dead – that the *tock tock tock* had stopped, that he was standing there in the deep wet snow of the burial yard watching a lone cross-country skier, who looked like an arctic soldier, pass between the tombs. Close to tears he turned to Grace, gripping her arm.

"I didn't want to hurt him, you know, not at all."

"No, I'm sure you didn't."

"Anyway, to tell you the truth, I thought I'd die laughing when you said, 'Welcome to the scene of the crime.'"

"It was something my mother used to say."

"Your mother went in for crime?"

"No, no. She was very prim, very proper, and very poor. It was words she picked up from the movies."

He touched her gloved hand and she took off the glove as the driver opened the limousine's door. She touched his cheek. Crede helped her into the back seat and then stood looking off through the bare trees, looking at the trail of the arctic skier. "What are you looking for?" she asked.

"Nothing," he said. "It's just, for some reason, I remembered my mother telling me that 'It's God who's a sneak. He's sneaking around in our lives.'" And then, "She liked to talk about a necessary dignity. Anyway, I think you should go on alone. I need to walk."

He leaned into the limousine, toward the driver, and said, "Take the lady to wherever she needs to go."

He closed the door and walked away, going toward the other side of the burial yard, deliberately taking very deep breaths, opening his lungs to the crispness in the air, realizing that by the time he got out to Yonge Street and hailed a taxi, his own shoes would be ruined, he would be soaking wet from the slush, and would probably have caught a cold.

At home in the empty house, soaked to the skin, he stood in the hollow of the stairwell, shivering. He went upstairs to his bathroom, stripped off his clothes, and stepped into the shower stall, twisting the shower head to MASSAGE so that the pelting water would loosen his neck muscles, cranking the temperature dial to HOT, not just to burn the chill out of his bones but to steam himself clean of the glad-handing at the funeral Mass, the perfunctory piety displayed at the grave, and of Grace, who had expected him to want her.

After he showered, he put on the white terry cloth robe and stood in front of the bathroom wall mirror, drawing a large C into the steamed glass, and then he watched as a tear slowly formed on the glass and slid down through the C, leaving a trail glistening with mirrored light, like scar tissue, he thought.

"A mother knows when her boy is naked," he heard his mother say as he ran his tongue along the quick of his forefinger, the cut almost healed.

At last, the steam disappeared, leaving a ghost of a C on the glass.

Though he had shaved at seven in the morning, he shaved again – drawing the straight blade back and down his jaw and neck – till he was satisfied by the suppleness of his skin to the touch of his long fingers, and then, as if it were necessary for him to actually hear himself say words about his father that he had kept to himself: "You lousy backstroker. All your life you were swimming on your back, belly-up, swimming with the current, a dead fish," and he sang out,

> *The harder they come,*
> *the harder they fall,*
> *one and all…*

His robe fell open. He was standing straight up. He stepped back from himself in the mirror, startled again by his pale skin and how dark his crotch hair was. Taking hold of himself in the mirror light, he felt a hardening rush of exhilaration.

"It's in the blood," he said. "It's in the blood."

BUDDIES IN BAD TIMES

Arthur Aneale stood over the body of his friend, Trent. For two years Trent had looked sallow, hollow-eyed and frail, and yet now, lying dead in his casket he seemed only to be sleeping soundly, in the flush of health. That's a neat trick, Aneale thought, and wanting to talk about Trent, he drifted through the clustered men in the room, most of whom were dour and sullen, with some looking sick themselves. There was no one who seemed to be openly amiable, no one who seemed to want to catch his eye. By the front door, he sat down on a straight-back butler's chair and stared at his feet. Whenever he was by himself and feeling lonely he stared at his feet because they always seemed too big, as if they weren't his feet. His big feet reminded him of how lonely he was, and how cold it was by the door. He could feel the cold on his ankles. A burly man wearing a black leather Harley-Davidson jacket came hurrying in out of the wintry night and said, "You'll catch your death sitting here by the door."

Aneale turned into the room and saw that a tall young man was shuffling back and forth beside the open casket. He had a lean, pale face and he smiled as he paused to look into the crowded room, the eager smile of a man hoping someone would talk to him, and so Aneale got up and walked to the casket. "Are you one of his? Are you a relative?"

"Sorry, I'm not attached."

"Don't be sorry. It's too cold tonight to be alone, colder than a witch's tit," he said. "Let's get a drink." As if he'd been in the funeral home before and knew it well, he took the young man by the elbow and led him to a sitting room across the hall where there were tall stainless-steel coffee urns standing on an oak sideboard. "I've got a real drink here," Aneale said, grinning as he slipped a silver flask from inside his suitcoat pocket. He got two cups from a serving rack beside the urns and poured whisky into the cups as they sat down side by side on a small sofa.

"My name's Arthur Aneale."

"And mine's Jeff Trainer."

"I just could not tolerate it in there any longer," Aneale said, "all mope and no flounce. I mean, what is beyond belief is how he's lying there looking absolutely puckish. Like, I mean, *toujours* the little prince in his casket, whereas the real dead, let me tell you, are all those angry sluts skulking around in that room."

"I'm glad you look at it like that," Trainer said, his eyes shining. "It's exactly how I feel. But it's not for me to say." He leaned toward Aneale, and Aneale, loosening his tie, tapped Trainer on the wrist. "I don't know why when we die we agree to get laid out in a box so that a bunch of busy little bitches can gawk at us."

"It's certainly the custom," Trainer said, smiling.

"It's not my custom, not my little *frisson*, just in case you happen to be around the avenue when I die. It's bang the coffin shut for me, and bang the drum slowly," he said. "Here's to Trent, he was a peach."

"Here's to him," and Trainer raised his cup.

"He certainly would like this, the two of us sitting here so absolutely *très vite*, drinking to his health even if he did just die."

"That's how I feel," Trainer said. "I had my own intimacies with him but I certainly didn't know him like you must have, but he came across to me as being strong. Very strong. Of the earth. I certainly felt the earth in him."

"He loved his gardening," Aneale said.

"Really?"

"The last time I saw Trent he was looking lean as a whippet in his tank top in his garden, clomping around in his Greb boots, deadheading."

"Dead who?"

"Cutting dead heads off the flowers. Cut back, cut back, he always said, and they'll bloom better that way, come the spring."

"Really?"

Trainer, settling into the sofa, crossed his long-slender legs.

"Such is life, he used to say," Aneale sighed. "Cock of the walk one week, deadhead the next. Trent said that to me every time we took a trip." He told Trainer about a summer holiday that he and Trent had taken on the Gaspé Peninsula. "I remember there was a boy, just a kid, not exactly a chicken but close, we picked him up outside a ruined old church and this little sweetheart of a kid cottoned on to Trent, and the next thing we knew we couldn't get rid of him for the life of us and so we had to take him along." Trainer was listening with his head tilted to the side, as if he were comparing Aneale's memories with his own impressions of Trent. "I mean, the crazy thing was, we couldn't even talk to the boy, he only spoke French."

"I could have spoken French to him, *parlez-vous le ding dong*," Trainer said, laughing, as he held out a hand for no reason, just holding it out, letting it hang there, as if he were always ready to be helpful. Aneale saw that he had soft, very white, puffy hands.

Though he was dressed in a severe black suit and a silver silk tie and white French cuffs, he was wearing a red Mickey Mouse wristwatch. Aneale found the watch endearing. Trainer saw him staring at Mickey Mouse and said, "It's 9:15 in Disneyland. Mickey's going out to meet Pluto." He giggled and then, as if he didn't want any break in their conversation, he asked Aneale if he ever watched the afternoon soaps and *Dr. Oz* and *Dr. Phil*. "I'd like to think that we like the same things," he said, touching Aneale's knee, and he seemed so considerate, so unassuming and available, that Aneale said, "I'll certainly be on the avenue for a couple of weeks more. I mean, why don't we see each other? You, me, and Pluto?"

"I'd love to."

"You call me Arthur, I'm going to call you Jeff."

"Certainly wish you would."

"Let's have dinner, Jeff. At the Byzantium."

"I thought you'd never ask, Arthur."

"So let's just get secretarial for a minute and let's have your phone number," and while he was writing down the number in his *Gauguin in Ferrara* notebook, Aneale said, "Remember now, we've got ourselves a date. By the way, where are you from?"

"Where was I born?"

"Right."

"A dowdy little down-at-the-heels town deep in the Ottawa Valley."

"Well, no wonder I couldn't place your accent."

"My mother was part French," said Trainer.

"What do you do for a living? I mean, it's so absolutely boring to ask, but how did you run into Trent?"

"Me?"

"Right."

"I'm the undertaker's assistant."

"The undertaker?"

"Yes," he said with a soft, wry smile, waiting, as if he expected Aneale to be so uncomfortable that he might get up from the sofa, breaking their sudden intimacy. "You surprised?" he asked, touching Aneale's wrist again.

"No, I mean, well yes I am, a little bit. But after all, I mean, *toujours le monde*, there's men who are dying who've never died before."

Trainer threw his head back and laughed, but then he said, "I can't help myself. I look for that sour look, I've seen it before. Some kind of shudder." He tugged at his white cuffs showing pearl links set in gold and then he shrugged, as if entirely at ease with himself, suffering only a vague sense of resignation, of half-hearted regret.

"I was wondering," Aneale said, wanting nothing to impinge on their easeful warmth, "how'd you get the job?"

"I got it when I was fifteen."

"You mean you've been handling stiffs since you were a kid?"

"I sort of grew up with the dead," he said, smiling. He moved close to Aneale, telling him that there had been only one undertaker in his town when he was a boy, and often the undertaker had been so busy that he'd needed help. "Sometimes my father used to help him." His father had owned a small convenience store. The store had gone broke. An insomniac, he'd then worked as security at an all-night Chicken Shack on the highway out of town. "He was tired pretty much all of the time." Trainer sighed, perhaps a little too studied, Aneale thought, but nonetheless affecting.

"One day when I was fourteen, my father sent me over to the undertaker. He was too tired to go himself," he said. "After that, it worked out simple enough. When the undertaker couldn't get my father, he took me." While the other boys in town who had to work after school were delivering groceries or papers, he was busy embalming. "The whole thing really got going good when the undertaker said one afternoon that he needed a permanent assistant."

He chuckled, his eyes bright with the memory of that moment.

"You wanted to dress up stiffs for the rest of your life?"

"It's real interesting," he said simply.

"Don't you get tired of, like, touching the dead?"

"Listen," he said, eager to explain himself. "People don't understand what's got to be solved each time I go to work on a body. It's serious. They're persons. I don't want to do just a job. There's people who end up here in pretty bad shape, I mean, it's terrible these days. I can't tell you how bad some of the men look. Suppose I let them go out in their caskets looking awful? What'll their people who love them feel?" Aneale stared at him in wonder. "I've got to try to get a clear picture in my mind of what people expect to see," Trainer said. "I've got to find out what I can about the person I'm fixing. I'd never want to boast, but you might be awfully surprised by some of the results I've got while knowing almost nothing at all." He had his hand on Aneale's knee.

"You're absolutely out of this world," Aneale said.

"I'm glad you think so," he said, delighted. "Take your friend, Trent, I mean, he'd been quite sick. Big-boned, but when I saw him dead, what I saw, well, it was skin and bone country, he weighed only about a hundred and twenty pounds. So supposing I hadn't got a sense of him, hadn't got him right, how would you have felt?" Getting up, he said in a calm, measured intimate tone, "Come on back to the casket. I'll show you up close what I mean."

Aneale slipped his flask into his suitcoat inside pocket and followed Trainer back to the crowded front room. Several men were weeping. From others, a muffled laughter. And a couple of rough-trade youngsters were cruising the room, hoping to turn sorrow into a quick trick.

Aneale and Trainer stood beside the mahogany casket. They leaned over the body as if in heartfelt contemplation of the dead man's face.

"I'll bet he looks almost like you knew him," Trainer said.

"He took my breath away when I first saw him," Aneale admitted, confused because he was sure that two angry-looking men he didn't know who were in black suits and black shirts were pointing at him and whispering. He could feel their disapproval. He was sure of it. But then, maybe it was Trainer they disapproved of.

"It's not bad for the little I had to go on. Just a couple of snapshots. See how I've injected under the cheekbones. But if I had got close to him like you…"

"Me?" Aneale asked as Trainer put his soft puffy forefinger under Trent's chin and pushed the flesh up. "See," he said, looking into Aneale's eyes, his smile boyish, "there's a trick…tricks of the trade."

Aneale tried to smile but he felt a chill and buttoned his suit coat. His ankles and feet were cold. He was suddenly sure that Trainer, ingratiating and polite, had only been looking at him so intimately because he wanted to get a feel for his face. *Jesus Christ, he can't help it, he's been looking at me the whole time like I'm dead, like I'm already in one of his fucking boxes.*

"I think I should blow this pop stand," Aneale said, trying desperately to make a joke as he eased away from Trainer, embarrassed that he had uttered such a lame quip. "I think I'd better go."

"Okay, as you wish," Trainer said, checking his Mickey Mouse watch. "It's only ten after ten but no worry, we'll be in touch."

Aneale turned away abruptly, glad to say hello to one of Trent's old lovers, a grim, unshaven, and paunchy man who went in for chrome studs and leather hats. Aneale didn't like the man and felt only disgust when he said, "They're piling up on the other side." Nonetheless, he held close to him, keeping his back to the casket, and after a few minutes they agreed to step out of the "skank feel" of the funeral home, to stand on the sidewalk and smoke a Lucky Strike in the refreshing chill night air. Aneale, as his head cleared, felt rid of what had been a deeply disquieting unease in his bones. He was about to try an excuse that would allow him easily to say goodnight and go home alone when a man called from a car that had pulled up by the curb, "Mr. Aneale, Mr. Aneale."

Trainer was leaning out of the open window of the car, the neon funeral home sign lighting his face a lurid yellow. "Can I give you a lift, Arthur?" he called. "Go your way?"

Aneale was shocked, even a little frightened, to see him sitting there, waiting, so available, holding out his puffy white hand. "No, thanks," Aneale said curtly.

"He a friend of yours?" Trent's old lover asked.

"No, we were just killing a bit of time back in there," Aneale said.

"Well, we're all buddies...buddies in bad times. Talk helps."

In the morning, as the burial chapel bell tolled eleven, he stood at Trent's grave ankle-deep in wet snow watching Trainer attach a small wreath of lilies to the grey steel waterproof box that encased the casket. Aneale hunched his shoulders against the wind, tight-lipped and stern, feeling even more cold and alone than ever. Trainer, cradling in his open, grey-gloved palm a small crucifix that he had removed from the lid of the casket so that he could give it to the grieving family, looked trim and elegant in his tailcoat and striped trousers. He stepped close to Aneale as he moved around the steel box and paused to look intently into Aneale's eyes. Aneale, stamping his cold feet in the snow, lowered his head, refusing to look up. Touching Aneale's arm with the small crucifix, Trainer looked as if he might be offering a word of consolation to Aneale's ear when he whispered, "There's men who are dying who've never died before. I liked that. Very good. Very funny."

AND SO TO BED

All my friends call me Booker, not because I make book on the ponies or because I take after Booker T. Washington White, who was a slope-headed blues singer, but because I'm into books, not like a bookworm, but a dipper. I am a dipper. I walk up the beach of my mind looking for ashtrays in their wild state and POW. That's what I want, a POW on the page. So I buy two or three books a week and put my boots up and read them in the morning beside the window in my waterfront flat, which I get cheap because it's down by the warehouses where I've got a good view of the bay. Sometimes I go down to the docks and take a ferry to the island, just reading in the sun like there's no tomorrow, which I know there is because really I'm optimistic. I always hope for the best, and I do believe you always make your own luck. So I sit on the upper deck, dipping into a page when I've got an empty moment free from thinking. It's like picking a pocket, just like old Matthew Arnold, who was a kind of pickpocket, said it. The special moments when you see something real clear are everything, they're the touchstones. Some people touch wood, I touch stone.

But make no mistake. Old Booker is not touched in the head. Booker breaks loose in the evening. I mean, I try never to read at night 'cause reading is like the night air – there's strange creatures on the wing. So I prance and play, *Cool as the breeze on Lake Louise.* That's my song, and these days the song's getting sung at this small tiny nightclub that's got those plush velvet booths and an oval stage. Ovals always remind me of eggs. Big beginnings. And the new club singer, she's got this great billboard name, Empress Angel Eyes, and a long, loping walk with great legs like she just came in off the *veldt* out of some movie starring Meryl Streep doing another accent instead of acting. I like that. Anyway, the Empress showed me the other night an old picture of herself from years back playing the mouth harp and wearing little granny glasses. "You want to get anywhere," she says, "you got to look like whatever's going on. Granny glasses one day, décolletage the next. And I tell you," she said, sipping a double Scotch-on-the-rocks, "as singers go, Piaf had it lucky. Everybody wants to break your heart like Piaf except she breaks your heart better."

"Great God almighty," I said, "you're bang-on, you're right. Piaf's always been the touchstone."

"The what?"

"Once you've heard Piaf sing, you've heard the song," I said, and she says, "Yeah, I guess that's true…but you haven't heard me." And I said, "No, no, I haven't heard you," except I had, standing at the back of the nightclub the night before and she was no Piaf, nor was meant to be, but she could break my heart anytime, so – "That's a goddamn great insight," I said, and I meant it. "You're terrific, you know that?"

"No," she said, flat-out and deadpan like the thought had never crossed her mind. Which made me say, "Baby, you've got happenings going on, and happenings, in case you don't know, are when the light shines in your eyes full of surprise." She was wearing silver cowboy boots. She smoked Marlboros. Her corn-yellow hair had this great luminous glow in the lights from the stage. "You know what?" she asked. "When I was sixteen I slept with Janis Joplin the week before she died. I was just a kid, of course, looking for a little life. Action, you know." She threw her head back and laughed. She had these great full breasts and right away I wanted to make love to her.

"I got to be careful," she said, smiling.

"About what?"

"I been hurt a lot, man, so don't hurt me."

"You know," I said, "little moments like this are wonderful." I kissed her on the cheek, just this delicate little brush like she's got no heavy-duty trouble coming down on her from me. "Sometimes," I said, settling back so she could see she should relax herself, "I sit watching the water out my window – I live down by the waterfront – and all the little whitecaps are like special little moments, little moments like this."

Right then Eddie Burke, the owner of the club, who's heavy-set with these hooded eyes and a real sour temper like he sucks lemons to start the day and swallows the seeds, he sat down and said, "Getting to know my little Empress, eh?" He laughed, because actually we get along okay. I know he likes to gaff with the goof butts behind the tympani, and like all potheads he's possessive, which is why, when they get arrested, it's for possession. I like that. So he folded his hand over hers. "Before you," he said to her, "I had me an old black scat singer in here. I fired him in three nights. I found him fooling with one of the waitresses, man, and it wasn't because the old fucker was black. It was because he was old. I couldn't stand the idea of that old buzzard nosing around one of my tender tits." I laughed pretty much because Eddie expected me to laugh. Angel Eyes stood up and went to change for her show, and I said, "The world is too much with us, man." So me and Eddie locked hands across the table. After all, we'd been good casual friends for a few years, and good casual friends are hard to find. "I got a gut feeling for women," Eddie said, "and I'd really like to bag that woman, but mostly I like young girls. I shag young girls because I got a gut feeling for life." I saw that Eddie was a little looped, so I said: "*Nothing can be sole or whole / That has not first been rent.*" Eddie held my hand. He held it hard, with real feeling. "You're right," he said. "Don't nothing work if you don't pay the rent."

Eddie and I usually talked a lot upstairs in a small room where he had all these old Rock-Revolution posters on the walls, art deco mirrors and all kinds of love-shit stuff from the 1960s, like flowers and Mao doing his famous imitation of a dead moon with eyes, and this fantastic wrought-iron rack of scented votive candles in the shape of a heart. Eddie had stolen it from an old empty country church. "I don't pray but I'm all heart," he said, sitting there beaming at the lit candles. There were also two wide-assed easy chairs, some floor pillows, and a small brown rug.

On the first night that she was up there alone with me after her show, Angel Eyes said that the rug looked like a trap door, and she sat cross-legged on it. "One day you watch, I'm gonna drop outta sight," and I said, "Angel, you are outta sight."

So we sat drinking whisky, with me talking to her about old black blues singers I had met in bars, like Mississippi John Hurt and Otis Spann, both of them dead. She made me remember all my little stories about those guys and what I had read about them, and I told her these stories, like their deaths had really really touched me, which they had, they must have, because pretty soon I was sitting there as silent as a dog on a dead-end street, humming *How long's that old train been gone*, staring blankly, I guess, until she said, "Don't worry, man, someday the sun's gonna shine." I looked up and said nothing, but when she hunched forward in front of me on the prayer rug, I laid my hand on her shoulder like I was, in fact, the Book of Revelation, and I said, "Angel, you're the apple of my eye," and then I whispered: *"God appears, and God is Light / To those poor souls who dwell in Night."* Angel Eyes got all restless and shivery and touched my hand. "Man, God is dead," she said as serious as serious could be. "He's dead, and you ain't heard the real good news – we're free. Poems like that don't mean nothing."

"What they mean, if they don't mean nothing, is that everything's gone to hell, Angel," and I got to own up that I was wounded because she didn't seem surprised at all that I could quote so much poetry, like the woods are full of guys quoting poetry when there aren't even any woods anymore.

"You believe that?" she says.

"Believe what?"

"Hell 'n' stuff like that. You believe in God 'n' stuff like that?"

"Angel Eyes," and I tried to be reasonable, "that's not the question."

"Oh yeah, then what's the question on my mind?"

"Angel," I said, leaning close to her, "the question is, does God believe in me?"

"Oh, wow," she said, clapping her hands. "I like that, yeah, I can dig it."

"POW," I said, because I knew I'd got her, and suddenly she kissed me on the mouth, so sweet, so delectable, so delicious that I kept coming back night after night, figuring we'd get down to a little bootie, not to say some serious sex, but she kept an aloof air, and I mean aloof, while in that bar she's carrying on every night like she's open to any man who speaks to her, always listening like she's waiting for the right word to get said to her. Which drops the lead right out of my dick. I can tell you. Because I am nothing if not words. I know that for a damn natural fact. I am a word-smith. My word is everything. If I give you my word, I give you my heart. So after all these nights of stalling I've got to wonder, I've got to wonder if this woman's got any discretion. Is there any discretion in her ignition? I like that. Then, one night, I heard Eddie whisper to her, saying he really liked the way she spoke so softly, and she said, "Most women got voices that could cut glass." Eddie put his hand on the small of her back like he was the only proprietor of all the impropriety in the world, but she took his hand away, and I liked that, her shoulders back so that her breasts, sitting there so free under her sweater, looked full. And as she walked away Eddie said to me, "That's some tender tease trap I got singing for me, but she's playing too hard to get. I think she must be a little dykey." And I watched these other men like bird dogs hovering around her every night but I held to the shadows, trying to draw her eye to mine. Sometimes our looks did about meet and I smiled like I knew everything that there was to know, and one night I said, "I bet you got a dimple in the small of your back."

So early one morning after the two a.m. show, when Angel Eyes asked me if I'd rather go upstairs to drink with Eddie or sit and talk, I decided to hang out with her in the dark bar. "I wanted to sit with you tonight," she said. "I like your voice, you know that? Deep. I go by a man's voice." So we talked about this and that, keeping it light, but with my voice deep the way she liked it. When I got up to go home I touched her on the cheek and said, "You're still the apple of my eye."

The next night I sat down beside her and whispered a little poem to her:

The invisible worm
That flies in the night
In the howling storm,
Has found out thy bed
Of crimson joy:
And his dark secret love
Does thy life destroy.

She said she didn't know what it meant but it sounded wonderful. Then I told her about all the little things I'd noticed around that afternoon, my little white moments I called them; white, because they were what they were until we made them into what we wanted them to be, like walking on a quiet street and seeing what I thought was a dressed-up fifteen-year-old boy. "He was wearing a little suit jacket with peaked lapels and a porkpie hat, and it turned out he was a man of about seventy or so, and he had this rod with a little black box on the end of it in his hand, a battery box. Under the rod, moving along the sidewalk by remote control, I guess, was this tin car the size of his shoe, and I said, 'What're you doing?' and he said, 'I'm walking my car,' and he kept on going. He fucking well kept on going, walking his car." She laughed quietly and touched my hand, like for the first time she really cared, and I wondered what it was about a guy walking his toy car that would make her care.

"You're nice," she said. "I figure you talk just like those books you're always reading."

"Well," I said, "I try to be nice. Touch stone."

"Touch what?"

"It's just a little joke."

"You're very nice," she said and smiled.

"You don't know," I said, "how nice I can be. I've got shunts and bunts little girls don't know."

"Oh, I believe it," she said. She squeezed my hand and then went on stage, singing like she was singing for me: "*Never's just the echo of forever, / Lonesome as a love that might have been.*"

I went upstairs and drank whisky for an hour with Eddie and when I came down Angel Eyes asked if we shouldn't want to go together for Chinese food later on. The restaurant was a regular favourite all-night place for people who were in show business. The teapots were filled with cognac or champagne. Which is what show biz is. POW. Teapots of champagne. I like that. And there was this ventriloquist at the next table talking like Mortimer Snerd, "Snerd's Words for the Birds," – *Still waters runs wet* – and everyone laughed and got drunk. Eddie tried to tap dance, more tap than dance, because what he really liked to do was to dance on other people's heads. As the dawn came, Angel Eyes said, "The Empress wants to go home." Looking at me like there's no tomorrow, she says, "You making it my way?"

"Sure," I said, so surprised and drunk I found myself shaking hands with her.

Eddie scowled and I had this uneasy feeling that our friendship had just gone the way of a rat's lunch. We were no longer going to be casual on the beach. As Angel Eyes and I stood in the street, a real chill in the air in the dawn light, I buried my face in her hair, as much to keep from falling down as anything else, and whispered: "*The wan moon sets behind the white wave / And time is setting with me, Oh.*"

"Oh," she said, and I nestled in her arms in the taxi, my eyes closed to keep off the glare of light.

"It's real weird that I should be a singer," she said out of nowhere, "because my father was a mute."

"A mute?"

"Yeah. I would sing to him and he would sit there smiling with his mouth open."

"Nothing?"

"Nope. Not a word. It's weird, and I never told anyone that," she whispered, "so I guess I feel real close to you. Every time you speak I have to close my knees."

"Oh yeah?"

"You got that voice."

She lived in a small bachelor flat. I was tired and up to my eyeballs in booze and stood with my back to the wall as she unlocked the door. Inside, she got to undressing without a word and so I got undressed, too, saying, "Baby, this is gonna be the best. I told you we'd be the best and this is going to be it. Believe you me." When we were naked I looked at her and said, "Beautiful, you got great breasts." I felt like I'd been punched to kingdom come by drink and didn't know where my dick was. I was limp all over. She touched my throat, which made me jump, and then she lay down on the white sheets. When I touched the inside of her thigh she began to sigh, this slow humming, like *Amazing Grace, Ummmh* she goes, *ummmh*, and my blood was all in my head, in my eyes, and I mean, man, I started talking a blue streak and the Empress just lay back and said, "Gimme some, man," and I thought, *Oh Jesus, where are you when what counts is dead?* Then she was wanting me and I was trying to get hold of myself for all I was worth, which wasn't much since I was so soft, stalling with little whispers and *oodlie-koos, oodlie-koos.* And then I heard a bell ringing. "What in the hell is that?"

"Crown Life."

"What?"

"The insurance company next door, they got recorded bells that play over a loudspeaker every hour on the hour."

"My God," I sighed, playing for time, and so I sang out, "*The bells are ringing, for me and my gal...*" She opened her legs again and pulled me down and then she hooked her ankles over the small of my back and for a moment my mind went blank. I mean blank. No zip on the radar screen. And I had this strange feeling I was on a child's rocking horse. She was whispering little love words, rocking me in her arms, kissing my neck, and I was on a wooden horse going nowhere. And those blades of light came through the slat blinds, cutting my eyes, cutting into me, and I felt a little thickening. A little rise, and she was reaching for me and I eased into her and told myself that I had to keep moving, that I had to think about something else, either nothing or the whole world, hoping I'd harden up. I opened my eyes and saw in the light of the slat blinds that the headboard was a bookshelf packed with paperbacks. I got this terrific rush of relief. "Oh God, I want you," she sighed, and I thought if I could keep moving and remove my mind from my body, then maybe my body wouldn't let me down. It'd just keep going like I was not there and she was. So I began reading the names of the books, all my concentration on the book titles as I read back and forth across the shelf, worried in my mind, my hips humping up and down and I heard her little moan. But there was nothing there, not a title I knew, not one book, and I slumped and stalled and came to a dead halt because what little I had was leaving me.

I had nothing to say. There were tears in her eyes but she brushed them away. I stood up, feeling small. She lay staring at me.

I shrugged like Sheepish was my middle name, like there was no way out of the silence. "So, say something," she said, hunched forward, pinching the sheets, leaving puckers and creases.

"Come on," she said. "I been figuring all this time on us being together and I make the play and now you got nothing to say?"

"What's to say?"

"You could say you're sorry."

"Okay. I'm sorry," I said, standing still, my eyes closed.

"I hate men who say they're sorry," she cried, standing up so I could see how fine her long legs were. I stood there with my hands on my hips staring at the loose, rumpled sheets, each crease a little ripple, as if I was back beside my window looking down on the lake.

"Anything but sorry," she said, screwing up her mouth. "You could've said anything but sorry. That's the pits."

She suddenly leapt around the bed and hustled all my clothes and shoes into her arms.

"Come on, Angel," I said and held out my hand, letting her see how helpless I felt, like I'd lucked out and lost my touch. But she opened the door, so I tried laughing but she didn't laugh back.

"I told you not to hurt me," she said. "I believed in you, so you get out of here." And she threw my clothes and shoes into the hall.

"Okay, I'm not sorry."

"Then what are you?"

"How the fuck should I know?" I shouted like I was angry but I didn't know what else to say.

"You just sank like a stone," she said, stepping aside so I could pass. And even though I was bald-ass naked, I took one step, and another, and then I was out in the hall, staring in at her. She slammed the door. I could feel a real head cold coming on. "I ain't going to catch pneumonia for you," I yelled as I circled around real quick, picking up my clothes. My socks were back beside the bed, I could see them clear as day, and I was going to have to go barefoot in my shoes. I hustled up, dressing fast, afraid someone would see me and call the cops and report there was a man exposing himself in the hall, and to save time, POW, I pulled on my trousers and put my jockey shorts in my pocket. Luckily, my tie was knotted and I slipped it over my head, tightening it at my throat, like no problem, man, and strode down the hall. If I'd only had my socks on, I'd have been as cool as the breeze on Lake Louise.

ANYBODY HOME?

Leonard Cholet was a lean old doctor in his late seventies who had dyed black hair and a domed forehead. He wore loose, double-breasted suits with padded shoulders. He unbuttoned my shirt, tapping my chest, listening to my heart. "To you," he said, "a pounding heart is a problem. To me, a long time ago a heart murmur was more than I could hope for." Unopened envelopes cluttered his desk. I could feel his breath on my cheek. He tapped again. "Anybody home?" and the doctor laughed, saying, "Don't listen to me. I talk because there's nothing else to do at my age. You should listen to your own heart, eh? How's that for a little truth, except most people nowadays try to think with their head instead of their heart."

He had a perfectly pressed three-point white handkerchief in his breast pocket. The old floor creaked as he walked back and forth. I closed my eyes. For a moment there was silence. I lifted my hands. "What you got there?" he said. I opened my eyes and looked around. "Where?" He laughed. "Between your hands. You look like you're holding something." I shook my head. "Memories maybe?" he said. "I got memories. Memories are made of what you're looking at. Me, what I hold onto." He took a flat wooden stick and his stainless-steel pencil-light. "Open your mouth. I got to look inside. You're tense, you know that. For a guy that looks so calm you're very tense." I closed my eyes again, listening to his creaking floor, creaking footsteps, my own footsteps last night as I crossed her parquet floors, *the walls white and the floors loose from dampness and there was only a tubular table holding the TV in the room,* "And say aah," the old doctor said, *dampness from it being in the basement,* "Aah," *and the white plastic padded headboard, foam-filled pillows, and she sighed, lay back and sighed so luxuriously, slate eyes, breasts lolling to the side, hips narrow, and small delicate feet, discreet little cries like being half-ashamed,* "Ahh," *and then blowing smoke, saying that at home around the house she liked to wear a Blue Jays ball cap when she hunkered up late at night doing her nails, hummed out of her skull, she said, by evangelical television shows, and she always slept till about ten, sleeping healthy, she said,* "Look, no stress marks, that's the selfsame pure skin I was a born baby with."

"But the only link," Cholet said, "with those years after the war – you hear what I'm saying – is my son, who's now like a big boot. With a hole in it. There's nothing wrong with your throat, but with him and his heart, there's something wrong. See, he likes to wear those yellow construction-worker boots with little steel clips on the toes. Me, I keep to my slippers with the sponge soles and my room with the lamplight like a small escape hole in the darkness. But for him, the way I look at it, it was a mistake my making a marriage, a man like me." He put the stethoscope, which reminded me of the black gumdrops I loved as a boy, into a case and snapped it closed, saying, "A man like me should never have married, but anyway she pretty soon went away, leaving my son to do something big, to live." The alarm clock went off, a toneless beeping, and Cholet hit the clock with the flat of his hand, and he turned away, making pencil notes in his little book. "You got a heart like a horse, so what's to worry for you?" I looked up at an old pewter lamp hanging from the centre of the ceiling, six sockets empty. Cholet, standing with one hand in his suitcoat pocket, lean and severe in the shadow-light, put his notebook away, saying, "I give you more powerful pills, don't worry. You want to calm down, you'll calm down." He lit a Gitanes, inhaling deeply, and for a moment, in that light, I thought, he's got one blue eye and one green eye. "So now this son of mine," he said, handing me my shirt, "he owns pigeons, some homing pigeons he tells me – cages up on top of the roof – and he says no matter what he does to them, doesn't feed them, twists a wing, it doesn't matter, they always come home to him, and others he's got are called carriers. To me, it sounds like a disease. He sends messages to I don't know who, maybe no one *settling down in her underpants with little wing bows, sparrow wings if they could fly, bare-breasted at her table, polish-remover bottle open, and spread her fingers on the table, long nails, rubbing them clean, the cap pulled down over her eyes.*

"Sometimes I put in a case of beer and a guy comes by. You don't mind me telling you, eh? I mean, we know what's the score. A little girl's got to be with a man every now and then but always they got that question, you know, moon-faced they look at you asking, Was it good? Was I the best? but never saying love, never a little love word, the last guy standing in the doorway on the way out, that's what he wanted to know before he can go, so I says, 'At least you got your dry-goods store, Henry, and at least you're a good bowler,' and his eyeballs popped like I poleaxed him. Anyway, what I worry about is my nails. If you ever been a typist, you know those big rooms all carpeted for quiet and a hundred girls plugged into headsets, the only thing breaking the rhythm is someone breaks a nail. But what you got to face is it's always guys who are already lovers who got to ask that question, you know, Was I good? which they've been asking since they got off the tit and onto apron strings. Just losers, which we all are anyway. You

play the game and you throw boxcars, you crap out, and maybe it's wrong, but it comes up boxcars," and standing by the window, Cholet, his coat rumpled from sitting all morning in his chair, hooked his forefinger into the ring on the dark green window blind and with a little tug he ran the blind up, letting in the late-afternoon light. He blinked and shied away from the light while I buttoned my shirt, standing in the shadows. "You've got a good heart, so look after it," he said. "I'll walk out with you."

Going down the stairs, a light scarf knotted at his throat because there was a chill in the air, he stopped on the bottom stair and took hold of my elbow, almost affectionately, and suddenly I felt a tenderness. He shook his head, saying, "The whole thing was a mistake, that's the truth. The big thing is maybe life itself is a mistake. God made a mistake. He didn't intend any of this, but somehow it works out in its own way, like my little table and desk, nice pine pieces. Twenty years ago I bought old chairs and things like that, secondhand, and one day a man who never paid a bill but just did odd jobs to look after his debts, he said, 'While you're away, Monsieur Cholet, I'll fix the furniture and when you come back you won't know where you live.'" There were bread crusts thrown on lawns and grey pigeons pecked at the crusts. Laundry had been hung on a front porch and two black women wearing bandanas were gathering fruit and tomatoes that had fallen out of a torn shopping bag. Cholet walked the inside line of the sidewalk, holding close to the walls. "I was going away, you see," he said, "for two weeks to fish, because one thing I like about this country is the dark water, back in a cove where it's calm like you can see the dust floating. And this man, he said while I was away he'd clean off the thick old paint so I'd see how beautiful the wood was. For two weeks I sat in my boat in the rain and came back to the tables and

chairs all waxed a honey colour, a room full of junk wood looking like a treasure, and he was right, I didn't know where I was,
and he said to me, beaming, happy, 'Monsieur Cholet,' he said,
'now these are just like you had roots,'"

*her spread fingers, leaning
on her elbows, working the little brush, cotton ball buffing her nails,
very calm and half-naked, wearing the baseball cap, and high-
heeled shoes lined up along the baseboard of the wall that had one
window at lawn-level to the street – some shoes expensive and some
fluorescent satin and rhinestone clusters on the toes.* "I got the inside
line on losers," she said. "Every day I listen to twenty losers at the
hairdresser's, ladies under the hair dryers who like to gamble, you
know, place a bet with the manicurist who's a tout for some bookie,
because it's private, you know. Gambling is private like playing with
yourself, get a tense little high with every bet, take a risk. I once knew
a girl who could just cross her legs and squeeze hard and get a rush,
the flush of the rush. You come down, go up, like in escalator land. I
walked along with old Cholet because I had nothing to do. I had
no one at home. *"It beats boredom, I mean, what's more boring than
crossing your legs all day,"* she said, *blowing on her nails under the
lamplight, hands almost a man's but long, tapered and beautiful like
clean bones in the light, and holding them out, palms up, spread fingers.* "See, I'm clean, got nothing to hide," *and she laughed and
clapped her hands, the whack sounding hollow in the white room.*
"You know those shoes," *she said, standing up,* "I don't wear them
nowhere, not even when I'm dancing 'cause I just like trying them
on. I put on some nylons, you know, expensive, and a garter belt, and
slip them on like I was a man looking down at myself trying on
ladies' shoes, except I'm the lady so I get a double rush, action both

ways, which is the gambler's dream. A win-win situation, so I can't lose."

Though old Cholet had been in his rented office rooms for years, no one called out to him, no one seemed to know him. He passed Ram's Curry Shop and Sam Mi's Trading Company, the walls hung with a hundred wigs and hairpieces. "Anyway," he said, holding up his hand like a cop as we crossed the street, "before the war I was a doctor in a part of Paris where there were clothing and sewing shops, poor and mostly Jewish, but I wasn't Jewish. I had a second-floor office up off a lovely wrought-iron stairwell painted white, like iron lace, and marble stairs, an office all frosted glass panels with pansies etched into the glass, a horsehair couch, and the first entirely naked woman I saw ever in that little room was in that frost light. Absolutely still she stood. I walked around and around her, stunned by the white curve of her belly. For some reason I thought, 'This is the curve of condolence,' above that blackness between her legs. Then soldiers came a few years later and herded all the Jews and me, too. They came right into my home and took me off in the trains."

He held me by the elbow again. "You know, you're a good listener," he said. "But the trouble with a good listener is you don't know for sure whether he's listening." He laughed and I said, "What can I say?" as we stepped into the grey light of the Parthenon Room. Cholet continued his story: "Anyway, I was no Jew. I went into a rage in circles, how could they do such a mistake, and terrified, I told them to take down my pants, they'd see, and when they didn't, I did. I held my cock, my own self out to them like an offering, my proof." He sat down with his back to the wall, facing the stage in the big empty restaurant. There were plastic olive-coloured leaves and grapes hanging from the crossbeams over the bar. The jukebox was playing and two north-country Indians were sitting alone in a corner, aimlessly rolling red dice along their table-cloth, calling out, "Six, your point is six. Make a six, six..."

"You see, I look back," he said. "It's like one day I find myself watching – because nothing could be hidden in the camps – a young boy and girl making love, and they had the skin and bones of old, old people, looking like they would have looked if they'd lived a long life. They made love furiously, whispering over and over love words and making love like lunatics, nearly killing them-selves because they had no more life coming. Some of us watched, and we knew what they were doing, killing themselves off quicker, which in a way we envied because we kept our hearts hidden. Otherwise I don't remember much except for the sound of the box-car wheels clicking on the rails – that doesn't go away – and baby shoes, piles and piles of little shoes. I'd seen men slide off what we called the flute, the board with the bum holes over the cess pit, fall off into the shit and drown. A terrible thing, a man swallowing shit. After I was out and on my feet, I'd lost an eye but I felt good because again I could smell tobacco on myself. I bought a suit, a good suit, heavy tweed, brown but with a green thread all through so it looked almost dark green. I had this one eye with an eyepatch and sometimes I found myself standing staring at myself in shop windows like the windows were mirrors, and before I got myself out of Paris I thought I'd get a glass eye. I was blue-eyed but I got a green eye to match my good Sunday suit, which seemed right in a wrong kind of way, like a joke on a joke. Like for a while I ate only kosher food, awful-tasting stuff, a non-Jew more Jewish than the Jews, but now I eat anything, junk food, it doesn't seem to matter, *as she walked over to the window wall and stepped into purple suede pumps, laughing and parading, then planting herself and angling her left foot like she was on stage, chin up, mockery-full of herself and full of nakedness and silence in the room, the feel of eyes, my smile, all the approval needed. She said her father'd had his own dream about her, too, "'cause he was in construction, and he loved being the boss 'cause he said life is for steadfast guys, that's the way he talked. He wanted nothing to do with windsucker guys, guys who had small dreams and held on to them. He made model airplanes, you know, paper and balsa wood, and he went into all these big summertime competitions on the island, trying to win and betting he would win. He was a big bettor on himself. 'Money talks and bullshit walks,' is what he said. So one day another flier says to me, can he have a date, and before I can say yes or no my old man says his daughter don't go out with no windsucker guys and laughs himself blue, saying, 'Walk, walk,' which was the nicest thing my father ever said about me," and down she sat with her legs stretched out, still wearing the baseball cap, staring. "It's all a gamble. Look at me, where I ended up. A hairdresser, and I make a bet on a horse every day. You'd be surprised how many women are throwing their bread away every day just to get a little action in their lives. You'd be surprised at what's humming under the hair dryers. I lose like everyone else except one day I parlayed a real payoff into some big bucks and I decide the hell with it, time to come up in the world, move out of this here basement and across the street, to a small apartment. So I take a place after talking to the super and I got no furniture, which you can see, so he says he'll help carry what's around, and I know he's hoping for a little action with me himself. He's got the mattress, a single size, you know, and I got the box spring, which weighs nothing, and he gets it across the street and I'm coming and then, right in the middle of the road carrying a goddamn box spring, a car hits me,* "But what happens," Cholet said, "even when there's nothing, what we called nothing, and this is remarkable enough in itself, when there was nothing to live for, even in the camp we played cards. We played with little dirt-marked cards, all the one-eyed kings and jacks passed hand to hand, hoping for a little luck, good or bad. It is so strange the way we become what we have shared, a little hope," and he smiled, crossing his skinny legs.

"What I mean is, now there are four of us. We're not friends necessarily, but we found each other here in this city that we'd never heard of before – men lucky to be alive anywhere, nobodies from nowhere, three Jews and me, and what am I? Nothing, and it's our home but not our home, so there we are playing cards every Friday night with a man, a young Chinese who's our pharmacist, in one of the guy's high-rise, very nice with all white rooms with white rugs, a round table. He plays poker almost every night, this Chinese. It seems gambling's in their blood. And stacked on the floor against the wall a foot deep on one side of the table are *Playboy* and *Penthouse* magazines from ten years back, and the same thing on the other wall, except it's *Popular Mechanics*, and if your cards are no good, you sit and take your choice thumbing through these books. *She laughed hard, circling the table, high heels clacking on the loose parquet floor, pulling her cap over her eyes, naked arms open,* "I ask you, someone who gets hit by a car while carrying a box spring is in big trouble, right? That's boxcars when you get hit while hustling a bed in the middle of the road. I mean, that's a signal, man. So I moved right back down here into the basement. I mean, this is where I live, the most roots I got, I guess, and I never gambled since because when you get a sign you got to go with it. No apartment for me. So I'm easy, very okay, I don't break my nails, I don't break my* *heart, I'm a good dancer and I got some nice shoes, right?* A young girl strode out of the kitchen, a jacket of beads and tassels draped over her bare shoulders. Cholet ordered saganaki and a salad of black olives and onions in oil. "Black olives with good spices, you know how hard they are to find?" he asked. "No," I said, and he said, "Say aah," and laughed. I laughed, too, and opened my mouth. He shook his head and smiled. "I like you. A little tense but you're all right. You would have been okay where I was. And here you are okay, too. What's to worry? You got a heart like a horse."

The small stage was spot-lit for the girl. Her cigarette burned to the filter tip in an ashtray while she danced. She clomped around in a circle, sometimes cupping her breasts, chewing gum. The Indians paid no attention, laughing, rolling the dice, calling numbers, "Crap, ace-deuce." "This doesn't go on long," Cholet said, eating olives and sipping brandy, and soon the girl was gone and he said, "The funny thing is, there are apartments above these stores and this bar and all the time, if you listen, there's a child above here. She runs up and down what must be a long hall. I don't know why I'm so sure it's a girl but I suppose it's because what she makes me think of is my son." Cholet lit a Gitanes and folded five dollars under the saucer on the table, nodded to the unshaven bartender, and knotted his scarf. *In the open doorway, her crossed arms under her breasts afloat in the lamplight, she said, "You know what's nice? Most guys you meet the first time all they got is yack yack about themselves, right? But with you there's no yack yack." "Maybe I got nothing to say." And she said, "Maybe so, but that's why I wanted to take off my clothes for you earlier, like a little present, you know, because if sometimes you got nothing to say it doesn't mean you've got to lie and say something." Her hand out, touching, wistful, "You got my number, right, if you want to call, okay? And you know what? I'm*

gonna put on my pyjamas and go to bed, and have a real good sleep.
Thanks to you, I feel real good," the door closing on the early morning,
and out in the street a low-hanging mist, dong of the bell in the city hall
tower and a damp coolness soothing in the air, coming home, looking
for some thread of light

and a neon sign flashed down the street. "So there we were, you see," Cholet said, walking toward the stone gate, "surrounded by magazines, motors, private parts. We are four old men dealing each other a hand in the middle of nowhere except for what we share, numbers, which make us closer than most men, numbers which are everything, and nothing tattooed on the arms. Last Friday we played till five in the morning and someone says it's the last pot, like a last chance at life, so all bets are doubled. And he says, 'You know what, let's play our numbers,' like you sometimes see people in beer halls playing with dollar bills, playing Bullshit Poker, where what they do is they pair up the numbers on their bills. And we laugh a little but it seems like a good joke at so late an hour so we bet, the four of us, no cards necessary. But now our Chinese friend is left out and sour because he's got no chance to get even on his losses. With each call there's more money and finally a big pot. So there we are facing each other, stiff in our white shirts still buttoned at the wrists, palms flat on the table, and the Chinese says, 'Okay, show what you've got,' but Jacob, he says to the Chinese like he's delivering a death sentence, 'There's some secrets you don't lie about,' and he calls two pairs, sixes and eights. But the way it works out, two pairs and Avrom's three threes are not good enough because I am three nines with a four and a five and so Avrom says, pushing all the money at me, smiling, 'Cholet,' he says, 'you're a big winner,' and I said yes, my heart beating, yes, and we all put on our coats like we always do at the door, laughing, and went home in the dark,"

walking away from her through the park, a misty night, street lamps in the elm leaves, with no lights on in the houses along the street except from my front window, the floor lamp left on when there was nobody else home. In the dark, I saw myself standing at the window, calm but hunched, my heart pounding, staring into my reflection, with her saying thanks to me for saying nothing and with me left wondering what was there to say to Cholet, except nothing.

POODLES JOHN

Poodles John owned a small clothing store. He was called Poodles because he always carried Benny, a small poodle, in the crook of his arm. He drove a big white car with old-fashioned fin-tail fenders. He had an easy smile and a little bulge of baby fat under his chin. In the late afternoon, with his car parked by the curb, he liked to stand outside the store wearing a one-button-roll suit – preferably a pearl-grey lightweight flannel – straight-last shoes, a white-on-white shirt, and in the winter a dark blue Bennie topcoat, narrow at the waist and flared at the hem. He thought that calling the dog Benny after his topcoat was still very funny. "Funny is as funny does," he always said to his clerks in the store. "Today we sucker the soft touches."

"You got the touch, Poodles?" his clerks said, laughing.

Poodles John lived with a woman a year older than himself, a handsome woman with auburn hair and full breasts who was in her late thirties. She had a loping walk. "You got racehorse legs," he'd told her, "and good lips, not those thin razor jobs like some women who'd just as soon cut your heart out as look at you." She no longer laughed when he tried to compliment her. "Old Luella's got the legs built for speed," she said one morning, smoothing her nylons, "but I'm slowing down. It's not the drop in the tits," she said, "it's under the arms that worries me."

Poodles liked the fullness of her body, remembering his mother before she died, the flushed warmth of Luella's flesh as she sat in front of the mirror listening to an alarm clock radio, keeping what she called, "A little calm before the storm." One soft spring night Poodles yelled, "What goddamned storm?" and Luella looked at him mournfully. "You only prove you don't know what's out there, waiting for us," she said, and Poodles told her he could not stand waiting for a bus let alone waiting for what he didn't know was there. Now he had to watch the wary look in Luella's eyes as she sat slumped forward on the side of the bed. He had admired the straight way she walked, her aloofness, and he always tried to walk with his own shoulders thrown back, sure that his ability to keep calm allowed him to handle other men wisely, the way he handled hookers and the clerks in his store. But now she said, "I don't know what I'm going to do."

"About what?"

"About getting old. I'm getting old."

"To me," he said, "you look terrific. We got nothing to worry about, me and you."

"You're such a con artist, Poodles," she said and shook her head. "Like you say. I got the racehorse legs."

"You better believe it, baby."

"I'm going to the glue factory, Poodles."

"This is no goddamn glue factory," he said, slamming his hand against the wall. "I ain't no scuzzbag and neither are you. I'm telling you to think good about yourself. I think good about myself and I think good about you. But if you wanta think bad about yourself, there's nothing no one can do."

He smoothed the lapels of his suitcoat. She put her head in her hands. He was worried she was going to cry. He picked up Benny and went out, driving slowly downtown. He took in two deep, calming breaths as he strode into the store carrying the dog. His clerks called out, "You got the touch today, Poodles?" He put the dog in its hamper behind the counter. "I always got the touch," he said, and the two clerks laughed. "Magic man, that's me," and he was pleased, going upstairs to the room he rented over the store. But as he stepped into the grey light of the bare room and saw the unpainted walls, the daybed and the card table, the phone and the slat blinds, all his good feeling drained away. *It's all her fucking fault, the bitch.*

Poodles closed the blinds. He ran a poker game in the afternoon in the upper room. He was a good dealer, stern-faced, and his fingers always fast. He broke open a new Bicycle deck and a carton of cigarettes. A long time ago an old dealer named Herschel, who never drank liquor but still died of cirrhosis of the liver, told him to give players a little something free. "It's a touch," he told him, "and they think they're among friends, and there's no one you can fade faster than a guy who thinks he's among friends." Poodles set out tinfoil pouches of potato chips along with the cigarettes. Emptying the ashtrays, he sat down, worried about Luella, who'd become so erratic, often breaking into tears that left him speechless. He'd had enough of keeping his mouth shut all his life, *what with all the shit and trouble it took to get a fistful of anything.* And he remembered bitterly when only a few low-life gamblers had come in the door and he'd had to scuffle and scramble, since he was running the game for a big Greek who had fronted all the money. He'd always had to try to skim something for himself while running the game and trying to take a little betting action on the phone at the same time. The players had complained about the phone ringing and he had sweated a lot. He'd stuck his betting slips, little roll-your-own cigarette papers, to his sweating arm while laying cards around and nobody liked that. *That was the ass end of it all,* Poodles thought, remembering how the Greek had come by and taken a lady's lipstick mirror from his vest pocket and hunched forward on the daybed clipping his razor moustache with small scissors, saying, "You're in the phone book, Poodles. You're Poodles Enterprises, but you're not turning shit. You take in loose change that don't pay the rent. You think, eh? You think what to do, Poodles, but until then, no more front money. You're on your own with your dinky dog. Do me a favour, eh? Get rid of the dog. It's humiliating, a big man with such a little dog. It's unnatural."

Poodles had opened up on his own, working three hookers in the Strathcona Hotel. He liked his girls, and one of them, Carrie, a girl with corn-yellow hair and small breasts, had real talent. Men asked for her and he appreciated her talent. He wanted his girls to do well, and one day when he was sitting with Carrie in her hotel room, her Kleenex box and washcloth on the floor beside the bed, he told her she was terrific, that she had a real gift, and it was too bad that she wasn't better-looking so that she could have made a big buck. Carrie only smiled and said, "Well, what're you going to do? You do the best you can." Poodles had been moved, and at the end of the week he gave her an extra fifty dollars because he now had six girls working for him, and he laughed, saying, "Never give a sucker an even break." *Suddenly I'm right where I want without really trying, he thought, which is I got a string of girls and my own ass ain't on the line in my own premises. So maybe I should say to myself that me and Lou should take a holiday.* At home Luella shuffled around looking glum and sometimes when he came up the walk he saw her staring out the window *like one of those women in ghost movies, always staring out the upstairs window.* One night he came upstairs and stood quietly beside her, looking down into the street through the thick leaves of a crimson maple. There was a light breeze. "Beautiful," he said. Someone had cut the grass and he could smell the sweetness. "Just take a whiff of that," he said, touching the small of her back. Then the man who owned the house came down the street holding hands with a willowy black girl and Poodles said disdainfully, "Jesus, even I draw the line at coons. No self-respect, man." Luella shrugged, indifferent to the little distinctions he drew between himself and other men. "Sometimes," he complained, "you treat me like I'm any low-class hustler." Because his business was now bigger, he knew he wasn't ordinary and so worried more about her when she refused to laugh at his deprecating jokes and made him feel that he had no right to believe he was a shrewd, respectable businessman. "I worry about you all the time, baby," he said, but she only muttered that she was going out for a walk.

At the end of the week he took her to Puerto Rico. It was the off-season and too humid and hot, but she had been so morose around the apartment, staying out later and later at night, that he had decided to get out of town. On their first morning in San Juan, he woke up and found her staring into the mirror as if they were still at home.

"Jesus, Lou. Six thousand miles and the sun's out and you're sitting inside in the room in the dark."

She was watching him in the mirror. He was taken aback by the mournful, almost pitying look in her eyes. He brushed his hair back with the flat of his palms. "What are you doing, eh?" he asked as calmly as he could.

"I was thinking about my father."

"And what?"

"He was a good man."

"So he was a good man. That got him a cup of coffee."

"Aw, Poodles, don't you ever think about your dad? Don't you ever think about anyone?"

"I think, baby," he replied, alarmed because she sounded as if she felt sorry for him. "All the time I think about you. I got you on my mind like a brick. The question ain't what I'm thinking but how come you're thinking what you're thinking, which I don't know about although I'm the guy you live with, and all of a sudden I'm the guy you don't talk to."

"That's funny," she said. "My father didn't talk to me either. Hardly ever."

"So maybe he had nothing to say."

She threw her shoulders back and smiled. He felt a little chill, the short hairs bristling on his neck. She stroked her throat and said, "All my childhood my father gave me dolls, Punch and Judy dolls, and puppet dolls on strings, and he'd dance the dolls in the air inside a box. They had big glass eyes, staring eyes like insane flowers that followed me all around my bedroom. Years later, you know, some nights when we used to go dancing with the spotlights in the mirror behind us, the lights looked like big flower eyes and sometimes I felt high, like I'd done some dope and felt filled with petals spinning there in the eyes of all the faces watching me."

The wistful longing in her voice made him reach out, surprised at his open extended hand, the puffy flesh, surprised at his sudden arousal, and he whispered, "I want you, Lou."

"Yeah, but do you want my mother?"

"Who's talking about your mother?" he said sourly.

"That's the point. My father would not talk about my mother. She went off when I was just a kid and he refused to ever talk about her. Said such talk would only hurt us."

"So?"

"So, the more and more I look in the mirror, the more it's like I'm finding my mother."

"Jesus H. Christ," he said, wanting to shake her by the shoulders. Yet what he really wanted was to let her make love to him, so he stood behind her, seeing himself naked in the mirror, pudgy and white and vulnerable, but she looked up at him and said, "It's like someone's moving in on me, another face, and I'm sure it's her face. I mean, I'm nearly forty and when I'm forty I'll look in the mirror and know who my mother was."

That afternoon she sat near the pool and out of the sun. She was silent and wore big black sunglasses. He couldn't tell what she was looking at. He was wounded and said, "You know what you look like? One of them women in movies whose husband's just been killed, sitting in church, you know, funeral wop, eh!" He laughed but she only touched her throat and he stared at the empty swimming pool. It was an acid green, a polished shining surface with a glare that hurt his eyes, and he said, "Goddamn, this is crazy. There's no one swimming." He leapt in awkwardly, and when he bobbed back to the surface he called out, "You do what you do, baby, but don't do it to me. Don't do what you're doing to yourself to me."

That evening in the casino, when he lost money at the crap tables, he said nothing but blamed her. She had killed his good feeling, his glow *like I knew when I walked in the door the glow was gone and the man in the monkey-suit smiled at me like I had "loser" written all over my kisser,* and he'd thrown the dice with no confidence. He'd had no luck and lay awake in bed beside her, angry as the whirring air conditioner drowned out the sound of the sea, and then she blurted out, "I always wanted to try hang gliding, that's what I wanted to do. Just like you see in the movies, that's the way

I wanted it. It must be perfect, drifting on the air currents like that, all alone up above everything, totally silent in the sun, just hanging there, the whole world clear. I read somewhere that that's what it's like if you die, and then you don't die but come back."

Poodles lay in the dark with his hands folded on his chest. "Yeah, and me," he said, "I wanted to be a winner, in a big way. I wanted to be a winner and instead I take a beating for two thousand and end up in bed with an out-of-work hang glider."

"You know what, Poodles?" she said, leaning over him so that her long hair brushed his bare chest. "You and the dog are a real team, you know that? You're going to end up with Benny in a basket. How about that?"

"So what?" he cried, leaping up and away from the frightening touch of hair moving across his body. "Who gets laid around here anyway?"

He turned off the air conditioner and went out to the balcony, saying, "So sweat! Take a little heat. You can stand to shed some weight."

"You bastard," she cried. "You'll be sorry."

He was sorry yet he said nothing more because he'd already said too much, and he sat in the plastic deck chair listening to the roll of the sea. The next day they went home.

As weeks went by, he spent more time in the store, needling his clerks and running his game and his girls and hustling cheap suits off the rack. He left ties, shirts, cuff links, and socks to the clerks. "That's what clerks are for," he said. "The extras, and always they should remember they're also the extras." Cradling the little dog, he referred to himself as an outfitter. "What you call yourself is what you are, at least as far as I'm concerned," he said to the clerks. He didn't let his clerks get close to him, but he was avuncular with his hookers, thinking he had a special touch with women and that he knew how to handle them. He called the girls, who were lean and young, his ladies of the evening. "And ladies," he said sternly, "there's always a fat man trying to get into a thin woman and we want some fat for ourselves."

He met the girls once each week in the Mercury Club on Victoria Street. It was a bar with a small dance floor and a jukebox, owned by an ex-boxer who was now a referee, who wrote angry letters supporting capital punishment to the newspapers. It was a bar popular among men in their late thirties and early forties, and he gathered the girls in the early evening when the bar was almost empty. Moxie Mensler, the boxer, would sit down for a moment, take his brown envelope of edge money for letting the ladies operate out of the bar, and then a waiter brought raw hamburger on a saucer. Poodles fed meat pinched between his forefinger and thumb to Benny as the girls came in. They smiled at the dog and one girl, who liked to wear a man's tie and suitcoat during the day, surprised them because she had knitted little wool pouches for the dog's paws, like little mittens for the winter. Poodles was so pleased with the pretty mittens that he put them on the dog's paws, whatever the weather. Now the girls all brought ribbons or little strings of bells to their meetings. Poodles liked the tone of these early evenings and he felt like a solid businessman *because I'm my own fucking man with collateral and collateral makes the man in other men's eyes,* which is why the bank manager in the branch he had banked in for a decade had suddenly come through the gate the other day and taken his hand, wishing him well. At first, Poodles had been afraid that something was wrong, but then he was pleased that he had kept control of himself, suddenly feeling that the man's hand coming out to him was like a confirmation, a blessing. He later told Luella that a bank manager is the one man who really knows how things add up. Poodles, standing there in the hush of the small bank branch, had decided to open up a new store.

Luella had little to say. He thought she was in a sleepwalking state. She would suddenly tell him strange stories about her father and how he had always calculated his life according to magic numbers: 5...8...17...28... "Who told him they were magic?" she said sternly. "And why would he believe it when the only magic he ever made was making my mother disappear out of his life?" Poodles thought for a moment, then said, "Every sucker's got a system. I got smarts." She stared at him sullenly and smiled, as if she had seen him in a new light. "That's right," she said, "you're too smart to get sucked in by anybody's magic, Poodles." She went out, as she did nearly every afternoon, to a private ballroom-dancing class where she said she was spun around elegantly by a young, slightly effeminate man who sometimes kissed her hard on the neck as he folded her back in his arms, *and she's got the nerve to tell me the only time she's treated elegant is by some lousy fag hustling in a dancing school. It's so corny it's disgusting.*

"Boys," he said to the clerks one day, "let me give you a little piece of Poodles' advice. The only way to handle women is leave 'em alone. Let 'em make up their own minds and then you don't get blamed for nothing, 'cause that's what most people get off on, is blame, to make you feel smaller than they feel small." The clerks shuffled uncertainly in front of Poodles, who was slumped in his chrome chair, lost in his own thoughts until a man came in wearing thick glasses and worn shoes. Poodles smiled, flattening his wide tie on his stomach. Suddenly at ease with himself, he took the man warmly by the elbow to the rack of charcoal-grey suits, and then moved him into the corner mirrors, tapped him on the bottom, and tucked him under the armpits. "Touch, touch till they're on their toes," he had told his clerks. "It's the privates, they're all worried about their privacy, but you got 'em up against the wall until you let 'em down real slow into $299.50, letting on like you believe in good grooming, until it's '$290 flat, wear it home, put what you got on in a box.'"

A little flushed and relieved to step away from the mirror and Poodles' soft touch, the man put on the suit and said, "Yes, yes, it's wonderful." His old clothes were under his arm in a box. As he went out, he paused to look at a more expensive sharkskin suit on one of the window dummies, then walked off into the afternoon light. Poodles sat back in his chrome chair, satisfied, sure once again that he knew how to size up a man, and said, smiling, "You watch. The first fucking rain and that suit'll go up like a window blind."

The clerks laughed appreciatively as Poodles sat with his hands crossed on his chest, basking in their admiring laughter. Then he reached down and picked up little Benny and stroked the dog's small nose with his forefinger. "See," he said, "how good old poppa Poodles is when he's going good?"

In the late afternoon he drove home slowly, satisfied that he was right to think well about himself. The dog was in a basket-woven hamper in the front seat. It was a misty, humid evening and the sun was a brilliant red. He shielded his eyes and drove a little faster.

Luella had laid out cold cuts covered with Saran Wrap on the table in the alcove dining room. She was buttoning a black chiffon blouse and looked slim and tailored in a black skirt and black alligator pumps.

"So," he said, "who's the funeral for?"

She shrugged and said, "I'm going out."

"Out, out," and he put down the dog. "What's out? Always these days you're on your way out, and every day you're got up more and more like a Turkish delight. What the hell's going on?"

"I'm getting my life together."

"You got a life? You and me is your life."

"Very funny."

"Who said funny? You call what you been doing an act? A bad actor okay, but take it on the road and you can forget it."

"I'm going out."

Outraged and afraid that if he threw her out to save his own pride she would never come back, he touched her shoulder, trying to surprise her with concern, but instead he scowled and said, "Calm down."

"I'm calm," she said.

"Yeah, but calm down."

"What is this? How calm can I get?"

"What do you want to do to us?" he asked. "What do you want to do to yourself?"

"What you don't do," she said.

"So, what's to do?"

"I want to feel fresh, all right?"

"Fresh. Fresh is for fruits, which is what you're maybe hanging around with too much."

"Inside, Poodles. I want to feel fresh inside."

"So feel, who's stopping you?"

"Nobody, Poodles. Nobody's going to stop me, that's the point. So lemme by, okay."

"To where?"

"Out."

"Ten years we live together and now it's like I don't get no rights."

"I'm going to Gimlet's."

"Gimlet's! What are you, crazy?"

"Sure I'm crazy. Old crazy legs is stepping out."

"A goddamn dog'd go in that joint with his nose in the air."

She slammed the door and he cried out, "You cheat on me and I'll break your legs. I'll take a baseball bat to your legs." He could hear her step fading on the stairs. "Stick crêpe on your nose," he yelled again, picking up a piece of salami. "Your brains are dead."

Poodles settled into his easy chair feeling sour. The phone rang and he took a bet on a baseball game in Cleveland. Then he sat alone in the silence, suddenly aware of the hum of the air conditioner. He was reminded of Puerto Rico, and wished that it had all gone differently, and maybe he should have talked to her about his mother, too. Maybe that would have cheered her up. He ate very little and poured himself a drink. He cradled the dog and stroked the back of its head. "It's like she don't expect me to be angry," he said to Benny. "What the fuck's that all about?" Benny licked the palm of his hand. He poured himself another drink and went out on the porch and sat on the small love seat they'd bought for summer nights. The sun was going down behind the garage roofs.

He tried to imagine Luella sitting at the cramped tables of the 24-hour strip bar, because the night he'd gone there he'd stared at a long-legged girl who had a flat belly, narrow hips, and small hard breasts. He had been filled with a lust that left him surprised. Her small behind with the little bush of black hair when she bent over had seemed so vulnerable that he'd said to himself, "Jesus, I'd kiss that." Afraid that he'd spoken out loud, he'd got up and hurried

278

home, *remembering how he'd always admired* Luella's aloof air, the way she held her head as if nothing in the world could startle her. Suddenly feeling desolate he leaned forward on the love seat, seeing her as a seductive woman who knew exactly what she wanted and how she was going to get it. "Goddamn," he said, and he wondered if she really had gone to Gimlet's. Maybe she had gone to the Twenty-Two, which was possible, because she had mentioned models and something about a young film producer. He'd only half-listened to her, thinking she was talking about dancing classes, but the Twenty-Two was the place these days for film hacks. *My God, for all I know she's into flicks.* Realizing that he had no idea where she was or what she was doing, he felt betrayed, and then helpless. "You got to always sleep with one eye open," he said bitterly. He poured anther drink, closed his eyes. *We had the world by the short hairs.*

He saw a woman sitting alone on a back porch on the other side of the garages. She was dressed in a white halter and white slacks. She seemed to be watching him, too, so he waved the bottle of rye and she waved back. He pointed, suggesting he should come over, and she waved again. He got up, a little excited, saying to himself, "Goddamn, I'm gonna steal me some pussy." He picked up the dog and went down the wooden back stairs into the darkening cinder alley between the garages. Then he was out in the narrow laneway, sure that if he counted four or five garage doors to the left he would find the right walkway into the woman's yard. But each opening was so shadowed he couldn't be sure, and he was in almost total darkness as he half-trotted from opening to opening, staring up at empty porches.

He took a drink from the bottle and decided to go home. Benny was whimpering. He hunched over and began to walk very fast. Someone yelled, "Hold it right there!" A sudden blinding light in his eyes, and slowly the light was lowered. He saw two cops standing back in the shadows of an open garage door and one said, "A little early for peeping, eh, fat fella?"

"What the hell you talking about?"

"We're talking about you."

"The hell you are. I'm no damned peeper."

"Sure, sure," the cop said. "You're just sneaking around behind houses with a bottle of cheap whisky because you and your dog got nothing better to do."

"It's goddamn expensive whisky," he said, full of resentment. For some reason he found himself remembering his mother sitting beside her radio, listening every Sunday to a man named Mournful Smith who whistled songs while playing the piano. He could see the polished black toecaps of the cops' boots. Wary, backing away from the light, he said, "I ain't up to nothing."

"Give us the whisky," one of the cops said. Poodles handed him the bottle and Benny leapt out of his arms, yapping at the heels of the cops. One of them whirled Poodles around and up against a wall, kicking his legs apart.

"For Christ sake, get your hands off me," he cried

"We got a touchy peeper." The cop began to pat down his hips, getting up close to him. "And call off your dog," the cop said and laughed.

"Look, I got a business. I live just down the lane."

"Yeah, and what do you do?"

"I'm an outfitter."

"A what?"

"An outfitter."

"What's that – a plumber?"

"I make suits."

"You know what I can't understand," the other cop said, "is how come you guys fool around in back alleys when there's all that naked snatch just waiting in the bars downtown?"

"I was looking for someone," he said. "There was someone waiting for me out there." He scooped up the dog.

The cop opened Poodles' wallet and took out a card. "Ignatius John Tacoma. So, what is it you do, Tacoma?"

"I own a clothing store. Where else do you think I'd get a good-looking suit like this."

"Stand straight and turn around," one cop said.

"Okay, so I'm straight."

"Maybe you're queer?" the cop said

"You don't got no call to insult me," Poodles said. "All I want is to be left alone. I got my privacy."

"How come," the cop said, "if there's nothing wrong you're sweating so much?"

"Who's sweating?" Poodles said. "I'm easy."

"Yeah, how easy?"

"How calm can I get?" he said, squinting into the flashlight. "I got nothing to worry about."

"We'll see," the cop said.

Poodles put up his hand, shielding his face. "What's to see?" he asked, but now that the glaring light was out of his eyes he saw that both cops were very young, almost baby-faced, and he was furious that he'd let himself be handled so easily. "Just like a fucking window-blind," he said.

"What?" one cop said.

"None of your damn business," he cried. "If I wanta spend my whole goddamn life down a back alley it's none of your business."

He was so angry with himself that there were tears in his eyes. "Lou'd just love to see me like this," he said and turned to see if her face wasn't there in the window.

"Who's Lou?"

"Wouldn't you like to know," Poodles said contemptuously.

"Go on home," the other cop said. "Get your act together," and both cops stepped back into the dark.

"You call this an act?" he yelled. "This is no goddamn act," and he shook his fist at the shadows. The cops didn't answer.

"You're crazy," Poodles cried, cradling the dog. Benny was licking his hand. "You got your dumb flashlights but you got nothing on me." One of the dog's little woollen mittens was missing. He didn't know how he could explain to the girls how he'd lost the mitten. "You don't see nothing," he cried, looking again for her face in the window. "An' you can't do nothing, 'cause I got collateral, man. I got collateral."

DARK LAUGHTER

It was late afternoon and overcast. The light through the tinted ceiling glass of the art gallery made the large plaster maquettes by Henry Moore loom up like bones and socket holes hollowed by the wind. The security guard in the archway was watching two men who were walking arm in arm, taking their time. They looked like old friends, but they had met only that afternoon beside the reclining nude with the huge hips and pellet head. They walked at an even pace, silent for a long while, a little shy but in step. Every now and then they paused, looked at one of the huge white plaster casts, and once the older man said, "This is desert stuff. I've never seen the desert but the man who did this has got a desert wind inside his head." He smiled, kneading the palm of his hand, as if the soreness of an old wound were there. He seemed a touch afraid of something, yet he was always smiling. "I'm dying," he said. "Some go quick. Me, I'm going slowly. It's the human situation, that's all."

The younger man said, "You mean you're really sick?" The older man, his breath somewhat sour, holding the young man close to him, said, "Do I look sick to you? All a man needs is a pinch on the cheeks for a little colour," and he suddenly pinched the younger man playfully, laughing, saying, "My boy, my boy, what did you think when you saw me coming at you?"

"Nothing," he said warily, feeling uncertain of what to make of this man who had started talking to him so intimately, as if he believed they shared something.

"Nothing? How can you think nothing when someone zeros in on you?"

"I don't know. I just thought, this guy's coming at me and I don't run from nothing. Never did, never will."

"Really, now. So what do you do?"

"I own a wrecking lot."

"A what?"

"Cars. Trucks. A regular wrecking lot, you know, where old cars go."

"A wrecking lot. And you come here?" The older man smiled.

"Why not?" he said, a little wounded. "I feel at home. I like all the whiteness, like these things are the blown-up bones of birds."

"Birds? They look just like cow bones or horses' bones to me."

"I only know about bird bones. I shoot birds."

The old man, rubbing the palm of his hand, stared at his open hand for a moment, and then pointed at a tall white totem sculpture. "It's like it's wearing a condom," he said.

"What?"

"It's like a plaster cast of a huge penis wearing a condom. By the way, where does a man like you shoot birds?"

"On the lot. Where else? Except I don't do it no more."

"Why not?"

"They learned, I guess, or maybe all those tiny skeletons lying around scare them away now."

The guard stood with his eyes closed, half-asleep on his feet, and then, as if alert and on the watch, he opened his eyes and looked quickly around, sullen and unsmiling.

"So why?" the older man asked.

"Why what?"

"Why shoot birds? Why would you want to shoot birds?"

"I didn't want to, I just did, that's all. I sit out there in the sun and there's nothing to do, except the sun's so nice on the hubcaps and fenders and such like, and the silence, I like that. And them caw-cawing crows and starlings just come and shit all over everything so I just take my time and shoot 'em dead because what I like best is silence, and when there's only the wind, and even better when there's no wind, except then you can always hear a fly. Somewhere there's always a buzzing fly." He was talking at the top of his voice and the guard had taken three strides into the hall, hissing at them and flapping his arms. The older man, smiling, said, "What's your name?"

"Abel," the younger man replied, putting out his hand.

"Really? Abel?"

"My father's joke. My father's a joker who never laughs. His name's Adam, so he called me Abel." The older man took his arm again and they began walking. The light had gone out of the skylight windows.

"So who's Cain?" the older man asked.

"Cain? What do I know? The whole world. Anyway, I got no brother. What's your name?"

"Luther."

"Luther what?"

"Luther Stahll."

"What do you do, Luther Stahll, when you're not zeroing in on people in public galleries?"

"I was a cop. A few years ago."

"A cop. You get busted?"

"No, no. Nothing like that."

"You quit?"

"No. I just decided I didn't want to talk to anyone."

"Just like that?"

"Just about," he said and tucked his head into his shoulder, an almost coy gesture, as if he were about to acknowledge some shameful secret about himself. But he was still smiling. "I was a swimmer, see? I mean a real police-games champion kind of swimmer. I could go longer and farther underwater than anybody knew. I used to spend my lunch hours swimming underwater, sometimes floating with my eyes closed like I was drifting toward I don't know what. I always had this sense that there was an unknown *what* out there in the silence, except it's not really a silence, you know, it's more like silent music would be if it could be silent. And one day I opened my eyes and I was staring into one of those big underwater round lights in the wall, a big eye of light swamping me, and I stared into it with my hands against the wall. I couldn't see anything and I had nothing to say so later I just sat down in my life like it was a room and I was alone and said nothing."

"For how long?"

"Nearly two years."

"My God. How could you stand it?"

"You're the one who's supposed to be so crazy for silence," Luther said.

"Yeah, but I gotta at least hear my own voice. I mean, sometimes I get up in the morning and I say, 'It's a hell of a morning,' and I feel good because I hear myself say it's a hell of a morning."

"Well, it's true. Sometimes I laughed."

"Oh yeah? Well, that's something," Abel said and stroked his long hair flat over his ears with the palms of his hands.

"It's everything," Luther insisted. "When I was alone I'd sit out on the front porch and I'd listen to myself laugh."

"What were you laughing at?"

"Not what. Who."

"Okay. Who?"

"God," he said, suddenly pinching Abel's cheek again. "See, a little pinch, look how healthy you look."

"Come on, lay off," Abel said, laughing shyly. "What the hell's God got to do with this?"

"Everything. I figure it's the one thing I learned being a cop. Try laughing at a cop when he's putting the arm on you and you know what he wants to do to you. He wants to kill you. But you laugh and there's nothing he can do. There's no law against laughter. It's your only revenge."

"You're not laughing," Abel said. "I don't hear you laughing."

"It's hard to laugh alone," Luther said and stood for a moment alongside a sculpture that was so polished it was almost glazed and there were cords of white string bound around the white body. "You know what I think when I look at this, and this'll make you laugh? It reminds me of a plaster cast like you'd put on a broken arm, all wrapped like a butcher does in a meat market. I figure there's a big side of red, living, healing meat in there and someday they'll take the cast off."

"That doesn't make me laugh."

"It doesn't?"

"No."

Luther linked arms again and drew Abel in close. "Listen," he said. "One day I went walking for the first time in two years, and standing on the curb I got so fascinated by the cars I stepped out and got sideswiped, knocked down like I was dead. A priest from some church, he heard the noise and he came running." Luther had hold of Abel by the arm and said, "I'm lying there like I'm underwater, that's how I felt, half-hearing everything, except somehow I knew I was okay, and I opened my eyes and this priest is over me saying, 'Do you believe in God the Father, God the Son, and God the Holy Ghost?' I knew right there, absolutely, that he wouldn't laugh when I said to him, 'I'm dying and you ask me riddles.'"

Abel broke into a sputtering, coughing laughter and Luther, as if he were relieved, as if a view he had of things had been confirmed, smacked his hands together, the smack echoing in the empty hall, and they were laughing together as he said, "I eyeballed that old priest and he had the strangest look in his eye, like some men do, you know, when they're down at the heels, halfbroke and come from families that used to have money. He had that bewildered, regretful look, and I thought, My God, man, you're more alone than I ever was, and I just walked away, laughing real hard as hell."

The security guard, hissing for silence, strode up to them and yelled, "Quiet. No disturbance is allowed."

"We're only laughing," Luther said.

"Then laugh quietly. This is a public place," the guard said sternly.

"I'm sick, my life's slipping away, and you talk like that to me," Luther snorted, smiling as he led Abel by the elbow toward the archway. "Come on, Abel, it's closing time anyway. We'll talk a little in the dark. It's dark out, you know. The sun's gone down."

They walked out laughing quietly to themselves, side by side, as if they were old friends.

A TERRIBLE DISCONTENT

When Collette came home after being away for a long time, the first thing she did was run her hands through old lacy underclothes in the bureau and put bobby pins into the little porcelain blue bowl she had won at school for elocution, and then she got up on the bed and looked at her legs in the dresser mirror. Men had always said she had good legs, and she smiled, but later standing alone in the street in front of a shop window she saw only her pale face in the glass, and the only life on Dupont Street was a preacher down on his hands and knees scratching scripture on the sidewalk with a stub of chalk. She thought how deeply she had missed men, except now they all seemed to be like her brother – lanky, sallow, twenty years old, and ill at ease in his grey serge postman's suit with the red seam-stripe up the leg.

She was most at ease with herself walking alone on the streets that seemed surprisingly idle and wide, and then down the lanes between houses and back gardens. It had been a dry August and all the yard tomatoes were small, a pink plum size, and the ruts in the lane were filled with white dust, the sun strong on the dead twigs and vines. Someone was burning trash and a crow flew out of the cloud of smoke, settling behind her in the high branches of a silver birch tree. She took a flat stone and threw it at the crow, the stone slashing through the dry leaves. The bird cawed like raw laughter but she didn't mind the bird's cry: it was people laughing, the chuckling sound they made behind your back that she disliked.

She shook her hair, long and loose, and laughed too, surprised at how loud she laughed, and the bird flew away and she thought, *There goes the last laugh, those black wings.*

She leaned on the old slat gate that hung by one hinge from the garden fence, and Simon was there in the shade of the weeping willow tree their father had planted the year Simon was born. Their father had spent weeks under that tree one summer when she was still a high-school girl, whittling and carving flutes. He had said, There's no point, at least not the point most people think is the point. Soon after, some papers arrived in a brown envelope and, a little later, a lean man who was wearing flight glasses shook his hand by the old slat gate, laughing slyly, saying, The beautiful thing is you old soldiers never die, no matter how old you get. The last she had heard, he was somewhere near the equator, probably dead because she got a yellow card postmarked Libreville saying he was *Missing in Action*, which was a funny way of putting it, she thought, for a man lying absolutely still somewhere. It struck her as she stared at Simon that he had their father's lidded eyes and flat sloping cheekbones, always licking his thin lips, with a smile that might have been shyness but actually was secretive, cunning, which she liked in him, the way he went hunching along the street, shuffling heavy-footed, so big-boned and young. He surprised her by putting his hand on her shoulder and said that the old woman was in a rage about her not coming back to fix lunch on time and said she was a shirker always trailing trouble like a tin can, and when Collette said she'd hop to it, yes sir, and made a mocking little motion, waddling like a wind-up doll, he said the old woman had hollered and pounded her cane because Collette was off mooning up the road, which she was, she said, but not mooning, only wondering why she had once thought that her star had fallen out of the sky, and she laughed.

The old woman, though she was blind, had always dealt from a Braille deck when they played cards at night at the kitchen table, saying since Collette had been a little girl, Grandma's got a right, and don't forget that. When they were children, though Collette did not know how, the old woman had always snapped a black queen on her as if she meant it as a mark, and now she was harping and pouting again, insisting that they play as if it were the old days, and when Collette said, No, the old woman stomped her feet, tall and stone-blind, eighty-two, and leaned on her blackthorn cane, glaring wide-eyed, her eyes the colour of spit or fish eggs.

Collette hated the old woman's bird that had been with her for years, a guinea cock she kept on a string leash, the nickel-grey feathers shining and the red comb jiggling when it high-stepped in front of the old woman, who threw a fistful of corn and called out to Collette, You're no good for anyone around here, and clomped up the porch steps, her guinea cock alongside her as she eased into the pine rocking chair. Collette stood out in the flower garden of foxgloves, poppies, and lilies, looking at the little bits of candy wrapper and an old nylon stocking that were blown up against the wire fence. She wondered how a woman could lose one stocking down a lane, particularly now when women were wearing pantyhose. *Maybe it was a woman with a wooden leg*, she thought, and laughed. And wouldn't that be a sight, she said out loud so that the old woman sat upright, erect and listening, but Collette said nothing more, enjoying the silence, the sudden expectancy of the old woman. She looked up and Simon was there with his nose to the back window, watching, and Collette wasn't at all certain why she had come home to the old iron-haired woman who had always been sour because Collette's mother had died delivering her into the old woman's hands on the kitchen table.

The old woman called out, Get lunch, will you, if you haven't forgotten how, and Collette took a swipe at the poppies with her foot, scattering the petals. Up in the window Simon was smiling, and under him on the porch the old woman caressed the neck of her cock. Collette fed the old woman buttered white bread, yellow pea soup, and poached eggs. The sun shone all day. There had been no rain. That night she lay on her bed, hands linked behind her head, a breeze bellying the window curtains, and the cool night air left her calm, at ease for the first time in a long while, except with the house being so quiet she could hear the old woman's rattling snore, and she even found herself listening to the creaking beams. The curtains rose and fell like some frail body barely alive and sighing. She felt a yearning, and not just for a man, because a man could have held her but the way she felt it would have been too hard and unknowing, and how could a man know since she could hardly say herself how she wanted to feel a rush through her loins but no ache, to be touched lightly and lifted like those curtains, bellied up in the air as if they held some living thing. She wondered whether she wanted a child or maybe childhood again, except that she never wanted to be a girl again. There had been so little that was childlike in her life, with the bony hand of the old woman always on her, as if by being born she had murdered her mother. As for her father, until he went away he had acted as if any kindness were a dull brown penny like the coppers she had flattened when she put them on the railroad tracks, the tracks two blocks away, unused now, the ties overgrown with scrub and weeds. As a girl she had put her ear to the rails listening to what was far away, and on the day she was told that her father had gone she went along to the old tracks and lay down and cried and listened as if she might hear him somewhere. The old woman hardly seemed to know he was gone, hard and locked inside herself, the way she had always had hard fingernails, poking into the bedclothes when Collette was a baby, nails the colour of the underside of a turtle she had once seen over in a pond in the Allan Gardens hothouse, which she thought was the loveliest place to be alone in the city, far from the old woman's cold and dry fingers.

Late at night years ago, in some sudden need, the old woman had taken Collette's braided head in her ropy arms and Collette had looked up and seen the loose grey folds of flesh drooping from the old woman's neck, her head high, just like a bird, her old woman's bones sharp and shining in the loose flesh. Except for silent times like that, the old woman had carped at Collette and Simon, whom she had always coddled and then ignored with a kind of contempt, just like their father – so droop-shouldered, morose, and always dressed in muddy browns, warming his bare feet before the electric fireplace in the living room during the winter – had ignored them, regarding them all with aloof suspicion.

Once, Collette had heard her father telling the old woman, as if he were cheering her up, that there was some unseen meaning in his wife dying in childbirth, that a death cannot mean nothing, and maybe the whole trick was in discovering what a death told you to do with your life, and, anyway, he wanted the old woman to know his wife was his wife forever. The irony was, Collette thought, that he seemed always preoccupied with sniffing around, a cabinetmaker who had loved the wet feel of stripped wood, the fleshy shine, and had ended up making dozens of little inlaid jewel boxes, stacking them around the house, empty, calling them as a joke his little coffins. When Collette had asked, Why, why this sniffing around, as if some corner held a clue to where her mother had gone, he had glared at her and said, Someday maybe you'll learn something about losing love, and she had said, I don't intend to lose anything, leaving him alone as he kept busy doing little more than brood. If anyone in the house asked him a question, any question, he got up with the newspaper and paraded through the house, reading aloud until his anger cooled down. Then he sulked, sorry for them, for himself, burrowing inside himself, and went away. An awful thing to do, she thought, so irresponsible that she wanted to kill someone herself, so she took to dancing and drinking all night, detached from the men she let make love to her, only afraid when she realized that she wanted a baby and didn't care who the father was. All her disheartened gaiety died, like the breeze in the curtains, the curtains suddenly limp. She looked up at the ceiling that was so white, so empty, with a little spider trekking slowly from the corner. She was going to get up and kill it, but she just lay there, tired and calm, closed her eyes, and went to sleep.

Simon came into her room in the morning where she was lying on her bed and sat by her feet. He laid his left hand on her ankle. He tried to hide that he was watching her in her nightgown, watching her breasts. She let the silence hang between them. He took his hand off her ankle and said, What do you think would happen if I were to leave, if I took a room or something somewhere else in the city? There had always been a dulled sensuality about him, some sly cunning to no effect, and she said, I don't know. Simon leaned forward, elbows on his knees, and said, What I don't understand, and he was licking his thin, almost white lips, is why you haven't gone for good, why you came back and why you're hanging in for a fight with anyone. She felt suddenly saddened and moved by him, sulking around on the edge of his own life, unable to leave because there had been so much neglect in the family, and so there he was on the end of her bed, slumped forward. A postman, she thought, with a bag full of dead letters, his sallow face staring, and she said to him, I've been alone with aloneness, and I just headed home because home's a point where you can see where you don't want to go again and being somewhere else would be just thirty minutes closer to nothing.

She got up and went to the old maple dresser with the oval mirror, and in the rim of the mirror there were yellow curling photographs from just a few years ago, a boy with long hair, Harry something-or-other whose father had owned a pasta store, one smirking face in a row of faces hardly remembered, and she brushed her hair, watching herself and Simon in the old smoky glass. Simon said, You dream about your men, I bet. He was crouched forward and his shirt was loose at the throat. She turned and put her hands on his neck, saying, And I bet you've got your naked women in your own mind, and he said, What do you think about? She rubbed his neck, moving her thumbs up his brown burned skin and into his hair, and leaned close so that he could smell her, almost feel her. Knowing that he wanted her hands on him warmed her so much that she was suddenly aware of the dryness in the room – dry wood all through the house, the stairs worn grey and bevelled by so many years of boots up and down except where there were knots standing up like carbuncles – saying softly to Simon, I sometimes see a man standing straight and his body wet and I run my fingers slowly across his chest, through the hair on his chest. With a little laugh she kissed him on the neck and pulled him against her. That's all, he whispered, so she pulled away knowing she had been unfair, but she stood there, shaping her hair with her hands and when he turned, his eyes on her breasts, she hated him for being her brother, and also because he didn't look ashamed at all, and without shame, she thought, we're nothing, and so she went out of the room and opened the porch door and found the old woman asleep, snoring, a rattling whine through the yard. The string leash had slipped from her hand and the guinea cock was strutting about in the dust. Collette went down into the garden among the lilies and poppies and the headless stems.

She took a pair of hedge clippers and began cutting the stems back, and the old woman, with the blackthorn lying between her legs, threw back her head and settled into a steady snore, like a giant insect, Collette thought. Then the old woman came half-awake and groped for the leash. Where's my cock? she cried, and the bird, hearing her, jabbed a leg toward the stairs, and Collette went toward the stairs with the clippers in her hands and the old woman bawled out, Bring me my cock, bring me my cock. Collette just stood there, uncertain, watching the bird step toward the porch, its head high, and she hooked her foot under its belly and hoisted it into the air, laughing, and the cock squawked and flapped and fell head first. The old woman leapt to her feet and screamed, Who's hurting my cock? while the bird whirled with its legs beating the dust. The old woman edged down the stairs, and Simon came banging through the screen door, yelling at Collette but she paid no attention. She and the cock eyed each other, its beak swinging slowly back and forth, the red comb flopping from side to side, its eyes never off her, the old woman yelling behind her as she levelled the clippers and took a step, expecting the bird to cut and run but the cock didn't move. There was only the throbbing in the loose flesh of his throat, and when she stood above the bird her hands shook and she could feel her own blood beating in repulsive time with the bird's stringy neck. The cock lifted its leg and took one contemptuous step and it was done, a slicing rasp of the hedge clippers. Blood swooshed out of the severed neck and she leapt out of the way, scared. The cock's body tottered, the blood in bursts, the headless body jagging crazily across the yard. The old woman, frozen in her blindness, let out a screech as if chanting to the bird in his dance, My cock, my cock, who's hurting my poor cock? and her whole face had collapsed, lips drawn back, baring her yellow teeth, tears down her cheeks, and the cock fell down among the lilies.

Every day afterwards Collette saw the old woman at the upstairs window and sometimes Simon stood beside her. She was in her bedclothes wearing her bedcap, and she put her long finger to her lips as Simon took her from the window.

It rained for several days and became so cold that some of the maple leaves turned yellow and red. When Simon came home from work Collette fed him, and then he took a tray to the old woman, sitting opposite her while she ate. The old woman did not come downstairs again. Collette told Simon to tell the old woman that she had taken the black queens from the deck, that the little game was over, but the old woman had said nothing, as if, Simon said, she didn't know what Collette was talking about.

Collette began going out alone in the evenings, sometimes taking the old blackthorn cane, which she thought made her appear interesting and elegant because she had read once that a young woman wanting to look mysterious should try to be a little sinister. She also found a wonderful black cape in mothballs in a bottom drawer, which she thought might have been her mother's. She wrapped herself in the cape in the evenings. Once, she wore it out to a big dance hall, though she didn't bother to go in but only stood outside listening to the music as if she were waiting for someone. One evening while she sat out on the porch entertaining a boring young man who lived four gardens down the lane, the old woman began rocking above, and he looked up at the noise from the rocking and Collette began to beat out the rhythm of the old woman's rocking with the cane, leaning forward and beating faster on the porch boards as the old woman rocked faster, trying to lose Collette. But Collette got ahead of her so that the old woman was trying to keep up with her, and it gave Collette glee, her face glistening, which frightened the young man, and she began to laugh. Then all of a sudden the old woman stopped. Tired out I bet, Collette said and lay back in the chair with the blackthorn between her legs, feeling fine. A few minutes later Simon came down to the porch saying, You should see her, she's as white as a sheet, and Collette said, She should see me. Turning to her young man she said, But of course she can't because she's blind, and Simon said, You oughta be ashamed of yourself, and he stomped off. Because he was looking bewildered and ill at ease. Collette said to her friend that he should give her a kiss on the cheek. He did, and then sat back with his hands folded around his knees while she sat looking out over the garden as the sun went down behind the two-storey houses.

THE COHEN IN COWAN

Cowan's my name, and in case you don't know, Cowan's cut down from Cohen 'cause Cohen meant you were a king but I'm a Cowan, which lets you know right away where I stand, which is on my own two feet, and where else, 'cause I used to be Jewish but now I'm very successful. Otherwise, would I have a black car like a regular mayor or a mortician if I wasn't successful? Mostly I know I'm okay 'cause I get no secret sweats in the night though I got a lot on my mind and sometimes the pressure is a cooker like you wouldn't believe. I don't owe no one in this whole world for what I got, which is to say my company from day one was a moneymaker I thought up in the shower room at the Y and where the idea came from is one night I'm watching the Oscar awards and this song *You Light Up My Life*, which I always thought was a Flick-Your-Bic commercial, wins 'cause it turns out it's a song about God. What I'm looking for's got nothing to do with God, it's got only to do with this company I put together as a dodge for tax purposes, out near the old cemetery and it has got to look legit. So in the shower after playing basketball I think to myself I'll get into the T-shirt business with T-shirts from Taiwan, to which if you send me a photo I'll put your face dead centre between your tits for all the world to see, which is better than all these Day-Glo slogans 'cause it's you yourself, which is when I get the company name when I hear myself saying U-yourself and that's where we all live 'cause nothing counts like old Number

One, which doesn't mean I don't have a Number Two, namely my wife who loves me a lot, but the fact is, I'm at my best alone in the Y and so standing the next day in the shower room I think, Why not lampshades with your face on your own lampshade, which my wife says is a little weird for a Jew but I say forget the Jewish problem and let the light that lights up your room light up your face. That's what we all want, to look good in a good light, and pretty soon there's so many orders I know I'm on a lucky streak, and sure enough one afternoon I'm out walking past one of these religious stores with prayer books and those beads and I stop dead in my tracks. I can feel for sure somebody's got their eye on me and pretty soon I figure it out, it's this 3-D holy picture of Jesus with the big heart bleeding, and my wife she says she's worried about lampshades being in bad taste, and there I am looking at this dripping heart with a red light bulb in it, which to me is really sick, but bleeding hearts are not my business except the world's full of bleeding hearts. But those big mooning eyes, no matter where I move, they follow me 'cause of the way they're printed in this pebbly plastic and BAM, like a light, it hits me. Put U-Yourself In The Picture With A Frame Of Simulated Walnut. I tell you this is terrific like you can't believe 'cause there's nothing people like better than the look of themselves on the wall keeping an eye on everything, and you think T-shirts are big. I'm getting photographs from the ends of the earth and I'm putting them through the same process so that their own eyes inside the frame follow them around the room wherever they go. I'm making big bucks, which suits me fine except suddenly I'm a businessman tied to an accountant instead of a tax dodge, and I don't want to be a businessman like that 'cause actually though I'm very respectable, you see, I'm a bookie.

Even more than being a bookie I like playing basketball, mostly by myself 'cause it's not that I can't keep up with the boys, being only thirty-six and I got what my wife calls a little pleasure-pillow paunch, but I don't like to complicate my life with too many other people who want only to make demands and one demand leads to another. So I like being alone, bouncing a ball on Sunday mornings at the Y when there's nobody on the floor, and usually there's only one old guy out that early jogging around the upstairs track like he's chasing his own shadow. He don't pay attention to me and I don't pay attention to him but we quit around the same time 'cause other guys are now on the floor and B-ball is really only terrific when you're by yourself 'cause when you're alone you can get this feather touch in the fingers, your whole body light like weightless, and you take off and float with the ball, looping it up off the backboard and BAM it goes swish. That's as close to perfect perfection as you're gonna get, knowing you're totally in tune between yourself and the ball, and before you even take a look you see it happen before it happens – which my wife tells me is almost mystical or musical, I forget the way she says I talk about it, but it's true. The only time I felt close to totally happy is the one or two times I got that feather touch in my fingers, like the little flutter I feel sometimes from my wife except my wife and me, who everybody says we were made for each other in heaven, one week we nearly come apart at the seams and, for Christsake, can you believe it, all over a lousy Christmas tree.

Which was not because I'm Jewish but the way I remember being Jewish, which in some ways is worse than being Jewish because it's always in the back of your mind and by and large what you remember is what you are, which is why I figure that what a person wants to forget should take care of itself, except there are some things you can't do nothing about and for me it's the smells I smell. Come Christmastime and I see Christmas trees what I think of is *shiksas* and what I thought about *shiksas* when I was a boy was pork, and when I think of pork I get queasy 'cause unclean's unclean, which don't make much sense 'cause actually I like eating great big *goyish* hams with pineapple rings. But what can I do about what I smell in my head whether it smells that way or not, so when my wife says she wants a Christmas tree so my two little daughters can open up their presents like regular kids, and I say they're not regular kids, she says why not, and I say 'cause they're nothing the way everyone else is something, and she says that don't make sense 'cause nobody's anything these days so what's the difference and what do I care, and I tell her I care and she says not about them and then I'm suddenly screaming pork and she looks at me for the first time in our lives like I'm crazy, which I suddenly feel I am, standing there in the kitchen going pork, pork, but there's no way I'm gonna be the first person who's Jewish or not in my family who has a Christmas tree in his house. For all I know what she wants is a star up on top like I'm supposed to be one of the three wise men wishing I knew which way to turn, which is the trouble with wise guys who got all the answers for everybody but themselves, 'cause they got stars in their eyes, which I don't.

Anyway, now I'm in the dark with my wife who is a looker and she's cut me off with absolutely no nookie no way and let's face it, I'm a very sexy person who doesn't like lying awake in the dark. So I'm sitting up downstairs half the night trying to figure out what's going on, staring at the turned-off TV tube staring back at me like I'm nuts, and there's my own face on the lampshade over the piano, all lit up. So I turn on the matching lamp on the mantelpiece and there's my wife all dolled up like Snow

White staring at me smiling on the lampshade, and between us on the wall my little girls are hanging in their plastic pictures looking at me no matter where I move, like the world's coming to an end over this lousy tree. I can't stand it 'cause my wife says why should people who're nothing sit around with nothing to do, especially when we don't care what's what with anyone, except I know we care 'cause we're screaming at each other the whole time, and I tell her we're making something outta nothing 'cause already I'm sleeping on the sofa and what's even worse everything's out of whack with me being a bookie 'cause now I'm losing.

And I want you to know bookies don't lose unless something is really wrong 'cause betting is the way I see things hanging together in a framework, and when I used to bet myself I was always looking for the sign when I couldn't do nothing wrong no matter how I played it, like the hand of God was with me, and lots of times I got the sign, but even when you believe you're so right you win big, you know you always got to end up losing, like no matter how successful we are we know we all got to die. One day I can see the only winner is whoever's collecting the bets 'cause the world's full of losers, so I got into being a bookie and right away I'm on the side of the angels and getting rich. Except now I'm sleeping on the sofa and every *putz* in town is picking winners and I'm going broke, and I figure it's all 'cause of that tree. So I'm driving home in a snowstorm the day before Christmas and there's this lot full of scruffy trees for fifteen bucks each, which is outrageous, but I buy one anyway 'cause I'm suddenly so excited like I haven't been for a long time. I can't wait to see my wife's face light up like I flicked her Bic when she sees this tree.

What I see as soon as I say hello is my wife standing with her arms crossed in the living room in front of a great big tree. It's all dripping with tinsel and tiny lights and there's a lopsided star up on top and my kids are sitting cross-legged in the corner looking scared but she's staring at my tree and I'm staring at her tree and all of a sudden we both start laughing ourselves to death, thank God, 'cause maybe I would've killed her for doing that to me if I hadn't done it to myself. After we stop laughing she says I can't just throw my tree away so maybe I should call the cathedral but I say what do I know about cathedrals, and she says that's exactly their business, looking after poor people who need a tree. I think I'm losing my mind when I call the cathedral and this priest is talking very softly to me saying yes, and what a blessing and don't I know there's plenty of families who not only don't have trees but they don't have turkeys either, and like I'm going crazy I whisper back to him, How about I buy them a nice big ham. He laughs real quiet like we're sharing some secret and says a turkey'll do just fine and he's very touched, and I tell him no, I'm the one who's touched, right in the head, and he gives me this little chuckle again, saying the Lord really does work in wondrous ways.

The only way I feel is like I'm bleeding to death when two guys from the church show up all smiles, and when I give them the cheque for the turkey the guy with the peak cap says it's a fine tree you have for yourself there, Mr. Cowan, and a fine Christian thing you're doing, and I'm smiling like my face is falling apart at the seams. Suddenly I want to yell Cohen, you creep, I'm Cohen, but my wife's giving me her little flutter touch on the small of my back and I get this loose feeling like everything's okay and pretty soon me and my wife are standing in the doorway like a couple of loonies saying Merry Christmas to these two guys carrying the tree to their pickup truck. Later we lie around with the kids gone to bed, listening for reindeer, and I say maybe I should come down the chimney and my wife says chimneys are a very bad joke for a Jew but I tell her for Christsake cut it out 'cause I'm already feeling a little lost like it is, lying there looking out the window at the really shining stars I never really saw like that before.

In the morning I can't believe it 'cause I'm lying there in this terrific sleep when the phone rings beside the bed, and I hear giggling downstairs that makes me think of summer and the water sprinkler on the lawn, but this voice is saying in my ear he wants to thank me especially, Mr. Cowan, for my kindness, and I don't know who the hell he is so I say he's very welcome but then I realize he's talking about how tickled he is by my tree and my turkey. He says he took a chance looking up my name in the book because there's got to be only one Adrian H. Cowan, which I tell him is true, and he says he can believe it and sounds so warm and pleased I'm suddenly sitting up smiling, asking him how it all looks and he's talking terrific, until he says so why not drop over, Mr. Cowan, and take a look 'cause it'd be a real pleasure to meet a man like me, which I say likewise I'm sure and I will and I hang up and think, Oh my God, I'm gonna hang myself, 'cause I can't believe how I've done this to myself, telling this poor guy I'm gonna come around and stand in his kitchen and stare at his turkey and tree, which is really my tree, and so I go downstairs and this I can't believe either. The whole room is littered up with paper and my little girls are laughing and yelling Daddy! Daddy! giving me gifts, and I can't stand it 'cause for them I got no gifts, but my wife says the whole day is this wonderful gift from me and what a wonderful man I am, and like she's at last telling me the biggest secret of her life she says she's already made a plum pudding.

Which is what happens when you give a little you get a lot and I've gone all the way from pork to plum pudding, so all of a sudden I feel like I'm sitting in a corner with my thumb in someone else's life and I really pulled out a plum, except this is no plum, this is painful, 'cause she says she's got Irish coffees and plum pudding at eleven o'clock in the morning for neighbours who don't care about Jewish, and why, I want to know, is this happening to me in my own house, that everybody is so happy when all I want is nothing except a little piece of the action and no talking to smooth-talking priests? I say thank you very much, I don't want to be a spoilsport, but I'm going to the Y while it's still early and play a little B-ball by myself. My wife, she taps me on the cheek like it's my *tuchis* and says she understands, smiling, when I know she don't understand at all, and I tell her for the last time that this is the way I am, which is nothing, and kiss her hard 'cause I'm holding her so hard I feel I'm gonna cry. And even when I'm in my big black car I feel I'm gonna cry, driving like I got nothing but time through the streets that are so empty.

All I can think of is going to see this guy with my tree, which is his fault 'cause I didn't call him, he called me, and actually he lives down close to where my father lived, which is not such a bad place except I haven't been there for years, and when I'm driving down the street I feel a little weird, like I'm moving back into my father's life which is my life, and suddenly I wish I had a son looking for himself in me the way I could look for me in my father if I wanted to, even though my father is dead twenty years, but still I got his old gabardine coat somewhere in a box with his long underwear that he died in when he fell down in the slush in the street and some cop said to me like I was someone else's son, the old *sheeny's* dead, which made me want to kill him when I was a young boy. Instead I grew up and got smart and changed my name to Cowan so my kids don't get that kinda crap in case I die in the street. Then before I know it I'm getting out of my car facing this number 48 like the guy on the phone said, and I mean this house is so bad it's nothing like my father ever knew, 'cause the veranda's slipping left while the house is leaning right, and I'm standing there in the street in my own very terrific suede coat with the fox-fur collar and BAM, it hits me like I can see this guy's face go out like a light. No matter how much he says he wants to thank me personally there's no way he'd like me looking down at his family beaming up at me and all of a sudden I feel this terrific sadness like I just lost my whole childhood, 'cause I hear myself humming, *I'm the king of the castle and you're the dirty rascal.* I know if I go in there, then there's no way I can come out clean, so I feel kinda left out like I'm trapped between what I done and what I can't do. So almost without thinking I lift my hand like I'm saying goodbye, and it's only when I'm back driving in the car that I see my hand in the air like it's a blessing the way my father used to bless me.

And I want you to know that it's not a question of counting blessings, but I can't remember blessing anybody, not even my own kids, which makes me feel even a little more sad. When I'm in the locker room putting on my B-ball shoes I know I'm all wound up and alive inside like I can't wait to get on the floor and then I find the gym is totally empty with not even the old guy running around the track, like he knew this morning I needed to be alone absolutely, and everything I do with the ball feels loose and I'm doing layups real easy and I get this weird feeling that whatever I want is right there at my fingertips. I start dropping in shots from fifteen feet and doing backhanders and scoops, crossovers and double pumps. I can't miss like I'm unconscious I'm so good, and then I drop this long looping hook shot like a rainbow from almost centre court, which I know before I even let it go it's perfect. For a minute I want to cry. I want the guy with my tree to be there sitting maybe in a folding chair with his turkey in his arms seeing this, 'cause suddenly I got the conviction that we're connected though I never seen him and he's never seen me, but somehow I know I got the touch like it was given to me maybe in the street when I had my hand in the air, which is what my father always used to do when he'd just put his hand in the air over my head and say nothing like he was real peaceful. And I'm thinking about this guy like he's there all peaceful with his face lit up, and suddenly I'm standing at centre court doing something I could never do before, which is get the ball spinning on my fingertip like it is the whole world, and I feel this terrific astonishment that I can't explain. I'm so surprised at being alive let alone I should have this special touch, which for once in my life I really know I got, 'cause for once I did what I didn't intend to do, which was leave the guy alone with whatever happiness he got from what I gave him. My only regret was he couldn't call me by my real name, which is Cohen 'cause now my name is Cowan, which lets you know right away where I stand, except standing there at centre court I didn't feel that I was me at all 'cause I don't exactly know who I am but now I know I'm not nothing.

PROWLERS

Slaverne Tuttle's mother wanted a girl. She loved the name Laverne, but when he was born a boy she settled for Slaverne and kept him in flowing curls until he was seven, when children on the street clipped his hair in the rose garden with a pair of pruning shears. His mother cried, but he took the clipping calmly. His father died during the war, parachuting behind enemy lines. Slaverne had only a faint recollection of a small man with steel-rimmed glasses, but his mother was tall with a slightly bent nose, a pastor's daughter, who became morose sitting alone listening for her husband's step. "He had a noticeable limp," she said. Slaverne grew up feeling sorry for his mother. One night he came home and found her drunk by the fireplace, dressed in her white wedding gown, and he said, "I am the man in your life, Mother." She cracked him across the face and wept as he tried to hold her, blood from his nose staining her dress.

It was only after she died that he began wearing her clothes. During the day he worked as a court clerk and he enjoyed the work, sitting at his own oval table, his slender fingers moving like spiders silently over the keys. Sometimes a judge asked him to read the evidence aloud. He always smoothed his closely cropped hair, quietly clipping his words. One judge told him testily that his thin monotone made all testimony sound the same. "The world is full of impassioned pleas," the judge said. "And none of us are the same. Never forget that." The judge had gathered his black robe and swept into his chambers, nodding at tight-lipped attorneys wearing white bibs. "It's due process," Slaverne told his friend Charlie, who was a long-distance bus driver. "You look at these people and you know it's all a question of who's in their high-heel sneakers. The cops strut around in crash helmets like space thugs, the hookers play pouting virgins. It's all a laugh. No matter how you look at it, life is a costume contest, Charlie, and don't you forget it. We're not weird."

He had met Charlie, who had a aquiline nose and hooded eyes that were languid and sensual after only a touch of eye shadow, at an indoor shooting range. They shared a love of high-powered pistols and the oiled sheen of the barrel as they stood side by side, insulated from the echoing shots by big padded ear-cups. Charlie was also good at pruning roses.

They agreed that he should stay with Slaverne after coming in off the road, and soon after he had his own closet in the small frame house set back from the street in a downtown cul-de-sac. The kitchen and music room looked out on the garden of roses, honeysuckle, and dogwood. Slaverne liked the garden because it seemed secluded. "Those are the enemy lines out there," he'd told Charlie, but sometimes drifters came down the cul-de-sac and fell into step behind him late at night. He often thought he was being shadowed, and one night he broke into a run, furious at people who would not leave him alone. When he got to the house and looked back down the dimly lit road, there was no one there. Disconcerted, he doubled back, watching for movement in the bushes. He knew there were always prowlers watching and peeping in the bushes behind the house, because on hot summer evenings with the windows open he had heard a twig snap or a muffled cough.

Charlie was easygoing and had a sensuous slow walk. He got out of his uniform as soon as he was in the house and put on lace underclothes and a little jewellery. He usually cooked supper wearing a brassiere, a short slip, and heels. He knew his legs were long and lovely. He seldom closed the kitchen curtains and Slaverne, sensing someone out in the dark, would see a shadow pass. He spoke sharply to Charlie about walking around half-naked as if they were alone and had all the freedom in the world. "We don't, you know," he said sourly. "Everybody's a criminal these days."

Charlie said he was sorry and closed the curtains and the drapes in the music room and curled up beside Slaverne on the cozy sofa. Slaverne kissed his closed eyes, but they were becoming more curt with each other. Slaverne thought Charlie was turning into a showoff, wearing a leather suit to a party one night with a parachute pack strapped to his back. There were several small bottles of champagne in the pack, and Charlie had been the centre of attention even though he was a short man, smaller than Slaverne, who was lithe and lean. "Look at me," Slaverne had said testily. "Here I am in my late thirties and I still look like a track star." He felt lethargic about their affair and he blamed Charlie.

"Maybe the trouble is you don't love me anymore," Charlie said one night.

"Don't be silly," Slaverne said. "You're beautiful."

"Who's silly? I take off my clothes and you look like you're looking through me."

"What can I say?"

"Say something."

"Maybe we've known each other too long, maybe clothes make the man," he said, crossing his legs.

"Since when is two years too long?"

311

"I mean, maybe we're used to each other, that's all. People get used to each other."

"Yeah, well not me. I never know what you're doing."

"Maybe that's the trouble," Slaverne said. "I don't get any surprises anymore."

"So, what am I supposed to do, hop-dance with a dildo?"

"Look, I'm just telling you I feel boxed in. Maybe we need to take another look at each other. What do I know about why I feel this way?"

"If you don't know, who does?"

Slaverne heard a noise outside. He parted the drapes and looked into the darkness, listening for footsteps. On another evening he had caught a glimpse of a man limping up the garden slope. He had called the police and waited nearly two hours for them to come, but they never did, and he went to bed with Charlie feeling angry and betrayed because the police hadn't taken the invasion of his privacy seriously.

He knew there were prowlers out in the garden every night, sitting on their haunches in the shrubbery. There were several small apartment buildings close by, and the peepers were looking for women who had forgotten themselves and left a little opening of light into their bedrooms as they undressed. Slaverne and Charlie now made love in the dark.

Then one day Charlie received an unsigned note in the mailbox from a man who said he had seen her through the kitchen window, "because there you were in your underclothes and didn't seem to care, so I'd like to say hello. It'd be terrific if you'd call the enclosed number at three in the afternoon on Tuesday. It's a pay phone and I'll be there and I'll know it's you and you don't have to feel self-conscious because we won't be able to see each other."

Charlie promised to keep the curtains closed but Slaverne sat around feeling sour because someone had stood undisturbed in the dark watching Charlie. "I don't count. I mean, if he's seen you, he's seen me, he knows I'm here. I'm the man of the house, but you're just supposed to phone some phone booth like I don't exist." He threw open the living-room drapes and stood scowling into the darkness.

A few nights later, Slaverne heard slow steps through the long grass. It was late at night and he and Charlie were dressing for a pre-Lenten ball. Some of the more dashing dowagers were expected and Slaverne had said excitedly, "We're going to prowl in the owl hours tonight." He was wearing a silver lamé sheath, a beautiful brunette wig, his mother's pearls, and red patent-leather shoes. Charlie, always a little late, was still in lace underthings. Slaverne parted the drapes and there by the kitchen window, pale, almost putty-faced, was a young man wearing round rimless glasses "That's it," Slaverne said, "that does it," as he watched the young man go up the slope of the back garden followed by a black-and-white toy terrier.

Charlie, who had washed his hair in the kitchen sink and had a towel wrapped around his head, told Slaverne to phone the police. Slaverne cursed and went to his bedroom closet and took down the pistol case. He came back into the kitchen, saying, "Don't worry, it isn't loaded." Charlie laughed. "You should see yourself." Slaverne stood handling the gun for weight, as if its balance were suddenly important, and he said, "I'm going to scare the living Jesus out of that punk, that's all." He went along the hall at a half-trot in his high heels, hoping no one would see him, hunching down as he went out the back door into the cover of the bushes.

He angled up the side of the slope and held close to a big sugar-maple tree, his heels sinking into the soft earth, certain he couldn't be seen. He held the pistol along the length of his leg and heard steps and the snuffling of a dog in the underbrush, and then there was a shadow on the other side of the tree. He stepped out and said in a thin reedy voice, "Hold it right there, you son-of-bitch." He was surprised when a tall boy, backing away from the gun, said, "You're crazy." Slaverne, peering at him in the shadow-light, said, "I am not." He was trying to sound reasonable, but he was suddenly afraid the boy, who he thought might be sixteen, would attack him. The unloaded gun was useless and he felt confused, but then the boy bent down and cradled the small dog. "You're crazy, lady," he said, "and I'm going home."

"You're not going anywhere," Slaverne said, his voice rising.

"Oh yeah," and the boy turned. He was clutching the dog to his chest. The frightened dog's little legs were pedalling in the air. "You bet I am so going home," he said. "There's no way no crazy dame is gonna shoot me. You're crazy but not that crazy." Hesitant, and then suddenly hurrying, he started walking around the house toward the street. Slaverne, trying not to hook his heels in any loose roots, got into step behind him, saying, "Maybe so, but get out of line and I'll knock your head off with this thing." The boy kept going. As they passed the music room window, Charlie, wearing a brassiere and half-slip, almost luminous in the box of amber window-light, appeared. He had brushed out his long brunette wig and he looked more beautiful than Slaverne had ever seen him, so beautiful that he wanted to stop and stand there in the darkness and stare. He had never seen Charlie in that light before, but the boy was leading him along the walk to the street and Slaverne was suddenly furious at Charlie for always parading in the windows and he screamed, "For God's sake, close the curtain. That's the end. Close the curtains and get out." He tried to cradle the pistol casually in the crook of his arm.

"Where are we going, lady?" the boy asked when they got to the road.

"What do you mean, where are we going?" Slaverne said.

"Where we going?" the boy said, darting across the road.

"The cops," Slaverne blurted out, hurrying after him.

"I don't see no cops."

"The cops are all over the place," Slaverne said, because every night policemen in yellow patrol cars came down the dead-end street and put parking tickets on all the cars. "Yeah, the cops," Slaverne said as he looked up and down the empty road.

The boy strode between some low bushes in a small park, going toward the busy downtown streets. Slaverne saw that city gardeners had cut back the bushes. He circled around, so he wouldn't catch his dress. It was Saturday night and he knew everyone would be crowding into restaurants after the late shows.

"Why the hell were you peeping, anyway?" Slaverne called out. He was several strides behind the boy.

"I'm not a peeper."

"Sure, you're just walking your dog."

"That's right," the boy said, "and there's no law against that, but I'll bet there's a law against you poking that gun at me."

"You were looking in my window," Slaverne said, shifting the pistol to his other hand. "And anyway, you want to look at bare boobs, the bars are full of naked bimbos."

"I don't drink," the boy said, "and besides, I'm underage. I'd be breaking the law."

"Are you crazy," Slaverne cried. "You're a peeper, I caught you peeping."

"No, I'm not."

"Well, maybe," Slaverne said, suddenly wondering what he would do if the boy could prove to the police that he was not a Peeping Tom. "What's your name?"

"You are crazy," the boy said over his shoulder. "You think I'd tell you my name?"

"Why not?"

"You're weird," the boy said, and then he stopped and turned around, circling Slaverne in the dark, staring at him intently, and suddenly bawled out, "Jesus Christ, you're a fucking guy. You're a fucking guy in a fucking dress."

"You're goddamn right and I'm just liable to do anything, you lousy little punk," Slaverne cried as the boy hurried off toward Cecil Street and all the Chinese restaurants. Slaverne followed. As they came out under the rippling neon signs, Slaverne heard his name called out. He looked back and saw Charlie hurrying in his bare feet, holding his long skirt with one hand and his high-heel shoes with the other. Slaverne and the boy, shoulder to shoulder for a moment by the curb, stared into the luminous red and yellow Chinese restaurants' lettering and the flashing headlights. Slaverne suddenly ducked his head, as if they were all on him, and he let the pistol dangle along his leg. The boy, surrounded by all the light and suddenly laughing, stepped into the traffic, and Slaverne was nearly hit by a taxi as he went after him, leaping sideways.

People stared. Slaverne ran across the street after the boy, but before he could threaten him, the boy turned. He had taken off his steel-rimmed glasses and he had muddy little eyes. Laughing, he said, "You goddamn stupid queen. Let's go to the goddamn police station, eh! You think the cops'll let a crazy freak like you go around the streets with a gun?" Charlie, having stepped into his high heels on the other side of the street, looking stylish and elegant, was parading through the cars, letting a lace handkerchief dangle in the air, stopping traffic. Putting down his little dog, the boy strode off toward the police station.

Slaverne kept stride for a few moments with the boy, but men and women seeing the gun suddenly stepped aside, glaring, and someone cried out, "What are you, lady, crazy?" He yelled, "Mind your own fucking business." Then the boy turned and screamed, "He's a goddamn freak. He's a goddamn guy in a dress." An elderly couple recoiled just as Charlie, wearing a black velvet dress with a scoop neck, took Slaverne's arm. The boy was now far ahead, looking over his shoulder, and then he ran off into the crowd, the terrier scampering after him. Slaverne was suddenly frightened and he cursed, seeing himself trailing his dress along a dusty courtroom floor, a white-bibbed attorney pleading, "None of us are the same, Your Honour." He lifted his slit skirt and jammed the pistol into his garter belt along the inside of his thigh. Charlie was giggling. Across the road, Chinese waiters, all wearing burgundy serving-jackets, were lined up along the curb, waving and laughing.

"It's all your damn fault," Slaverne screamed at Charlie.

"My fault? You charge out of the house like a crazy man with a gun and it's my fault?"

"I told you to get out. Get out of my life. You've humiliated me."

He grabbed Charlie by the shoulders and spun him into the darkened doorway of a grocery store. There were shining steel hooks in the window and two pressed ducks on white tiles under the hooks. "You tart," Charlie yelled. "You goddamn pretentious tart."

Slaverne, with all the neon light catching his silver lamé dress, cracked Charlie across the face and Charlie screamed, letting go a looping left. He missed and they wrestled each other to the curb, and Charlie, his nose bleeding, wobbled on his high heels and turned an ankle. Slaverne knocked him down. The waiters on the other side of the street yelled. One called out, "Yankee imperialists, go home."

A sloppily dressed man, a drifter, sauntered drunkenly along and stood over Charlie, who lay tangled up in his long velvet dress. The drifter said, "Aw, come on." Slaverne punched him in the face and the drunk collapsed and began to cry. Slaverne strutted into the street, crossing toward the waiters, smoothing his dress and hair, trembling. There was a little blood on his dress. He suddenly threw his shoulders back. He knew that his legs looked good.

"Well, it's a man's world," he called to the waiters, wheezing for air, his voice deep. There was giggling laughter. He adjusted his wig as a car came along and spun on his heel, hiking up his skirt, hitching a ride with his thumb out in the air. The driver hunched forward over his wheel and stopped. He reached across the front seat and opened the door, smiling smugly at the waiters. Slaverne saw Charlie crawling along the curb, his velvet dress torn at the shoulder. Slaverne slipped into the front seat and, with his face framed in the side window, he blew the waiters a Hedy Lamarr kiss. As the car sped off, the waiters broke into applause.

MELLOW YELLOW

The McBrides lived in a comfortable house in a row of red-brick houses on the south side of Amelia Street. There were tall sheltering elms and a stone wall on the north side of the street, a wall that enclosed the old cemetery. Beyond the cemetery was a railroad track, a single line that was used only early in the morning when Marie-Claire would waken to a low train whistle and get up to draw back her bedroom curtains and look out over the stones – many of the thin slabs tilted and broken. She'd played in the cemetery as a child. She had never been afraid of the graves, not since she'd stretched out on her stomach and called down into the earth and listened, called again, and listened. No one had answered. She'd decided that no one was there, that she was safe inside the walls, so the first time she'd let a boy touch her naked body had been in the long tufted grass, lying between the stones. But he'd been so frightened of the dead and her white body in the failing light of dusk that he'd suddenly stood up and run away to the doorway in the wall.

At nineteen, her full breasts trembled when she walked quickly. She had long legs and auburn hair down to her shoulders. Boys whistled at her when she walked down the street. She didn't mind. Sometimes she put two fingers to her mouth, as her father had taught her, and whistled back. She didn't like young men her own age. She liked men who were old enough to be serious, but that didn't mean she liked old men. Older men weren't serious, she said. They were worried about dying. She never thought about death, even when she went for a walk in the graveyard. She felt wonderfully alone and at ease with herself among the stones, alive and eager to see the world. That's why she thought the morning train whistle was like a call, and on some mornings as the train rumbled slowly past the yard, she leaned against her window and let out a low muffled wail, calling to the train, giddy with expectation as she went down to breakfast where her mother said to her, "Whatever in the world are you going to do with your life?" and she said, "I don't know, but I'm going to live it."

She brought Conrad Zingg to the house to have supper with her mother and father. She had been seeing him for several months and her mother had said that she wanted to meet him. "This is Conrad," she said, and her mother smiled because he was tall and slender with a lot of black hair, a firm mouth, and steady dark eyes. "Call me Connie," he said, taking her father's hand but smiling at her mother. He seemed very sure of himself, very amiable and yet aloof. "Yes, all my friends call me Connie," he said and stepped back, shoving his hands into his suitcoat pockets. Her father stepped back, too, disconcerted. "Connie, eh," he said. "Connie what?"

"Connie Zingg."

"Zingg? What kind of name is Zingg?"

"Viennese. My parents came from Vienna when I was a child."

"You grew up here, then?"

"This is my town," he said.

"And here you are," Mrs. McBride said, "at home in our house for supper," then to her husband, "And doesn't Marie-Claire look happy." Conrad said, "Zingg went the strings of her heart." Mrs. McBride laughed, and taking him by the arm she led him into the small dining room. Marie-Claire was startled. She felt a tinge of betrayal. She didn't think they should be talking about her heart, taking for granted how she felt, even though she had wakened that morning wondering, listening to the train, if she didn't love him.

She tried to think of how she would tell him after supper that he shouldn't joke about her feelings, but then as they stood by the table her thoughts drifted back to the afternoon they had spent together on the bay. They had laughed and laughed, riding the ferry, not getting off, but pretending that they were docking at all the great cities. As she had stared at the sunlight on the choppy waves, she'd felt that she was wonderfully safe beside him, safe in the shelter of his self-possession, safe to dream that she could be anywhere she wanted to be in the world. "Well, sit down," her father said. "Marie-Claire, she says you work at being a traffic consultant. What's that?"

"I design the traffic downtown."

"You dress it up?" her mother said.

"No, no," he said affably. "Computers. I work out the timing, the red and green lights, trying to get the flow."

"Stop-and-go," her father said.

"Right."

"You're in charge of the stop-and-go?"

"Right."

They ate their supper. It was a good supper of pot roast and potatoes. Marie-Claire was pleased because her mother was happy. She knew her mother was lonely for company. She also knew that her father was morosely uncomfortable, eating with a stranger in the house. He didn't like having strangers in his home. He thought a home was a safe place for friends where he didn't have to explain himself. He did not have many friends. But Conrad had been very attentive to her father's silences. He had not talked too much or been overbearing. At the end of the evening, after saying goodnight to her parents, he kissed her lightly at the front door and said, "Salt of the earth, your people. Salt of the earth."

Her father was still at the table as she passed to go upstairs, content that she'd shown her parents that a successful young man could be attracted to her and want to court her, but her father called out, "It doesn't work."

"What?" she asked, startled.

"The stop-and-go. Any damn fool can see that?"

"Nonsense," she said angrily.

"He may have designed it, but it doesn't work."

She got into bed feeling wounded, as if her father had passed judgment not only on Conrad but on her. For a moment she wanted to rush downstairs and say as cruelly as she could, "What do you know? What have you ever designed?" but she was naked in her bed and too tired to get dressed again. "Tomorrow is another day," she said and went to sleep.

She admired Conrad's confidence, and how sure he said he was that he had a future. Her mother and father had always talked about the future as a day to be afraid of, a day when everything would go wrong. As she listened to Conrad talk she tried to keep a grave expression on her face. She wanted him to take her seriously. He talked about traffic, and how his control of where and when people went was crucial to the control of chaos. "Red and green, in themselves they don't mean anything," he said. "It's like right and wrong. We agree to agree about what's right, and what's wrong. Red and green. Life's that simple, and that hard."

"I like yellow," she said, though she'd never thought about it before, and in fact, with her auburn hair, she did not think she looked good in yellow.

He laughed. "You're priceless," he said.

"So are you," she said, sitting cross-legged on a sofa in his apartment, watching him throw darts at a yellow and black board he had put up on the door to the hall. Sometimes, he would quietly play by himself for an hour, touching each steel tip of a dart to his tongue, counting down in his head as the darts hit the board. "You've got to not only learn how to count down," he said, "you've got to think backwards." She did not understand why he wanted to think backwards or how he could watch darts programs on the sports television network, sometimes for two hours, hardly saying a word to her. He would glance at her as if he were going to speak, but all too often he had the back of his hand against his mouth. He liked to sit with his hand like that, and once she had said, "Are you chewing your knuckle?"

"No, of course not," he'd said, and he'd put his hand defensively down on his knee, but she had seen that his knuckle was red, almost raw.

"Do I frighten you?" she'd asked impetuously.

"Don't be silly," he'd said. "A slip of a girl like you?"

"Do you want to arm wrestle?"

"I'd break your wrist," he'd said, rubbing at his inflamed knuckle. "Yes, I would."

"No, you wouldn't," she'd said.

One evening, he asked to meet her a little earlier than usual so that they could take a walk before going out to supper. She wore a simple black raw silk dress. His hair was cut. He was very erect as they passed several expensive stores. He gave her an approving smile and folded her arm under his. Then he stopped by a jewellery store window and asked which ring she liked, and when she said she wasn't looking for a ring, he grew sullen and distant.

"I don't like diamonds," she said. "I like pearls."

"Diamonds are a girl's best friend," he said.

"Not this girl. And I don't like red roses either," she said, trying to take a light impish air. "Yellow, white, anything but red." He said nothing. For some inexplicable reason as they walked along the street in silence she felt guilty, as if she had failed him.

She asked him where they were going.

"Why, we're going to The Senator."

The Senator was an expensive supper club, a sophisticated jazz lounge. He led her up the stairs and through the door, and she let him hold her hand as if he were guiding her, certain that there was a grace in her stride because she had studied how all the models in the fashion films on television walked. She could see that he was pleased with her because he walked beside her with his shoulders squared, an almost stern and disdainful look in his eyes that might have frightened her if she hadn't been so sure he was like this only because he wanted to have her.

The head waiter pointed to a side table, but Conrad took the waiter's arm firmly and nodded to the front. "We'll sit down by Mr. Jackson, thanks. He'll be glad to see us…"

"But, sir…"

"No buts about it."

"Sir —

"Thank you…"

Conrad, with a quick wave of his arm, almost as if he were directing traffic – which made her laugh gaily – led her through the close tables and then when they were seated he leaned across to her, before they ordered drinks, and said, "Today is my birthday."

"Your birthday... Why didn't you tell me... I should be taking you out... I don't have anything for you."

"You're all I want," he said, looking directly at her.

She put her head in her hands for a moment and let out a low, quiet wailing sound. He looked perplexed. "What was that?" he asked.

"That's how I whistle in the dark," she said, trying to laugh.

He looked very grave and she thought he was watching her as if he were trying to trace her thoughts. She sat back in her chair. The week before, he had told her that she had to make up her mind about their future, and had given her until his birthday to decide, but she was sure he hadn't told her when his birthday was and hadn't given it any thought at all. Only now, with the steadiness in his eyes, did she realize that he had been serious.

She pouted. It was ridiculous to suddenly thrust such a decision on her. How could she decide? They had been close, had had wonderful moments in which she'd felt both safe and free, and they'd made love several times, but he had never really talked about love. He had never said that he loved her though he had said one night that he valued her more than anything he had in the world. She had wanted to cry when he'd said that, but now she thought, *He's never said that he actually loves me,* and she resented his restraint and his self-assurance. *Well,* she thought, *when he mentions it, then we can talk it out.*

J.J. Jackson, the pianist, came to their table. He greeted Conrad warmly, calling him Connie, and said, "You got yourself a fine-looking lady. *Fine.*" Conrad asked him to sit down, and before she could say tartly that she thought she had a *fine*-looking man,

Jackson told her that he had met Conrad in night traffic court. He said he'd been charged with "something really stupid, entering into a left-turn lane when the light was already yellow, stopping and then turning against the red." Conrad, who was waiting to argue his own traffic ticket, had suddenly offered to appear as a witness for him. "He was some kinda brilliant," Jackson said. "He had that judge all turned around inside his head, with the time of this and the time of that, and how this and that were impossible. Finally, this here judge, he says, 'How do you know all this?' and he says, 'Because I designed the whole system, Your Honour.' I thought I'd laugh till I died at the look on that judge's face." Jackson smacked him hard on the back. "My main man," he said. "My ace boon coon. Who then said to the judge, 'I have my own ticket, Your Honour.' But the judge he says, 'Out. Forget it. No more.'" Conrad accepted this display of admiration and warmth with ease. He looked so satisfied that she wondered if he hadn't seen Jackson's wry smirk and wondered why he would let anyone smack him so hard on the back. When Jackson left, Conrad settled into his reserved aloof air, the back of his hand against his mouth. She reached out and touched his free hand that was flat on the table and he smiled again, looking directly at her, a silent resolve in his eyes.

She shrugged and said, "What's it like being a boon coon?" and turned to enjoy the music, clapping enthusiastically after one of Jackson's solos. The crowd around her was clapping loudly, too, so she put two fingers in her mouth and whistled. She was anxious that she might be acting like a young girl but it was the only way she felt she could maintain her sense of herself. So she whistled again and wanted to cry. She couldn't understand why she wanted to cry and why he refused to say anything to her.

They left the lounge and walked home, taking the side streets that were quiet in the night. It had turned cool and she was shivering, yet she didn't cuddle against him as they walked. She didn't feel she could because he was walking with his hands in his pockets. He talked about baseball and a woman who was trying to swim across Lake Ontario for charity, for crippled children, and he seemed not only concerned about the children but quite content with her, but she knew he was not content and she thought he was not being honest, not being fair. She was angry and refused to walk all the way home in resigned silence.

"Would you like this to be our last night, Connie?"

"That's up to you…"

"No, it's not," she said fiercely and wheeled away, but somehow she knew that if she said any more he would just smile at her. She knew she would never forgive him if he smiled at her in her rage. She remembered how he had smiled at her in The Senator, as if he were being patient with her. She was tempted to put two fingers in her mouth and whistle at him. Instead, she punched him on the arm. "You're something else," she said.

"And so are you."

They stood at the bottom of the stairs to her veranda. He was suddenly talking to her again, as if they had not been silent almost all the way home, and he was talking about how he hoped to move out of traffic control into policy planning for the whole city. "But never into politics," he said. "You just get your brains beaten in in politics and beaten in by any clunkhead who comes along." He told her it took courage to plan the future, to go to the top. "That's the way it is at city hall," he said. "The politicians, the dorks who don't know what they're doing, they are on the ground floor, the planners are on the top floor." He kissed her lightly on the cheek.

Then, after a moment in which he held her hand, looking down as if he were meditative and shy, he said, "Goodnight, Marie-Claire..." and began to turn away.

"Connie...just a minute, Connie..."

There were tears in her eyes.

"Connie, don't go away yet..."

He turned to her eagerly, expectantly, and she felt very young, very unknowing, beside him. He seemed to have counted on her calling out.

"Connie..."

He touched her cheek, as if his touch could help her out of her confusion, but she didn't feel confused. She felt bullied by his silence. She wanted to slap his face and tell him he was pig-headed and arrogant. "I guess I'm just yellow," she said.

"What?"

"Yellow."

"There's no need to be scared," he said.

"Who said I'm scared? You don't know what I'm talking about, do you? You don't know where the hell I'm coming from."

She turned and walked calmly up the stairs and into the house, leaving him standing on the walk. For a moment, as she peeked through the lace curtains covering the small oval glass window in the door, she thought he was going to come up the stairs and her heart leapt, but he turned and walked across the street and stood against the cemetery wall. At first, she thought she could feel him willing her out of the house, to come to him, and she was afraid. Then, as she watched him stand for so long in the shadows with his back to the wall and his hand to his mouth, she thought he looked lonely and lost and she was sure he was waiting for her, as he had waited all night, because he couldn't bring himself to cross the street, couldn't say that he wanted her, couldn't say that he loved her. She felt a sudden urge to comfort him, to go to him and hold him and say, "You want to arm wrestle? Never mind, you win," but then she thought with contempt, *He'd be scared stiff if I ever took him off into the graveyard at night.* She turned away from the door, shut off the hall light, and went into the kitchen, where her mother and father were having their bedtime cup of tea.

As she saw them sitting so quietly at the table, as they had sat for years, she felt more confident about her life, and yet she also felt ashamed that she had not been more of a friend to her mother and father in their home. She kissed her startled mother on the forehead and then, full of a strange new mellowness, she draped her arms around her father's neck and said, "You're right, it doesn't work."

"What?" he asked, astonished.

"The stop-and-go. It doesn't work."

She went upstairs to bed. She couldn't wait to go to sleep and then wake in the morning to the call of the train whistle coming to her across the graveyard.

THE MUSCLE

Livio Scarpadello was late for school because of the morning walk he'd taken with his father, a long walk, and when they were in front of Settimio's Café, where there were chrome coffee machines in the window, his father had insisted that they sit down at one of the small Arborite tables and have a thimble-cup of good strong espresso. He'd smiled and patted Livio's hand as if it were the old days of bleaching morning sunlight in the village. Then they had hurried along the street to the dowdy red-brick school and at the door he'd said, "Livio, you listen, always listen to the teacher."

His father had been a stonemason in the hills outside Taormina, and his father loved stone, the way it captured light and held it – "like life itself," he said – speckled with colour and yet it could be a dead weight, almost as heavy as a dead body, except stones never sleep. Though the real secret of stone, he said, like the stone he'd cut for the village fountain, was when you held it to your ear. If you listened hard you could hear water, water locked in the stone. Livio always wondered why the village men sat hunched against the stone with their legs stretched out, never listening, not even to each other, as they laughed and joked and got quietly drunk on black wine in the early evening.

When Livio got to the classroom he hung back at the door, not because he was a little late but because Mr. Beale, the history teacher, always made him feel small and unimportant, made him feel like a stranger who could never belong in this new world. Yet it consoled him to know that all the students felt unimportant when Mr. Beale was teaching.

Today he was talking about Rome. He was a tall and easy-going man with a confident air who collected ancient glass bottles, which he sometimes brought to class so he could show the students how all the impurities in the once-clear glass had caused beautiful lace-like discolourations. He liked to amble back and forth in his tweed suit, talking in a rambling, authoritative way about history, and sometimes he would open his long arms wide as if he were offering his students all the wisdom in the world.

Livio hoped he could sneak into the room without catching Mr. Beale's eye. He never wanted Mr. Beale to single him out again because the last time Livio was late Mr. Beale had said sarcastically, "Where did you come from?" as if he had never seen him before. "You don't belong here, do you? Ah, you do, you do. I believe that's true," and all the students had laughed. Later, between classes, they had called out, "Where you from, Livio boy?"

But he hesitated too long at the door. Mr. Beale saw him and cried out, "Come in, come in, you're among friends." Someone at the back of the room snickered as Livio sat down, hunched forward, listening to Mr. Beale, who was suddenly standing in the light in front of the big window, opening his arms.

"Livio, you should know about this. I bet you know all about Rome and Carthage, yes? So, the great question is: Did the Romans make a mistake? Was it a mistake to wipe out Carthage?"

Livio looked up, wondering, a little wide-eyed, shaking his head.

"Carthage," Mr. Beale repeated, dryly.

"Yes," Livio said.

"Delenda est Carthago," Mr. Beale said.

"Yes."

"Was it a mistake, eh? Was it in their own interest to kill off their enemy forever?"

"No, Carthage no mistake," Livio said, smiling.

"Wrong," Mr. Beale said, turning away. "These things always seem so simple, but life's complex, boys," and he turned back to Livio for a moment with a wan smile and then went on to explain that the Romans should have worked out a deal with the Carthaginians in the same way the Americans had come to terms with Germany after the war. "Because you can't get blood out of a stone. You've got to get your enemy in debt to you, make them thankful partners, because you can't feed off yourself surrounded by people entirely alien to you, which is what Rome ended up doing. And you won't find that in your books." The class was over. Mr. Beale looked pleased with himself.

He put these difficult questions to Livio every day and sometimes Livio stared and said nothing, not sure what was going on. One day Mr. Beale, throwing open his arms, said, "Livio, you pay attention. Always you listen. You gotta to listen," and the boys broke into loud laughter. Mr. Beale smiled and patted one of the laughing boys on the back as he walked to the blackboard.

Livio sat rubbing his knuckles, but then he thought about his father who was no longer a stonemason but only a bricklayer, uprooted from a village that had been left behind, broken and empty, and now he was living with his wife and son in a damp basement flat, laying bricks and working like a day labourer, never complaining.

When Mr. Beale went by and tapped Livio on the shoulder, saying, "You do well, Livio, you get better every day," he sat locked in silence, confused and angry. He remembered a little mute boy everyone in the village had made fun of. His father had told him that there were voices inside the boy, deep inside, and all he had to do was open up the boy's mouth and put his ear as close as he could and he'd hear them. He'd hear strange old grandfathers whispering. And one day Livio had pried the frightened boy's mouth open, staring down into the dark gaping hole that smelled so sour he had turned away, surprised as the boy broke into tears, his mouth hanging open. Livio, sitting very straight in his seat, felt like crying, afraid that Mr. Beale might come and force open his mouth. Closing his eyes, Livio drifted off into a dream of village evenings and how he used to amuse his father and the men around the fountain with the little trick muscle in his wrist.

Later in the afternoon, Livio rolled up his sleeve and felt the two little cords that ran down his right wrist. He put a thin dime on the cords, clenching his right fist, slowly turning his wrist. The cords tensed and then a small muscle popped up, the coin flipped over and landed on his wrist. Livio smiled. The boy sitting behind Livio poked him and said, "Hey, do that again." Livio shook his head. "Come on, I want to see that again."

Livio put the coin on the cords, clenched his fist, and turned it as the boy leaned forward. Livio, suddenly at ease, laughed with the boy as the coin flipped over.

"What's going on there?"

Livio slumped down in his seat, but the boy leaned into the aisle and said, "Livio has a trick, sir."

Mr. Beale, buttoning his jacket, came to their seats.

"Let's see your trick. What kind of trick?"

Livio shook his head.

"Come on, we your friends. We gotta see everything you canna do." Mr. Beale turned to the class. "Don't we, class?"

They all shouted yes and the boy behind Livio pushed him. "Go on, show them."

Livio looked up and saw Mr. Beale, aloof, stroking his neck, the light on his narrow face from the big window, and Mr. Beale said softly, almost soothingly, "You show us your little trick, eh, Livio?"

Livio put the coin on his wrist. All the boys were watching him. The muscle popped up and the coin flipped over. The class was silent and then someone called out, "Do it again."

Livio quickly put the coin back on his wrist, but Mr. Beale said no to Livio and wheeled on the class with a wave of his arm. "We don't a turn thisa room into a circus." But there was no laughter. "We can't have this in the middle of class," he said sternly. "We've got work to do."

"But you said you wanted to see it," a boy cried out.

Mr. Beale shrugged, as if what had happened was of no consequence because they were all friends and it was over, but Livio suddenly stood up and thrust the coin out at the teacher, who, startled, waved Livio aside. Livio held out the coin to him again.

"You want me to try your little trick?"

Livio nodded and sat down. Mr. Beale rolled up his sleeve and put the coin on his wrist. Clenching his fist, he twisted his wrist back and forth, yet the coin stayed still. He flushed, little blotches of red breaking out in his cheeks as he stood staring at the profile of a sailing ship on the coin, his long arm extended, his hand white. The class started to laugh. Humiliated by the laughter, he tossed the coin into Livio's lap and went back to his desk, picking up a book and then putting it down. He began to write all the dates of Caesar's conquests on the blackboard and he told them to memorize them.

When class was over, the boys gathered around Livio. The tallest, Abner Such, who was muscular but usually shy because he wore thick glasses, smacked him on the back and asked him to do the trick again. Livio shuffled, embarrassed. Mr. Beale, trying to be friendly and part of the good feeling, called out, "You don't want to forget the football game, boys." No one paid any attention. Livio saw the teacher lift his arm as if to speak, but the boys were all laughing and Mr. Beale sat down. The room cleared and Livio and the teacher were alone.

With a loose smile on his face, Mr. Beale stood up awkwardly, as if wanting to be bigger than Livio. Feeling uncertain for a moment, Livio finally looked up, smiling. "My English pretty good, eh?" he said helpfully. "I think I do pretty good."

"Very well, you've done very well."

"I think it's so."

Livio didn't know what to do. There was a button missing on the teacher's jacket sleeve, and Mr. Beale stood twisting the loose nub of thread. He seemed to be waiting for some snide little word from Livio, sure that it was coming, but then Livio suddenly reached out and took Mr. Beale's hand. His own blue wide-open eyes had a vulnerable look, yet his grip on Mr. Beale's hand was firm. "I don't hold no bad feelings, Mr. Teacher," he said. "You neither, I think, eh?"

"No, no. Of course not, Livio," he said stiffly, as if sure he was being mocked in some new way by a boy who deeply disliked him.

"Sir, it's only a trick," Livio said, fumbling for the right words. "I practise. You practise, too, sir, eh?" And he took the dime out of his pocket and put it in Mr. Beale's hand, the one he was holding. "Take it, sir. Friends now, eh?"

"Well, now, see here…" Mr. Beale began, his face flushing again, and because of the way Mr. Beale was staring at him, Livio felt uneasy. Mr. Beale looked lonely and disappointed, a look Livio had seen in the eyes of men slouched around his father's fountain, and he wondered if the teacher knew that stones never sleep, and sometimes are heavy because they're full of water that you could hear if only you listened..

"Livio," Mr. Beale began, and then his hand tightened on Livio's, the grip so tight it was painful. "Thank you. Thank you very much." Looking at the coin he said quickly, "Yes, Livio, I'll hold on to this."

A DRAWN BLIND

Oldham Amis lived in a yellow-brick house with a peaked slate roof and a pillared front veranda. He'd inherited the house from his father, a seemingly cheerful man, who had made a small fortune through a company he'd called Tubs-R-Us.

"What do people want?" his father had asked. "They want to cover things up, that's what. Like they'd never been there."

He'd gotten rid of claw-footed, cast-iron old bathtubs for customers by encasing them in plastic baths instantly moulded into place.

"The baths look like nothing special but they fit where you want 'em to fit."

He had freely spent his money on travelling, going on expensive cruise ships "with the boys." He'd put a lot of money into a chain of retirement homes for the elderly. "They're the future," he'd said. He'd also bought a dozen very expensive stone grotesques carved by a friend in the mortuary business, decorating the front lawn with stone unicorns, fawns, lion cubs, and grimacing dwarfs. Inside the house, he'd insisted on hanging a brass barometer on the wall over the tub in the bathroom, saying, "Good to know what pressure we're under and when."

Mrs. Amis had kept to herself through the years. She'd her own easy chair where, night after night, she'd sat with scented handkerchiefs in her sleeves, which she'd used to touch her temples while she'd read romances by Mazo de la Roche. When her husband, whom she always called "Mr. Harold," died of a heart attack in a gay Church Street sauna, she'd gone out to the garage, gotten a tire iron, and smashed all the stone animals on the lawn. Oldham, in his early twenties, had come home to find her sitting under the barometer, running boiling water into the open tub, the room dense with steam. Harold had left his estate to his son, not to his wife.

Oldham, who had a part-time position lecturing in history at an evening college, had kept his mother company in the late afternoons, and had tried reading aloud the gossip in newspapers, but she'd become, like other widows on Walmer Road, a secret drinker, and her mind had wandered as she'd sat wrapped in a blanket on the veranda, drinking Baileys Irish Cream from a china cup, pretending it was tea. He'd sat in silence, his long legs crossed, because there was little more he could say to her. She'd only cared about Slavs and Jews and their noisy children who had been moving onto the street from the South Market.

"Don't you see," she had cried out one evening, touching her temple with a little white lace handkerchief, "we're all fakes, like Mazo de la Roche. Did you know her actual name was really Mazie Roche? They're overrunning us, those scum. Listen to them. And we deserve it, no backbone, any of us."

Sometimes when the children were playing street hockey she'd call the police and in a little while a patrol car would ease around the corner and a cop would tell the noisy kids to get off the street.

"That's all that's left to count on," she'd say, "the police."

When his mother died he was certainly financially secure but he kept on teaching the history class every Wednesday night. He liked talking to the class about the mistakes generals made, how history, especially when men were at their most optimistic, was always in decline. In a small book about a courtesan who'd inexplicably committed suicide, he found the epitaph he had carved on his mother's headstone: *TIRED of THIS ETERNAL BUTTON-ING and UNBUTTONING.* His father's old friend, the mortician, was offended, but he didn't care. He began to collect books of epitaphs as a special kind of history, and when he found out that the hill his college was on had been called Gallows Hill, because the blue clay had been used to make the bricks for the first death house in the city, he felt a warm confirmation of his sense of how things secretly hung together, and that was the pleasure he sought in all his books, a confirmation of how he felt about life. Outside the college class, he didn't talk to many people and didn't change his mind about many things. His house was filled with all kinds of books and their clutter irritated him. He didn't want to reread them and yet, because they had been expensive, he couldn't bring himself to give them away or throw them out.

Then, in a subway station, he saw the ticket-taker in the glass cage reading a paperback novel. The man, rather than set the book down and mark his place, would just tear off the cover and then tear off the pages as he finished them, dropping them into a waste can, whittling the book down to nothing. This seemed so sensible to Oldham that from then on he read only paperbacks, and even when he sat reading on the front lawn, he placed a little waste can down beside his right shoe.

One evening while he was listening to a baseball game, the sun filtering through the silver birch trees, the living room in a lovely rose wash light, he sat drinking brandy in his Sheridan armchair beside the old upright radio and he wrote notes to himself in a neat cramped hand in a book bound in black leather. For nearly three months he'd been keeping a journal, not what he did from day to day, but quotes and small reflections. Listening to the ball game and Mudcat Grant, who was pitching a no-hitter, he wrote: "The deepest root desire we have is to project totally ourselves, cookie-cutter shapes of who we are; hence, Adam's rib becomes Eve so that he can copulate with his image of himself, and the Virgin, she conceives her son out of herself; love thyself as thy neighbour…"

He took off his round steel-rimmed glasses and sat with his eyes closed, half-brooding, half-listening. By the seventh inning of the ball game he was so caught up in Grant's no-hitter that he suddenly realized he was sitting in total darkness. He wanted to share his excitement because he was on the edge of his chair, hanging on every pitch, but he found himself touched by a bitter sweetness and surprise and a flutter of panic because he'd never seen himself as so absolutely alone. He stood up, remembering the time as a boy that he'd gone sailing with his father in a rented boat in Toronto Bay. He'd lain down behind his father at the wheel, refusing to look at the heavy waves that smashed the boat broadside, and with his eyes shut he'd repeated, "Jesus Mary and Joseph," just like he'd heard his mother moaning one late evening alone in the kitchen, but on the boat his father kept calling out, "Nothing can go wrong, Oldie, old kid," and nothing had gone wrong. Oldham had been ashamed but his father had said, "You got to feel the pressure of fear to find out what it is and once you know, then you know how to handle it." Now Oldham, in the dark of his living room, smiled, feeling buoyant and unafraid and at ease. He went out for a long walk, forgetting about Grant and the baseball game.

The more he thought about being alone, the more he liked it. He didn't want to talk to women for too long and he was glad he didn't have to get to know his once-a-week students. Standing in a crowd or sitting at a bar, his sense of his own apartness gave him a feeling of security, as if he couldn't be touched, and also a sense of self-discipline. Of an evening, after delivering a paper to his class – looking back, his favourite was about tombstone jokes – he'd go to the movies or a club if there was a good Dixieland band on the stand. Once a week he had supper in the Oak Room in the King Edward Hotel, usually milk-fed veal or medallions of beef in wine and mushroom sauce. Then he walked along to the Dundas Street strip-joints, watched a show, and hired one of the hookers who lined the lounge walls every night. He liked his no-nonsense approach to the whole matter, and though he kept his little notes to himself in his leather-bound book, he was sure too much reflection, too much analysis of the self, was a kind of self-hatred. He was delighted one night when he found a quote, unattributed, in a collection of epitaphs: "Nowadays not even a suicide kills himself in desperation. Before taking the step, he deliberates so long and so carefully that he literally chokes with thought. It is even questionable whether he ought to be called a suicide, since it is really thought which takes his life. He does not die with deliberation, but from deliberation."

Late one night there was a soft rain, more like a mist, and when he went to sit on the veranda around midnight, the street lamps glowing up in the caves of maple leaves touched him with an almost sensual longing, not for anything lost in the past, because he had no particular regrets, but it was a kind of projected homesickness for the future – a wondering whether in the midst of his calmness he was already into his decline, a wondering whether he was going to end in a fog like his mother or die in a wrong place like his father. He tried not to think about how and where his father had died.

As he sat with his arms folded across his chest, hugging himself because he felt an evening chill, he stared at the houses across the road, thinking they were like a row of crypts in the night. He looked up and down the street for lights in the windows, looking for some sign of what went on in all those darkened rooms, because the big old homes were now rooming houses filled with blacks and haggard whites.

He started walking late at night when the streets were empty, nearly everyone asleep, except for those few random lights in windows with the blinds always tightly drawn, making the light seem secret and more mysterious. He found himself making up little scenes, imagining what was going on behind those blinds, as if he'd walked quickly by an open doorway in one of the downtown hooker hotels and seen bodies caught in a flash of light and then they were gone, no names, forgotten. This left him with the same feeling as he had sitting down to supper in the Oak Room, where he was part of the place and yet apart. He didn't want to meet any of the people who lived in the houses any more than he would have spoken to people in those rooms in the hotels, but he liked thinking that there were transient lives being lived in the half-light of those rooms, lives as mysterious as his own, because he thought with a sudden rush of satisfaction that if anyone were to pay any particular attention to him, surely he would seem a mysterious self-enclosed man to his neighbours. Motorcycle policemen going by slowly at one and two in the morning gave him quizzical looks as he sauntered along the sidewalk in his tweed jacket.

One night, he heard the low, mournful wail of a horn, and as he stood listening it sounded like someone playing *The Last Post*. He went out into the street just in time to see a woman in slacks running away through the shadows toward Dupont Street. There was a light in the big front room on the second floor in the house across the street. Someone was pacing back and forth behind the drawn blind. Out on the balcony, a man stood playing a trombone, the horn angled up into the air. A short bald man dressed in slippers and a dressing gown sidled up to Oldham on the lawn and said, "Must be up there, I bet."

MERMAID

He woke up hearing the ocean. He closed his eyes as if he were still asleep and listened because he was nowhere near an ocean. He had been born in a concentration camp, survived the camp, and made a life for himself selling insurance. Now sixty years old and having never been to an ocean, he was in bed with a woman who thought she was old because she was thirty-eight, and he thought she was young because she was thirty-eight. It was her bed; the pillows were of soft down.

"Do you hear the ocean?" he asked. He had never slept all night in anyone else's bed.

She opened an eye. Her left eye. It was a pale ice-blue. It was a blue clock, he thought.

He couldn't remember her having blue eyes.

"Yes," she said. "I love swimming in the ocean."

"You do?"

"Yes."

He was worried that if she opened her other eye it would be blue, too.

"I was sure you had brown eyes," he said.

"Right. Because I'm a mermaid," she said. "All mermaids have brown eyes."

She laughed. Her teeth were very white and the tip of her tongue between her teeth was pink. She drew his head down to her belly, between her thighs. He took a deep breath.

He could smell the ocean.

He tasted the ocean.

"Only great men have ever slept with a mermaid," she said and opened her other eye.

It was blue.

"You're no mermaid," he said.

"Welcome to the real world," she said.

"No, no," he said.

He was still strong, lean, and muscular. He made a fist and showed her the inside of his forearm, a tattoo.

It was a mermaid.

"You've got a mermaid tattoo on your arm," she said.

"No, look very hard," he said, and he drew her head down to his arm.

She said his skin smelled like smoke, she had smelled it all night. He said, "No, just look, look hard."

She looked and at last she said, "Numbers. There's numbers inside the mermaid."

He said, "Yes, they disappeared in my little mermaid."

"Why'd you do that?" she asked as she lay back in her soft bed. She looked almost unbearably young to him.

"Because I am alive and she is now my real world. She has brown eyes, and those others who gave me the numbers are dead and they had blue eyes," and he leaned over her, lightly kissed her eyes closed, and said, "Now we make love again."

EVERYBODY WANTS
TO GO TO HEAVEN

A man can die of fright in his dreams. That's what Cecil said he did, describing how he had died and how being one of the living dead was just like doing the dead man's float, face down into the water, drifting with his eyes open. He'd sit in his chair for hours, staring straight ahead, slumped where his wife sat him every morning before she fed him cornflakes, a poached egg, and toast. Once a day she mourned for him. She stood in the kitchen with her eyes closed and rocked back and forth on the balls of her feet, holding a slice of bread before she put it in the toaster, moaning low, a deep moaning for a woman so small. Sometimes she crooned to him. He seemed to like that, which wasn't surprising since he'd always been a crooner around the house himself. She still dressed him in his green golfing slacks and canary yellow sweaters and the shoes with the little leather tassels. He'd been an actuary for an insurance company. Cecil Klose, the actuary, calculating the odds on death. "I'm always the first man in with the odd man out," he'd said. "Cecil," she said, "you were a heroic man. Until the day you died you lived a totally boring life." She chucked him under the chin.

He didn't look at her. He didn't blink. Then he said, "Transfer, please. Transfer. I want to change cars."

"I work hard looking after you," she said, glaring at him. "I'm steadfast to you, and I always was, working hard like I was about to go out of my mind, and now you talk to me like you've gone out of yours." She stroked his damp brow with a terry cloth hand towel. "You may have died to all intents and purposes," she said, "but I know you're still in there, thinking." She stirred a glass of orange juice that had been standing so long that the pulp had sunk to the bottom. "Real fresh-squeezed," she said, stirring the juice with a swizzle stick. "Good for the vocal cords."

He had always sung around the house, especially after closing an insurance contract. "You want to know who stands between the beginning and the end?" he'd always said. "It's me, Mister In-Between," and then he'd stood crooning like Frank Sinatra, *"Don't mess with Mister In-Between."* He had a dozen Sinatra albums. "It's not the voice, it's the timing, the phrasing," he'd said. "It's like me doing a deal, the nuance is everything."

She made him drink the orange juice and then wiped his lower lip with her finger.

She took a deep breath.

She puckered her wet lips and ran her hands along the inside of her thighs as if she were aroused. She was not aroused. Both of them now slept in the winterized back porch that was just off the kitchen – he, on a sofa bed that hadn't been closed back into itself for a year, and she, on an old camp cot. She sat down beside the small back porch windows. There were streaks of sunlight on her face. The square windows were screened by climbing sweet peas and hollyhocks, and there were coloured wicker baskets full of thimbles and balls of wool on a pine table. She put brass thimbles on the fingers of her right hand. She started thrumming on the table, a steady rolling as if trying to find a tune, something maybe he would remember and like, *The Boulevard of Broken Dreams.* She began to whine as she thrummed, and this whine became a low keening wail. Then, with a nod to no one, she pulled the thimbles from her fingers and lifted his arms so that they stretched, open-handed, straight out from his body. "Time to do something useful. Time to do the wool." She dropped a loose coil of red wool over his left hand, and then across the gap, over his right hand. In a dry whisper, he said, "I'll tell you how I died..." She drew the skein of wool taut. "No," she said, "not now, there's work to be done. Three balls to get done this morning, red, yellow, and green." She glanced at the huge hamper in the corner. It was full of balls of wool. "I'll tell you how I died," he whispered. She tried not to look at him. There were tears in her eyes. "You can die later," she said. "This is not a game."

"I was washing," he said, "taking a shower, the steam piling up, clouds..."

"That's no fun, talking about that, not now, Cecil. No games."

He'd been good at games. He'd liked dressing up in his green slacks to go out and play golf. He'd liked to play games with children.

His favourite game with the children on the street had been to stand on the sidewalk and let them see a cellophane-wrapped peppermint candy in his hand. In his open hand. He'd held his hands over his head like a boxer being introduced. He'd shown them his closed fists, and then his open hands, empty, and he'd laughed heartily, always pleased when the children had reached for his empty hands, pleased that once again he'd fooled them. "They know I'm a fun guy," he'd said. "I fooled them."

"Fun?" she'd cried once. "What the hell is fun? What is fun?"

"Fun," he'd said, looking at her as if she were crazy, "is when you feel good and you feel good when what's good for you gets done. The trouble is," he'd said, staring directly at her, "some people like to feel bad and feeling bad spreads around like the common cold. The next thing you know, you're in bed for a week, or for life."

"In these arid hours," she'd said.

"What?"

"These arid hours."

"Arid, arid, what kind of word is arid?"

She had never answered that question. She took a deep breath and still didn't answer the question. She kept unwinding wool from the skein around his hands, making a ball. She looked through the porch glass into the tendrils of sweet peas and morning glories. She saw petals of light. Radiant light. And delicate stamens held in the silence of the light in the glass. She knew how to hold on to silence. She could keep silent for days. "You're a wind-sucker for silence," her father had told her when she was a girl, "but so is God with His Word in these arid hours."

She again took a deep breath.

"His Word? What'll it be like?" she'd asked her father.

"It'll be like one of those water bugs you see on a dead calm day on a pond, coming at you like a snub-nosed bullet…"

"I stepped out of the steam," Cecil said. "I stepped out and took a towel and wiped a big circle clean in the mirror and suddenly I was enclosed, enclosed by the circle so that I didn't know where I was except I was gone… Just like that, I was gone, into a dream. I knew it was a dream because I've never felt so right about anything in my whole life, like everything was where it was doomed to be, so I was terrified."

"Terror," she said. "What do you know about terror?"

He said nothing. She said nothing. He stared straight ahead, his hands wrapped in another coil of wool, yellow. Often when they sat like this, so still that she thought she could hear dust falling in the sunlight through the windows, she would begin to laugh, quietly, a dry crackling laugh, and then her laughter would become deep and throaty. When he had first known her he'd thought that every time she laughed she was going to tell him a secret, but she had never told him anything, not anything he thought was a secret, not anything deep, nothing dark or shameful. He had yearned to hear something shameful. But there'd never been anything dark about her. She had beautiful pale skin and pale blue eyes and was sparrow-breasted.

"Little birds for breasts," she'd said ruefully after they'd made love on their wedding night in a motel, "and I don't think they'll ever sing." He'd sat alone in the toilet until dawn, getting drunk on a mickey of Alberta Premium rye whisky, and then he'd told her that a bird in the house means a death in the family and as far as he could see she had twin death for tits. He'd fallen asleep, snoring. She'd put a quarter in the vibrating machine and watched him shake on the bed for twenty minutes. She was angry because she couldn't find any more quarters in her purse. She remembered her mother had told her, "You want to set a man straight, you give him a good shaking." She had cried for three days as they'd driven through the countryside from inn to inn, honeymooning, and for three days he'd said over and over again, "I don't know why I wanted to sound like I hate you. I don't." She'd stopped crying and said, "You do. You hate me. Why did you marry me?" Trying to laugh, he'd said, "You were the only woman I ever saw who wore open-toed shoes – your big toes sticking out, painted red." He'd laughed. He had a measured laugh. Like a metronome. *Heh huh, heh huh.* She'd said, like she was suddenly talking about something else, "Remember Jayne Mansfield?" And he'd asked, "Why?" And she'd whispered, "Decapitated. She had the biggest birds in America and she got decapitated in a car accident."

"Heh huh."

"At times like this it's just best to take a deep breath," she'd said. "Breathe in, breathe out, like a breath of wind in the garden."

She sat, breathing deeply in, deeply out.

"The garden's full of nests," she told him, peering through the porch glass and the climbing flowers, as if she were announcing a discovery.

"And I could hear a bird that morning, after I showered," he said, staring straight ahead. "I could hear one lone bird once the circle had closed and it wasn't singing, it was whispering. Everything was all steamy white and there was a bird whispering and the bird was so big that all the whiteness was inside the beak of the bird. I could see the sun in the bird's throat. But it didn't give off any light, only a glow with no reflection, and then it went out, so there was only a dim, gold, band-like rim. Though there was no sun I could still see walls of sheer ice a way off in the distance. I knew they were the walls of the universe. I knew I was in the mind of God. I was so scared I wanted to cry, but everything was so brittle in the cold that I was afraid to cry because my bones would break if I even breathed. Then I saw how lucky I was, because I knew I had died and nothing could be worse than being afraid of God, being dead and not knowing that you had died."

"I'm not afraid of dying," she said. "And I'm not afraid of God."

He said nothing. There was a little spittle at the corner of his mouth. She tossed two balls of wool into the hamper and wiped the spittle away from his mouth. She wiped his brow with a damp cloth. He had always been meticulous and now she was meticulous with him. There was an Arborite tray attached to his chair. She put both his hands on the tray, palms down, fingers spread, and then unzipped a small black leather pouch, taking out scissors, tweezers, and a short pearl-handled nail file. She began to clean his nails, to probe under the nails and to push the cuticles back, so fiercely that thread-lines of blood appeared along two of the cuticles. She dabbed the blood away with cotton batten. "No, God means nothing to me," she said as she stood up, went to the sink, and took down a mug, soap, and a straight razor. She had learned how to strop a blade. He had always used an electric shaver, but she liked the sound of stropping. There was something sensual about it. It aroused her. And she liked to strop the blade in front of him, though he never altered his gaze, never looked at the leather or the blade. But once she'd got a lather in the mug and had brushed it onto his jaw, what she really loved was shaving him – the clean track through the white lather, the feel of the sharp blade against the stubble, the rasping sound. It was the sound, and the feel of the sound in her fingers, that she loved best, as she shaved his throat clean, particularly around a mole that was over his Adam's apple, a mole she'd never noticed until she'd had to shave him.

"I don't know how I never saw that mole," she said.

There was so much about his body that she had never noticed, had never seen before. "Transfer, please," he said. "Transfer, I want to change cars." She took off his slippers and put on his brown shoes with the leather tassels. She changed his clothes every morning after breakfast and every evening just before the eleven o'clock TV news. She also washed him on the porch before bed, washed him and examined every part of his body, surprised each time by the hard boniness of his feet, the yellow of his toenails, the patch of black hair in the small of his back. She had spread his legs and stared for a long time at his scrotum and penis, soft and shrunken back into his body. He was not circumcised so she'd drawn the skin back, washed him with a small face cloth, and found herself smiling at his limpness, and one testicle hanging lower than the other. It was the left one. Her mother had told her that a woman's left breast was always lower than her right because of the sorrow and disappointment in a woman's heart. She wondered if the hanging testicle was the mark of a man's sorrow and disappointment, too. She suddenly bent down and gave his penis a pecking kiss. She'd never kissed his penis. He'd never asked her to. Now she kissed and stroked him but nothing happened. She couldn't arouse him. She was enraged. "Look at you. Mr. In-Between, Mr. Fucking In-Between," she said, astonished at hearing herself say *fucking*. She had never said the word aloud in her life, she had only mouthed it in the dark. Standing up, she folded her arms and began to moan and sway and rock back and forth on the balls of her feet as if in deep pain, a pain in her marrow, and then she slowly drew the blanket up over his still body stretched out in the sofa bed, tucking the blanket to his chin as she said bitterly, "Death was always in you."

"Transfer, please."

"No, you don't get off that way."

"Transfer, I want to change cars."

"No, you've got to live with the truth just like I've got to live with it. The truth is the truth. You can't change the truth. We can't change anything else, why should we want to change the truth? That baby died in my womb. That baby had death in him, the death that's been in your seed from day one, the death that you've got in you."

"Transfer, please."

"That life in me, that breathing life was dead before it had half a chance. You're a carrier. I miscarried because you're a carrier."

"Transfer, please, *heh huh*. Transfer." He blinked, blinked again, and began to sweat.

"Oh Cecil, Cecil," she said, suddenly laughing and patting his hand. "It's all in the phrasing, isn't it?" She let out a piercing scream. And then another. And another.

The phone rang. It was an automated voice, the telephone company offering new long-distance rates. *Stay on the line for further information…* "No, thank you," she said and hung up. She stood drumming her fingers on the phone's cradle.

"And I stood waiting, waiting," he said, calling her away from the phone. "The bird was whispering but it wasn't words, and then I saw what I knew was one of God's thoughts, a thought for me. It was right there, standing in front of me, in front of the hollow sun. It looked like a wolverine, one of the animals of His mind, who'd come to have a word with me, slavering, an amber light in his black eyes. *For such is my beloved.* That was the word, the words I heard as the wolverine drew his claw like a razor from my throat to my gut and opened me up, hauling my innards out, and then the animal entered into me, closing the wound behind him, until I could feel it, this living cannibal thought, possessing me from within, devouring me, until at last I knew I was seeing nothing with my own eyes, I was no longer me. I was terrified and dead and born again as this wolverine, and I knew that the landscape I now saw was blood-red, as red as it had been white, and I heard the word, *live in the blood*, knowing I had died, that my body was like that gold rim of the sun, a closed circle, empty at the core…"

He lifted his hand and drew a circle in the air. She put her hand up and touched the line of the circle. He'd always loved circles.

That's why he'd always given children on the street soap-bubble blowers. "There," he'd said as children surrounded themselves with the diaphanous globes, "is perfection in the air." He'd also been able to draw perfect circles and he'd always carried newly sharpened HB pencils in his breast pocket, and whether he'd been at work or whether he was watching reruns of *The Honeymooners* on television on Sunday mornings, he'd always drawn circles on a legal-size pad, saying, "Leonardo da Vinci could draw perfect circles. He was a southpaw, too. Said it was the sign of the greatest artist in the world, freehand circles." And he'd carried three stainless-steel half-shells in his suitcoat pocket. His insurance clients had loved to play the shell game, trying, as he'd moved the pea around under the shells, to guess where the pea was. He'd been very quick. "The pea is like your heart," he'd said. "If you could find the pea real easy, there'd be no mystery." That's why, when he'd held candy in his hands over his head, he had told the children, "Go ahead, find my heart." He'd happily shown them an empty hand after they had guessed wrong. Then, to make them feel foolish and grateful, he'd always given them the candy anyway, with his little laugh, *heh huh, heh huh.*

"That's really what I can never forgive you for, Cecil," she said as she lifted his arms and began to wind more wool.

"I'll tell you how I died," he said.

"Never mind," she said.

"Doing the dead man's float."

"Grateful, Cecil, you wanted me to be grateful."

"I'll tell you how I died…"

She wound the wool taut. "When I wash you, clean you, I don't want you to feel grateful."

"Transfer, please."

She took the wool from Cecil's hands and put his hands down in his lap. She listened for the postman's step. It was very quiet. She listened hard. The postman didn't pass by. The disability cheques were late. She was angry. She looked at his fingernails. They were clean. She thought she might cut them back even closer. She began to hum, and then sing:

> *Love and marriage,*
> *love and marriage,*
> *go together like a horse*
> *and carriage...*

He stared straight ahead, a little spit at the corner of his mouth. The spittle reminded her of one of her spinster schoolteachers. The spittle disgusted her, the more she looked at it. She was seething with anger and screamed, "Wipe your mouth." He didn't move.

She took off her gold wedding band. She was surprised at how easily it came off. His ring was more difficult. She yanked it over the knuckle. She weighed the two rings in the palm of her hand and then held them up to his eyes between her thumbs and forefingers, like spectacles. "Look," she cried. "Look. Just like the sun, just like the sun you saw in God's mind. Empty. What do you think about that?"

"Please," he said.

"What?"

"Please. I want to get off."

"Oh, yes, I bet you would like that, wouldn't you? Instead of being on this stupid porch."

"Transfer, please."

"You'd like me to really look after you, wouldn't you?!"

"Please."

"But I can't kill you, you're already dead."

"Heh huh, heh huh…"

"What else can I give you?"

"Such is my beloved," he said, and she laughed and crooned, *"I can't give you anything but love."* Then she sang:

> *Dream awhile,*
> *scheme awhile,*
> *you're sure to find,*
> *happiness, and I guess…*

He began to growl. He had never growled before. He sounded like an animal, an angry animal. He was wide-eyed with no expression on his face, growling.

"Stop it," she yelled.

He growled again.

"You stop it," she said, as if warning an animal. "You better stop it."

His growl turned to a guttural snarl.

She got up. She thought she should make some toast before sleep. And tea. And take a deep breath. Instead, she went to the kitchen drawer beside the dishwasher. Years ago, he'd put a handgun in the drawer. He'd been worried about someone breaking into their house in the dark. But no one had ever threatened them, almost no one had ever knocked on the front door at night. The gun had never been fired. She wasn't sure if there was a bullet in the chamber.

She stood facing him with the gun in her hand. "I'm telling you to stop it," she said, "to go away with your growling." She looked hard into his eyes. They were bloodshot. The snarling grew louder, there was drool at the corner of his mouth.

She lifted his left hand, because he was left-handed, and put the gun in it, closing his fingers around the butt, and then she turned the gun back toward his mouth. "I'm warning you," she said, "for the last time." He curled his lip, snarling. She pushed the snub-nosed barrel into his mouth, her hand on his, her finger on his, up against the trigger. "Stop it," she cried. His head was tilted, his eyes wide open, and she was sure that she saw him hiding down a deep hole inside the dark pupils of his eyes. "Cecil," she said, "I knew it. I can see you. You're in there. There you are."

The bullet blew off his jaw. There was blood all over the chair but none on her. She stepped back, leaving the gun in his hand. "Cecil," she said, "Cecil, dear Cecil."

The police found her standing on the front porch wearing only her kimono, holding a feather duster. She was dusting the air. The open kimono had slipped off her shoulders, so that she was naked to the policemen as they came up the walk, startled by her being naked, by her big bush of black hair for so small a woman, and how boyish her body was, and one of the cops said, "Jesus, she's got no tits at all." She was crooning quietly:

> *I can't give you anything but love, baby,*
> *That's the only thing I've plenty of, baby,*
> *Dream awhile...*

WILLARD AND KATE

Willard Cowley lived with his wife, Kate, in a sandstone house. There was a sun parlour at the back of the house and the windows of the parlour opened onto a twisted old apple tree.

"Everything alters," he often told her, "under the apple tree. One by one we drop away." He was a well-known scholar, big-boned and tall, with closely cropped grey hair. "It's the job of wizened old teachers like myself," he said, smiling indulgently at his students, "to tell the young all about tomorrow's sorrow." He was officially required to stop teaching, to retire. He was sixty-five. Kate came down to his office. "You needn't have come," he said, but he was comforted to see her. She said the sorrowful look in his eye made him even more handsome than he was. "A lady killer, Willard, that's what you are."

"I've never felt younger," he said as they walked home together.

As the weeks went by, they went for a long walk every day, and he talked about everything that was on his mind. "A mind at play," he said to her one afternoon, "and I don't know whether I've told you this before, but it is not a question of right or wrong, really – a mind at play is a mind at work." She had soft grey eyes and a wistful smile. "Yes, you've told me that before, Willard, but I adore everything you tell me, even when you tell me twice." They often stopped for a hot chocolate fudge sundae at a lunch counter that had been in the basement of the Household Trust building since their childhood. She loved digging the long silver spoon down into the dark syrup at the bottom of the glass.

"You and your sweet tooth," he said. "It'll be the death of you."

"Someday you'll take death seriously," she said.

"I do. I do," he said.

"How?"

"I think I'd like to die somewhere else."

"Wherever in the world would you like to die?"

"It's strange," he said, "we've always lived in this city but now I think I'd be happier somewhere else, out in the desert."

"There's no ice cream in the desert," she laughed, softly humouring him.

"Well, it's only a daydream," he said. "It's not how I dream at night."

"What do you dream at night?"

"About you," he said.

"But I'm always right here beside you."

"Yes, yes," he said, "but think of where we could go in our dreams, think of what it would be like watching wild she-camels vanish into the dunes."

She threw her arms around his neck and said, "Yes," kissing him until they were out of breath.

"What a couple of crazy old loons we are," she said.

"Thank God," he said.

Her eyesight was failing, so at night he began to read the newspapers to her. They got into bed and he read to her as she lay curled against his shoulder. "Oh, I like this," he said. "'A politician is like a football coach. He has to be smart enough to understand the game and stupid enough to take it seriously.'"

"I like that, too," she said, laughing. "I don't like football but I like that."

"That's why you'll never be a politician," he said, "thank God." He linked his hands behind his head, letting his mind wander, suddenly perplexed because he couldn't remember the name of the pharaoh at the time of Moses. He heard her heavy breathing. Before turning out the light, leaning on his elbow, he looked down into her face, astonished that she had fallen so easily into such a sound sleep because in her younger years she had often wakened in a clammy sweat, panic-stricken, mumbling about loss, about eyes that had not opened, saying she could hear her own screaming though she was not making a sound. He couldn't imagine what dreadful fear had welled up within her during those nights, what darkness she had sunk into, and he wondered how she had managed over the years to stifle that fear, tamp it down. Perhaps in her fear she had gotten a dream-glimpse of their stillborn child. He had forgotten why they had never tried to have another child. He only knew he had never wanted another woman. This gave him sudden joy and a sense of completion in her. He was close to tears as he looked into her sleeping face, afraid that she would go down into a darkness where she would not waken and he whispered:

Child, do not go
into the dark places
of the soul,
there the grey wolves whine,
the lean grey wolves...

In the morning, after he had two cups of strong black coffee, he read the newspapers aloud. Any story about old ruins and the past lost in the dunes of time caught his eye. A few months before he'd retired he had written in *Scholastics: A Journal of New Modes* that the psalms of David were actually based on a much older Egyptian sacred text, now almost entirely lost. This meant that David was just a reporter of what he had heard somewhere on the desert trails, and so Willard was pleased one morning to read in the paper that nearly all the archaeologists at a conference in Boston had agreed that the Bible was not history, that no one should pay any historical attention to anything written before the Book of Kings. "The whole thing," he said to Kate, "may just be theological dreaming. The whole of our lives, our ethical and spiritual lives, may be a dream. A wonder-filled dream in which we defeat death by turning lies into the truth." When she asked him how a lie could be the truth, and how everything that was true could be a dream, he said, "I think that maybe all through history we have become our own gods in our dreams. We create them and then they turn around and taunt us. Maybe Christ on the cross is really a taunting dream of death and redemption, a dream in which Christ has to stay nailed to the cross because we don't dare let him come back to us again. We don't dare let him come back and live among us like a normal man because then there'd only be a dreamless silence out there without him in it, a great dark silence." As he said this he felt a lurch in the pit of his stomach, a slow opening up of an old hollow deep in himself, but this hollow didn't frighten him. It was an absence that he had long ago accepted, just as he had accepted the absence of children in their life. He had learned to live with this absence but he could not bear to see Kate in pain. One morning when he was wakened by her moaning in her sleep he felt a frightened pity as he looked down into her sleeping face, pity that she had had to suffer her own attacks of darkness, attacks of absence, in her sleep. He touched her cheek and whispered, "Kate, you're my whole life. Thank God."

One afternoon, when the apple tree was in bud and the hired gardener, who had tattoos on his arms, was cleaning out the peony beds, Willard laughed and pointed at the gardener. He told Kate that he'd been studying a book of maps of the Middle East a friend had given him years ago, and he'd discovered that there was a small city near the Turkish border that was called, after Cain's nephew, Enos, and since the men there had always marked themselves with tattoos, he said, "The mark of Cain was probably just a tattoo."

"You mean Cain's pruning our rose bushes?"

"Yes."

"Willard," she said, "you are a notion," and she smiled with such genuine amused pleasure and admiration that tears filled his eyes. He held her hand, breathing in the heavy musk of the early spring garden.

"With you, Kate," he said, "I always feel like it's going to be possible to get a grip on something really big about life before I die. I'm very grateful."

"Oh, no," she said. "No one in love should be grateful."

"I can't help it," he said and felt such an ache for her that he had to take several deep breaths, as if he were sighing with sudden exasperation.

"Don't be impatient," she said.

"I'm not. I was just suddenly out of breath."

"And soon you'll be telling me you're out of your mind."

"That goes without saying," he said, laughing.

"That's what everybody says happened to Adam and Eve," she said. "That she drove Adam out of his mind because he wanted the apple and she ate it..."

"And look at us now."

"A couple of old lunatics," she said, lifting his hand to her lips. "And that's not gratitude, that's love, Willard. You've always been the apple of my eye."

He stood beside her with tears in his eyes.

"Some day," she said, brushing his tears away with her hand, "I'll tell you what I really think."

"I bet you will," he said.

"Yes."

To distract her, to hide his emotions, he riffled through a sheaf of papers on a side table. "You know what? You'll never guess," he said, fumbling the papers. He was excited. He wanted to please her. "I've come across the most wonderful creation story…"

"Creation?"

"Yes, yes," he said, flattening a piece of tawny onionskin paper on the table. "Professor Shotspar translated this for me years ago, from a flood story. It was written down somewhere around 1800 BC, in Akkadian, which in case you don't know is one of the oldest languages in the world, and it's exactly the same flood you'll find in *Gilgamesh*. But this is about the gods and how they got around to creating man – Lullu, they called him. How do you like that? And it's about how they created all of us so we'd knuckle under and do their dirty work, their mucking up…

> "When the gods, before there were men,
> Worked and shed their sweat,
> The sweat of the gods was great,
> The work was dire, distress abiding.
> Carping, backbiting,
> Grumbling in the quarries,

They broke their tools,
Broke their spades
And hoes…
Nusku woke his lord,
Got him out of bed,
'My lord, Enil, your temple wall is breached,
Battle broaches your gate.'
Enil spoke to Anu, the warrior.
'Summon a single god and make sure he's
put to death.'
Anu gaped
And then spoke to the other gods, his brothers.
'Why pick on us?
Our work is dire, our distress abiding.
Since Belet-ili, the birth goddess, is nearby,
Why not get her to create Lullu, the man.
Let Lullu wear the yoke wrought by
Enil.
Let man shed his sweat for the gods.'"

"Maybe that's where *he's a lulu* comes from," she said, laughing.

"That's good," he said. "Damned good. I guess we're a couple of lulus."

A week later they were sitting in the sunroom parlour having a glass of dry vermouth. There had been a heavy pounding rain during the night and it was still raining. The garden walk was covered with white petals pasted to the flagstone. He should have noticed that Kate was growing thin, eating only green salads, Emmenthal cheese, and dry toast. At first, sipping her vermouth, she'd grown giddy, and then, as if sapped of all energy, she said, "I'd love to be sitting somewhere down south in the hot sun." He turned to her and said, "But you've never liked the sun." She was sitting in a heavily cushioned wicker chair with her eyes closed. He touched her hand. She didn't open her eyes. He went back to reading Conrad, a novel, *An Outcast of the Islands*. Suddenly he stood up, staring into the stooping branches of the apple tree, bent by the weight of the pouring rain, and then, just as abruptly, he sat down.

"Listen to this," he said: "'*There is always one thing the ignorant man knows, and that thing is the only thing worth knowing; it fills the ignorant man's universe. He knows all about himself...*'"

Willard dropped the book.

"What's the matter?" she asked, opening her eyes.

"Can't you see?"

"See what?"

"If I seem to know so much about everything, maybe that's only a kind of ignorance. Maybe I don't know anything about myself."

"Don't be silly," she said sternly.

"Silly?" he said. "I'm deadly serious."

He sat staring out the window, into the downpour as tulip petals in the garden broke and fell. He stared at the headless stems. She rose and went upstairs and took a hot bath. She lay in the water a long time, slipping in and out of sleep, until she realized the water was cold and she was shivering. When she came back downstairs he was still sitting by the window, facing the drenched garden.

"Willard, for God's sake, what's the matter? You've hardly moved for hours and hours."

"I don't know," he said. "It's a kind of dread, or something like that. A dread..."

"It's silence, that's what it is."

"I suppose it is. The vast silence. Maybe we live in silence forever. Maybe when we die that's all we are to hear. Silence. The word is dead. Maybe that is what hell is."

The next morning she didn't get out of bed. He brought her tea, but she only drank half the cup. "Perhaps it's a touch of flu," she said, but she had no temperature and no headache. Her hands were cold. He sat holding and rubbing her hands. She smiled wanly. "Oh, I missed our good talks yesterday," she said.

"It was only a pause," he said, trying to be cheerful.

"That's right," she said, and she closed her eyes.

"It was a hard day on the garden, too," he said.

"Yes."

"All this dampness, it's not good, not healthy."

"No."

"It gets into the bones."

"Yes."

"Dem bones, dem bones, dem dry bones…" he sang, trying to be gay.

"Dem dry bones…" she whispered.

"Did you know, Kate," he said, leaning close, seeing that she was drifting off into sleep, "that they've started digging near to where most people think the garden of Eden was, and there's an actual town that was there around 6000 BC? And that's a fact," he said, wagging his finger at her as she lay with her eyes closed, "because there are so many ways of dating things now, what with carbon 14 and tree rings, dendrochronology they call it, when they cut across a tree and read the rings. And then of course they match it with an older tree, and that tree with an older tree, all the way back to the bristlecone pine, 5,000 years ago, in fact even longer. And then…"

She was sound asleep, smiling in her sleep. Her smile bewildered him. He had never seen her smile in her sleep. He wondered what secret happiness, found in sleep, had made her smile.

One week later she was taken to hospital. She had a private room and a young doctor who spoke in a hushed monotone with his hands crossed inside the sleeves of his smock. "It's a problem of circulation," he said. "The blood's just not getting around."

"Oh dear," Willard said and sat in the bedside leather easy chair all day and into the early evening until Kate woke up and said, "You shouldn't stay here all this time."

"Where else should I be?"

The day she died, her feet and lower legs were blue from gangrene. And in great pain she'd quickly grown thin, the skin taut on her nose, her eyes silvered by a dull film. She panted for air, rolling her eyes. "Willard, Willard," she whispered and reached for him.

"Yes, yes."

"Talk to me."

"Yes, Kate."

"There. Talk to me there."

"Where is there?" he asked desperately.

After her cremation, to which only a few old scholars came and none of his former students, Willard wandered from room to room in the house talking out loud. He kept calling her name, as if she might suddenly step in from the garden, smiling, her hands dirty from planting. In the late afternoons he sat by the open parlour window, talking and reading and gesturing. But then early one evening he got confused and said, "What did I say?" He couldn't remember what he had said, and when Kate did not answer, the dread that he'd felt the month before, the fear that the hollow he'd so easily accepted was really a profound unawareness of himself, seized him in the chest and throat so that he was left breathless and thought he was going to choke. He was so afraid, so stricken by his utter aloneness, that he began to shake uncontrollably. He sat staring at her empty chair, ashamed of his trembling hands. He was sure he heard wolves calling and wondered if he was going crazy. He decided to get out for some air, to go down to the footbridge that crossed over the ravine and then come back.

Later that week, Willard went for a long walk in the downtown streets, along streets that they had walked, but he couldn't bring himself to go into the lunch counter. All the faces reflected in the store windows as he passed made his mind swirl, but when he stepped through the subway turnstiles, to the *thunk* of the aluminum bars turning over, he told Kate out loud and as clearly as he could that he was now absolutely sure, as he had promised her, that he was on to something big, a simple truth, so simple that no one he knew had seen it, and the truth was that all the great myths were based on lies. He'd actually been thinking, he'd said to her during the short cremation procedure, that to live a great truth, it is probably necessary to live a great lie. "After all," he said excitedly as he stepped through the last turnstile, "the Jews were never in Egypt. There was no Exodus. The Egyptians were fanatical record keepers and the Jews are never mentioned, and the cities that the Jews said they built, they did not exist. They were not there. There was no parting of the sea, no forty years of wandering in the desert... I mean, my God," he said, shaking his long finger as he forgot where he was going and didn't see that people were staring at him as he went back down an escalator, "what does anyone think Moses was doing out there for forty years? Forty years. You can walk across the Sinai in two days. And Jericho, there was no battle. No battle took place because there were no great walls to tumble down. There was no city there back then, not at that time," and he threw up his arms, full of angry defiance, standing on the tiled and dimly lit platform of the St. George subway station.

"Sorry," Willard said to a cluster of women who were staring at him, "I'm very sorry." He hurried back to the escalator, travelling up the moving stairs, craning his neck, eager to get out into the sunlight. "I just don't know what I'm going to do, Kate," he said in a whisper. "Talking to you like this, I forget. It's so fine, I just plain forget, people looking at me as if I were some kind of loony."

It was painful for him to stay at home all day. He kept listening for her voice in the rooms, embarrassed by the sound of his own voice. He sank into grim, bewildered silence, sometimes standing in the hall in a trance, a stupor, certain that he was losing his mind. Sometimes he slept during the day and once dreamed that he was walking on his shadow, as if his shadow was always in front of him, a shadow made of soot. It whimpered with pain. He stomped on his shadow till he was out of breath. He was afraid it was the soot of a scorched body. He heard her voice, and saw her sitting with her elbow on the windowsill, picking old paint off a glass pane. She was feverish and kept calling for ice. "Ice is the only answer." He woke up terrified. He locked their bedroom door and made his bed on the sofa in the library. For a week he slept on the sofa, drinking several glasses of port, trying to get to sleep. He could see from the sofa a hem of light under the bedroom door. He'd left the light on, a bedside reading lamp that she'd given him for his birthday, a porcelain angel with folded wings. On two evenings he was sure that he heard her voice in the bedroom, a voice so muffled that he couldn't make out the words. Then one night while he was keeping watch on the hem of light, half tipsy, half asleep, it went out. He was panic-stricken. He took it as a sign that she was in trouble, that she was really going to die, and he fumbled with the old key, trying to get it into the lock, whispering. "Hold on, Kate, hold on, I'm coming," cursing his own stupidity and cowardice for trying to close off the bedroom. Willard felt ashamed, as if he had betrayed her. When he got into the room, breathing heavily, he discovered that the bulb in the lamp, left on for so long, had burned out. He had seldom cried before, and only once in front of her. Now, standing before her dressing-table mirror, he discovered that he was dishevelled and haggard and he was crying. He began to sing as cheerfully as he could:

> If I had the wings of an angel,
> over these prison walls I would fly,
> I'd fly to the arms of my poor darling,
> and there…

He moved close to himself in the mirror and curled his lip with contempt. "You're a coward," he said and then lay down and fell asleep on their bed. In the morning he dressed with care, putting on an expensive Egyptian-cotton shirt and camel-hair jacket. He went out into the bright noon hour and found he was relieved to be walking again with a sudden jaunt in his stride, downtown among the crowds. He began to sing: *I'll take you home again, Kathleen…* But then he grew suddenly wary and stopped singing, trying to make sure he heard himself before he spoke out loud. He kept looking for himself in store windows to see if he was singing or talking at the top of his voice.

In the Hudson's Bay underground shopping mall, he came to a halt so abruptly that an old woman was unable to avoid bumping into him and spilled her bag of toiletries. He didn't notice. He stared at a portly black man standing by the checkout counter. The black man was talking into a cellphone, and farther along the mall, another man had a cellular phone close to his cheek. Willard realized that for weeks he'd seen people all over the city talking and nodding into phones and no one paid any attention to them. "Nobody knows who they're talking to," he cried. "Maybe they're not talking to anyone," and the old woman, picking up her rolls of Downy Soft toilet paper scattered around his feet, looked up and said, "You're not only rude, you're crazy," but he hurried off.

At Rogers Sound Systems a young salesman, with a Jamaican accent Willard had trouble understanding, tried to interest him in the latest models of cellphones. Willard was surprised at how compact the phones were. When the salesman said, "Look, this one even has its own built-in flashlight," Willard said, "A phone is a phone. How complicated can that be?" The salesman shrugged. "In that case, we have older models on sale, half price."

Willard bought one of the sale-price models. When the salesman tried to advise him, saying, "About all those old-fangled buttons, man—" Willard cut him short with, "Never mind. I think I can figure out a phone." He strode out of the store and set out for home, eager to get talking to Kate.

As soon as he got to the footbridge he tapped a green button and, holding the phone close to his ear like an old walkie-talkie, began telling Kate a joke he'd heard many years ago: "How these two old ladies had promised each other that the first one to die would come back and tell the other what Heaven was like, so after Sadie died Sophie waited and waited, and just when she gave up, Sadie appeared in a halo of light and Sophie said, You came back, so what's it like? And Sadie said, You get up in the morning and eat and then you have sex, and then it's sex before breakfast and afterwards sex, and before lunch and then lunch and more sex and sex before a snack before goodnight and then sex, and Sophie said, Sadie… Sadie, this is Heaven! But Sadie said: Heaven, who's in heaven. I'm a rabbit in Wisconsin." He laughed and laughed but with the phone tucked against his cheek, so that no one paid any attention to him. "Oh, I'm in fine fettle," he said. "This walking clears the lungs."

Willard stood on the footbridge over the ravine. He had never stopped to look down into the ravine before. He'd always been in a hurry to get home, his head tucked into his shoulder against the wind. He was surprised at how deep the ravine actually was, and how dense and lush the trees and bush were. The city itself was flat, all the streets laid out in a severe military grid, but here was the ravine, and of course there were ravines like this one that ran all through the city, deep, dark, mysterious places, running like lush green wounds through the concrete, the cement surfaces, and he felt sheepish. "All these years, and I've never been down in the ravines. Who knows what goes on down there. Can you imagine that, Kate?" He began to walk slowly home. He looked up and down the street. "All this is beginning to trouble me. Everything's beginning to trouble me," he said. "Everything seems to be only the surface of things. Everything is not where it's supposed to be. I mean, Abraham was always Abraham, some kind of old desert chieftain from around the River Jordan, but that's probably not true. All the actual references that I can find say he lived in Heran, in Anatolia, and that's a place in southern Turkey, close to where Genesis says Noah's ark ended up, settled on Mount Ararat, and that's not in Jordan, that's in eastern Turkey. The whole thing seems more and more like a Turkish story, a Turkish delight," and he laughed and quickened his pace, "because Abraham's descendant, a man called Dodanim, became the Dodecanese Islands, and a guy named Kittim is really Kriti, which is Crete, and Javan is really the Aegean, and Ashkenaz… Everyone knows the Ashkenazi are from north of the Danube. The whole thing, the whole story, took place somewhere else farther north. It's not a desert story at all, that's why the Jews weren't seen in Egypt…they weren't there, they were out on the edge of the world."

He was so out of breath from talking and walking at the same time that he had to stop walking. He had a cramp in his wrist from clutching the cellphone to his cheek. He was relieved. There was no one on his street of tree-shaded homes. He put the phone in his jacket pocket. Then he suddenly shuddered and choked back tears. All his talk, he felt, was wasted. He was alone. He was alone in a well of silence. "Jesus," he said, "even Sadie came back and said something." He felt abandoned, he wanted to hear what Kate thought of all his talk, all his daring insights. A man coming around the corner with his dog on a leash hesitated because Willard looked so frantic, but Willard shouted, "And a good day to you." The man hurried on.

Around noon on Easter Sunday, Willard put on a lightweight tweed suit that he hadn't worn for years. He went across the footbridge and strode along Bloor Street, revelling in the strong sunlight. He hadn't been out of the house for days because he'd been working in his study on several cuneiform texts. He'd hardly eaten. He'd done very little talking to Kate, but now he felt fresh and bold and self-confident as he walked among well-dressed women.

"It's a wonderful day," he said to Kate, holding the phone close. "And I've got wonderful news. I've finally figured this thing out, yes ma'am… The answer's right there in what looks like a contradiction that's built in at the beginning, right there at the start of

Genesis, where God says he's made man in his own image, and then, in the second chapter, there's no one around. Everything's empty. So whoever he'd made has flown the coop."

As the red light changed to green at Church Street, he stepped off the curb, saying, "The whole place is empty, man is gone, and what that means is that for nearly a million years, man trekked around chasing animals, naming them, hunting them, but suddenly he got smart. Ten thousand years ago he got smart. He wanted a garden. And a closed garden is something you've got to cultivate. And man shows up in Genesis again, and he was Cain the cultivator, who'd taken off from the old happy grazing grounds of Eden to work the earth in a new place, the new civilization where there was nothing. That's what the new Eden was, not a paradise of two witless souls lying around under an apple tree, but Cain, the tattooed man who had the courage to build a closed garden, a city out there on the edge of the world. Cain the civilized man, the marked man…" and Willard raised his arms, facing into the sun. The women in their Easter outfits shied away from him. "That's when man became magnificent, Kate. That's when he went into the dark to create his own world, to create himself. That's the first time he had the guts to take his own word for everything."

"Oh yes, yes," a tall, lean woman with big owl glasses said. "Oh yes." She was smiling eagerly. He quickly brought the phone closer to his ear. He wanted to be left alone. He wanted Kate. He waved the woman with the owl glasses away and as he did so, his thumb slipped onto a red button. He had never pressed the *red* button before, but now he suddenly heard Kate. She was calling him. "Willard, Willard, what's been the matter with you?"

"It's you!"

"Of course it's me."

"I knew you were there. I knew it," he cried triumphantly.

"You knew? You knew where I was!"

"No. Where are you?" he whispered, stepping through a crowd of women on the sidewalk.

"I'm here. Right where I said I would be. I've been screaming at you for weeks, and you didn't hear a word."

"I never dreamed that all I had to do was touch the other button. I never pushed it. I never heard you."

"But I heard you," Kate said. "Can you imagine what it's been like listening and listening and I couldn't say a word…"

"But I never thought…" he said.

"That's all you've been doing, Willard," she said, calming down. "Thinking."

"I've been talking to you."

"A blue streak, I'd say."

"Don't be upset," he said.

"I have a right to be upset," she said. "Sitting here like a dumb bunny for weeks."

"Never mind," he said.

"I mind. And locking our bedroom door, that did not help. I was yelling so loud at you I thought I would die. I was hoarse for two days, I lost my voice."

His thumb was aching from pushing back and forth. "We're just wasting time talking like this," he said.

"Time is not my problem," she said.

"I have been dying to know for weeks what you think."

"What I really think?"

"Yes."

"Truly?"

"Yes."

"I think you are," and she paused, and then with quiet gravity, "simply magnificent. I can't imagine living without you. I hang on every word."

"You do?"

"I would never lie to you."

"Thank God you're still alive," he said.

"Nobody wants to die," she said.

A KISS IS STILL A KISS

An old blind man shuffled his feet under a chokecherry tree, trying to get out of the shade of the tree, tapping his white cane as he hunted for the sun, for a warm bench in the park where other men lay sprawled asleep on the grass, their hats in the crook of their arms and empty beer cans between their legs. A seagull stood close to the sleeping men. Another perched on one leg on the stone sill of a large display window across the road from the park. The window was on the ground floor of the Household Trust Tower. It was noon and a woman sat at a carillon inside the window, and because there were speakers in the high branches of the trees in the park, the old man could hear her playing. He sang the words as he tapped his cane:

> *You must remember this,*
> *A kiss is still a kiss...*

He kept tapping until he began to feel strong heat on the back of his neck, sunlight by a bench at the foot of a two-storey wall that had been painted to portray ochre fields and green foothills, clouds and white birds, and leaping out of the sky was a rainbow that fell to root behind a bench where a young woman sat alone, her face tilted to the sun, alone until a young man sat down beside her. He was in his late twenties. He wore a black felt hat and had gathered his long black hair into a tooled silver clasp at the back of his neck.

"You're looking good," he said to the girl. She was wearing high-top black policeman's boots and a mottled battle-fatigue jacket that bore a hand-stitched patch over her heart: *May The Baby Jesus Open Your Mind And Shut Your Mouth*. Her head was shaved clean except for a hedge of yellow hair and she had braces on her teeth.

"You some kind of Indian?" he asked.

"No way," she said. "No Indian looks like this."

"Maybe not."

"You a doper?" she asked.

"Nope," he said.

"Only a doper would figure me for a Indian. I don't look nothing like those guys sleeping on the lawn."

"Right."

"Fucking right," she said, and tilted her face to the sun again.

"This park's a good place for punks, eh?"

"Whatever you say, man," she said.

"You a punker?"

"Get real," she said and closed her eyes.

Hunched forward with his elbows on his knees, he said, "You mind what I wanta ask you?"

"Talk's cheap, man."

"How come you got those Tinkertoy tracks on your teeth?"

"My braces?"

"Yeah."

"My old boyfriend, he figured they were prime, man, so prime he got himself some braces, too. He don't need no braces. He don't need nothing. He got himself beautiful teeth. He don't care about nothing. He's just doing what he does."

"What's he do?"

"He don't really do nothing."

"Me, too," he said. "Not if I can help it."

"Perfect," she said.

"What's your name?"

"I don't deal in names, man. Not with strangers."

"What kinda paranoid is that?"

"The right kind, man. The right kind because I got the fucking facts."

"So tell me your name, for a fact."

"What for?"

"For nothing. I can't talk to nobody that's got no name."

"I ain't nobody."

"Right."

"Cindy," she said. "Cindy Wichita."

"That ain't a name, that's a town."

"I can't help that, man. How can I help that?"

"That's a town in the movies."

"I ain't no movie, man. No way. No stupid movie is happening inside my head. If you're so smart, what's yours?"

"Abner," he said. "Abner Deerchild."

"Fucking unreal," she said. "Absolutely fucking unreal."

"What?"

"You got a Indian name."

"Right."

"You panhandling or you on the pogey?"

"I just kinda steal, you know, like I steal what I can."

"Like, you're a real thief?"

"I just look out for myself."

"Keep your eyes open."

"Right."

"So don't fuck my head, man," she said.

"Why would I do that?"

"I don't know, like, suddenly we're talking to each other, so just don't do it."

"Okay."

"So what's with you? How come you sit down beside me, like outta the blue?"

"Nothing. Nothing I'd want to say right out."

"Why not?"

"Not right out."

"Why not?"

"You might get mad."

"Big deal."

"I better not."

"Why not?"

"I'd like to fuck you."

"Very funny."

"I'm not trying to be funny."

"Yeah, so why not?"

"Because I'm not."

"So why you want to fuck me?"

"You got great hair."

She laughed. "There's some dudes," she said, "some dudes who lose their lunch looking at my hair. Lose their fucking lunch. Freak out, they freak out. That's what everybody is, scared shitless of their own shadow and they figure right off the bat that I'm their shadow." She opened a canvas sack beside her on the bench and pulled out a floppy leather-bound book. She put it on her knee. "Check it out. This here, that's my grandmother's Bible."

"Bibles weird me out," he said.

"Bibles are the word."

"They still weird me out."

"This here's the light," she said, tapping the book cover with her finger. "When you got the light, when you got the blessed fucking light beaming on you, you don't get so scared of your shadow, you don't get so scared in the dark."

"The dark don't scare me." He smoothed the nap of the crown of his hat with the flat of his hand, straightened the orange feather in the black suede band, and settled the hat on his lap.

"I don't scare," he said again, leaning back and stretching his long legs and crossing his leather cowboy boots.

"Everybody's scared," she said.

"Not this dude."

"Sure you ain't a dope head?"

"No way. I got my shit in gear."

"You carrying some shit?"

"Naw."

"Know where I can get some?" she asked.

"I told you, I don't do dope."

"You ain't never done dope?"

"I done dope, every dickhead's done dope, but I don't do no dope now."

"Too bad, man. Like, I could die for some shit right now."

"If I die I'm gonna die like I wanna die," he said.

"Don't matter which way you wanna die, man. When you die, you're dead."

"Nope," he said.

"What nope?"

"Not my grandfather. He's not dead."

"Who's your grandfather?"

"He got himself hung," he said. "Hung for murder, out by Bowmanville. The judge, he promised he'd let us lay his body out in the old way, up in the air in a tree. But the judge lied. He fucking lied. A priest buried him."

"Don't shit me, man. Nobody sticks dead bodies up in trees around here."

"Look," he said, nodding toward the men curled asleep on the grass, their faces swollen, "we're drinking ourselves fucking dead so that when we die you can bury us in the ground." He laughed and then spat. "That's what you lard-asses want. You wanna trap our spirits forever."

"Like fuck," she said.

He leaned closer to her. "But the dead don't stay dead. My grandfather's not dead. There's been graves opened." He was very close to her, whispering. He saw the old blind man sitting in the sun under the rainbow. The old man was smiling. "Even in the cemetery right here downtown, over by Parliament Street" he said, "there's people who've dug open graves so the spirits are free."

She bent over and rubbed the dust off her boots.

They heard the carillon, a new song, and the old man sitting on the bench tapped his cane between his feet and sang:

Sometimes I'm happy,
Sometimes I'm blue,
My disposition
Depends on you...

She suddenly gave Abner a pecking kiss on the cheek. "I don't kiss so good with my braces on," she said. Her hand was on the Bible. He covered her hand with his.

"I haven't been kissed like that since my little kid kissed me."

"You got a kid?"

"I been a daddy since I was sixteen. Ain't seen my kid for two years, but I ain't seen my own daddy since I was six. Unlucky six."

"I wish I had a kid," she said. "I tried once to get a kid but I got trouble in my tubes, you know, so I pray and I pray a lot."

"I don't pray your kinda prayers," he said. "They pray," and he pointed at the men asleep on the grass. "They all got rosaries."

"I ain't no Catholic," she said.

"Neither are they."

"This here's my grandmother's Bible. I'm her kinda Christian."

"No shit."

"I wouldn't shit you about Jesus."

"What kinda Christian?"

"Not one of them weird Pentecostals, man. They's always looking for blue smoke on the floor," she said. "That's what my father is, and my mother, though she just goes along for the ride, like she's scared, too, collecting prayer cloths, always on the road pretending she's Rose of Sharon looking for the next miracle."

"She got some kinda road map for miracles?"

"They got an old bunged-up trailer, that's what they got, and they're always looking for some brainless preacher who's just got the gift of tongues."

"I got the gift of tongue."

"I'm talking miracles, man."

"Me, too."

"Don't make no mistake, man. Don't play me for dumb. You remember Dumbo. He was a baby elephant. He had big ears. I don't have big ears."

"You're looking for miracles."

"I believe I'm a miracle, like, we're all miracles."

"Hello!"

"All of us being here is a miracle, man, and some of us are even washed in the Blood of the Lamb, except most people are fucking well scared of being alive." She opened the Bible. "See," she said. "Second Timothy, one: seven, *'For God hath not given us the spirit of fear; but of power, and of love…'* I'm not scared of no love." She put the Bible back in the canvas sack.

"Let's split," he said.

"Where you wanna go?"

"Around."

They walked past the painted foothills, past the old blind man, out onto a boutique mall where office clerks on their lunch hour from Household Trust were browsing among racks of polyester Blue Jays hats, plaster lawn pigs the colour of candy floss, satin embroidered BEAVER cushions, and desktop models of the SkyDome designed to hold elastic bands or paper clips. At the end of the mall a balding man, wearing wide red suspenders over his yellow shirt, beckoned to them. There was a sign above his head: *Put Your Polaroid Face On A Genuine Porcelain Plate.* "Come on," Abner said, "it's only a couple of bucks. It'll be like getting married."

They sat on a plush red velvet sofa. "Everybody comfy?" the balding man asked. He took their photograph. Then they picked a purple and gold-rimmed plate from a display rack. Their Polaroid print was trimmed and pasted over the white moon in the centre of the purple plate.

"That's sweet," she said. "Real sweet."

"You bet your sweet ass."

"My ass ain't so sweet," she said coyly.

"I like your ass."

"I like my hair, and I like your cowboy boots," she said.

"You two should be honeymooners," the balding man said, handing them the plate.

They put the plate in her canvas sack beside the Bible and walked down the mall past Winners and Sadine's Dry Cleaners and two sapling lindens set in cement boxes, the trunks wrapped in protective plastic webbing.

"You wanna go up to the glass house?"

"No prob," she said.

They crossed the mall to the brass doors of the Household Trust Tower. He sang along with somebody's boom-box blasting in the tower:

You can't always get what you wa-ant,,
You can't always get what you wa-ant...

They rode a chrome escalator to the second floor, a glass-enclosed garden of shrubs and dwarf trees and shallow pools, ferns, pink hydrangeas, laminated benches, and serpentine walks made of interlocking ochre bricks. They sat down on a bench in the wind-less and humid air. Nothing moved, no leaf, no fern, no breathing sound in the dense ground cover. All they could hear was the rush of motor-driven water in a pond.

"I think I love it here," she said.

"I could see you'd like this kinda outdoors thing," he said and stretched his legs, then smoothed his black jeans along the inside of his thighs. "I mean, it's peaceful, like it's almost really real, you know."

"The trees are maybe real," she said.

"Yeah, but really real is still not like this."

There were little bronze deer standing in a pond close to a tiny red bridge.

"Can I ask you something? I mean, seeing as how you asked me about my braces."

"Okay."

"I was looking at the guys lying on the lawn, you know."

"Yeah."

"And one of them woke up and was looking at me."

"Right."

"He was looking at me like I was weird."

"Right."

"You know a lot of white men?"

"Some."

"What d'you call white men?"

"What d'you mean?"

"How do you call them? White people?"

"Lard-asses."

"No, like in your own language. You got a fucking language?"

"It don't come out in my language like *white people*."

"What's it come out like?"

"It's a long story."

"How long's long?"

"Pretty long."

"So, I got all day."

"What my grandfather told me is white people got no colour, so the word we use is *K'ohali*, it means a certain part of animal fat, right, like the white part of the fat, the colour of fat people, lard."

"I ain't fat."

"All white people are fat, like, you know, you live off the fat of the land."

"Ain't no fat land around here, man."

"Shit, all you white people got life ass-backwards."

"You're telling me I'm ass-backwards and you're, like, sitting here like a regular goddamn fucking warrior clomping around in cowboy boots?"

"That's got nothing to do with nothing."

"My boots are better anyway."

"You probably like this glass shit-box better than the woods, all the trees you never seen."

"I seen trees."

"What d'you mean trees?"

"Trees."

"This goddamn city's got trees in those cement boxes, it's more like what we call a wilderness. I got to watch out for animals going by, like that fucking car, because maybe it'll swallow me up or run over me and kill me." He put his arm around her, cradling her. "Salvation for the nation, that's what I say, the United Iroquois Hour…"

"You Iroquois?"

"Ojibwa. Way north, Lake Superior."

"You miss the water?"

"Life goes by calmer when you're close to water."

"We got water all around us."

"These goddamn piddly pools ain't water."

"I don't mean here. I mean in all the windows."

"What the hell you talking about?"

"There's waterbed stores all around here."

"So?"

"Half the city's out there sleeping on their own fucking little lakes."

It was very humid in the enclosed garden. She laughed as she undid the buttons to her fatigue jacket. He saw she had a small tattoo, a cross, between her breasts. "I meet this guy a week ago," she said, "and he tells me he's got five waterbeds. Couldn't stand them, except his wife and kids love 'em and every night he says he's dreaming he is drowning because he's never learned to swim and when he told his wife they had to get rid of their waterbed because he couldn't sleep, she told him he had to learn how to swim."

He laughed loudly. A young clerk with a pencil moustache, who had bleached his close-cropped hair, snorted with irritation, closed his cardboard carton of sweet potato fries, and moved down the path to a Chinese waterfall wheel.

"Can you swim?" He still had his arm around her and he could smell talcum powder on her shaved head.

"No. And I don't need no lesson," she said fiercely. "I already been saved."

"I was just talking." He hugged her again.

"Absolutely no one talks to you fucking Indians except us street angels, so be nice. Like, don't pretend, man. Like, we're all part of the same thing, the same fucking grateful guys."

"Goddamn."

"You guys are like ghosts. You listening up, man? All the dead fucking Indians who are still alive, you're ghosts. You figure that out, man, you're all mostly brain dead."

"Who's brain dead?"

"You, otherwise you wouldn't ask me questions like you ask me."

"What questions?"

"I'm not scared of you or anyone, except Jesus. I'm scared of Jesus, so I don't try to pretend nothing."

"Who's pretending?"

"You better not be."

"I'm not."

"Okay," she said, mollified. "That's cool."

"We're cool?"

"Yeah."

"You're not mad at whatever you were mad at?"

"No."

"Can I ask you a question?"

"You wanta know how I shave my head?" She opened her canvas sack. "I got a straight razor."

"A real question."

"There's no real questions, man."

"Sure there are."

"So ask me."

"You're saved, right? Born again."

"Right."

"How did you know you were saved?"

"What do you care?"

"I want to know."

"See my boots." She stretched her legs. "That's my old boyfriend. He taught me how to varnish my boots. He was in the army."

"Okay, I love your boots. I love your hair and I love your boots."

She crossed her legs. There was a long slit in her denim skirt. He could see the white of her thighs. She rested the canvas sack on her knees. "I got this big window in my bedroom, see, facing east, man, and there were these cross-bars in the window and the sun used to come through the window in the morning." She laid her hand on the sack, on the Bible in it. "And one morning standing in the sun I could feel the heat, man, and the shadow of the cross from the cross-bar in the window on me, on my boobs, and like, I felt full of joy. I knew right then that I was saved, that I had the mark of the cross on me, and I bear witness, man, I bear witness to the joy in the Lord wherever I go."

He pursed his lips like he was thinking hard and cracked his knuckles.

"You think that's joy, eh?"

"That's what I felt that day," she said.

"One day at a time, right, that's what I say."

"Right."

"One day."

"Absolutely fucking right," she said. "Dead on, man."

"I got myself a joystick," he said and spread his big hand over hers.

"You looking to fuck me?" she said.

"I don't wanta just fuck you."

"So what then?"

"I wanta give you that baby."

"What baby?"

"The baby you said you was wanting so hard to have."

"You watch out. Don't go bullshitting me. Nobody just fucking-well has babies."

"Sure you do. That's what real fucking's for."

"The final days are coming, man, so don't go bottom-feeding on me, man."

"My grandfather, he told me that all the time."

"What?"

"The world's gonna end."

"So, how?"

"He told me when I was a kid, he told me to take this here little pail outside and bring some sand in to him. And when I did, he poured the sand into piles and said these are the cities and there'll be bigger cities in the future and then there's gonna be a punishment, but the only thing we don't know is when we're gonna get punished but it's gonna happen."

"That's great, being a grandfather like that."

"They hung him."

"That's what you get for going around murdering people."

"He didn't go around."

"He went somewhere."

"The priest said he went to Hell."

"You know what I can't figure about you?"

"What?"

"Why a guy who should hate cowboys is wearing cowboy boots, and you think my hair and braces are weird." She laughed, gathered her canvas sack, and got up.

"I stole them off a white drunk," he said.

"You're fucking kidding."

"He was lying drunk in a crapper in a bar so I took his boots off and left him my sneakers."

They went down the escalator, came out in the mall, and saw the lady sitting at the carillon in the Household Trust Tower window. She was smoking, and then stubbed her cigarette in an ashtray and started to play:

The first time ever I saw your face
I thought the sun rose in your eyes...

They walked through the park. A shadow from the tower had fallen across the painted ochre fields and the white clouds and the rainbow. The blind old man was slumped on a bench, sound asleep in the sun, snoring. Others were still huddled on the grass under the shade trees. It was two o'clock. The lady at the carillon shut down the loudspeaker system. It made a pop, like a pistol shot heard from a long way off.

"So where's home?" he asked.

"The Bond Hotel on Bond."

"You kidding me?" he said.

"Cindy Witchita never kids."

"I copped a bed there a couple of months ago," he said. "Or maybe it was last year." They walked arm-in-arm toward the old hotel, passing pawnshop windows cluttered with fishing gear, clocks, chairs hung from the ceiling, wedding rings, birthstones.

"What room you in?" he asked.

"319, man."

"Really?"

"End of the hall."

"We were neighbours when I was there, so how come you never visited me?"

"Because I didn't live there then, man. Anyway, I always mind my business. I don't bother people."

"Me neither," he said.

"Too many nosey people always butt in."

"When I wake up at two in the morning it's what I wanta do. Butt in on somebody's life."

"Somebody might be sleeping."

"Right, so I don't do it. Instead. I chase dust bunnies across the floor or I make me a coffee instead."

"Then you really don't get no sleep."

"It's not the coffee that keeps me awake," she said, moving closer to him.

"It ain't booze either."

"If you got nothing to do and go to sleep too early, man, you wake up too early, so what're you going to do?"

He laughed and squeezed her hand. "You ain't scared of me, eh?"

"I never been scared of nobody's love," she said.

"You still look like all the goddamn Mohawks I ever seen in the movies," he said.

"Yeah, but they weren't real Indians like you are, man." She skipped up the hotel stairs, surprisingly light on her feet in her shiny policeman's boots.

Once they were in room 319, he set his broad-brimmed black hat on the straight-back chair's seat, the only chair in the room. She draped her battle-fatigue jacket over the end of the bed and took the purple china plate with their photograph from her canvas sack.

"Where'll I put our picture?"

"Top of the TV."

"Nice," she said. "We look real nice, man. Happy," and she took her grandmother's Bible out of the sack, put it under her pillow, and began to undress.

"How old are you?"

"Nineteen," she said.

"Spring chicken."

"Don't call me no fucking chicken, man. I hate chickens. Only pimps got chickens."

"Sorry," he said, drawing off his tight black jeans. Naked, he stepped back into his cowboy boots.

"I gotta tell you this," she said. "My real name's Alice." She sat on the edge of the bed, pulling off her boots. "You were close. Cindy's a name I stole from a movie star."

"Yeah, well, my real name's Falling Moon Feather. Goddamn priests at the mission school named me Abner."

"They hurt you? Those fucking priests." She lay down on the narrow bed, tucking the other grey pillow under her hips.

"Naw. This guy, Father Eudall, he used to give me whisker rubs and kiss me a lot but he never hurt me."

"I had an uncle named Abner."

"Was he cool?"

"He married a moron, man, like she was a big woman, you know, but she had a real fucking midget mind. He always called me his little Alice and touched my tits, always telling me how unhappy he was, and how fucking unhappy God was, always touching my tits."

Falling Moon Feather knelt on the bed beside her.

"Take your boots off, man," she said, laughing. "You gotta take your boots off."

"They're not my boots," he said and kicked them off toward the window where a seagull was standing on the windowsill. Falling Moon Feather said he was sorry that there was no music for them to hear in the trees as he brushed his lips against her breasts and throat, his long black hair falling over her face. He kissed the cross tattooed between her breasts.

"That's nice," she said.

"That's what Father Eudall taught me," he said. "To kiss the cross."

"I knew there was something totally right between us," she said. "I knew right away when I was sitting there with my eyes closed."

"Me, too."

"You didn't have your eyes closed."

"No, but I knew. I was watching a blind old man sit in the sun and when I sat down beside you, even though he couldn't see us, he smiled at me. Like it was a good sign."

"How come you ditched your kid's mother?"

"She turfed me."

"How come?"

"She's a good woman but a good woman can go bad. Her heart can go bad on her."

"What's in your fucking heart, that's what counts."

The seagull rose from the sill and flew off into the red sky reflected in the glass wall of the Household Trust Tower.

"Except now she says I should go home to her because she hears I'm happy."

"She's unhappy…"

"She's unhappy because I'm happy."

"That's the way it goes, man. Most people aren't happy unless we're unhappy."

"I tell you, Alice," he said as he kissed her and entered her, and she accepted the weight of his body in her arms.

"What?"

"Unhappiness is fucking overrated."

THE STATE OF
THE UNION

I don't know how to tell a story so I'll tell what I know. This is what
I knew when I was sixteen:

> *The spider's kiss,*
> *a wrench in the womb,*
> *a petal falls,*
> *my face in the water by the white reeds.*

I was sitting down on a rock by the pond. The house was up
the hill. We lived on Humberview Crescent. It was dark. At my feet
there was a branch, and a spider waiting in the white throat of the
branch.

There were always frogs in the big pond. I always listened to
the frogs at dusk. There were hundreds of them on all sides of the
pond – shrill lost souls drowning in the darkness – frogs who'd suddenly found themselves upright with hands and feet, sinking,
clutching at the water, trying to walk on the water, flailing, beating
the water with their tiny hands as they sank, and at my feet, a spider in the white throat of a branch, waiting.

It was the white throat, the white reeds, the whiteness that fascinated me. And the frogs trying to walk on water.

We could see the pond from our living-room window – an
elbow of black water, black because it was so deep. More than a
hundred years ago, when the pond was on the edge of the town

limits, a company of grenadiers on a forced march, trying to get into town before night fell, cut across the pond in a mid-winter mist, marching in single file through the deep snow over the ice. The ice broke and they all died, drowned. They went down like a long chain into the cold water. In the summertime, when swans on the pond ducked their heads into the water, I always thought they were looking for the dead soldiers. They weren't. Still, there are some people who say they can hear the soldiers crying out at night. I can't. But I could hear my mother. She often cried at night in her bedroom in the dark. I think my father beat her though I never saw bruises on her body. He did not look like a man who would beat a woman, so clear-eyed, a good nose, and his white hair. He was too young to have white hair but it had turned white during the war, Korea, and he had medals from the war. A row of medals. He wore them on police parade or at police funerals; otherwise, they were kept on the living-room mantel-piece. My mother polished them. If anyone spoke admiringly of them, however, she smiled, a wry smile. If she laughed out loud, that seemed to enrage my father. I never laughed at my father but there still seemed to be something he refused to forgive me for. "He is a man, that father of yours, who's got a lot of resentments, a lot of secrets," she said. She had a lot of resentments and secrets also.

One day, she had just let the screen door slam behind her when she told me, as if I weren't her son who might be shocked, that she was in love. She was feeling sorry for herself, or not so much sorry as vulnerable – soft, she called it. "I'm a soft woman," she said to me, "so soft, you see…and I want only the best for us all." No sooner had she said how soft she was than a red beetle crossed the concrete stoop, a hard-shelled beetle, and I said, "Should we kill it?" "Yes," she said and didn't blink an eye as she stomped it dead with her shoe.

"That'll do it," I said.

"You bet." She scraped the sole of her shoe against the stair. "I'm going out," she said.

"Will you be back soon?"

"Maybe."

"Should I lock the door?"

"No."

"Why don't you ever lock the door?"

"I never have, not in all the years. It's just not been my way, no matter how strange it seems. No, I've never locked a door in this house, never, and it's not because I'm looking for loads of family or strangers to come in. I'm certainly not looking for that, no sir, but as for locking people out, you can't lock a thief out. You can lock a fool out, but not a thief if he really wants to get in, and besides, I keep all the locks off the doors, not because I want to keep evil from getting in, but to make sure evil can get out..."

She touched my cheek, looking wistful. "Now do your mother a favour and give her a big kiss."

><>~><

There was a snowstorm, the snow thick and wet. At about three in the morning it stopped. It turned cold and a crust hardened on the snow. My mother and father were asleep. I pulled on my high black boots and went out walking down the centre of the street. There were no lights on in the house windows. There was only the deep white snow, and the crust was a brittle shell shining in the light of the street lamps. The crust bellied and broke under my boots, black boots that sank into the clinging softness of the snow, and the only sound up in the black branches of the trees was the cracking of the crust, breakage, the sound of small murders, and I could hear the halftone of hands whispering in the dark...

><~><

My father bullied his way out of my heart. At least he tried to. He was a big man, a sergeant of detectives. He broke men's legs, two or three times, he said. He was never charged. He told my mother, not as a confession, but just as a matter of fact across the breakfast table, that he'd broken men's legs with a crowbar. He was a burly man who would moan and pout if his eggs were not properly poached. He would also glower at himself in the mirror. And then touch his face gently, as if he expected his face to shatter. "There's a tiny little criminal, a real creep, a puppet, dancing in all of us all the time," he said. He saw darkness in everyone. Sometimes he said he saw faces in the mirror, black faces with popping eyes. Black faces enraged him, not because they were black but because the faces were always there in the mirror. Sneering at him. He said this to me one afternoon. He told me that he couldn't tell anyone else how he saw them sneering because they'd call him a racist. The men whose legs he broke were black. They were cocaine dealers. Black snowbirds, is what he said. "I broke their wings. I told them I'd rip their beaks off, too." But the worst, he said, were the Vietnamese. Saigon shivs, he called them, his voice shrill. Sometimes when his voice was shrill like that he sounded afraid. Womanly. It was hard to imagine him ever being womanly and afraid, not with the glints of amber in his grey eyes. But often when he was afraid his hands trembled. "Shakey Jake," he said, trying to laugh. "Shakey Jake McDice." That's when he got most cruel, when he was afraid and his hands were shaking, and he was trying to make fun of himself.

"Most of the time a man gets what he deserves," he said as he sat gripping the arms of his heavily tufted chair.

"Sometimes he does," my mother said. She slipped off her shoes, studied the turn of her ankle, and said, "Sometimes I think I deserve better than I've got. I don't know who to blame. Problem is, without blame, who are we?"

"I don't want to know," he said.

"You don't?"

"No."

"You don't want to know."

"Nope."

"You don't want anybody to know how crazy all this is?"

"I'll tell you how crazy this is. This is as crazy as it gets. It's like you never letting us lock all our doors, that's crazy," he yelled. He got up and strode from the room and locked all the doors. "Safe and sound," he said. "I'm a cop. I know what's going on." She got up and threw his golf clubs through the windows, breaking the windows one by one. "I'll break your legs," he yelled. He closed his eyes and began to tug and pull at his hair. "Not likely," she said, "not bloody likely," and she went out and got in her car and drove off. She loved her car. She loved her racing gloves. She wore her racing gloves in the house. She loved to talk about camshafts and carburetors. "I love empty roads," she said, but she didn't want to go anywhere. She just wanted to drive, full throttle, by herself. She'd drive along the lakeshore expressway in the middle of the night and get speeding tickets. They were yellow ribbons that she laid out beside his poached eggs in the morning. He put them in his pocket and said, "What you better remember, what you want to remember about freedom, is that you get nothing for free." He narrowed his eyes. The leper's squint, my mother called it when he narrowed his eyes. "Nothing," he said, "Nothing, nothing, nothing."

><~~><

Waking in the morning, I was always excited, always sure that something crooked in the air was about to correct itself. I was an optimist. I believed that there was something like an open seam in space, a seam that opened onto a scream of outrage, a silent scream that I could almost hear. I could feel this scream. I could feel the outrage. It sometimes made me cringe with pain. But whenever I was in pain I took a cold shower, shivering afterwards as I put on a heavy white terry cloth robe, certain that I could outlast, outlive this pain. Every morning I was certain, certain that the crooked would be straight. That's when my father went to work. Unless it was raining, he walked to work. On those good mornings I opened my bedroom window, always surprised by the slant of morning shadows on the lawn, shadows that were a dun colour, earth tones full of promise. *"Dun is the colour of my true love's hair,"* I used to sing, trying to make a little joke. "Dun is the colour of my true love's shit," my father said the one time he heard me. Then, right away, he apologized. "Sorry," he yelled, really angry. I cranked up the lever to the sound system in my room as my father came out onto the walk and I sang along with Engelbert Humperdinck, singing as loud as I could in front of the open window, the street booming with our blended voices, a splendour of sound that my father took as it was intended, as a taunt. He understood that I despised Humperdinck. I'd tell him, "Anybody who sings like that is a dink." I cranked the sound lever to full. Feeling the treble reverberation trembling my bones, I lifted my open arms, as if welcoming someone's embrace. I threw my voice as far as I could and went off-key.

⤚∼⤙

The moon trailing flowers is the clock's nursery rhyme. From the other side of the moon the world is in a blind (a half-rhyme...). I made a list of my father's favourite songs. I called it the Humperdinck list: *Release Me; Our Love Is Here to Stay; Someone to Watch Over Me; There Goes My Everything; But Not for Me; They Can't Take That Away from Me; The Last Waltz; I'll Never Be Free; Time Out for Tears; Please Send Me Someone to Love; Am I That Easy to Forget?; So Lonely I Could Cry; Mixed Emotions; I Apologize; A Man Without Love; Don't Say You're Sorry Again; In My Solitude; Don't Explain; Winter World of Love.* These are the songs of Engelbert Humperdinck. My father knew them all. He said over and over again that he loved Humperdink. He loved listening to them with my mother. He loved golfing. He swung at my mother with a golf club. Such is love, such are the songs of love. The frogs are good dancers.

⤚∼⤙

Mrs. McGuane lived down the street. She had married late, in her early thirties, and then her husband, who she said was a mining engineer, had died in a north country plane crash in the winter. "Icing on the wings," she said with a look full of bemused sadness. "Icing on the cake, now it's around my heart." She told me this with a sensual laugh, as if she really liked the sound of the words, and of her laugh. My mother told me some months later that none of this was true. She refused to tell me what *was* true, except to say that Mrs. McGuane's husband had some kind of connection with the church but was, in fact, dead, and her own family had left her well off. Mrs. McGuane hired me to dig up her garden. On hot days I stripped down to my waist and I sweated and I sweated until I was sopping wet. She used to watch me. One day she invited me in for a glass of water. She didn't bother with the water. She drew her finger down the sweat on my chest and opened my trousers and began stroking me, slow at first, and then hard as I stood there, staring at a kind of glee in her face until three or four jism shots went looping through the air to the tile floor. "Surprise, surprise," she said and went to get me a glass of water. My thighs were shaking. I thought I was going to fall over. She held the glass of water out to me, smiling benevolently. I knew she was not benevolent. I could feel that. She would be good to me, but not benevolent. I worked every second day in her garden. On those days she took off her blouse or sweater and brassiere and sat cross-legged on the floor of the breakfast room. She didn't take off her shoes. She had light freckles between her breasts. She said her husband had never noticed that. Another day, she draped a silk shawl around my bare shoulders, and the next day she made me wear a single strand of pearls at my throat. Then she asked if she could make up my face – eyeliner and lipstick. The lipstick was bright red. She gave me a silver hand mirror from her dressing table so that I could see my face and told me to watch my face while she knelt and sucked on me until I came in her mouth. I watched my face, or the face that was in front of my face, the parted red lips, the socketed eyes. The next time, I watched her, a woman who might have been my mother, on her knees before me, moaning at prayer. I told her that I wanted to make love to her, that I didn't understand why she wouldn't make love with me even if maybe I really didn't know how to make love, but she said, "Why would you want to do that?"

"Don't you like sex?" I asked.

"Not afterwards," she said.

"Maybe I love you," I said.

She sat very still, staring at the floor, and then narrowing her eyes, said, "If you keep that up it will change everything for the worse. No talk about love allowed."

She asked me what I thought about when I was coming. I said I didn't think, I heard things.

"What?"

"Frogs," I said. "I could hear them drowning in the darkness."

>~~~<

My father always looked at a person like nothing could be simpler than what he was thinking. He had a mind that was machine-tooled. He had a turnstile in his head, whipping around back and forth, *gu-thunk, gu-thunk,* a head full of contradictions, at least they were contradictions to me, which is why I could not read his mind. Maybe my mother could. Not me. He said he hated TV, how TV got inside your head, yet on Sunday mornings he always sat watching the *Crystal Cathedral of Tomorrow*'s *The Hour of Power*, glass on glass walls, piles and piles of glass sheeting and mirrors, the smarm of salvation, a salvation that was all coiffure and self-esteem. And he always brushed his hair before he sat down to watch, as if someone in the Crystal Cathedral might look up from a pew and see him on the other side of the tube. He didn't watch because he was religious. He watched because he had a yellow-dog eye, a jaundice in his eyeball, and a contempt for preachers and he relished his own contempt. He could get high on his contempt. Almost nobody deserved his admiration. Nobody. Except maybe General Patton and Ronnie Reagan. And Joe Frazier. And Gordie Howe. He liked Gordie Howe. He hated Muhammad Ali. Always called him Cassius Clay. And he thought all preachers were a crock. That was his word. Billy Graham was a crock, and politicians like Pierre Trudeau were a crock, but the Pope, any Pope, was even worse. Buckrakers for every pooch in the world in a black suit. As for the local politicians, he would lie back in his La-Z-Boy chair and say, "The mayor's a bumper sticker. Got all of what he knows off the back of a puffed wheat box. You can buy him by the yard – give him a set of used dining-room furniture and he's yours." He felt he was going good when he said things like that, and when he was feeling real good he would insist on taking me golfing or bowling. I didn't like going bowling because even as a child I thought that anyone who wanted to run quick short sprints in rented shoes while carrying a twenty-pound ball was slightly demented. He was smart, he was meticulous, always spanking clean, keeping his nails pared. He was attractive, and mysterious, because you never knew what was going on behind those grey eyes. He was the worst kind of secretive man; he seemed so open, so abrasively friendly. He liked to say, smacking me on the shoulder, that he had the common touch, but if anyone said that he was common, then he was on them as quick as white lightning in a water glass. That's what my mother told him, sitting in her bath soaping herself, and she blurted out as if she'd been brooding on it for years, "You're common, Jake, common." Then she yelled to me, "Your father's totally common." I walked into the bathroom and stared at my father. He looked like he'd been slapped behind the ears with a two-by-four, he was so furious he was smirking stupidly. He had a right to be furious. After all, he loved her, at least he said he did, and he insisted she loved him – though she'd told me she also loved somebody else. "I've taken somebody else to my heart," she'd said. My mother's breasts were splotchy with soap. She slid down into the water up to her chin to hide them from me, her head floating on the water, and he said, "I will kill you, I'll lop your fucking head off." He laughed. A tinny, high-pitched laugh. She had sloe-eyes. She looked up and said, "You don't scare me, talking to me like that. God scares me, I'll admit that. I don't know how to talk to God and He doesn't know how to talk to me, but you don't scare me." No matter what she said, she was always smiling, smiling though she was more often than not hurt and bitter. Smiling was something that she had learned in school, along with two and two are four and little ladies don't sit with their legs apart. Smile! She nursed a powerful sense of being wronged. "Your mother," my father said, looking at her like he was looking at a criminal, "and all her friends like her, are only busy being busy. Busy while they're unloading all their hyped-up complaints and self-pity and grief on any unsuspecting stiff who'll listen to them. Bleating on and on about how something pure inside themselves has been defiled. Defiled, the goddamn cock-wallopers."

The next day he sent her roses in the morning, roses in the afternoon. "Your father is crazy." She was slicing bread with a long bread knife, wearing her leather racing gloves. "You know what's the matter with him?" she said. "He feels he's been overlooked.

That's what really gripes men like him. They're all fascists, they feel they've been overlooked. That's all Hitler was, a man who felt overlooked." I watched from the window. There he was in the garden. I wondered if he felt overlooked. What did he really know? Did he know that she was soft, soft in love?

It was Sunday afternoon. Every Sunday afternoon she put on a record of somebody with a Russian name playing Chopin's *polonaises*. He was standing in the backyard by the peonies, wearing golfing trousers tucked up at the knees, leaning on his putter. He looked ridiculous, especially for a cop, a hard-nosed cop. I went out to talk to him, to ask him how his golf was going. "My game, my game," he said. He whispered to me about holes, holes-in-one, rabbit holes, holes in space, holes in the heart, home being where the heart is. And about the menace of rootless, homeless men and women in the cities, and how the government was like the homeless, always looking for a place to roost in our lives. He hunched toward me as if he were afraid of the flowers, as if they were insidious listening devices. It was the first time that I ever felt sorry for him. "The walking dead are loose in the land," he said. "Fucking bureaucrats." My mother was at her window, smiling. I wanted to break the window, break her glass face. She was smiling as if she'd just looked in the Lost and Found and discovered that we were gone and she was glad. I was surprised at such anger in myself, particularly as I loved my mother more than my father. I hated him for the bullying yet seemingly sad man that he was. It was the sadness in him that made the bullying so false, so brutal, so much a cover-up. As he broke a man's legs, I knew that his heart couldn't have really been in it: he always wanted to cry when he hurt people, he was always feeling sorry, for them, especially for himself.

Mrs. McGuane had a collection of ceramic frogs. They sat on her kitchen windowsill, on their haunches. They had bloated round bellies, small heads, mouthpiece lips, and holes in their haunches. Ocarinas. I learned to play them. I played *Somewhere Over the Rainbow, Blue Moon,* and *Harbor Lights,* Mrs. McGuane's favourites. She said she'd bought the frog ocarinas in New Orleans, that she'd gone there after her husband's death and had fallen in love with a black woman. "Actually, I wouldn't call it love," she said. "I just wanted to look at her, look at her naked. I didn't want to touch her, didn't want her to touch me. It was more like adoration."

She said she'd decided that she wanted me to look at her; and I agreed not to touch her. She led me upstairs to her bedroom. It was a long narrow room, pearl grey, the walls, the carpeting, the covers on the bed. All pearl grey. She told me to sit with my back to a big bay window that overlooked the garden. "That way I can hardly see you in the light." She slipped off her dress and was naked except for the high heels. She had shaved off all her pubic hair. She stood about three feet in front of me with her hands on her hips, her legs apart, staring over my head into the light. She didn't move. She had a bruise on the inside of her left thigh. She said, "You can do yourself if you want. Don't young men like to do themselves?" I said, "No." She said, "Good, you can just look at me."

The next time, she was waiting for me in the back sunroom with her makeup kit and she made up my face again – lipstick and eyeliner – and led me upstairs. After slipping off a silk robe with a shawl collar, she told me to put the robe on over my clothes. I sat wrapped in red silk, licking my red lips. Then she handed me one of the ocarinas. As she stood in front of me, naked, I played "Somewhere Over the Rainbow" on the frog.

"You look very much like your mother."

"Excuse me?"

"Though not as beautiful."

><~~~<

Isn't our soul the spider, which weaves its own body in the throat of the branch?

><~~~<

My mother liked to pretend I was a singer, but she wasn't stupid. She knew better. She just wanted to anger my father. I knew I was not a singer, though as a boy I had been a soprano, a beautiful voice in the choir at St. Peter's Church. I sang the solo at Christmas and at Easter. It was the *Seven Last Words* that we sang on Holy Thursday that I loved best. It was a time when all the images in the church, all the crosses, were wrapped in purple shrouds. Seven last words inside the shroud. *Eloi, Eloi lama sabachthani. It is finished. Father, forgive them, they know not what they do.* "They know not what…" After Thursday's *Seven Last Words*, on Good Friday, they took the mourning shrouds down, and there was the cross. The cross fascinated me – the rigid dove-tailed intersection of the lines, the precise intersection of pain, in suspension. And I saw that the hanging body made a different shape than the cross itself. The crossbar went straight out, east to west, but through the sag of his body his arms were uplifted, his body hung like a *Y*…feminine, in his dying he was like a singer, maybe Judy Garland, embracing her defiant silent note...

Then my voice had changed. The hair on my body turned black, abdomen, knuckles, toes. I waited for my voice to deepen, and it did, but when I tried to sing it slipped in and out of alto, falsetto, baritone. I'd lost my voice. It could not be found. That's when I began to sing along with other singers, especially my father's favourite, Engelbert Humperdinck (his other favourite was Zamfir, the man who played echoing wooden shepherd flutes), and my mother joined me. We were a duet. She had a throaty, husky voice for a small woman. Standing by the window in my bedroom we'd sing *Time After Time, A Sunday Kind of Love* and *What a Difference a Day Makes,*

> *twenty-four little hours,*
> *only sun and the flowers*
> *where there used to be rain...*

My father resented it. I had no talent. He'd said so. I had the *aptitude* for talent. That's what he said. "The world's full of men who'd like to be Lucky Luciano but they can't cut it. They hold up one gas station and spend the rest of their lives in jail. All they got is an aptitude." He'd come home and stand on the lawn and stare up at the window. I sang. One day, he went to the garage and got out the old lawnmower. As I stood there singing, he scowled as if he'd been sullied, as if someone had dumped dirt on his head. He put his head down and began pushing the old mower across the lawn, the blades clattering, pushing it faster, louder, till I stopped singing but he didn't seem to hear that I'd stopped and he kept pushing the mower till Mother stepped out onto the stoop and cried, "Jake, your heart, you'll hurt your heart."

∼∼

It was right around then that I acquired a limp. It was like a hitch in my thoughts. It was quite funny. Every time I had a serious thought I had to laugh, I was limping so hard. That was also the time I saw an old black blues singer, Brownie McGhee. And he had a huge limp, one leg shorter than the other, from polio it looked like. And when he left the stage he was singing *Walk On*, riding his hobble leg up and down. Everybody wanted to cry at his pain but I wanted to laugh because he knew how to play his own pain into a performance, into pleasure. I went out of the blues club limping a huge limp, and laughing, and someone told me I should be ashamed, imitating a man with a mockery like that, and I was ashamed, not because I was limping, but because I couldn't sing. So I went home and sat in total silence in the empty house and I remember saying to myself, "All I want is to be happy." I was in my mother's room, staring at one of those glass globes of hers, those glass balls, and inside the globe there was a house under a perpetual falling snow. I realized I was never going to be happy, not in that house. Still, it was my home, my family, even if in the summer time the snow still fell. But the swans would never duck their heads and look for me. That was clear. There were three tall urns sitting on the floor at the far end of the room, filled with dried flowers and bulrushes. I picked up the globe, rocked on the balls of my feet, took a stride, and bowled the glass house down along the carpet, crashing the ceramic urns. *Kapow*, a dead hit.

That summer, I read the following statement in a book. "Dying each other's life, living each other's death." – Heraclitus. I didn't then know who Heraclitus was, and frankly didn't care. A few pages on in the same book I found a diagram. I liked it, though I'm not altogether sure why. I took it to a copy shop and had a copy enlarged 300 percent and pinned the copy up on my bedroom wall.

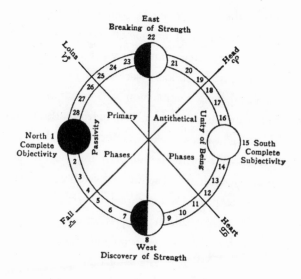

Mrs. McGuane phoned and said the sky was a strange teal blue. I still haven't bothered to find out what teal blue is. She asked me to bring one of my mother's silk robes and a pair of her sunglasses to the house. "You mean a dressing gown?" I asked. "Yes," she said, "and her pink bedroom slippers that you just step into, with the little pump heels." I didn't know how she knew about those pump heels but I brought them in a Shoppers Drug Mart plastic bag. As soon as I stepped inside the back door she told me to take off my clothes. I did, and then she slathered my cock with a clear liquid grease from a tube, H&R Sterile Lubricating Jelly. It was exciting, the slipperiness. Then she led me up to the bedroom. The drapes were drawn, it was a summer afternoon but it could also have been winter in that air-conditioned shadow-light, except that I could hear cicadas in the heat. She was naked under her own robe, wearing only a garter belt, which she took off and put on me. I was surprised that it fit me so well around my waist, and looking down at myself, so erect between the loose black straps, I felt an intense rush of pleasure in my loins, a satisfaction with myself. She draped my mother's blue raw silk robe over my shoulders, closed a little clasp at my throat so that it was like a cape, and then told me to put on the sunglasses as she carried the slipper-pumps to the full-length mirror on her closet door and set them down on the carpet facing the mirror. I stepped into them and wobbled for a moment because they were too small. She stepped between me and the mirror, with her back to me so that she could see us in the glass, so that she could hold my eye as she bent forward while reaching back between her legs, drawing my cock toward her buttocks, one of her hands up on the mirror. Then with my cock up against her, she put her other hand to the glass and said with a fierceness that almost frightened me, "Fuck me." I took hold of her hips and entered her, reached for her breasts, and began to fuck her. I had to kick off the slippers. She didn't notice. She was smiling, and as I really began to hump her from behind, she cried, "Fuck me…" and began to sing almost blissfully, at least it sounded blissful to me, *"Georgia, Georgia, the whole day through..."*

Georgia, my mother's name.

>━━◁

Pale, pale footprints of the barefooted trying to find their pale way in the snow. I dreamed that. A step, a step, toward something someone might call a truth, a word or a glance. A bullying curse. The bite of truth. Sometimes that's the way my mind worked, and works. Still. Bop. Bop. Bop. Word. Word. Word. That afternoon I went down the hill to the pond. The swans were swimming. There were several old men sitting on benches and children playing along the walkway and a Mister Softie ice cream vendor was parked under a weeping willow. The old men were smoking White Owl cigars. One was wearing a paper White Owl wrapper as a ring. In the two o'clock heat the still pond had an oil-like sheen. Hues and tones of pond-slime green and yellow. It was very peaceful. Standing beside the Mister Softie machine, there was a life-sized Coca-Cola bottle. It was made out of some kind of vinyl, except for the cap, which was wood. It came walking toward me. I could see the shoes underneath the bottle bottom. It walked right up to me, and just above the hyphen, there were two eyeholes. I was sure I could see two eyes inside the eyeholes. Eyes. I heard a deep, not harsh, but gravelly voice. "You tell your father, we're gonna get him. He won't see us coming any more than you saw me coming, and he'll get his." Then, the Coca-Cola bottle turned and walked away. I didn't know what to do. I couldn't call the police, or attack a bottle. Maybe he had a gun. I went back up the hill and into the house and sat in silence in my room for a long time. I put on Engelbert Humperdinck and opened the windows. Just before six o'clock as I was singing, my father came striding along, looked up, went into the garage and got the mower, and started mowing the lawn. He seemed to be furious with me, thinking whatever he was thinking, *gu-thunk, gu-thunk*. Whereas I had felt only afraid for him, hardly thinking at all, and so I went downstairs and out onto the lawn, the Humperdinck song still blaring out into the street. I told him about the warning from the Coca-Cola bottle. He looked at me a long time, a direct, almost disdainful, disbelieving look, and then he punched me hard on the shoulder, a short crossing punch that sent pain shooting down into my fingertips. "I told you when you were a pipsqueak kid, never talk to strangers and now I'm telling you, above all, never talk to Coca-Cola bottles. And if you do, then make sure they take the Pepsi Challenge first." He laughed loudly at his joke.

><><

Mrs. McGuane blamed everything on sunglasses. She said that Aristotle didn't wear sunglasses. Luther didn't wear sunglasses. But her husband did. He was John Cletuse McGuane, a Presbyterian preacher, and he wore sunglasses. That's what she finally told me. He wasn't a mining engineer whose bones were now encased somewhere in the ice. She said he'd risen quite rapidly in his church, both as a preacher and because of the pamphlets he wrote, especially about Judas. In one of his pamphlets that she gave to me to read while I was sitting in the sunroom, he wrote: "In the early Church, in Egypt – and mind you, the early Church was much closer to the present spirit of Pentecostalism than anything in

Catholicism since the authoritarian Council of Trent – Judas was regarded as a saint. The argument was simple and straightforward. Jesus, the Christ, the Son of God on the Right Hand, was all-knowing, and therefore knew what He became Man to do; His end truly was His beginning, His intention was to die, and so early believers said that He came to kill Himself for our sins. In His own mind He was a suicide. The apostle who understood this was Judas, who took upon himself the mantel of scapegoat, and out of love for Jesus, and in perfect imitation, hanged himself. As a matter of fact, the great theme at the heart of sacrifice – running through Judas to Jesus to Peter – is the efficacy of betrayal."

I could hear frogs running for their lives across the pond water. Mrs. McGuane said that after he delivered a sermon like this on Judas on Easter Sunday, a shouting match took place in the church. Though the sermon was startling to the parishioners, it was nothing compared to the shock of his suicide a year later. His body was discovered at dawn in Gzowski Park on the lakeshore, facing the water, hanging from a tree. His hanging had its own peculiarity. He had climbed into an old maple tree, had tied his ankles to a branch so that when he fell into the air he was hanging upside down. He'd then slit his wrists with a razor, his blood draining out of his outspread arms. She showed me some newspaper clippings. Someone had suggested that his suicide was an imitation of the death of Peter, who had asked to be crucified upside down because he was not worthy to die as his Lord had died. Someone else said his suicide was a deliberate mockery of the Cross and the Church by a man who'd lost his faith or his mind or both. Several neighbours were interviewed and among them, my father, who said enigmatically, "*Rien de rien*, he must have no regrets."

My father had discovered, of all things, Edith Piaf. He'd started singing *La vie en rose* around the house. I didn't know what to say.

><~><

When I was a kid, I used to go down to the pond and catch frogs. Every ten minutes I could catch a frog. I'd rub my finger down its back, soothing it, and then put a straw up its hole and watch it swell and swell until it was swole up. Then quick as a whip, I'd stuff a little cherry bomb in where the straw had been and I'd light it and lob it out over the still pond, toward one of the swans, like a hand grenade. If I'd got the timing right it would explode in mid-air. I didn't know why I did it. I didn't know why I enjoyed it. I just listened to the shrill cries of the frogs at dusk and knew I'd never run out of frogs. One day, an old man stopped by the water's edge and told me I was evil. I knew I was not evil. Whenever I came home from the pond I felt heartbroken. All I could see before they exploded were the little arms of the frogs, wide-open, embracing the air, full of hope.

><~><

It wasn't until my mother started wearing tailor-made buckskin suits with beading on the sleeves and came home with a hickey on her neck that my father turned really sullen and silent. He had nothing to say. It looked like whatever he'd had to say had been taken from him. He'd sit there and stare at her and she'd stare at him but he didn't do anything. She'd brush her teeth and then hunker down over a plate of dry toast, looking more and more morose. She'd brush her teeth again. Late one afternoon I saw in her eyes for the first time the laughter like a skull laughs. Knowing laughter, the laughter of someone who's come unlatched. Finally he said to her, "What's that on your neck?" and she said, "Love bites, love bites back." Every day, she ordered boxes of fresh-cut flowers. She kept putting flowers all over the house. "Why don't you order in some coffins, too?" he said. He looked like he was going to cry. I felt sorry for him, and hated him. I didn't want to feel sorry for my father. She put on and then took off her racing gloves, going nowhere. He started prowling the house, opening dresser drawers, sifting through her underclothes, opening closets, not looking for anything, just sifting, like he was rehearsing his training at cop school, sometimes talking out loud. She said, "I loved you, maybe I still love you, but I don't care." He took his putter out of his golf bag and went into the living room. "You don't care. You don't fucking care." There was a lime-green portable plastic putting hole on the rug in front of the fireplace. He dropped a ball on the rug and lined up a putt. "If it's any consolation," she said, "it's a woman." He stroked the ball straight into the hole.

"A woman," he said.

"Yes."

"Anyone I know?"

"Yes."

"Who?"

"Eleanor McGuane."

"Eleanor fuckin' McGuane?"

"Yes."

He broke her head with his putting iron, blood all over his white shirt and the white rug. He called the police, warning me not to interfere. "Don't fucking interfere. Don't get in the way." When the police came, and the ambulance men, too, he was sitting up close to the television set though it wasn't on, staring into the blank grey tube, and he was listening to shepherd flutes, softly humming along with Zamfir. I wanted to haul the old lawnmower up into the room and mow everything there was on the floor around the room to make him stop his humming. I could feel a silent scream in space, my space, a scream of outrage. I knew nothing was going to correct itself, no seam was going to be healed, nothing crooked was going to end up straight. He just sat stiff-lipped, hardly said a word to the police, and they treated him with something that looked like baffled awe. I was suffocating, swallowing words although I didn't have anything to say, almost hysterical, as they wheeled my mother out on a stretcher. She was still breathing. I could see I was going to be all alone. Whether she lived or not. Alone. As my father stood up to go to the patrol car, I cried, "Don't worry about me, Dad," and he said, "I am not worried about you, I'm worried about me." A cop standing beside me said without looking at me, "The goddamn selfish fuckhead," and I said, "No, no, he doesn't mean it like that, not like that. That's just Shakey Jake talking."

><del><</del>

I think, *My father tried to kill my mother*, and then I am swamped by shame, which makes me laugh, and then I fall silent. I limp home.

"Despair is silent. But even silence has a meaning if the eyes speak. And if despair speaks, then we are not alone." My mother's eyes are on me, my father's eyes are on her. I watch as they watch me.

We are not alone. We are a family.

SILENT MUSIC

He woke in the morning and had a little orange juice. He went to the front sunroom of the old family house. He sat in his ladder-back chair and stared at the rag rug and then he went up to the window and stood close to the glass, looking into the pane, listening *to the birdsong along the back of my earbone, the soundless sound Mother said was heaven-sent, sitting in her hair curlers in front of the window with the worn lace curtains frittered to pieces from too much sunlight and washing, staring through strings of light and pinholes at the black dog out there on the other side of the window,*

and unless your eye hears the dog's lower lip dripping spittle, his tongue hanging there between two white teeth, unless you hear his breathing how can you know the heat of him on your hand like the heat from the firebox when I was a boy, Ansel Mohr in his mid-thirties, *and Mother had her own birdsong along the back of her earbone, tapping it out on her little triangle in the old folks' band like an inkling of something left out of her life when she knew what was left out was love, except she always called me her love child since a father was nowhere, never known by me, so I guess what was left out was the word of love spoken,* which he had heard on a cold winter night when he was a child, the firebox in the kitchen stove blazing, and she was huddled over the telephone, talking in a low voice: "I am grateful, you know that, but it's been hard, so alone, and never your voice even, let alone a touch."

Ansel had gone into his bedroom, to the bunk bed his mother had bought on sale, saying, "It'll give you an extra place to play, like a sandbox, a little bed-box in the sky," and sometimes he slept on the bottom, sometimes on top, always aware there was an empty box above or below, and he found his teddy bear under the bed. He loved his teddy bear. He slept with the bear every night. Then he went to the bathroom. He took his mother's only bottle of perfume and doused the bear. He waited until she had hung up the phone, sitting in the shadows with her head in her hand, staring at the floor. He gave her the bear. Surprised, she held the bear at arm's length, startled by the scent, and then, seeing the empty bottle in his hand, she flew into a fury. She squeezed the bear and it cried out. She opened the firebox door and hurled the bear into the fire, where, for a second, he saw it come alive as a torch, on its back, and he closed his eyes as she slammed the door and went to bed.

Early in the cold morning, when the fire was out and before she woke, he opened the grate and sifted the ashes and found a small round silver voice-box filled with little holes, which he wrapped in a white handkerchief because he thought it was the teddy bear's heart, *and sometimes I listened as if the pockmarked moon could speak, a peering eye blinking as baffled as my mother, the echo eye of her sitting there sucking on her pain like an all-day sucker, sweat-faced in front of the fire, full of disdain, of disappointment, or sitting in a deck chair in the garden, splay-legged in the shade of huge sunflowers, smiling and whispering to herself. Years later I offered her the silver voice-box while she was knitting, the needles clicking like clocks gone crazy, syncopated to the stitch dropped, and she laid down the knitting and said, "What's that?" turning it over and reading* Acme Toy Company, patent pending, *always this impending dread, sometimes looking down at my feet to see if my legs are there, spinning around to see if suddenly he's there, the faceless face between my hands lips moving, staring into nowhere in the silence between my hands, turning around to see that one day she wasn't there either,* and when she died the Requiem Mass was celebrated in a stone church. It rained. The slate roof glistened through the black branches of maples. There were a dozen parish people he did not know: white-faced women in loose sack suits, a man with his trouser cuffs rolled into his socks, and the smell of Old Spice, Cepacol, and incense, and there were old ladies, and men from the rest home carrying white straw boaters. They held on to each other's hands at the ringing of the bells, the suffering Christ with His arms wide open, leaping off the cross, ecstatic, and choirboys sang as Ansel came down the aisle behind Father Cooper and the tight-lipped professional pallbearers, a dryness at the core, remembering his mother long before she had begun carrying bundles under her arms, back when she had, over a cup of tea, told him, "Life is all patchwork,

and if your father had ever married me that would have been the end of the Mohrs. But here you are, you're a Mohr, and that means there's meaning still in this house, though it's not much of a house, frame and all, but the fire in the kitchen is nice. I always liked an open fire," *an open wound, suppuration of silent words, a long line of fathers foreskinning for all they were worth, unknown, unsaid, alone in ice-cold space as we're all alone in the absence of God with only His mother, the mother of God, out there in black face, alone herself, the queen of the world,* and when he was a boy, he'd found that nearly all the women on the street were secret drinkers, and sometimes they screamed at each other and stomped around their front lawns. Sons and fathers were dead from the war and women were left alone. Young boys sometimes found wine corks between pillows on a sofa, or Mrs. Gladdery in her rose bushes on her hands and knees, little thorn cuts on her bare arms, saying, "No, no, naughty boy," soft yet firm when she sunbathed on the flat tin roof of the back of her house and she had him run his hand along the inside of her thighs into the hollow but never let him touch her like she touched him,

and one day she rubbed him, saying didn't he do that before going to sleep like her little Stuart did, and she said he had to promise he'd never tell Stuart about being up on the roof, "But of course you don't talk to anyone, do you?" and she laughed, *her robe hanging from a spike, like the old limp red inner tubes in the garage down the lane, dead snakes, where, after the war Mother found a snakeskin floating in the rain barrel and three dead birds and she put the skin into the stove and nailed the birds to the porch wall and the skeletons were hanging there all summer whenever I went past a fat middle-aged man down the lane who always sat on a three-legged stool in front of a garage, loose-mouthed and laughing quietly, wearing a string undershirt, and making endless paper planes out of a pile of newspapers at the end of the lane by the under-pass,* a damp stretch of darkness under railroad tracks and thirty or forty trains went through every day and he used to stand under the bridge, the rumbling of the freight train wheels making him tremble and shake, the weight of the sound almost painful and yet he wanted it, and when it went away he scrambled up the gravel embankment and stood watching the caboose disappear, *and maybe Father was a caboose man,* and one day his mother said, "I will say this, he could play the piano like the devil," *showing me a pile of sheet music, grey walls of paper like the grey walls of*

Silverwood's, a long dairy building with loading doors and ramps back when milk wagons were horse-drawn and the short street was covered with spilled milk – sour and yellow-white – curdled cheese and horse piss and dung, road apples the other boys had called them, with sparrows feeding on the dung, and then a man usually appeared leading a line of horses and Ansel stared at the shaggy hair around their hoofs and their slow walk with sometimes huge erections, and the men gawked and turned away, frowning. The horses looked as if they were laughing, their lips curled back like the laughing man making paper airplanes *and up the hill there was a huge castle stone house behind walls,* and he knew from his mother that a man named Pellatt had bankrupted himself building that house, though he wasn't sure then what bankrupted meant *and anyway*

         it was the name Pellatt I liked because I wanted a pellet gun and maybe when my father showed up I might shoot him in the leg, not to kill, only to wound, and when sometimes Stuart and I went on scouting missions through the brush along the walls, they got to the top of the hill, to a garden of flowers in diamond patterns. One day a lady appeared in a long dress and Stuart whispered, "Look at that. A princess, a real princess." As she turned around Stuart said, "Oh shit, some princess," because, with her hooded eyes, she seemed tired and worn down, and she looked to Ansel just like his mother and the women who drank too much because they were sitting by themselves waving lace handkerchiefs at children, and all his life with every woman he met he smiled sadly as if he understood their loneliness and need for a little comfort. He became good at comforting lonely women, though he was not sure he had ever been able to comfort his mother, because even as a child with his head against her breast he had heard her heart pounding and had looked up, listening to her whisper about the colour of dawn before the sun, and the same grey, except with lustre and a little pink, that she had seen in pearls when she worked for a while in a jewellery store, and glass *how she loved glass* and a blue vase she'd bought, an egg-blue that turned rose in the sunlight, and she said, "That's the way life could be if we only had the strength, and I've all the wonder in the world but no strength." Then before she went to the rest home she said, "And the truth is, I've loved my disappointment, kept it close like fine silk and now I'm going to lie down in it. A silken shroud is not to be sneezed at,"

and he walked out of the church behind the casket into pouring rain, and a high east wind blew the rain into the headlights of the few cars going along the road toward the cemetery, past Red-bone's Bar-B-Q, an old movie house turned into All-New Asian Age Rubbing Parlour, a stone war memorial to the fallen in the Korean War, and Heritage Used Cars. She was buried beside headstones covered with wet fallen leaves, neon crosses, and a plastic Sacred Heart on a tin prop. The hard rain was slanting. Father Cooper said the prayers, and coming from where she'd eventually ended up, the members of her old folks' band knelt in the pouring rain. A woman said to her friend, "She was a true Christian in the Christian community."

"Oh, and outside, too," her friend added.

Father Cooper and the old men and women stood close and chanted, "Hear us, O Lord... Hear us," as they bent head first into the rain under black umbrellas suddenly blown up and inside-out by the wind, up into the air like huge black tulips, *and in the cat's*

*eye a dead bird, like once at the lake the trees lichen-lined down the
north side of the trunks, lace, mildewed green, always lace in decay-
ing grace, and the fox snake in the low-hanging branch curled around
a bird's nest like an old bicycle tire looped on top of itself, waiting cold
in the strong sunlight, the nest, her nest, her bare breasts, that naked
young girl one time and how she stood there still sticks in my mind,
high-heeled, calf muscles hard and me hard, smiling little girl, and
me hunching down in front of her sucking on her breast, the little
indent in the nipple, her fingers inside my collar fingering my hair
and my middle finger hooking up inside her, warm, thumb on her
hair almost silky until she says, "I'll do you there on the white rug. You
see, I like you," and I could hear worms in the walls and Mother
singing* rub-a-dub-dub, three men in a tub, *and why were dirty old
drinking men called rubby-dubs afloat in a washtub, thankful for her
down there prayerful between my legs wondering what to do what to
do, not so much who, as why, why at all am I anywhere in this whole
world actually here* in the kitchen where he sat down with one of
his mother's hat boxes. But he didn't open it. He folded his arms
and listened, wondering if the voice he heard could be his own.
The phone sat angled off the hook. He heard the low hum and
then the warning bleeps. He didn't know why he kept the phone
now that she was dead. It was of no use to him. He hung up the
phone.

There was a saucer on the table, a slice of dry toast, orange
peels in a cup, a loose mound of envelopes and bills, an old wind-
up alarm clock with a little bell on top, and a big moon-faced magnifying glass. When he opened the hat box he found a newspaper
picture of his mother as a young woman, the newsprint yellow and
crumbling, with no date, no explanation. The clipping had been
closely cropped. She stood smiling in a dark dress with many

pleats. He held the magnifying glass close to the paper. She looked happy. There was a crease and a stain on it from a raisin in the bottom of the box. There were torn pieces of blank paper, an earring, a narrow black velvet sash, a dried-up wrist corsage, and a folded piece of lined schoolbook music paper.

There were no notes. No clefs. No sharps. He walked down the hall to the living room and stood by the long narrow windows. There was a plate-glass mirror over the mantelpiece. His hand rested on the brocaded back of his mother's old easy chair. Then he picked up one of her pressed-glass bowls, the pale shades of pink in the glass turning dusky rose and violet in the light *strange for a woman who settled for so little to like so much changing light,* and he sat humming, staring at a line of small portraits on the mantelpiece, found earlier in another one of her hat boxes. He didn't know who they were. There were no names written on the backs, nothing, *the grace light of zero, life saved so that it might die, like Mother, quiet and calm as grass, which she stood on, heels thick and round on her walking boots leaving little holes, zeros, a voice-box for worms in the grass, her black boots, polished, a walking woman, always forgetful of everything except when she walked alone at nights when she deliberately stepped on a sidewalk crack,* whack, *when she came down hard with the shoe leather, unafraid, like she was daring bad luck to take a shot at her, the way she also always walked under ladders, and brought home the black cat, cradling it even though she was allergic to cats. She had this narrow sense of herself, fierce like the sharp tin propeller blades we used to whiz up in the air when we were kids,*

like when one day Billy Mitchell whipped through the garden with a short-handled broom pole, cutting everything in sight down and Mother cuffed him so hard she split his lip, because she wasn't going to let him get away with doing whatever he wanted to do. Billy was always getting his way, something he had learned from his grandmother, old Mrs. Hunter, so fussy and proper with her silver spokes on her polished-up gentility Ford, back when there were also wagons on the streets, horse-drawn, Silverwood's wagons, and horseballs on the street, and her grandson Billy, he used to, when he wanted his own way as a child, stand on the street and rub road apples down all over his head til Mrs. Hunter, screaming, gave him anything he wanted. He'd stood there smiling, smeared in shit, and that's the way all the Billys make their choice, smearing themselves in shit in the sunlight so they can do their damage, and though nearly two feet of snow had fallen that week in the season's last March storm, he went out for a long walk browsing through the stores, watching cops in their white crash helmets like punk hoods and hopheads, their wraparound face visors, shining plastic eyes deflecting all light,

and Ansel carried himself with an air of deliberate well-being though he felt he might be coming apart at the seams. As he walked he closed his eyes and named all the stores – Swepples Drugs, Danforth Radio, Adanac Cakes – and when he went into Woolworth's he saw on the wall, over Stationery Supplies and Fine Toiletries, a painting reproduced on canvas, a wobbly white church looming up out of a dark sky full of stars like big sunflowers. He liked it, the almost childish lunatic gaiety. There was only the plate-glass mirror over the mantel, his mother's mirror, because she said it made the room bigger, filled it full of light, and she had painted the walls white to help the light but he preferred the front and back porches, like little houses, each window a small screen alive with shadows, and he bought the painting and carried it wrapped in a big brown paper bag under his arm.

The next morning it was cold and clear and the sunlight on the deep snow was bright. He took down the mirror, unscrewing the chrome clamps. He hammered a nail into the wall and hung the painting, wondering why his mother would rather have had an empty mirror than a *church no matter how wobbly because life itself is wobbly, so you need some certainty, some confirmation of how things really are, because there is nothing, absolutely nothing else, Mother, between us and the dirt we do ourselves, the damage we do in doing damage to others,* so he decided to store the mirror in the tool shed at the end of the garden. It was heavy and he carried it out in front of him like a placard. The snow was deep and unbroken. It glistened in the strong sunlight. Walking with his head down watching his step, he suddenly thought he must look ridiculous and he looked up into the mirror but all he saw was a blinding flash, an explosion of light.

He stood with his arms out, holding the light, unable to close his eyes or find his face. He dropped the mirror, which sank like a blade into the snow. All he could see was light and snow and empty sky. The milkman found him like that, white-faced, drained, standing staring with his arms straight out, and the milkman led him back into the house and sat him down, "Don't worry, Ansel, it'll all come back, you'll see," but he sat staring, hardly eating day after day, and some neighbours came around and talked for a while and left shaking their heads. Sometimes he got up and stood close to a window, looking into the glass as if something were there. Every day the milkman said to him, "Don't worry, nothing lasts forever, you'll see," but it did last into the spring when one afternoon old Father Cooper came around. He opened the door and Father Cooper touched him on the shoulder and slipped inside without a word, a wistful look in his eye, and then he walked toward the stairs, his hands in his pockets. He smiled at Ansel. "I knew your mother, you know, years ago." He looked up the stairs, and then he shrugged, saying, "We all like to think we've played a part." Ansel, bewildered by the familiarity, stepped back into the living room. The old man followed, saying, "In case you forgot, the name's Cooper," and he reached out and touched Ansel on the cheek. Ansel sat with his arms folded across his chest *and whisker rubs, I'd forgotten the whisker rubs when I was a boy, young Father Marshall, those big blue lonely eyes chalking up his angels of perfection on the blackboard, the points of isosceles piercing the heart of God, three persons with pointed heads, he'd said, laughing, with all the best lonely intentions in the world giving his boys whisker rubs cheek to cheek, the affection of the loneliness of priests that I'd forgotten* and old Father Cooper said, "I see you've no TV in the living room. It's a bad thing, these TVs in the living rooms. TVs everywhere. Cuts down on the talk, and no talk's no good. Black-and-white TV on the good old days was absolutely worse. The good old days were worse. I hate black-and-white."

They sat in silence. There was a strong wind and the branches near the windows swung in the wind and cast shadows across the floor.

"I'm a Nosy Parker," the old man said.

Ansel nodded, smiling.

"Is that yes or no?"

The priest, shifting in his chair, saw the painting over the mantelpiece. "Fella that painted that picture, I know all about that. He cut off his ear, but I guess you know that, too. Clean as a whistle. Guess he only wanted to hear half of what was going on. That's what it's like to be a priest, you know. A woman gossiping is just a loose lip, but her secret she keeps in her heart. That's what you hear in confessional. You hear the secret half of what's going on, one ear to the grille, you know."

Ansel squinted and stared at the cornflower stars, his eye filling with flowers, spinning flowers that left him light-headed. "And well, now," the old priest said, settling into his chair, "we do the best we can. It's all you can ask," the light from the windows catching his freckled forehead. He closed his eyes and sat still for a long while. The house was silent except for the wind and Ansel heard a creaking in the walls. A crack in the plaster ran like a vein down to the baseboard. There was dust along the baseboard moulding and, in the corner near the foreleg of the old radiator, a thimble, *Mother's little cup, needle pusher, leaning into the mahogany mirror on her dressing table, looking not at herself but into the past for some clear moment, some insight into the hang and shape of things. She was, pouring little shots of straight rye, a charwoman's drink she'd always said, into her thimble, giggling, throwing them back and she probably used that thimble to mend the rips in my life,* and then the old priest rubbed his cheeks as if he'd just come out of a little sleep and, with his chin resting in his hand, he said, "You know, I've got a theory. I was thinking about this all day today. Of course we've all got theories, but it seems to me that any man's the

432

hero of his own little world, his dreams, right? And there's nothing a woman would rather believe in than in a man's dreams about himself but the trouble is,"

and the old priest loosened his collar, "the trouble is most men have little or nothing to say for themselves. They're thin in the storyline, and it's why they change women, because they've got only these few small stories they've got to tell over and over. And if they're married, a woman soon knows she's heard the best he's got and there's really no more to say, no more dreams, except the woman can't ever let her man see in her eyes that she knows his dream life is over, and this is why men take off with other women, not just to sleep with them, but to tell their one or two little stories about themselves again, wanting to see that wonder look come into a woman's eyes." The old priest leaned forward, elbows on his knees, his mouth set, holding his head. He waited. Ansel blinked and licked his lips. Then the old man, closing his eyes, said, "You ever seen an owl in a tree? You ever tried talking to an owl in a tree?"

Ansel shrugged and the old man smiled and patted his hands together. "That's more like it. I can't hardly get a word out if there's no response. I just came by because I can't stand you sitting here gawking into nothing all alone, and since I've stood talking to an owl, you got to admit that's pretty interesting, too, because there's nothing quite like the unblinking eye of a sitting owl."

Ansel nodded.

"Owls keep down the night life."

Ansel nodded again.

"Sometimes I think God's an owl," the old man said. "An owl in the night. Except that's only after I read about Abraham and suchlike. Blood sacrifice. It's blood that binds the old books together."

Ansel opened his mouth, and then closed it.

"During the day, of course, he's not there at all. The owl, I mean. God's there, that's for sure. Of course a lot of men don't believe that, maybe even yourself. Maybe that's what's going on, what with your mother gone and all, but I figure not believing's a kind of impotence. A man gone impotent is a strange bird."

Ansel laughed and shook his head, smiling.

"No, no. Not that. I mean real impotence. It's in the heart," the priest said. He stood up and shook Ansel's hand.

Ansel opened the door. "Home, my boy," the old priest said, "whether you hang yourself or your hat, is where you are, and you are what you are."

Ansel sat in the living room. It was July now. He was sweating and he stripped down to his shorts and went out onto the back porch. A white gravel walk led from the back porch to the tool shed. Outside the shed door a wooden piccaninny lawn boy stood in blue breeches and a red jacket. The eyeholes had been drilled clean through the head, and though the mouth was drawn at the corners, without the eyes it was hard to tell whether the mouth was set in contempt or laughter. There were huge sunflowers down the length of the garden, golden yellow heads, big dark centres, the only flowers in the small oblong backyard. He sat on the porch whetstoning an old hand-sickle. He was in a white wicker chair, naked except for his white undershorts, sweating in the stifling heat. From time to time he wiped his face and shoulders with a towel and then he drank a glass of cold milk, *the other day,* as if he were talking to the old priest, and suddenly he wished the old priest were still there as he touched his thumb to the sickle blade,

I read how a fellow had his whole yard cemented and then he laid that over with outdoor carpeting, glued her down, good emerald-green car-pet, and once a week he went out there vacuuming his lawn clean as a pistol, wearing a white handkerchief knotted around his forehead in a sweatband. His toenails needed clipping. He smiled, spat on the whetstone, and patted the flat of the blade on his thigh.

Two sparrows landed on one of the huge sunflowers. The spar-rows were pecking the dark brown centre. *They know I'm here,* looking around, suddenly struck by his loneliness, *not the birds, I mean the flowers, how I feel them feeling me sitting here whetstoning, those stems there, thick as a man's forearm,* and the sun caught the blade with a flash of light and the birds flew away. He sat very still with a wry little smile, staring at the head of the blackface lawn jockey whose feet were anchored in a bucket of cement buried under the lawn, *and only last week, cutting the two flowers down right above the root, carrying them shoulder-high* remembering how he'd suddenly picked them up and started whipping them around over his head, *waving great big yellow daisies, thrashing the empty air,* and he had got the old hand-drill and reamed the eyeholes through the lawn Sambo's head *and I knelt down and looked through to those little holes of light on the other side, thinking, What's that, greener pas-tures? and laughing not to myself or the big sun hole up there, the white hole, white holes in every black pane of glass at night, but just laugh-ing, laughing at the street all entirely empty except maybe a girl, a woman hurrying home, and how come right now I hardly can think of women, the dip like a thumbprint in the low small of a woman's back, the weight always lacking in small breasts, gone, lightweight, being light-headed and haven't had a hard-on for who knows how long, nor want one in this absence, the peak roofs of the dark houses in the moonlight, gravestones gone from Mother's yard, dreaming of how*

I have tried to love, holding on, hoping only for a little thumbprint, some stamp, veracity while the ice worms work their way. He got up and went into the kitchen. He took a carton of cold milk from the refrigerator and carried it along the dark hall by the stairs out onto the front porch. He sat down and hunched forward in his chair, covered with sweat. He poured his glass full of milk. He had a big man's body. He got up, *funny,* and walked back through the dark house to the garden porch, *I've got myself in protective custody.* He held the sickle shoulder-high, aiming the blade at something in the air, and *sometimes thinking it's my head or theirs, those sun-sucking sunflowers, just sucking up all the sun.* He hooked the sickle's point into the newel post, letting it hang there like half an ice tong. There was a heat haze over the tin roof of the tool shed. *The trouble is it's simple. No endings. If there's an ending then everything falls into place, falls because you know where you're going, which is why I figure I never know where I'm going. Anyway,* and he folded his arms across his chest, the lines around his mouth being two deep shadows, *the* clomp clomp *down the hall of my footsteps, tunnelling, that bewildered mole's smile of mine I see in the mirror, and then I come out here into the light that glitters like particles of snow lifting off ice except it's summer, glittering sparkles of light in my eyes like sparklers on firecracker night, the way we used to write our names in the air with sparkling wands, names, light no one else sees, and I don't know how the light hit me, like lightning in the eyes, God or a great gap of nothing. Who knows? I don't know if this is God's grace or the end of everything, except how calm I feel, this huge nothing or silence a satisfaction like the wasted fullness after a woman and yet the feeling that somehow there in the glass between me and the black dog, something hangs, suspended, hidden, like a truth, a word, a word that'll open up between me and what's out there on the other side.*

He sat for a long while and then pulled the sickle point out of the post and ran the flat of the blade along the back of his forearm. *Something about a blade sun-heated, the feel on the skin, like the shock of ice water, a shock almost soothing. I've done that, up to my neck naked in ice water and there's nothing you can think, so numb, it's just soothing, you're iced, it's the end, and one of these days I'm going to ice those sunflowers. I get sometimes so I can't stand their great big heads, overgrown costume jewellery, flowers for the way things are, someone all the time sucking you dry, and I feel them actually feel the way I'm feeling,* as he laid the sickle down on a small side table and smiled, knowing that he was soon going to cut them all down to their roots. He opened the screen door and took up the carton of milk again and *Ansel, you get yourself ready, mother's milk, the milk of human kindness.* He shook with silent laughter and then shrugged standing out on the porch, sopping wet, unmoving, staring, his mouth drawn at the corners, *no song, singing, no one and between the dog saliva and semen, my lost face in the light. I have lost myself in the light, looking, and all there is is compassion, somewhere from someone, a word beyond anything I might say if I could about this complete nothingness which keeps my eye more alive than ever before, so that even sleeping spiders in their webs sometimes look like opals in the light.*

He sat for three days listening. He wondered if the voice he heard was his own. He had never heard his own voice.

He got up and dressed.

He combed his hair.

There was a blue jay in the tree outside the window. He had never seen a blue jay before. It was almost a week since he had combed his hair. He was surprised at how well he looked. He'd lost weight, the loose jowly flesh.

He stood, listening.

I have nothing to say, as later that week he walked along the river road, coming upon a small church wedged between storage yards and foundries, and he stood inside the church, *I have nothing to say,* staring at an unknown woman, *raven-haired and high cheekbones, sitting in a pew, eyes closed, humming a low mournful tune, keeping time with her foot, a light tapping on the marble floor, the sound of tap water dripping in the night, her hooded eyes* staring at the ceiling of the cold brick chapel, a plague-procession fresco, bodies twisted in pain by buboes, flagellants whipping themselves in rage, howling with the death lurch, and in front of the altar rail a carved Christ caught in mid-stride with big bony feet and a haggard peasant's face with a round little mouth, a short man wearing an off-the-shoulder carmine velvet cape, naked except for a gleaming gold-leaf loincloth *and you are nothing, so fish-mouthed, zero,* and one night on television he had heard a man say, "You want to know how successful someone is then just count the zeros after his name," and then, after a nod and shuffle, a shrug and a quiet laugh, the woman said, Yes, sure, why not? She would love to take a walk with him. And so they, both curious and smiling, headed toward Ansel's home.

The wind made an easy lisping noise along the edge of the river. They went down the slope of a hill behind an ironworks, along an unused path, and there were broken drain tiles, wire, a rusted bolt, groundhog holes, and rough grass giving off a chill. She stepped lightly ahead, half guileless, half brazen, and said, "I feel just like when I was a girl and put on heels for the first time, knowing that when a man looked at me in heels he didn't see little girl legs and that gave me pleasure because there's nothing better than being a woman," *and who knows what Mother would've said to that, trying to fill the narrow rooms of her life with light, staring into the eye of her own unhappiness, sometimes strangely satisfied, with her unhappiness, so it seemed.* "When I was a little girl," the leggy woman said, "my father used to wash me every night and dry me with a great big towel. Then one night when he was drying me he handed me the towel and said, 'Dry yourself between your legs,' and though I was a little girl I somehow knew from that moment on I was a woman. I mean, then and there I made up my mind I was a woman, and felt very sad about that thing between me and my father being gone because he could not touch me. That's what I was thinking up there in the chapel, that I wanted him to touch me," *pretending to pray,* and she had reached out and touched the toe of the haggard Christ and then had begun to smile and laugh in the chapel hush, and had whispered across the pews to Ansel, "What's the matter, the cat got your tongue?" *and in the cat's eye always a bird,* past, to be, in the mouth of the mute Christ in his gold loincloth, and the sky was overcast and grey. She had an open easy laughter, and she said, "Imagine me saying that and I always wanted to leave a man speechless so I guess you're my man," as she later lay down, *upstairs naked on your back, and you said, "There's blood, but all births begin in the vacating blood," and the next night with you staying over like you had every right to be there, "on your own time, on your own dime," as you said while I was kneeling between your legs as you shoulder-rocked the way children push themselves through water on their backs, backwards, all sourness emptied out, tasting, smelling the skin folds, breathing words into that mouth.* "But I guess it is the loneliness,"

she said. "I just went in and sat down, cool like it was, not because I never go to church or anything like that but I was thinking about me and my girlfriends. I mean, we're all married and though we're all happy we're not happy, you know what I mean. So we spend a lot of time together, which is good, and our husbands like it a lot because it keeps us out of harm's way from men and what for us was just getting together for a few laughs turned into more than a few drinks, with at first a little touching and then a lot and nobody takes it seriously except it's serious. And now we actually strip down, sometimes pretending it's a kind of fashion show and it is beautiful, you know, the way a woman can be so tender to another woman. You get a funny kind of companion sense of yourself. Even a couple of our husbands know what's going on, including my own, but he prefers it that way because it's no threat to him so it leaves me sad the way we all have to do these things in life without thinking," *and what is that? To be free of thinking and empty in the head instead of this impotence of the heart while suddenly so alive in the cock.* So I just took off a couple of days ago, walking, you know. Everybody takes off."

She stayed with him for two days, saying, "He'd never look for me out this way because I don't know anybody around here and nobody knows me and you're really nice treating me just like I was a princess or something," on the back porch, a grey squirrel running through the hacked-up flower beds. The grass was brown. He smiled. There were anthills in the lawn, pustules of sand. She was lying on a sun cot. She had taken her clothes off but still wore high heels. She had two small scars close to her light reddish hair.

"You know what's nice with you?" she said. He looked at her. Her eyes were closed. "There's no questions asked. That's what's nice. Not that I figure there's ever a real answer to a question, but I can see you got lots of books and stuff around so you must be up to something inside your head, but mute, the way you are, you're not always heaping it on me, see?"

She sat up. She had dark nipples and her heavy breasts sloped sideways *and what's it like with mother's milk suspended in different directions and a vacancy between the legs?* as she said, "Except there's a thing I'd really like to know, without prying or nothing, but I figure you cut down all those dead sunflowers lying out there or else you got a nutty neighbour, so why would you do that, leaving them there like dead rope or bodies lying around, you know what I mean?" He touched her breast and she took his hand and wet his finger in her mouth so that his touch on her nipple was wet. She undid his trousers, drawing him out as he lay back remembering his boy's bunk bed, his bunk box below, the haunting presence of an absence above, and he stared at the row of empty narrow planting boxes on the porch rail. She swallowed his semen as he lay beside her, shaping silently words she could not see, *grace lights of zero,* and looked at himself, limp, *all stems fall down, and bridges,* and later when they were upstairs lying in bed, when she thought he had gone to sleep, she got up and went down to the telephone and he sat on the top stair listening.

"In the heart, that's where. A little something… I know I'm crying… Yes."

She came back up. He was in bed in the dark. He could see her in the doorway, hands on her hips. She sighed. He did not move. She folded her arms. Then he sat up and she sat beside him. He touched her hair and kissed her cheek. He kissed her on the neck, then shrugged and let her go, and she said, "Well, I've got to move on. It's how it is."

In the ochre lamplight she leaned over him, her hair falling around her face, kissed him and said, "You're in my heart, I can hear you in there." Then she was gone and he stood at the window, staring into the dark caves of leaves in the maple trees.

In the morning, there were ants in the kitchen. There had been no rain and the garden earth was grainy. A little boy had come to the door in the afternoon selling small Red Cross flags on behalf of Crippled Civilians. He had bought two and stuck them through the eyeholes of the lawn Sambo. A country singer was singing *"just another scene from a broken dream"* on the radio, *and that's bullshit. Nothing's broken, just bent. Altered, by owl light.* It was ten to nine. He was listening. He stood up, looking out the window. He preferred glass in the dusktime, the ebony reflections he could see of himself and also see through as if he held all the landscape inside himself, the way he held his mother's words before she'd gone into the rest home. "And you are groping," she had said, "and groping's no good. It pours down on you. I can see the dark right there in your eyes, which is wrong because the sky's got a glaze, and if you look up you can see that. Look up. Anybody can see that, while I got what's important to me right here in these bundles, and I need a rest and when you need a rest you go to where people rest, which is a rest home, so that's where I'm going."

She had moved into the home, after burning old dresses and all her high-heel shoes in the firebox, along with a carton of papers, a quilted blanket, and a small lace tablecloth smelling of mothballs *sitting spread-legged on a stool, and where was the fat-bellied man in the string undershirt making paper airplanes sitting on his stool surrounded by rubber snakes and Mother laughing at the snake in the tree and the gulls down by the lake,* and the rest home was down by the lake, so every day she saw gulls with slate-grey wings ripping at dead fish, dead from eels and oil slick. There was an old empty wooden shack on the beach and each morning she went down the path between tall pine trees, carrying her bundles. She kept her stool in the shack and sat and waited until the sun burned away the mist. The gulls came with the glare. She cradled her bundles against her breast and sometimes scullers appeared on the water from the rowing club, men hunched forward and skimming the water, their blades nicking the water. "And you don't know why I'm thinking what I'm thinking," she said, "but then it's not necessary to know. We all pretend to know too much. The more we talk, the more we think we know. You're you, that's all. You are, and that's everything because nothing is nowhere and you're here. That's a fact. Look at it this way. You got more secrets from me than I'll ever have from you." He visited her every Sunday. The caretaker stood at the door. There were old people in all the rooms, whispering *like shedding light.* He found her sitting in an easy chair. "I was just sitting here," she said, "staring through that open door and it struck me that maybe an open door's like a coffin upright, you know. Someone was telling me the other night that at the old Irish wakes they used to stand the body upright in the open box to be among the people in the dining room so a body wouldn't miss the dancing." They got up and went into the hall with all the elderly people who were walking with their arms linked or holding hands. Some bedroom doors were open and women sat in their chairs facing the hall. One afternoon, he saw an old man with pure white hair embracing an old woman. She was wearing a pale blue dress. The woman was fumbling with his trousers.

"Some things never die," his mother said, shifting the bundles under her arms, and she led him to the music room, glass-roofed and full of light. A dozen men and women were milling around music stands, and they all wore white straw boaters. He stood in the doorway as his mother took a chair close to the back windows, stacking her bundles. She smiled at him as she squared her boater on her head and opened up a black leather case, took out a gleaming triangle, which, as everyone else sat down, she held up, framing her face, and tapped with a little silver rod, giving a precise *ping like a bullet note, and was Father Marshall somewhere with his ear to the wall, listening, chalking angles on a blackboard, isosceles perfection piercing the heart of God*, and he saw that the saxophones, clarinets, flutes, and the small slide trombones and trumpets were golden-spangled plastic, and the caretaker, hushing the shuffling players, lifted his arm, and then they began to play *Darktown Strutters' Ball* – the sound nasal and whining and yet sometimes whistling and sweet – and the old men and women hunched forward, earnest and intent, puffing their cheeks, wagging their elbows. His mother beamed when she hit one clear note on the triangle, and then she picked up her bundles and together they walked out onto the lawn and stood under a linden tree. There were several old couples promenading, nestling against each other. The light through the leaves dappled the lawn and Mother, *she never wanted to have friends but only a genuflection before her special sense of her own self*, said, "You should come to Sunday Mass some morning because we play at Mass and I ring the bell when the priest lifts the cup. I don't care much about the Mass but sometimes I think the sound of that bell is as close to the sound of God as we'll ever get." They walked through the tall pines toward the lake and the small dunes where there were wild plum trees and dried roots hung in mounds of sand. They sat on a ridge of salt grass, her bundles beside her, *containing maybe a man's name who played the piano in a red caboose like the devil*, as she touched his hand, *and it was an unabashed touch of tenderness*, he thought, wondering why that morning he had suddenly stood up, taking a hammer and, striding to the shed, he had opened the door, hammering the old plate-glass mirror to pieces, the shards of glass catching the light on the ground like glittering knives, *an explosion of light in the loins of shrivelled men and women staring into the white abyss hole, fingering life, and does Mother even now do what she hasn't done for years and does she hide her bundles, her secret, under the bed, breathing what words into the gumming mouth of which old man, and to what music?* and one Sunday, he found the caretaker at the door. "She wasn't at Mass, and nobody noticed until the priest raised the cup and there was no sound. She's not in her room either or down at the shack." Ansel ran along the beach, past the rowing club, and then he saw the seagulls circling slowly, *their birdsong along the back of my earbone, her inside her hump of clothes there on the sand, hip ajar, one shoe straight up, pointing, the heel bottom a pinpoint I heard like a little hole letting air out of the sky,* and "You are, that's all," she had said, "and nothing is nowhere but you're here," where he found her sprawled flat on her back and face up to the sun, arms spread wide and the bundles free. He closed her eyes and reached for the bundles, down on his knees, moving around them like a prowler, putting out a tentative hand. He ripped them open, bewildered as he dipped his hands into a confetti of tiny pieces of scissored paper, and on each little piece there were notes, quarter-notes and half-notes, *clefs and all the soundless sound she said was heaven-sent,* and he filled his hands, hurling the scissored music into the light, the sun high like a flower of mirrors where it glittered white, and the paper notes swirled around his head *and maybe she was right* as little clouds of notes curled and fell, covering his hair, his shoulders, and all her body. And as he knelt, inside his skull he heard the word of love. He didn't know if it was his voice. He had never heard his voice.

COMMUNION

The old man had a hunch to his shoulders as if he were under a heavy load. Even on hot days he wore a suitcoat to hide the numbers tattooed on his left arm. In April, he came to the church of Our Lady of Perpetual Help. He was late for Sunday Mass, coming in after the sermon. He stood at the back of the crowded pews under the ninth station where Veronica wipes the face of Jesus.

The old man had withdrawn his left hand into the sleeve of his suitcoat. As if he were an elderly war amputee, he extended the empty end of the sleeve as a welcome to a fellow latecomer, who called him brother and then dipped two fingers of his hand into the piscine. The old man did the same with his right hand but did not make a small cross on his forehead.

At the ringing of the *Sanctus* bells, the old man got into line among those who had confessed and been granted absolution. After a few shuffling minutes, he stood at the altar railing in front of the priest. He put out his right hand to take the host that had been proffered to him. He held the wafer in his open palm, stared at the dry white O as it lay across his lifeline, lifted it, and felt it settle on his tongue. Letting his left hand fall free from his sleeve, he bit into the host. Wanting to swallow this God down, he gathered his spit and did.

UP UP AND AWAY
WITH ELMER SADINE

1

Elmer Sadine was sent to Saigon and assigned to a squadron of Phantom F-4s, but he did not see battle action. He saw sullen men under propeller fans in bars, sitting on the edge of their chairs waiting for the end of the war, for their flight home, men who sweated too much as they talked about morphine sulphate. Elmer hitched a ride on a helicopter recon flight and as the gunship followed a mustard-coloured river, he fired off an M79 launcher and watched a rocket grenade explode in a clump of trees. A lance corporal laughed. "Now," he said, "when it's all fucking over they're sending us the sharpshooters." Elmer was offended. "Up your ass," he said. The lance corporal punched him in the face and stuck his .45 in Elmer's mouth. "Suck this," he said.

Elmer met a nurse, a woman older than he was. He met her outside a whorehouse. She asked him how he'd got his swollen eye, and if he wanted her to look after it. The whorehouse was surrounded by old vines and flowering trees. He didn't know the name of the flowers but he said they looked like orchids. "Damned beautiful." The nurse said they weren't orchids, the trees were common as weeds in Saigon, but the real little flowers were in the whorehouse. She told him she had worked for two years with medivacs near Da Nang but now she was living in the whorehouse and looking after the young girls, testing them for infection. "It's my penance. Our guys carry more shit in their veins than the world can handle," she said. None of the girls was older than thirteen. She tested Elmer and then made love to him. She liked to undress him in her room and she was meticulous about his body. After they made love she fondled and washed him tenderly, which aroused him again, but she smiled readily at his arousal and turned away. "Too much of a good thing makes you stupid," she said.

One day when he came by the whorehouse she swallowed a green capsule and told him he could watch as a child prostitute made love to her. The child smelled of Tiger Rose Pomade. Then she sent the girl away and undressed him, made love to him, and washed him. He forced her back onto the bed, bruising her wrists. "You're raping me, you know," she said. She laughed, sang snatches of songs, and then she cried a little. She wouldn't kiss him.

"You're wired," he said. "Fucking wired."

"Never mind that, never mind the girl. It was just something to do," she said, "something before the weeping and gnashing of teeth."

"The gnashing of teeth?"

"Yes."

"What if someone's lost his teeth?" he said, trying to make her laugh.

"Teeth will be provided," she said.

He went back to his room and got drunk and wrote her a note, saying he couldn't see her anymore. "I don't believe in much and you don't believe in anything," he told her. He blamed her for their breakup but he did not send the note. He burned it. For some reason he kept the ashes in an envelope. He put them with his military papers and went for a walk in the night, close to a rancid, stagnant lagoon where there were thousands of refugees' shanties. He was carrying a .45 under his raincoat. He fired a single blind shot into the dark toward the shanties. He didn't know if he'd killed a refugee or not. Two days later, the whole shantytown went up in flames. A cooking stove had exploded. Then most of his squadron were shipped home. The nurse went with them. He stayed on and took a room for a week in the whorehouse. He slept with the children, grew a moustache, and then left. He plucked a flower from a tree and pressed it between his papers.

2

When he came home from Saigon, his father, Albert, a successful stockbroker, said, "I know you. You don't want a job, you want a position. You should go into local politics." His mother, Ethel, thought that was a wonderful idea. "I'd love to see your picture in the paper," she said. "Yes, and you could present yourself as something of a war hero," his father added.

"A hero?" Elmer asked.

"Sure. Nobody knows who our heroes are now, a picture in the paper, a sign of the times," his father said and laughed.

"You're laughing at me."

"No, no, I'm laughing at the times."

"Your father loves you," his mother said.

"You're my only son, I've left everything to you," his father said. "What else can I do?"

"Nothing," Elmer said.

He knew his father was not mocking him, that his father loved him. But he also felt his contempt, perhaps because his father had a quiet sneering contempt for everything. He was glad he did not feel close to him. It was safer to talk to his mother about his father because she was always in a cheerful mood, even about her own disappointments. Whenever he'd had an angry word with his father she would bake a big cake, chocolate or maple walnut, and after that he and his father would sit at the dining room table in silence and eat cake while she sat in the kitchen and sang quietly:

She wheeled her wheelbarrow
Through streets broad and narrow
Crying cockles and mussels
Alive alive-oh...

Every October, his parents took a short holiday; they drove into the Caledon Hills to see the changing leaves.. His father drove a Buick – they wouldn't have any other car – and they stayed in regular motels as long as the motels had swimming pools. They never went swimming. "But sitting by a pool drinking your morning coffee kinda makes it feel like California, or the movies," his father said. Since Elmer had just come home from Saigon, they asked if he wouldn't like to come along. "No," he said. "I've seen jungles full of trees." They said, "We thought you might like to visit with us," and set out. As they drove along route 401, they were killed, crushed when a transport trailer truck broke an axle and overturned onto their car. The truck, carrying tons of watermelons, burst into flames, the diesel lines rupturing at the fuel tanks under the trailer. In the intense heat, hundreds of exploding watermelons blew open the trailer doors.

They were crushed and burned; *scorched*, the police said. Their bodies were put in bags and then in closed caskets. "Gave up trying to get watermelon seeds outta their bodies," the mortician said. "I understand," Elmer said. "I guess you would," the mortician said, "you being in that war like you said." As Elmer stood at attention in his airman's dress blues, he looked down into the twin graves, and what he suddenly remembered was a black soldier in Saigon, a grunt who had bobbed his head drunkenly, saying, "Life's like a black woman's left tit. It ain't right, and it ain't fair." As Elmer left the graveyard, the minister asked, "Well, Mr. Sadine, what'll you do now?"

"Politics," he said.

"Really?"

"Sure."

"Well, that's some job."

"I don't want a job, I want a position."

He shaved off his moustache and settled into the house. It was a big house with many small rooms. He did not like to sleep in his own bed. He left a light on in their room all night, and usually kept their door closed. Sometimes, stretched out on a sofa in the study, drinking several glasses of whisky to ease himself to sleep, he stared at their bedroom door. One night, for no reason, he opened it and went in and looked under their bed. There was a bugle, his father's. He'd never heard his father play the bugle. He left it there and entered politics.

3

His election slogan was: UP UP AND AWAY WITH ELMER SADINE. He stumped the narrow row houses of Ward 9, the downtown ward. He talked about family values in public life. He wore his flyer's wings on his lapel. He made speeches at several Legion Halls but did not find it easy to be with other airmen, other fighter pilots who had fought in other wars. His eyelid fluttered when they talked about air strikes and carpet bombing. He shuffled his big feet. When he was asked one night why he had wanted to fight for another country in another country's war, he said that he had nothing to say about war because war was like a black seed that they all carried in their bones, everybody, Americans or Canucks, and whenever he said this he broke into a cold sweat. He could not blame the sweat on fatigue or dreams of a free fall through the air in flames. Whenever he had to talk about war he felt dead on his feet at the podium.

The campaign lasted six weeks. The voting results in the ward were close. After a recount he was elected as alderman by nine votes. He'd run in Ward 9 because his only opposition was a florist with a lisp, and also because he had been born on the ninth day of the ninth month. He appeared at a breakfast prayer meeting one week after the election and said that he hoped to serve the city for nine years. He said that while standing under a cold shower that morning, he had brooded on the number 9, looking for a meaning, and he had seen that no matter how you looked at 9 in all its multiples, it always added up to 9 (9 x 8 was 72, which was 7 + 2, a 9; and 6 x 9 was 54, 5 + 4, a 9; and 9 x 9 was 81, 8 + 1, a 9). No other number, he said smiling happily, was so self-contained. "I can assure you, I'm my own man," he said.

The next morning, his photograph appeared in the newspaper: OLD NUMBER NINE TAKES HIS SEAT. He was startled to see such a big picture of himself in the paper, and though he knew his mother would have been pleased, he was slightly offended. He was not old. He studied his face in the mirror. He was a young man.

He had his father's nose and eyes. He looked hard and long into the mirror. He heard the grandfather clock in the hall chime. He'd been looking into his own eyes for nearly ten minutes. "Son-of-a-bitch," he said. He laughed loudly at that and then he remembered that his mother had always said, "The loud laugh bespeaks the vacant mind."

He started wearing flight glasses, not just on the street and to nursing homes and old folks' homes, but to council meetings. He wondered what people thought. "I like them," his secretary said. "They give you a certain *je ne sais quoi*, a certain élan. They go with your wings." He thanked her. He decided to look up those words to see what they meant. He asked her to write them down. That's what he told his secretary to do when anyone asked him a question, "Write that down." He soon had a large filing box full of questions. He'd say, "Oh yes, I remember you, the question you asked." He did not pretend to have answers. He gradually became known as a tight-lipped spokesman for reduced taxes. "There's no such thing as loose change," he said. "There's loose morals but no loose change." During Lent, a reporter from *Your Catholic Neighbour*, writing about morals in civic life, asked him what he believed in. "The number 9," he answered. The reporter did not laugh. "Don't worry, I won't quote you," the reporter said.

4

Three years later, the mayor, Mort McLeod, who had been elected to bring casino gambling to the city, suddenly died of heart failure in The Dutch Sisters, a cheap lakeshore motel. It was whispered in the council cloakroom that he'd been found in bed with a high school baton twirler. Sadine had only contempt for cloak-room gossip. *Shitheads*, he said to himself. Then he told several newspapermen that he was his own man, a *hands-on man*, "And I trust what I can touch, what I can see. I trust these sandstone walls, that battleship linoleum." During the conversation with the newsmen, he said to a startled fellow alderman, "That's a fine door, a fine glass door you've got there, and the mayor was a fine mayor."

The Requiem Mass for the mayor was said in the cathedral. The De La Salle College Drum and Bugle Corps blew their silver bugles at the elevation of the host. Sadine wished that he'd had bugles blown over his mother and father's graves. Taps. We're all fallen warriors, he thought as he stood at the cathedral's centre door beside the Monsignor. He said to the Monsignor in a loud, clear voice, "Good work is public work. And the public work is our private work. And our work was the mayor's." The Monsignor looked doubtful but smiled and said, "I'm sure you must be right." Sadine, as he shook hands with the parishioners, felt a sudden bond with the Monsignor. Though he wasn't Catholic, he thought he might start coming to church. His eyelid began to flutter wildly, so he put on his flight glasses. The Monsignor turned to him and made the sign of the cross, saying, "May the Holy Mary, Mother of God, and all Her angels and saints, bless you." Sadine went home feeling pleased, so pleased he was sure something was going to go wrong.

5

As the sitting alderman from the central ward he was asked to take over the mayor's chair until an election could be called. "I'm just sitting in," he said expansively to a news photographer, "sitting in for the next eight months or so." He agreed to meet with a rakish old Chinese real estate broker at Bistro 990 on Bay Street. The broker said, while winking and spooning ice cream into the bruised mouth of a delicate-boned young man, "A fool and his money are soon parted. I should like to play the fool in your life." The broker offered Sadine a trip to Hong Kong if he would help to ease the stringent garbage collection regulations in Chinatown. Sadine said, "I've already been to the Far East, thanks." He declined cash, but a week later he accepted shares in an established chain of funeral homes that asked for his help in the rezoning of several new parking lots. "You name me a better bet than death," the broker had said. Sadine, now that he had such a secure income, decided to invest the money he'd inherited from his father in an old store in the east end that needed refurbishing, calling it Sadine's Dry Cleaning store. The store's motto was: *Let the Mayor Take You to the Cleaners.* His aides said the motto was a political mistake because he wasn't really the mayor, but he said, "You don't understand how popular a dumb joke can be."

As acting mayor he refused to support the extension of an elevated cantilevered concrete skyway along the east-end lakeshore. Trying to make a joke, he said the skyway would desecrate the memory of the dead mayor by casting a shadow over The Dutch Sisters motel. Then he stood up in chambers, stroked his chin, and said: "Taxes. Taxes. Taxes. Stupid." and sat down. Later, at a large fundraiser in Little Italy, Igidio Ciparone, a construction executive, said, "How do we get this guy's nose into joint?" Ciparone's wife, a woman who had plump, swollen arms, said sourly, "Look at your shoes, Sadine. Only a low-flying bore like you would wear shoes with such thick heavy soles." He shuffled his big feet and looked down at his shoes, wondering why anyone would be interested in the weight of his footwear, and he said, "Sensible people wear good solid shoes." He went home. "A lot she knows," he said. He went out to the garage, where there were rows of shelves on the walls, the shelves lined with model airplanes. He'd started building the planes shortly after becoming an alderman. Sometimes he stood in the unlit garage and stroked the taut paper bodies of the planes, chanting in a whisper: "Up up and away with Elmer Sadine!" Sometimes, while waiting for the glued struts to dry, he wondered why he'd never played with model planes like these as a boy. He wondered why his fondest childhood memory was sitting beside his mother, holding her hand, watching squirrels run across the garage roof and up into the branches of the big sugar maple. "Tree rats," she'd said. "Just common rats who look loveable because they have bushy tails and run around in the air." He felt a cold chill. He missed his mother. He went back up to his study and sat down and doodled several 9s on a piece of notepaper. After half an hour, he said, "When all's said and done, there's nowhere to go but up."

6

He ran for mayor because it was expected of him. But he'd lost interest, going from meeting to meeting feeling lethargic, bored, and angry at his own lethargy. It was how he'd felt in Saigon on the night when he'd gone out to the shanties beside the lagoon and fired a blind shot into the night. His mind wandered on the hustings. In the middle of a speech to the Knights of Columbus, he suddenly started talking angrily to his nurse in Saigon. "Teeth will be provided," he declared. There was loud questioning. "You mean clackers?" someone yelled. Everyone laughed. He didn't care. He was deeply upset because he couldn't remember the nurse's face. He could smell the flowers around the whorehouse. He remembered the smell of a child-whore's hair, Tiger Rose Pomade, and her fingers. He remembered the final two days in Saigon, lying in bed with three little girls as they stroked and kissed him and giggled. He could remember the mayor's face, though they'd never had a conversation alone, but he couldn't remember the nurse's face. He was sure he could remember his mother's face. Or perhaps, he thought suddenly in a panic, he was confused. Maybe he could remember the nurse but not his mother.

He went home and had several glasses of whisky. An empty whisky glass fell out of his hand and he heard his mother say, "Oh dear! You're drunk." He heard his father laughing in the bedroom. "Son-of-a-bitch, I'd kill you if I knew where you were," he said. He went and got the bugle from under the bed and blew a loud *BRAAAK*.

The next day, as soon as the polls closed, he conceded defeat. When asked by a reporter how he felt, he said, staring straight into the TV camera, "I have no shame at how I did." He was astonished when the reporter turned to the camera and said, "Well, there you have it. At last a politician who admits he has no shame."

7

Though he was still a young man, Sadine quit politics. He wept when the Organization of Funeral Home Directors, at a lunch, told him that they would make sure a small, little-used park close by his house would be named Sadine Park. He felt so good he stood up and cried, "Up up and away with Elmer Sadine!" Everyone laughed. He went to the bank. He was told by the manager that he was in a very good position financially. He opened one more Sadine's Dry Cleaning store, across the road from another funeral parlour, this in the west end. "Widening my view of things." He did not change the store's motto: *Let the Mayor Take You to the Cleaners*. He thought that it was still a very good joke.

When he wasn't at his stores, he stayed at home and worked in his study at a long pine table with an X-Acto knife and boxes of balsa strips and tubes of glue. Then he went out to the garage. The garage was empty because he didn't drive a car. There were more than fifty model planes on the shelves. Every Saturday, he went to Sadine Park on the edge of a ravine. He flew his planes in the park.

One morning a tall, lanky man came into the park through the gate and pointed at Sadine with his walking stick. Sadine was standing by a cluster of honeysuckle bushes with several model planes at his feet. He stepped back into the bushes but the man came directly to him, reached over the bushes and grasped him by the hand. "The name's Mellens, Martin Mellens. I wanted to meet you. I wanted to know what kind of a neighbour of mine sleeps with a light on in his house all night." He said he lived in a coach house down near the old iron footbridge that crossed over the ravine.

He was older than Sadine. He had long spindly legs, a tanned skin that was tight on his skull, and cropped hair. Sadine stared at Mellens. He didn't like his house being watched. "I was sure," he said dryly, "that I was out of the public eye." Mellens laughed, took his hand again, and said, "My young Mr. Mayor, I'm not the public, I'm your neighbour." He strode back to the gate, calling out, "And if I can't be your neighbour, I'll be your friend." Sadine, seeing the older man's spindly long legs and boyish bounce, thought, *The man walks like a water spider who's run out of water.*

Sadine asked the postman about Mellens. The postman said he was Russian, a widower whose young wife had died after giving birth to a son, and the baby had died, too. But when he asked a neighbour across the road, the neighbour said, "No, he is not Russian, he's Latvian. And not only is there no baby, but the wife, a young woman, she ran off with an evangelist who goes in for holy roller services, preaching out of his motorhome church." The neighbour laughed. "She swapped Mellens for a Winnebago," and he slapped his thigh at his own joke.

8

On the next Saturday, Mellens knelt by the planes at Sadine's feet. He helped inject fuel into the tiny stainless-steel motors. He grinned. As the humid afternoon passed, he mopped his brow with a big white handkerchief and told Sadine that he had made his money in the nursery business, not shrubs and flowers, but a pesticide he had developed that was not toxic but killed grubs. "I don't mind telling you, I've got a streak in me that's a touch flamboyant. See this, my walking stick? That's a grub," he said, putting the ivory handle of his stick into Sadine's hand. The handle had been carved into the shape of a maggot. "Mellens is the name, grubs are the game." He laughed. Then, late in the afternoon, he suffered short uncontrollable fits of shaking that started in his hands. His whole body shook. He grinned and said, "Pay no attention. It goes away." Sadine was glad to hear that. Without thinking, he began to sing:

She wheeled her wheelbarrow
Through streets broad and narrow
Crying cockles and mussels
Alive alive-oh…

"Sometimes," Mellens said, interrupting Sadine, "there's a pain that comes with the shaking. It's almost as if it were right in the centre of my bones. Unbearable. Nothing works on it. Aspirin. Cocaine. Nothing."

Sadine stroked his chin. At last he said, "You should try morphine sulphate. Get your hands on that. I've seen how it works in Saigon. I was in Saigon."

Mellens began to stop shaking. He leaned on his stick.

"You were?"

"Sure."

"Must've been quite terrible."

"Nearly got killed. Charlie punched me in the face, stuck his pistol right down my throat."

"Jesus."

"Nearly shit myself."

"I'll bet."

"Nearly fucking shit myself."

"I'm sure."

"Long way to go to shit yourself."

"They say travel broadens the mind."

"Right. Well, it concentrated mine. I was tonguing the hole in the barrel."

"Jesus," Mellens said, looking at him with what Sadine thought was a wry smile. Sadine suddenly feared that Mellens knew he was lying, about Charlie, about ever coming close to getting killed, and

Sadine, astonished at himself, wondered why he had twisted the truth of the story.

"The travelling I like to do now," Mellens said, "is the cruise ships. You ever been on a cruise ship?" He fitted a fuel injection needle into a motor. Sadine said, No, he had not. Mellens told Sadine that he had met a young woman on a cruise to Curaçao. "Changed my whole life." After a night of shipboard dancing, she'd come to his cabin. She'd started to sing and snap her hips as she undressed, and he'd begun to shake. "It was like having a high fever. She held me all night, asking me no questions." She had towelled the sweat from his body until dawn. Drained and calm, he'd fallen into a deep sleep. He'd slept through the whole day and into the next night, and then they'd gone dancing again. They'd made love. She'd come home with him, home to his house, and they'd got married. "But now I'm not with her. I don't sweat, I don't dance, I just shake." He laughed as one of Sadine's model planes, a Spitfire, circled over their heads. It flew in low. The motor's ratcheting noise forced Sadine to yell out, "You're a lonely man."

"I suppose I am," Mellens said, smiling.

"I suppose you are," Sadine said.

"It's kind of like tonguing that hole you were talking about," Mellens said.

9

Sadine sat at night by his bedroom window, staring into his own reflection in the dark glass. He distrusted Mellens, a man so free with his feelings, so openly full of himself in the generosity of his friendliness. "Alive, alive-oh," his mother had sung. "Crying cockles and mussels..." Sadine poured himself a glass of whisky. He felt the soundless weight of emptiness in the house. He'd never felt this emptiness before. He thought of his mother. He had come home once late at night and found her wearing a black bonnet with jet sequins, peering through the bay window curtains, whispering, "Albert, Albert, fly away home, your house is on fire, your son has no shoes." He'd laughed. He'd always had shoes. His mother had been drunk. She'd looked up at him and said, "Don't you know how to pray, son? So you can put on the shoes of the fisherman?" It was very dark. He saw himself in his bedroom mirror. He wasn't wearing his shoes. He was in his bare feet. Everything was still. He blamed Mellens for this sudden weight of silence in his house. He walked into his parents' bedroom and looked around. There were no more bugles under the bed. Nothing else had been touched. His mother had always been cheerful, wary and cheerful, sometimes almost feverish in her cheerfulness. He realized he'd never gone to see the Monsignor, never gone back to the church to Mass. "Taps." He decided that a lone bugle blown in the night might be the most beautiful sound in the world.

He went back into his bedroom, rummaged in a drawer and found his military papers, and lifted out the pressed flower, dry pink petals with streaks of mauve. He held it to his nose. There was no smell. He began to cry, remembering Mellens' laughter in the park, the sweet mournful look in his eyes as he'd talked about his wife, talked about how beautiful she was. "She came out of nowhere to me," he'd said. Then Sadine laughed as he lay down on his bed, seeing the spindly legged Mellens coming out of nowhere through the park gate, wagging his walking stick at him in the air. "I wanted to know why my neighbour sleeps with a light on in his house all night." Sadine got up, went into the bedroom, and turned off the light. "Fuck you," he said.

10

As Sadine walked into the park, Mellens was standing by the honeysuckle bushes, singing happily, quietly to himself:

There's a husky dusky maiden in the Arctic
And she waits for me, but it is not in vain,
For someday I'll put my mucklucks on and ask her
If she'll wed me when the ice worms nest again.

"What kind of song is that?"

"That! That's you. You're from here, this country, that's your heritage," Mellens said, and immediately put his head down and went to work on the motors. Sadine stood back. The sun was shining brightly, so he put on his dark flight glasses. "Heritage, my ass." He'd been watching old war movies on television the night before. He was tired, and he was irritated because an elderly couple had begun coming to the park, sitting on a bench close to a clump of lilac trees. They sat watching Sadine every Saturday, pointing at the planes, laughing. Mellens completed the fuel injection. Sadine sent the radio-controlled planes up into the air. The planes, swooping and dipping, rose and circled the rim of tall spruce trees around the park till he checked his stopwatch for fuel time and drew two of the planes down to a safe landing. The old couple under the lilac trees applauded, but they snickered cruelly when the last plane ran out of gas and plummeted to the grass, crushing its nose cone and a wing. He couldn't stand the way the old couple giggled. Mellens, wagging his cane, said, "Don't let those crazy old coots get to you." Sadine nodded. "Okay," he said as Mellens picked up the fuselage and then carried the broken pieces of the plane back to Sadine's garage.

11

In the garage, with rows of model planes parked behind him on plain pine shelves, Mellens stood staring up into the stillness of wings suspended from the ceiling by black linen threads. "You know what this is like? It's like staring up into Alaska," he said.

"I've never been to Alaska," Sadine said.

"You should go."

"I don't want to go."

"I went for a cruise once to Alaska," Mellens said. "All sorts of people sitting there in chairs beside windows that were sealed up so you could see the big high slopes full of trees but you couldn't smell the air, sitting there sealed in amber. I sat down to say 'Hello' to some of these kindly folks in their golf shirts and pretty soon the man beside me, he said, 'Well, there are a lot of them trees out there,' and he rubs his hands together and says, 'Do you think that those trees is natural or man-made?' and I said, 'I don't know, they must be natural.' So he says, 'Now that's what I was saying to Edna, they gotta be natural, because if they was man-made they could never of got 'em that close together.'"

Sadine laughed. He felt a pang of envy, wondering why he'd never had such easy conversations with strangers, or if he had, why he couldn't remember them. His memory never seemed to give him what he wanted. He could hardly remember anything his mother or father or the nurse had talked about, and when he visited the managers of his dry cleaning stores he had little or nothing to say. Only the week before, a prominent funeral director at a curling tournament supper for funeral home handlers and embalmers had patted him affectionately on the shoulder. "Our man's a born listener. It's a gift," he said. "Now if only my wife had the gift."

"I wish I could remember a joke," Sadine said to Mellens.

"You do?"

"Yeah," he said as he laid a line of clear glue along a balsa wing-strut and secured a joint, searching his mind for a joke. "I remember at this curling tournament they asked me what I thought about curling and I said it looked to me like a bunch of caretakers with attitudes sweeping up the ice. They thought that was pretty funny." Mellens howled with laughter. Sadine was taken aback. "You want to talk about ice," Mellens said, "the miles and miles of ice up there in the glacier bays? Sometimes when the air is squeezed out of the ice the ice absorbs all the light into pockets of turquoise. It all looks like the broken fingers of the earth. That's where only the ice worms live. It's a big brutal serenity out there…"

There was a drop of glue on Sadine's forefinger. "That's funny," he said as the glue began to harden.

"What?"

"I just remembered something else."

"What?"

"Something I did. Like what you're saying."

"What'd I say?"

"Where you were, a big, brutal serenity, except this was out on the prairies." He peeled the glue from his fingertip. "Empty space, that's what it was. Whatever that great big thing was, it didn't care a hoot about me. That's what I remember – an emptiness so tight in my chest I was almost afraid to breathe." He paused and then winced, as if he'd got a sudden pain in his side. "I hate my father," he blurted out. "I hate the prairies and I hate my father." He moaned, staring up into the dark well of the garage, into the wing spans. Mellens said nothing. Sadine took a deep breath, shrugged, and said, "He was a kind of caretaker and he sure had an attitude."

He did not go on to tell Mellens how afraid he had been of that prairie emptiness, how he had walked up and down the streets of the town, filled with panic. He'd hired a hooker at the hotel and taken her to his room, and there she'd led him into the bathroom so that she could wash him. "A girl's got to keep clean," she'd said, and the fondling with warm water and soap had aroused him. The girl had held him in the palm of her hand. "You can play with that," he'd said. "Sure," she'd said, "and I can whistle a happy tune on it, too."

Mellens, lifting one of the fragile planes from a shelf, turned it over in his hands, a Stuka dive-bomber. Sadine remembered how grimly he had made love to the hooker, till he had rolled over exhausted and heard her say as he fell asleep, "My God, ain't you something."

He had wakened in the prairie hotel feeling so refreshed that he didn't care when he found out that the girl had taken fifty dollars from his wallet. "She was damn good for me." After that, every Friday night back home, he had booked a room and a hooker at the King Edward Hotel, and always had a dozen chrysanthemums delivered to the room. He liked the lush expansiveness of flowers. Sometimes he tore a handful of petals from the flowers, spread them on a pillow, and then went into the bathroom. "Cleanliness is next to godliness," he said, laughing as he stood by the sink, wearing his flight glasses, waiting to be washed. "Up up and away," he said, aroused.

Mellens held the frail body of the Stuka against the garage light, running a finger along the wing tips. "I'm glad you've come back," Mellens said.

"What?"

"Wherever you went in your head."

"I was thinking."

"I am sure you were."

"I was."

"Thinking of what?"

"Soap," Sadine smiled.

"You were thinking of soap?"

"I was," Sadine said.

"Soap."

"Yep."

"I was in the war, too," Mellens said. "You know that?"

"I didn't know," Sadine said.

"Not your war. The World War."

"You're kidding. That makes you old enough to be my father."

"Not quite."

"Where're you from?"

"Riga."

"Where's that?"

"Latvia. I ended up in the gulag. Hard labour. What was hardest was to live with how filthy everyone was. Shit. Lice. You don't know how lousy life is till you know you've learned to actually sleep with your own lice. To lie in shit and sleep with your lice. Nobody dreamed about whipped cream and eclairs in there, we dreamed about soap. And one day, a particular guard said to me,

'My garden is dying. You fix my garden and I will get you a box of soap, a big box.' I fixed his garden and I got this box of a dozen bars of soap."

"So you became a gardener."

"Me and the worms, we made a life."

"And here, too?"

"Right. Here."

"In my mind, in worm country. Wherever the ice worms are, up in Alaska. Anywhere. That's where I am. Ice makes you wonder, you wonder about wormholes," he said, holding a slender Phantom F-4 up to the light. "The physicists, they say the universe is a great big transparent sac like a skin and there we are in this sac except there are wormholes out there, holes that go right through the world's skin out into other worlds." He circled Sadine, saying, "We could get out of this life alive, we could almost get out of this world alive if we could find the wormholes." Sadine heard a sharp, brittle crumpling sound and Mellens, with a sheepish smile, held up the Phantom F-4, the belly spars collapsed in his big fist. "Damnation," Mellens said, "now that's dumb." He handed the broken plane to Sadine, who yelled, "You've broken it!"

"So, it can be fixed," Mellens said, shrugging.

"It's broke," Sadine said, surprised that he was so angry.

"If it's broke, fix it."

"Fix it. The man says fix it. He's got no shame," Sadine cried. "You've got no shame."

"Shame," he said. "You want to talk about shame?"

"No. There's nothing to talk about," Sadine said.

"Why not?"

"Because I've got nothing to be ashamed of."

"Then shut up," Mellens said. "It's a paper plane, for Christ's sake. There are bigger things," and as he turned to leave the garage he laughed and sang,

> *She'll be waiting for me there*
> *With the hambone of a bear*
> *And she'll beat me*
> *'Til the ice worms nest again.*

12

A week later, Sadine had to go downtown. He needed to get new leather soles put on his shoes. He took a taxi rather than walk past Mellens' house. In the shop, a man at the counter said he wanted a pair of riding boots repaired. He was wearing a red hunter's jacket, a hard, black riding cap, and was carrying a bugle. Sadine spoke to him and the man explained that he was the bugler at the racetrack, that he took the bus out to the track every noon hour, going in full dress because it meant curious people always talked to him. He liked to talk to strangers. "Never had a lonely bus ride yet," he said.

"How hard is it to learn to play the bugle?"

"Learning to blow is one thing, learning to play the bugle is another."

"My father left me his bugle. He left it under his bed."

"No kidding," the bugler said. "The only time I put my bugle under a bed, it was a woman I loved so much I never wanted to get out of her bed."

"You're kidding."

"Look, learning to play your father's bugle, that's nothing. It's the bed that's a problem," the racetrack bugler laughed.

At home, Elmer put the bugle to his lips. He had the peculiar feeling that he was kissing his father for the first time. He blew into the bugle, making a loud, braying flatulent sound. "Fat fucking chance I can play this thing," he said and laughed. He went downstairs and out to the garage and began to rebuild the Phantom F-4, paring the balsa strips with his X-Acto knife. When he was done, he set the plane on a table. He stared at it a long time and was surprised that he felt no satisfaction. He felt grim. He felt he was being watched. He was sure he'd caught a glimpse of his mother's face in the overhead well of wings. "What are you doing there?" he screamed. He brought both fists down on the plane and crushed it, shaking his head because he felt a sudden tiredness, a lethargy so deep in his bones that he wanted to lie on the floor and cry. He wondered if he had actually killed anyone on that night when he'd fired into the shanties by the lagoon.

On Saturday, he went to the park with only one plane. He flew an F-86 in low circles over the trees. The old couple, seeing how grim and tight-lipped he looked, left him alone. Mellens did not appear. The air was humid. The plane had no lift. It crashed. Sadine walked home carrying the broken wings, disheartened, his eyelid fluttering. "Some goddamn pilot," he said. He was astonished that a stupid argument with Mellens had left him so troubled. He poured himself a drink and opened his mail and was startled by a big white pamphlet that had 999 embossed in bold black on the cover. He remembered telling the reporter that all he believed in was the number 9. Then he realized he was holding the pamphlet upside down, that it was an evangelical tract promising the imminent end of the world under the sign of 666 – *the numbers of the apocalypse.* "Three 6s are 18," he mused, "and 9 and 9 are 18, so maybe it'll all even out."

He opened another Sadine's Dry Cleaning store and then went to the bank with a large unexpected dividend cheque that had come in from the funeral home company he had incorporated. "Boy, the dead are really dying," he said. He was so pleased he booked a room in the King Edward Hotel in the middle of the week. The girl turned out to be very young, probably too young, which was dangerous, but Sadine felt incredible arousal as she crouched on her hands and knees and he mounted her from behind. Then, almost immediately, he became preoccupied with the taut smoothness of her skin and his own flabby paunch, and though he thought, *I'm still young*, he heard himself wheezing for air. He wondered if he was bored. He wondered what had been in the green capsule that the nurse had swallowed in Saigon. He decided he would ask for two girls on Friday so that he could watch them. "It was just something to do," he remembered the nurse saying. With a loud laugh, he gave the girl a hard slap on the buttocks, and then another slap. The girl leapt up. "None of that fucking shit," she yelled. "None of that fucking shit, man. Nobody hits me," and she gathered her clothes, dressing so quickly that Sadine, still on his knees with his eyes closed, didn't realize she was dressed until she was at the door. "No, wait," he cried.

"Wait for what?" she said, her hand on the doorknob. "This bitch is on wheels, man."

"I wasn't trying to hurt you."

"Who the fuck cares?"

"I do."

"Don't give me that shit, man. You gonna beat on me? You think I was born yesterday, man?"

"No, I was," he said.

"Very funny."

"No, it's not," he said. "It's not funny at all. I wish it was funny. I wish I could tell you a joke."

"This is a joke, this whole fucking night's a joke."

"No, it's not," he said.

"So what d'you want?"

"I usually get washed."

"Washed?"

"Yes. With soap."

"You want me to wash you?"

"If you want."

"No, no, no, no man. It's what you want, not what I want. It's what you pay for."

"I don't care anymore. I'd just like you to stay, that's all."

"What're you gonna do if I stay?"

"Nothing. Talk. You can talk to me."

"I don't talk. I fuck."

"Try talking."

"What's to tell. It's all shit. I don't shovel shit for dead men."

"Nobody said I was dead."

"I didn't mean you were dead, man. It's just a way of saying. Don't take it personal."

She came to the side of the bed. She looked at him very shrewdly, smiled, and stepped out of her high heels. "I ain't telling you nothing, man. I bet you could do me dirt. I ain't telling you nothing about me."

"So don't."

"Nothing."

"Whatever you want," he said.

She took off her dress and lay down beside him. "I can tell you about tricks, all the lunatics I meet," she said.

"Whatever," he said.

"Like you," she said.

"What?"

"You're a lunatic."

"Is that true?"

"That's a maybe."

13

When Mellens came through the gate, Sadine was embarrassed because he knew he was smiling warmly, but he didn't mind being embarrassed. Mellens, striding across the grass, began to talk at the top of his voice, wagging his grub-handled cane. "What a trip, what a trip. People of our kind, Sadine, our kind, successful, big rolls of fat under their arms and under their chins. They play bingo! They play bingo. Can you believe it? All afternoon in that cruise ship, not caring about the sea, and when the bingo caller called out, 'Under the I, two little ducks – 22,' they all cried, '*Quack, quack.*'" He hooted with laughter. Sadine quickly sent a Hurricane fighter plane roaring straight up into the air, driven by a new booster motor.

"'Under the O – twin 5s, the number 55, and so big,' and what did these fine people of ours call out? – *Dolly Parton!*"

He told Sadine stories about his trip until the sun sank behind the trees. All the planes landed safely. As they walked home along the heavily treed streets, past limestone rockeries, they were sub-dued and reflective, but inside the garage, as Sadine shelved the planes, regretting that there was no repair work to be done so that they could stay there, Mellens said, "You know the strangest thing I saw? You should've seen this ship's casino. It was sitting there totally empty except for this nice-looking old man at the end of the craps table, and when he threw the dice, the croupier, he calls, '*Hard Eight,* your point is 9.' The old man had his cane hooked to the edge of the table and it's a white cane. He was blind, he's a blind man shooting craps all alone. And when the old blind man says, 'Double my bets,' the croupier took his money from the rack and counted it out very carefully and I felt right there, felt what I'd never understood before – the complete wonder of human trust, the trust in life as it is. Life as it is is better than no life at all. A blind shot in the dark. That's how we learned to sleep in shit with our own lice. I could see it in the cane hanging on the lip of the table as though it was hanging on the edge of the world, a crazy blind man, beautiful, in a world he'd never seen."

"A blind man shooting craps!"

"Yeah, and a winner."

"He made his point?"

"Yeah, and later, I thought about you."

"You did?"

"Your planes. Once we left Acapulco, I was standing on deck late at night somewhere outside Panama City and all these planes are coming in, lights blinking, and I thought of you, that light you keep on all night in your house."

"Not anymore," Sadine said as he stepped out of the garage into the pale shadows of dusk. Mellens followed, his cane clacking on the interlocking brick driveway.

"It's strange," Sadine said.

"What?"

"How one thing leads to another." He walked down the driveway, suddenly wanting to tell Mellens that he was seriously thinking of really learning how to play his father's bugle. Instead he said, "One night I was in Calgary for some aldermans' convention or other, staying out by the airport. You could see all the landing lights from the window, and I hired a hooker…"

"You went with a hooker?" Mellens said, grinning, so that Sadine could see the line of his dentures.

"A girl who wore silver stockings and had braided hair with little beads in it, and a sequined purse. Funny how I remember that."

"What was her name?"

"I don't know. I never asked. She was from Detroit, I know that. She was a black girl from Detroit and I suddenly told her I wanted to watch the planes come in, I wanted to stand out in a field in the dark somewhere while she was doing me and watch the planes come in. So she drove me to this side road and said, 'There's no planes at one in the morning,' but I said, 'There are always planes.' I stood there staring at nothing in the sky happening while she knelt down to do me and the next minute there were these great goddamn rabbits going by in the night, a herd of rabbits."

"Don't be crazy."

"Big like this," and Sadine opened his arms.

"They must've been hares."

"Who cares? They were the ghosts of something going by."

"You're seeing things."

"Sure, I was seeing things," Sadine said. "I'm hauling my pants up around my throat and I'm seeing things and they've got big red eyes."

"Maybe they were ghosts getting out of town."

"They were going straight downtown. They were screaming. You know that? Rabbits scream, and all of a sudden, standing there holding my pants so I wouldn't fall down, I yelled, 'Sweet Jesus, get me out of here!'"

Mellens laughed and put his arm around Sadine's shoulder. "I'd never have guessed that you've got this low-life taste for hookers." Sadine stiffened, offended. He would never be able to make Mellens understand that his use of hookers was essentially a practical matter, that he'd always left the hotel rooms feeling braced and buoyant. Cleansed. It was nothing personal. He'd learned in politics that people who took things personally ended up wounded, enraged, and belittled, but he wanted to protect himself so he tried to sound light-hearted. "I give her the number nine," he sang, "drive it home, drive it home." They stood side by side on the sidewalk, smiling like secure old friends. He wished, as he stepped out of Mellens' embrace, that he'd never told him about the rabbits, their screaming and their red eyes.

14

Mellens telephoned later in the week. He said he was sick, a congestion in his chest. As Sadine hung up, he realized that they had never talked to each other on the phone before, and though they were neighbours who'd met for weeks in the park, they had never been in each other's house. "Probably a good thing, too," Sadine said. He took Mellens' call as a sign, a warning. Late one night, after several glasses of whisky, he thought he heard Mellens' step on the stair, and then was certain he heard Mellens talking to his father in the bedroom. He thought they were arguing and he put down his whisky, got up, and stood in the hall to listen. He heard nothing. They had stopped. Perhaps they knew he was there. "They're fucking hiding," he said. In two weeks, in early October, he talked to Mellens again. Mellens phoned and asked, "You still there?"

"Where else would I be?"

"In the grave."

"Don't be ridiculous."

"That's what's left," Mellens said.

"What?"

"Being ridiculous."

On Saturday, Sadine was shocked by Mellens as he came through the gate, wizened and yellow under the eyes. "Sick, sick as a dog," he said, pulling the shawl collar of a woollen sweater-coat close to his throat.

"With what?"

"With life, with nothing."

"Nonsense."

"I'm dying," Mellens said, jabbing his cane at Sadine. "Get going. Let's get this act of ours up in the air."

Sadine had to wait as the elderly couple strolled across his take-off path. He was shaking, his eyelid out of control. He suddenly wished that Mellens had met his mother, had met her before she had put on her black bonnet with the jet sequins. "My mother was a lonely woman," he said. "Today, she would probably have baked us a cake. She had this peculiar faith in cake."

"You don't say."

"Yes. The more I think about it, she was very lonely. She used to sing *Alive, alive-oh...*" He sent a Mirage bumping across the grass and up into the sun. "So you're feeling really sick?"

"The ghosts got me, I guess."

"Ghosts?"

"Those rabbits of yours. My wife, she came home and got me, too."

"You saw her?"

The Mirage swooped low over clumps of dogwood bushes. "Sure. It was just like she'd come back down a wormhole and stood there at the foot of my bed."

"She's come back to haunt you?"

"That's exactly what I said the first time I ever saw her. *Here is a haunting beauty.*"

"I don't believe in ghosts."

"If you've got no ghosts, you've got no life," Mellens said grimly.

"I still don't believe."

"Sure you do."

They heard a smack. Under the lilac trees, the old woman had slapped the old man, knocking him down, and now the man was up and shambling from the park, weeping. "Ah, young love," Mellens said. His laughter made him look so gaunt that Sadine was ashamed that he'd ever been angry at him. "Wait'll you see this," he said. "I've been working on it for weeks." He drew a cloth back from a sleek black swept-wing plane. "Stealth," he said.

"What?"

"It's a Stealth bomber. No radar can track it."

"Really."

There were twin motors in the belly of the bomber. It rose slowly, in a long, graceful low-flying arc. "You know what I've been thinking about while I've been sick?" Mellens said, shielding his eyes from the sun and following the flight line of the plane.

"Remember that trip to the glacier bays, those glaciers growing like they do at two or three hundred feet a year, their damned relentless lifeless growth…"

"Mellens, for Christ's sake!"

"What?"

"We're trying to have some fun flying planes."

"You fly and I watch."

"Right."

"Because you got your wings," Mellens said, chuckling. "But I've got your number. Yessir, Mr. Mayor."

"What number?"

The Stealth bomber pulled straight up over the trees, their leaves all changed in colour, pulling into the sky and disappearing in a sun flash.

"You want to see something, look at that," Sadine said proudly. "Look at that," and the black plane reappeared out of the sun, diving at high speed.

Mellens yelled out, "There it goes! Heading straight for the wormholes!"

"Cut it out. You and your goddamn wormholes," Sadine cried, making his cry sound like a warning as he looped the plane back over their heads.

Mellens drove his cane into the soft earth. It stuck and quivered. "Yeah, well, old pal, old number 9, you know what? Everything is up for grabs. I don't think any Viet Cong stuck a pistol in your mouth, and you know what else? Maybe I've never been on a cruise ship." Eyes closed, he'd gone red in the face. "What d'you think about that?"

"Nothing."

"What d'you mean, 'Nothing?'"

"Be careful," Sadine said.

"I'm too old to be careful. Careful gets you a cup of coffee."

"Then be nice."

"Nice. What's nice? What a dreadful word, nice."

"Get a life!" Sadine suddenly screamed out. "For Christ's sake. Get a life."

Mellens hurried across the lawn. "I told you I'm dying." He left his walking stick in the earth. He turned at the gate. "You remember, Sadine, there's a great big white silence out there," he cried. He went through the gate and Sadine sent the Stealth bomber, its twin motors shearing the stillness in the park, straight up in the air again. But then it went into a series of tight turns that he had not sent by signal, so he levered a new flight pattern into the control panel but the bomber widened its circles and picked up speed until it levelled off. It crossed overhead and disappeared between the tops of the yellow, ochre, and red trees, heading downtown. Sadine took off his flight glasses. He stood rooted to the ground for a long time, staring off between the trees, waiting for the plane to come back. "Something about those leaves," he heard his father say. "They're so beautiful they make you wish life wasn't the way it is." He picked up the Mirage and the control panel and he drew Mellens' walking stick out of the ground. The ivory grub handle was warm in his hands. He felt so heavy-footed he used the cane for support on the walk home.

15

All week he worried about what to say to Mellens and what to do about the plane. He scanned the newspapers to see if there might be a story about a model Stealth bomber that had showed up out of nowhere in a child's backyard, but there was no word, and he had no idea where to look for the plane. A week passed and he decided that he had to see how Mellens was feeling. When he telephoned, a woman answered. She said that she was his wife. "Are you a friend?" she asked.

"Yes," he said, almost defiantly.

"Well, in that case, the burial is tomorrow morning. You'd best come."

16

Sadine drank six glasses of whisky but did not fall asleep. He dreamed that his mother was hiding a cowering Mellens under her pleated white skirt, and then he saw Mellens as a scrawny long-legged boy in a Soviet gulag work camp, grinning as if he'd known that they would meet, saying, "Sadine, Sadine, teeth will be provided." Sadine was sopping wet, shivering. "For Christ's sake," he said. He heard his mother singing, his mother who had bathed and washed him as a child. He thought of the women who had washed him and then taken him in their mouths, swallowing his semen. His seed. He had no children. No one to wash. He'd never wanted a child. Mellens had told him, "No, no children. No." They shared that. And the black seed they carried in their bones, he could feel the seed inside his body, soot along his bones. "But at least I'm still alive," he said. He got up, his hands shaking as if he'd been accused of something shameful. He went into his parents' bedroom and lay down again and went to sleep.

17

When he awoke in the morning, he began to shiver, dreaming –
though he knew that he was awake – that he was lost alone on the
runway of a wilderness airport in a snowstorm and there were red
warning lights all around him. But then he realized that the warning lights were eyes, the red eyes of the dead, the dead who were so
white he could not see them. He could see the whiteness of everything, including the dead, and yet he could not see anyone. He was
certain that Mellens was standing in front of him but he couldn't
see him. The clarity of seeing nothing stayed with him as he showered and then put on his dress blue uniform, folded away for years
so that it still smelled slightly of cleaning fluid. He was a little
flabby and the belt was tight but he hadn't put on too much
weight. He drank a cup of black coffee and called a taxi. He sat in
the back seat of the taxi with Mellens' cane across his knees. He was
in a cold sweat again, trembling. He had pricked his thumb, drawing a drop of blood as he had fastened his wings to his lapel. He'd
sucked his thumb to stop the bleeding. He was still sucking his
thumb as he got out of the back seat of the taxi.

18

He crossed the grass to the graveside, his shoulders back, his head
held high. There was a minister at the grave, whose red-white-and-
blue Winnebago was parked under a weeping willow, and there
were six professional pallbearers. He noted that they were not from
his funeral home. A young woman who had long blonde hair was
wearing a veil. Sadine could not see her eyes. There was a white

orchid on the lapel of her black suit. He was wearing his flight glasses.

"You must have been a very good friend," she said, noticing the cane that he carried under his arm. "If he gave you his walking stick you were a very good friend."

The minister ended a brief prayer, asking flights of angels to carry Mellens home. He blessed the coffin as it was lowered into the earth.

Sadine wanted to do something. He was furious with himself for not having learned to play the bugle. "I would have played 'Taps'..." he said. The veiled woman looked startled. "Pardon?" she said. Then he tore the wings from his lapel, ripping the cloth, and he dropped the wings down into the hole. The metal clunked against the coffin. His feet sank into the soft, loose earth. His eyelid fluttered. "From time to time," he said, "we flew together."

PAUL VALÉRY'S SHOE

I have tried as hard as I can to tell stories, not necessarily what I'd call true stories, but stories that have a true feel to their ending, true to how I feel in my heart. What happens is that I start a story with a particular face, a particular phrase, and soon thereafter I have a page or two – or ten or twelve – but coming to where the story has to end, the only thing that ends is my knowing what more there is to say. I sit staring at the dance of dust in the light. Sometimes I'll keep typing, searching for that shoe that Paul Valéry said is out there waiting for the story that's true to itself, the perfect fit. But no matter how bold my start has been, soon there's nothing more to say and I end up shelved in my own head. The hours pass and I try to peck out a line, a paragraph. I keep trying to look for the ending back in the beginning. I refuse to take the easy way out of the story by just killing off the main man or the woman in the story because that is not an ending. That's just death. That's just having absolutely nothing to say. So what do I do, caught between nothing to say and no ending because I don't understand my beginning? I sit here in this room with these ridiculous old curtains on the window, curtains that remind me of my childhood because they are worked with an appliqué of the letters of the alphabet, the promise that the alphabet contains. And I am sitting in this dark room lit only by a lamp on the bed table with the stand-up mirror on the table, trying to tell this particular story about a writer who is actually starving to death while he is writing the story of how he is eating himself alive – refusing under any circumstances to quit on himself or his story because he is too much of an optimist, as all storytellers have to be optimists, because they believe that there is that shoe out there that fits. They can't help themselves from starting a new story because they know that somewhere in the beginning there is an end – as I believe that there has to be an end even for this tawdry, shameful story that I'm trying to write – a story as cramped as these two tiny rooms where I sit and catch inadvertently an appalling glimpse of my sneaky little face in the bedside mirror, the face of a dolt sneering back at me – sneering because that dolt knows that I still believe the phrase "a petal falls" is a touching, moving phrase – sneering at me, his eyes shining bright in the gloom, as I'm sure my own eyes are shining, the eyes of a starving man, chewing like an anxious girl on my knuckle, too stupid to feel pain, and then chewing on another knuckle, as if coming to an agreement with that dolt about a phrase could save me, could spring open the light that is in all the little phrases I have hidden away in notebooks – the lines of conversation overheard and written down, lines so quick and easy to whoever said them, quick as the curl of a lip, quick as an eye dropped in sleep, all, all of them, the words, seeming at first as fresh and alive as fireflies at night but turning to ash in the morning, ashes in the mouth whenever I've sat here like I'm sitting here now, day-after-day, TAP TAP on the keys, hearing "a petal falls" – "a petal falls" not eating for six days now – stroking my wrists, stroking the mildew-like tracing of my own veins in the skin, so delicate, not believing that any of what is now happening is true. I mean, could I actually die of hunger, die out of want for a story, die at the only point in my storytelling life where I actually have an ending, die because in fact I have absolutely nothing left of myself? Could I actually end by eating my own heart out? Could I end up, after more pages pile up and pass, being so light-headed from hunger and typing and licking between my tendons in this hour that is so cold that it takes my breath away, eating what is necessary, possible, getting down to the heart of who I am as I ease one word, and then another, into a shoe – a shoe that fits as I end my story, yes, end it by saying, yes, with utter storytelling simplicity, yes, how much I hate to admit I love the words "Once upon a time…?"

A SELECTION OF BARRY CALLAGHAN'S WORKS
ARE NOW AVAILABLE IN DIGITAL FORMATS

BARRELHOUSE KINGS is the unique story of two Canadian writers, each well-known in his own right: Morley Callaghan and his son, Barry. It is a stunningly written recollection of the world in which Barry Callaghan grew up – the world that was Morley's milieu as a writer and became Barry's as their lives dovetailed. Along the road toward that dovetailing, Barry encounters an incredible cast of characters: Becket, Muhamad Ali, Brownie McGee and Sonny Terry, Golda Meir, Pierre Trudeau, mobsters and several song-and-dance men. Unforgettable, this is an autobiography that will stand the test of time.

THE **EXILE** eBOOK *SERIES*

BARRELHOUSE
KINGS

BARRY CALLAGHAN

A MEMOIR

E№ 356   www.ExileEditions.com

RAISE YOU FIVE is periodic writing about the most complex ideas, rendered in prose of utter ease and clarity – prose from a man who believes all writing, at its best, whether it is a book review or meditation on evil, is a kind of storytelling, and that storytelling is what keeps it alive.

RAISE YOU TEN As a man of letters, as a poet, novelist, and personal journalist, Barry Callaghan is a singular presence in Canada. Always a storyteller, a *flaneur* "secretly attuned to the history of the place and in covert search of adventure," he is also a public scholar in the tradition of Edmund Wilson (his extraordinary portrait of Wilson concludes this volume). Unflinching before the harsh complexities of our time, *Raise You Ten*, like *Raise You Five*, is, as trumpeted by the *Globe and Mail:* "Literary criticism and cultural history of a high order, in turn joyous, acerbic, celebratory."

RAISE YOU ON THE RIVER is a masterfully written volume of essays and encounters that includes extended pieces on widely varied subjects such as Margaret Atwood, Hip Hop music and Emily Dickinson, Joyce Carol Oates and Céline and Saul Bellow, the cities of Calgary and Munich, basketball star Vince Carter, blues performers Otis Spann, Sunnyland Slim and Muddy Waters, painters John Meredith and William Ronald, Apartheid and the secret police in South Africa, Robert Graves, boxing and literary buffoonery, and more – all concluding with an extrodinary letter/report from inside a brutal battle, the 1970 Black September civil war in Amman, Jordan.

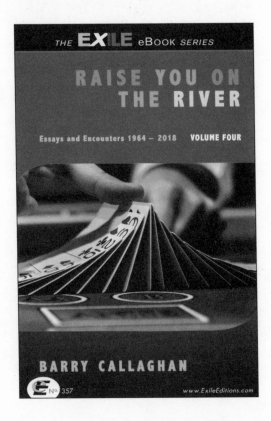

THE **EXILE** eBOOK SERIES

RAISE YOU ON
THE RIVER

Essays and Encounters 1964 – 2018   **VOLUME FOUR**

BARRY CALLAGHAN

No. 357   www.ExileEditions.com

BESIDE STILL WATERS is a passionate love story, with its roots in Toronto and its resolution in the dark heart of contemporary Africa. Adam Waters' search for the woman he loves, who has mysteriously disappeared from their hotel room, takes him from the casinos of Puerto Rico to war-torn Gabon and a leper colony deep in the African bush. Counterpointing Adam's quest are his memories from boyhood, and of his father, wandering jazzman Sweet Web Waters; his experiences as a war correspondent; and the girl who becomes his lover, dancer Gabrielle. Callaghan confronts the pure joy that can be in sexuality and the evil that is inherent in the nature of growth itself, by combining the excitement of an adventure story with the exuberant love of language.

HOGGWASH Barry Callaghan and Joe Rosenblatt, poets of perspicacity, pizzazz, and probity, have been combative, ecstatic compadres for over forty years, with Callaghan donning an array of chapeaus, the man of *belles lettres* and Hogg *flaneur*-on-the-hoof from Smooth City, while Rosenblatt decades ago declared his unconditional allegiance to the buzzzers, chirpers, and purrers of the natural world, and to remain at peace by his pond, aloof from the human horde. This most unlikely pair are conjoined by their shared dedication to the Word, drawn from their nether surreal and noumenal worlds. *Hoggwash* is a convergence by epistle in a tribute not just to their enduring friendship but to the life of the imagination itself.

THE **EXILE** eBOOK *SERIES*

HOGGWASH

The Callaghan and Rosenblatt
Epistolary Convergence

Nº 327   Introduction by Catherine Owen   www.ExileEditions.com